Because He Loved Her

Cefolù, May 2023.

Because He Loved Her

FIDELMA KELLY

POOLBEG

Published 2022 by Poolbeg Press Ltd
123 Grange Hill, Baldoyle
Dublin 13, Ireland
www.poolbeg.com
Email: info@poolbeg.com

© Fidelma Kelly 2022

The moral right of the author has been asserted.

© Poolbeg Press Ltd. 2022, copyright for editing, typesetting, layout, design, ebook

A catalogue record for this book is available from the British Library.

ISBN 978178199-491-7

www.poolbeg.com

About the Author

Fidelma Kelly is from Ireland. Linguist, opera *aficionado,* dog-mammy and elder carer – she has worked in education, opera, public relations and property. An English Literature and French graduate of Trinity College Dublin, she later returned to TCD to complete an M. Phil in Applied Linguistics. She speaks French and Italian fluently and has spent extended periods in both countries, in particular in her beloved Sicily. Her love of languages frequently informs her fictional settings.

Her previous work has been shortlisted for the RTÉ Radio 1 Francis MacManus Short Story Award and the Memoir category at Write by the Sea Kilmore Quay Literary Festival in 2021. She was a finalist in the Irish Writers' Centre Novel Fair competition in 2017.

She has contributed features to the *Irish Times*, the *Sunday Business Post Magazine*, the *Irish Daily Mail* magazine and Writing.ie. Her first novel *Sweet Lemons* was published by Poolbeg in 2021.

For more information about Fidelma and the philosophy behind her work, visit her website at *www.fidelmakellyauthor.com.*

Acknowledgements

I owe this book to many influences – not least of which are the drizzly Saturdays spent on the side-line of muddy rugby pitches throughout the second and third decades of my life. As I grew older and obviously softer, I opted for the comfort of the covered stand, in the slicker, professional era of the game, but I have never lost that passion of my early rugby-supporting years.

My love affair with Sicily continues: it was a pleasure to research and write a large section of this novel on the eastern coast of the island. Thank you, Taormina!

Thanks are also due to the Irish Writers' Centre Novel Fair competition and judges Anthony Glavin, John McKenna and Nadine O'Regan who chose the first draft of *Because He Loved Her* as a Finalist winner from among hundreds of entries.

To my early readers Ethel Dwyer, Margaret Meehan and Ester Tossi: thank you for your time, reactions and linguistic advice.

To my fellow Curtis Brown Writing course participants, who offered an international perspective and fresh and frank insights that helped forge the final shape of this novel.

For feedback and commentary, heartfelt thanks go to fellow authors Catherine Dunne, Lisa Harding and her Blackrock Writers' group, Vanessa Fox-O'Loughlin, Daniela Crowe and editor-in-residence at West Cork Literary Festival Kishani Widyaratna.

An author needs a publisher like a dance needs a dancer. Thank you, Paula Campbell and the entire team at Poolbeg Press for your continued support – in particular, Gaye Shortland, my good-humoured, patient and perfectionist editor.

For Raymond Lambert
Lausanne & Dublin
1949-2022

Part 1

SUMMER 2022

Chapter 1

Johnny

Allenbeg, Tipperary, Ireland

I never really liked my son-in-law. When he first landed on my doorstep, I pretended to – for Vanessa's sake – and to keep the others off my back, but he was a snooty gobshite. This morning, when Tommy the postman pulled his van right into my yard, I knew he was on the trail of a bit of gossip. His outstretched hand held an expensive-looking white envelope cautiously, as if it contained anthrax.

'How's Johnny? Nothing dreadful – only this posh-looking one – I'd wager an invite. Mind how you go!'

And, with that, the small green van turned and was gone.

I suspected immediately what it was. I had heard of Rob's plans to remarry some weeks back, so the wedding itself wasn't exactly a surprise. The surprise was that I was to be invited.

I felt the need to fortify myself and went down to the kitchen to make a cup of tea. I filled the kettle and took the tea caddy from the cupboard. My hand shook as I dipped the spoon into the musty leaves. I let the spoon drop and found myself back in the hallway, turning the hefty envelope over and over in my hand. This cruel piece of communication had a sender's sticker on the back – somebody called 'Roche' with an address in Greystones, County Wicklow.

The shrill of the kettle was insistent, so I ripped the seal as I wandered back down the steps to the kitchen, accidentally tearing the sender label in half.

I don't know why it *hurt* to see Rob Cunningham's name in print on the invitation, but it did. I suppose it was the finality of the break with Vanessa and our family that provoked the jolt. In the beginning, I had given him the benefit of the doubt – the sportsman in me, I suppose. And he was also from a rural background on his mother's side, though their holding was a much grander affair than mine. I guess I was relieved that at least he wasn't one of those poncy city-slicker types that Vanessa had occasionally dragged home from some fashion event or other in Dublin. I could never fathom how a good solid business degree had led her into such a silly industry. Not to mention the stint modelling and judging Miss Ireland and the like, where she had met Rob at a selection heat in some hotel bar, when he was out with a group of teammates.

'I'm bringing a friend down on Sunday, Daddy,' she had said, laughing into the phone, not long after she started dating him. 'You'll like him – he's sporty.'

She failed to mention his chosen game, which had never been my code, but Rob was a natural sportsman and a ball was a ball, despite its shape. We ended up on that first afternoon having a kick-about, Vanessa included. She had been a fairly handy minor footballer, before she began to worry about rebounding balls bruising her face and gave it up for more genteel exercise. After lunch, I had suggested the game to break the ice a little, as the visitor maintained a degree of formality with me, which I was not used to.

'Here, Rob, this one's yours!' and I hoisted a high ball for him to field.

He ran across the paddock in an impressive sprint and caught the ball neatly.

'Right back at you, Mr Walshe!' and he leathered the ball with the force and trajectory of a much younger man. There it was again: '*Mr Walshe*', even on the football pitch!

'For God's sake, Rob, would you call me Johnny! You've eaten my dinner, you've drunk my beer.' (I wanted to add: 'and you've had your hands all over my beloved daughter and have probably screwed her', but I thought that might have been too much on our first encounter.) 'I think we can dispense with the formalities.'

'Well, actually, I didn't drink any beer – I don't drink alcohol – but, alright, if you prefer Johnny, that's what I'll call you from now on.' And with that he passed the ball deftly to Vanessa, chasing and half-tackling, half-hugging her as they fell onto the grass laughing.

I knew it was only horseplay, but I felt an anxious knot in my stomach all the same.

———

He wasn't what I expected. Vanessa's previous boyfriends had been tall to match and surpass her own considerable height. Rob was shorter – stocky – with disproportionately developed shoulders. In her bare feet, they were about the same height, but once in heels she dwarfed him – it may have been a bit male chauvinistic of me but I found it strange.

He seemed shy for a city club rugby player, with his soft baby-face and ordinary-looking mousey-brown hair. Not being an expert on these matters, I had to accept the opinion of my son's wife – that he was 'attractive but not too much so' – and was what the women would describe as 'good husband material'.

He certainly wasn't a stunner like my Vanessa – even I could see that – but then I was biased on the subject of my only daughter's beauty. I am not ashamed to admit that I tuned in to *Morning Glory* on the telly only on the days she was presenting and followed every toss of her head in admiration. But the thought that she might seriously be in pursuit of a husband – with all the changes that implied – had thrown me off balance.

It's not that I hadn't expected her to marry *eventually* – particularly to marry well – someone who would continue taking care of her the way I had done since her mother passed away when she was only ten but, as she blossomed into an interesting and entertaining young woman, it had been just the two of us at all the sporting and social events. I had begun to depend on her company.

Sundays were always my day. A match followed by dinner, or depending on the kick-off, lunch followed by a quick race to some sports ground or other. But since she'd met Rob, Sunday was now *his* day, as was Saturday and Friday evening and the entire weekend, if the match was an away one with Saracens or Treviso or in some other out of the way place. Occasionally, my son Davey and his wife Karen travelled with them, compounding my sense of abandonment.

Davey didn't hold back. 'Dad, you're being unreasonable,' he said more than once. 'You can't wrap her up in cotton wool for ever. You've had a monopoly on her time for long enough. You're starting to sound selfish now. And, besides, Rob seems like a decent bloke.'

He had also had the heads-up from Karen that I was shortly to receive a visit, in which Rob planned to do the old-fashioned 'asking my permission thing', before he proposed marriage. It all seemed dreadfully rushed. I said as much to Karen.

'Sure, they're not together any length of time. Is it not a bit soon to be announcing engagements?'

She gave that serene smile that women smug with themselves do and retorted: 'When you know, you know.'

Women talk a lot of shite most of the time.

———

It was an unseasonably frosty night in October when Rob came calling. I prepared myself for the chat Karen had anticipated. I can recall my feelings of nervousness, as if I were the one to be interviewed and not the other way around. I went to the trouble of changing out of my everyday clothes and dressed in a smarter outfit. I cleaned a couple of crystal tumblers and put them on a tray with a jug of water and a bottle of whiskey, and then I remembered he didn't drink. Besides, he had a good stretch of road ahead of him to training camp in Limerick, and I didn't want him to think I encouraged that sort of thing. I cleared away the glasses, threw out the water and shoved the whiskey back onto the bookshelves.

Tea was the way to go. I headed down to the kitchen to prepare a tray, then I thought he was probably a coffee drinker, and all I had in were granules. Where was Nessa when I needed her? This was the sort of thing she usually handled, just floating easily around the kitchen, fetching and preparing things methodically, all the time chatting to her guest as she did so, whereas I was unused to the social niceties of entertaining and any company but my immediate family, who usually catered for *me* when they were at home. I cobbled together some sort of tray, with a packet of shortbread biscuits I suspected had been there since the previous Christmas and were probably stale and, as I was carrying it back up to the sitting room, I heard the rattle of the cattle grid and saw the flash of headlights. Somebody rapped on the window. I checked it was indeed him – too many attacks on isolated farmhouses these days – and then headed for the front door where he was waiting.

'You made good time – if you were still in Dublin, that is, when you phoned me.' (I knew I was rabbiting on but I couldn't stop.) 'Come in, come in out of the cold. That's a hoar frost for this early in autumn.'

'Yes, it was bad enough in parts – unexpectedly.'

I watched as he hesitated in the hall, wondering if he should remove his waxed jacket and put it on the wooden hat-stand, a yoke that hasn't had a coat that doesn't smell of mothballs placed on it in years.

I felt a curious satisfaction at his discomfort. 'Here, take off your coat.' I pointed to the newel post at the end of the stairs. 'I have a good fire on inside. You'll appreciate the extra layer better when you get back into the car.'

Rob almost leaped out of the coat and draped it over mine.

'You're probably wondering why I'm disturbing you in the middle of the week like this—'

'I have a fair idea.'

'Well, it is – as you know – Vanessa's birthday next week, and I had hoped – well, as part of her present – to buy her an engagement ring.'

This all came out in a rush, most unlike the normal pace of his speech.

'I thought as much.'

'Would you be agreeable to the idea?'

'For God's sake, man, this isn't *Pride and fuckin' Prejudice*. Are you asking me if I'm OK about you marrying Nessa?'

'Well, *she* has a bit of a say in it as well. We shouldn't presume.' He relaxed a bit and grinned. 'Are you making tea?' He nodded at the tray.

'You'll have a cup?'

'Yes, please.'

'I'll put on the kettle.' I pointed in the direction of the kitchen.

'I'll come with you.'

I was uncomfortable at this suggestion. I didn't really want an audience, but I could hardly say as much.

'You know, if – and I feel quite confident that she will – if Vanessa accepts my proposal, I don't really want a long engagement.'

My future son-in-law watched as I set about making tea.

'Why the rush?' I blushed immediately when I thought of the implications of my question. 'I mean, you're not going out very long. By all means, get engaged – move in together if you want to – isn't that what all you young people do? Give yourselves a chance to get to know each other better, without the pressure of a wedding and setting up home and all that.'

'I'm quite traditional about these things. The home will come with the marriage.' Rob took the heavy teapot out of my hand. 'Besides, when you know, you know.'

Here we fuckin' go again. 'I suppose you do.' I carried the milk and sugar up the steps behind my daughter's fiancé.

But did I? Did *I* know if he was right for my precious girl? After a half-cup of too strong tea and a soft biscuit, Rob had taken his leave of me, satisfied that it was all systems go. He had my seal of approval. He looked like he was about to attempt a hug on the stoop of the door, but accepted the hand I offered instead. I'm all for a firm handshake but his grip was so over the top that I had to shake the circulation back into my fingers long after he released them.

I waved at the retreating Land Cruiser, a bit redundantly given it was pitch black in the yard, and went back inside. And, as I did, a sense of desolation engulfed me and I felt uneasy. What exactly had I agreed to? What did I know about this man who I was about to hand over the most important thing in my life to? I mean, an hour before I didn't even know if he preferred coffee to tea!

I grabbed the bottle of Paddy, sat in my chair, threw the dregs of the revolting beverage into the fire, and filled the good cup with an unmeasured tot of whiskey. I was inconsolable.

I sat there for what seemed hours, topping up the fire with turf, and with logs whose sap hadn't fully dried out and which spat and sparked in derision, hissing *'foolish old man'* and causing me to jump each time. If this was such a momentous happy event, why did I feel so sad? I liked Rob well enough – well, as much as any father likes the man

11

who is about to take away his only daughter – and Nessa seemed to be completely sure about him. *Was* I being selfish, as Davey frequently asserted – wanting things to stay the same and having first call on her?

With the second glass of whiskey, I tried to look at the more positive aspects of what had just happened. I would have a new family member and perhaps grandchildren in the not-too-distant future. (Rob seemed to be a man in a hurry.) There was all the excitement of a wedding to look forward to, though the thought of that awkward handover at the top of the church aisle terrified me. I needed to adjust my feelings accordingly before seeing Vanessa for her birthday, since the last thing she would want would be her da blubbering and making a show of her in some fancy restaurant in Dublin. It wasn't all bad; it could be a good year after all.

It was. At least some parts of it were. The months and months of build-up to the wedding, the volumes of magazines she purchased and the sheaves of torn-out pages with dresses and shoes and the lord knows what, stuffed into folders and thrown all over the house. I suppose had her mother still been alive, I wouldn't have been so involved, but Vanessa was used to roping me in as her second opinion on all kinds of things. This was no different. Meetings with florists, and rehearsals with musicians, vats of ribbon dyeing in the shed for table arrangements, trial hair-dos, trial make-up, arguments about seating plans, gifts arriving, neighbours dropping in. Suitcases being packed for a spectacular holiday immediately after the event and that final nostalgic jaunt in the car to the pretty hillside church – just her and me.

And yes, despite my best intentions, I did some blubbering in that church.

Twice.

I pick up the stiff white invitation from the table. It has a kind of imitation linen weave going through the paper and the printed bits are in gold apart from the blank line for my name, which is written in a fancy black script. *'Mr John Walshe & Guest'*. And *guest*! They probably think I need minding in case I get drunk and disorderly. It's for some date late August. The venue and even the bride's name barely register with me. **RSVP before July 20th**. It's not even the end of June now. She's fast out of the traps this . . . Tamsin. Odd name.

I wonder about the preparations over in Wicklow. Are there bits of material everywhere and practice floral arrangements? Have the tiers of the cake been baked yet? Or maybe they're having that trendy one with the chocolate biscuits. What will the bride look like? *Will she look like Vanessa?* A part of me wants her to be a replica – but an

13

inferior replica and, ungraciously, the other conflicting part wants her to be as ugly as sin, to punish Rob for what he had, and what he carelessly lost.

I guess I'll see for myself in August. That's if I can bear to go.

Chapter 2

Davey

South Dublin, Ireland

Karen was in a quandary about our invitation. When I got home from my business trip to Italy, the second thing she did was hand me the damn envelope. (The first was a hug and a welcome-home kiss.) Since Vanessa, we have stopped taking for granted that I will return home safely from every journey.

'What do you think?' she asks.

I'm still digesting the information – the scenic Wicklow hotel, the popular last Saturday in August. This was no low-key affair put together at the last minute. To secure that hotel on such a busy date – this was at least a year in the planning – even longer, if they had their booking deferred due to pandemic restrictions.

'What do you expect me to think? That Rob is moving on quickly from his heartbroken state?' I toss the invitation onto the table.

'I mean, should we go? It seems odd that he's including us.'

'He's still my brother-in-law and we've always maintained contact – admittedly less so since the hearing . . . and Tamsin . . . but he still touches base every so often. Didn't we get tickets from him for the internationals? And he dropped in presents at Christmas?'

'A lousy box of chocolates and a plant – don't get carried away. I don't know . . .' Karen picks up the invitation and frowns. 'I'll have a chat with Johnny about it. I'm presuming he's had one? It seems a bit . . . insensitive somehow. We should really be led by his decision.'

'Did you hear from Dad when I was away?'

'Not since this would have landed. He phoned on Monday about when I was dropping back the accounts. But they're far more complicated since he opted for the tillage incentive scheme and sold off most of the herd. Then there's Michael the farm-hand's altered salary due to their arrangement for him to manage what remains on the dairy side. I actually *do* need more information, which is probably better explained in person. We could pop down on Saturday – use the books as an excuse?'

'Surely Michael has that stuff up on the computer? It seems ridiculous Dad doing it all by hand. I've tried a hundred times to convert him to technology but, no, it's still the laborious ledgers.'

'He won't change at this stage of his life. Besides, it makes him feel he still has some involvement in running the farm.'

'Rather him than me. You know I've always hated the financial side of my job.'

'It gives him something to do in the evenings. You forget how lonely he's been since Vanessa.'

'But she was living in the city . . . *before* . . . it's not like she was at home with him.'

'I know but, apart from her soup-run night, or her TV morning slots, I suspect she was there more often than she let on.'

'Sounds a bit needy on her part.'

Karen pulled a face. 'Why do you say that?'

'Ah, she was always too attached to Dad. I said it to him umpteen times – it was his responsibility to put a bit of distance between them.'

'That's easy for you to say. You were at boarding school when your mother died. She was only ten, left on that farm with a depressed Johnny and a herd of cows that he could hardly cope with. It was inevitable that they would grow to rely on each other.'

'A reliance that Dad needed to discourage as she became an adult woman . . . I need a shower.'

Karen opened her mouth as if to continue our conversation but I was gone. My temples were throbbing with a tension headache and my right shoulder ached from dragging that carry-on bag through the interminable corridors of Fiumicino airport. The new client had relocated his factory to an industrial park north of Rome, inconveniently a two-train hop from the city, where some lunatic driver had picked me up at the station and did his best to rearrange my bone structure as we rattled over the last twenty or so kilometres to the plant. Although the business side of it had gone well, I found the generous entertaining of my Italian counterparts exhausting and my stress was compounded by our less than satisfactory communication in pidgin English and Italian.

Loath as I am to admit it, since Vanessa's death I have developed an irritation with Italians. I know this is irrational, that my colleagues in the food industry are innocent of any negligence towards my sister, yet I can't help it. Their cheerfulness and light-hearted bonhomie offend me. They never seem to discuss any issue in depth – whether it's global warming or yet another collapsed coalition government, or – the subject closest to my heart – the seemingly bizarre Italian legal system. They had been extremely sympathetic back in the summer when it happened – phoning and emailing their condolences, and for several months after constantly enquiring about my father and her husband and how they were all doing. Then suddenly, the time for sorrow was over and normal life resumed, with our interactions confined either to business deals or the concerns that filled *their* days – the goings-on of children and grandchildren, the next holiday they planned to take, where they had eaten the most wonderful *pesce spada* the previous Sunday.

Over the last three years, I have envied their ability to be shallow. At home, my family paid lip-service to it being time to move on, but neither Karen nor I have really done so. In the first year, we had the expectation of some answers and had followed the enquiry closely but, after the preliminary hearing, we slumped back into a depression, while Karen and I carried the additional burden of guilt at having proposed Taormina as the honeymoon venue in the first place.

———

'You just have to go – it's the most romantic place in the world!' I can still hear myself enthuse.

When Rob and Vanessa began to plan their wedding within a fairly tight time-frame, it was inevitable that we would be asked for suggestions. I was perceived as a semi-expert on Italy, given that I imported their food and wine and travelled to a different part of the country on a monthly basis. When the subject of suitable honeymoon venues for early July was raised, Karen took control.

'Davey's right. It has to be Taormina.'

Rob seemed unconvinced. 'Is it on the sea? What about all that Mafia business?'

Karen laughed, her eyes sparkling with excitement, her cheeks flushed as if she were already in the hot July sun.

'Yes! Just a short funicular ride down to the most idyllic crescent of a bay – and there's your nearest beach. And as for that other business, well, they're no worse than our own home-grown criminals, except in Sicily they wear posh suits.'

19

The glamour of it all had attracted Vanessa, and she and Karen had escaped to the office to check out possibilities.

Karen and I were mad about Sicily, having spent our first summer there as a student couple. We had systematically back-packed and cycled our way around the island, picking up work as we went – she, because she was multi-lingual and prettier, working in the many coastal town restaurants – and me, because I was sporty, English-speaking and reasonably well put-together, as a tour leader for short-stay visitors who fancied a mountain-climb or some sea-kayaking.

Many years later when we married, Karen's well-meaning godmother who worked in the luxury tourism sector, treated us to our honeymoon at a five-star gated resort on the Caribbean Island of Aruba. Whilst it was opulent and wonderfully relaxing after the manic months prior to the wedding, it lacked colour and character, and our hearts ached for the passionate chaos and authenticity of our beloved Sicily. As early as the long-haul flight back home, we resolved to rent a place for as many weeks as we could afford the following year, on our favourite Italian island.

I still smile when I think of all the grotty one-bed hovels in which we stayed in various coastal resorts during our earlier visits. It has only been in recent years that our affluence allows us to afford the better hotels of Taormina, the resort of choice of royals and celebrities. I suspect it's that sense of having 'arrived' at where she had really wanted to stay all along, that has turned Karen into a kind of zealous one-woman tourist board for the town.

Between the two of us, we had talked the honeymooners around.

'Is this going to cost me a fortune?' Rob, draping his arm affectionately around Vanessa's shoulder, asked the question jocosely but, I felt, with serious intent.

'Probably. Italy *is* expensive, but it's quality, man.' I smiled at his worried expression. 'Besides, it's worth it. *Nessa's* worth it.'

This seemed to copper-fasten it for Rob. His anxious expression dissipated and, giving my sister a sudden squeeze, he acquiesced with an assertive nod of the head.

'Yes, that she is.'

When it came to them actually booking dates, we were all so excited by the thought of Sicily again that we decided to go on holidays with the honeymoon couple. Well, that is not strictly accurate. First problem was that Vanessa wanted to bring Dad with them. Despite my pointing out the inappropriateness of this, my sister dug in her heels and insisted that she had always taken him on holidays, for who else had he got to go on holidays with? This holiday was, she declared, to be no different.

Uncomfortable at the thought of our new-in-laws'

reaction to the proposed threesome, Karen and I decided to take a holiday at the same time, contacting our usual haunt – Hotel Giulia on Corso Umberto in the town – for two rooms, allowing the newlyweds plenty of space in a separate panoramic hotel.

But Dad, on seeing the pictures of the hotel's entrance, wasn't keen on joining us in effectively the main shopping street and, ever the countryman, had asked for somewhere less busy – 'farther out'. Our resident tourist information officer had her doubts about billeting him in a separate hotel, pointing out he was sixty-four, he spoke no Italian and he hadn't travelled much. Yet she knew better than to go against Johnny, and when she showed him the images of an old-style hotel in the village of Castelmola, perched high up, overlooking but not *in* the bustle of Taormina, he was sold.

We three would stay a week, accompanying Dad on the journey back, whilst the honeymooners remained. That was the plan.

So, when my beautiful only sister fell over a fence and down a rocky outcrop, resulting in her death, it was my fault that she was there in the first place. This would never have happened had she been on a flat sandy beach in the Caribbean.

Karen shared the responsibility. 'Oh my God! I encouraged her to go for La Villa – practically carved out

22

of the rock – because it had the prettiest view! Had I known!'

Men plan; God laughs. Though I hardly believe God would be so nasty as to plan that particular outcome.

———

As I put on fresh clothes for the evening, I wonder why I'm thinking so much about the planning and lead-up to Rob and Vanessa's honeymoon. It's not just that I am fresh off a plane from Italy – I'm always there. My work depends on frequent visits to the various producers, so that part of my life has had to continue as usual even in the direct aftermath of her death – but this last visit was different. Knowing that Rob was about to go again – to get married again – stirred up conflicting emotions. As I walked to the boarding gate earlier today, passing all the tourism promotion billboards, I couldn't bear to look at the Sicilian one with that archetypal photo of Mount Etna taken from the amphitheatre in Taormina, because Taormina is now a dirty word, an unmentionable place in our house.

'Dave – your dad is on the phone. He wants a word.'

'Thanks. I'll pick it up here.'

'No, he's on my mobile.' Karen was already on the stairs.

'You're alright. I'm coming down.'

I meet her in the hall.

'What's the form like?' I half-whisper, half-mouth at her.

She waggles her hand meaning 'so-so' and, for Johnny's

benefit, enunciates loudly, 'He's wondering what I'm doing with his accounts!'

I take the phone. 'How are ya, Dad?'

Silence.

I think we have been cut off, until I hear that distinctive deep intake of breath which precedes crying. Somehow, he controls his voice and manages to speak through the gulps.

'Wasn't it awful to get that fancy old invitation? I hear yours arrived as well.'

'Well, you knew it was on its way.'

'Still, all the same. Kind of line-in-the-sand time.'

'That's one way of looking at it.'

'And I *didn't* know the invitation was on the way – I knew there was another *wedding* on the way, but I thought he would have had the cop-on to leave us out of it.'

'You can always *not* go.'

'Is that what you and Karen are doing?'

'We haven't had a chance to discuss it really. I'm just in the door from . . . a business trip.'

'The whole thing is very upsetting.' The gulping had started again and, this time, he made no effort to disguise it. 'I just feel . . . I feel like Nessa's completely forgotten –'

'I wouldn't say that exactly.'

'—that he's moving on much too quickly.'

There really is no answer to that.

'Look, why don't we take a spin down to see you on Saturday?' I say. 'Slowcoach has some queries about your figures, but she should have the bulk of them done by then.'

'I'm not in the mood for company.'

'Fine. That settles it. We'll have a late pub lunch Saturday about two, so wait for us. Will I put Karen back on?'

'No need. Say goodbye to her for me.'

'See you Saturday.'

Karen comes back out of the kitchen, her hand extended for the phone. 'So, we're going visiting?'

'Yes. He's quite upset.'

'I thought he sounded a bit off. Not surprising. You and I'll have to decide on our strategy for this damned wedding before the weekend.'

This was something I wasn't ready to tackle just yet. 'Come on. I'm hungry. Dinner first. Anything but pasta!'

'Have you any new wines for me to try?'

'There's a couple in my bag in the hall. What are we eating?'

'Steak.'

'I have just the one!'

And then, before I go to fetch the wine, I wrap my arms around Karen, inhaling deeply her Karen-smell, burying my cheek in her hair, because dreadful unexpected things happen to people in unexpected places, all the time.

Chapter 3

Bishop Joe

Waterford City, Ireland

When I was transferred to the diocese of Waterford and Lismore, I was greatly relieved. It was a fresh start, an agreeable part of the country and at fifty-three years of age I was young enough to mould the job to my liking, to make a mark on my new parish.

I like this south-eastern corner of Munster – the beauty of the landscape, the diversity of the people. On arrival, I was immediately surprised by the various nationalities living here – not only in the city of Waterford, but more interestingly, out in the many smaller towns and villages which comprise the diocese for which I am responsible.

Most of all, I love the fact that it isn't County Clare. What had started out as the dream job – my first posting as bishop in a terrain which I had been familiar with since I was a boy – had ended in torment. Every working day became a nightmare and I closeted myself away from those with whom I should have been mingling – people who depended on me for solace and sustenance as they rebuilt their lives having fled war-torn countries or struggled to claw back what they had lost in the last economic crash. What galled me most was that my untenable situation had been brought about by others – and that, although deeply embroiled in the saga, I had done nothing to provoke it.

But proverbial mud does actually stick, and I found myself bombarded by questions about the story on a daily basis as I went about my more mundane duties. I tried and tried to smile and treat each enquiry with a combination of levity and grateful sympathy, but after several months, I was developing rictus: I just couldn't keep a genuine smile going.

We all know what happened at that point, and the embarrassment of my crisis will never leave me. I was left with no option but to step back from my position and do what I should have done in the beginning: take a career-break until the fuss died down.

Which is why, this morning in the sun-infused diocesan office of Waterford and Lismore, I became incensed when I discovered this accursed invitation in my in-tray, a Post-it stuck to the back: '*We'll have to meet up soon to go through the ceremony. R.*'

I suppose it wasn't very ecclesiastical of me but my gut reaction was to scroll down the contacts in my phone and to bawl my nephew out of it. I did.

'Hi, Uncle Joe, how's it going? Did you get my invitation?'

'You know I did. That's why I'm calling.' I intend to

phrase it as diplomatically as possible but it still comes out as: '*What the hell are you thinking of? You know I can't possibly be involved in this wedding.*'

'But you said you would . . . ages ago . . . you know it won't be the same if you're not the celebrant!'

'Rob! Think about what you're asking. *You* are not the only one entitled to a new life.'

'But Tamsin's mother has her heart set on it – us being married by a bishop.'

'Tamsin's mother might have to review her position. And, anyway, I am not a commodity to be purchased. You can do all the commercial stuff with the wedding planner you've no doubt employed, but my services are not for sale.'

'*Wow!* Where's all *this* coming from?'

I could hear the dismay in Rob's voice.

'Uncle Joe! You've always had my back. I thought you and I were pals.'

'We were. We *are*, but I have concerns.'

'*Concerns.* What's that supposed to mean?'

'You know full well what I mean. And, apart from that, it's all a bit precipitate.'

'In English, please. I'm only a thick front-row rugby player. Think of all the head injuries.'

'I mean you're rushing into this.'

'Tamsin and I are good together. I can't wait any longer. I thought you of all people would grasp the concept of "the sanctity of marriage".'

'Don't go calling me on that one. Remember, I *am* a

celibate. I took that vow. It's part of the deal. Your commitment to such an ideology is very much a personal choice and has very little to do with me.'

'I can't believe I am hearing this. That a Catholic bishop would advocate promiscuity!'

'Slow down there, don't twist my words. What I am saying is, that I am not hooked on this philosophy of "waiting". A sound marriage needs to be founded on a good sexual relationship.'

'You're a joke!' Rob sounded as if he was about to cut the call, but then he rebounded: 'So, the deferred physical relationship with Vanessa before we were married made no difference at all in the eyes of the Church?'

'Rob, your personal relationship was just that – personal. It was a judgement call for you and Vanessa.'

'But what happened to the rules? If I choose to follow the rules and my partner refuses? Are you – a Catholic bishop – telling me that I should defer to her even if it's against my beliefs?'

'No, but forcing someone to do something against *their* beliefs is equally wrong.'

'So, sex before marriage is fine by you? The more the better!'

I needed to put an end to the direction this conversation was taking.

'Look, Rob, I only rang to suggest that another celebrant officiate. It would be easier for you two as well – the less there is in common with your first wedding the better.'

'And who are we going to find at a couple of months' notice?'

'I'll make a few calls. I'll get you somebody great.'

'That's hypocritical. I thought you didn't believe the marriage should happen at all, yet you're perfectly willing to pass the responsibility over to someone else. You just don't want all that stuff about Vanessa's death being dragged up again, with your name in the middle of it.'

'*No, I bloody well don't!*' I yelled. I took a deep breath and made an effort to tone it down. 'Your lifestyle . . . is your choice and has consequences – *had* consequences – bad consequences for me, because of your high media profile. The last thing I need now is to have my face all over the papers, with some sort of smart-aleck caption like "*Re-Match*"!'

'There won't be any media. Tamsin agrees. She has warned the wedding planner and her photography buddies that it's a private event.'

'And you are naïve enough to think that word won't get out? That even if you actually manage to cordon off the hinterland of Greystones, that one of your guests won't post it on social media? I'm surprised at you, Rob. These days, there's no such thing as a private event.'

'I don't know what side of the bed you got out of this morning but you're very grumpy – or maybe' – he sniggered – 'maybe you didn't get to bed at *all* last night. Out for a midnight stroll again?'

It was time to swipe the call to its conclusion. He had no right to bring that up. He could bloody-well find his own replacement minister, which shouldn't be a major problem given that he was practically a member of the clergy the way he went on! No doubt he was still in contact with some of the guys he met during his brief sojourn in Maynooth University.

———

Even a casual mention of my breakdown upsets me. At the time, I hadn't realised I was spiralling out of control so rapidly. In the months immediately succeeding Vanessa's death, of course, like the rest of the family, I was distressed and angry at the seeming injustice of the loss of a young life on the cusp of so much. I railed at God and questioned why he had doled out such misery to her particular family. But then I got on with living and, apart from coping badly with the curious enquiries of my neighbours and diocesans, I thought I had put it behind me. I had even begun to forgive God.

However, after the hearing adjudicated that there was no case to answer, doubts niggled and distracted me. I certainly wasn't myself. I became a preoccupied, functioning depressive, fulfilling my role in a manner and overseeing that my obligations were attended to, but inside I was still in torment. My concentration was shot; I couldn't process more than one small task at a time and, then, not even well. Back in Killaloe, the Church finances still permitted the luxury of a full-time secretary and he was

31

constantly spotting errors and returning edited documents for signing. In the end, I relied upon him to draft what was needed from scratch, and I hardly read the letters before scrawling my signature at the end.

———

The sleep-walking began about three weeks after hearing that confession.

I shouldn't even refer to this: I am breaking the 'Seal of the Confessional' i.e. 'client confidentiality'. But I know that's what set it off.

I had been a seasonal sleepwalker when I was a young boy. By seasonal, I mean I only ever went rambling when my parents took me off on *their* rambles to a holiday cottage or a caravan park in the summer. The change of bed and the stress of different and more cramped accommodation seemed to make me restless, and the ease of access to escape outdoors was facilitated by a seldom-locked door. Following too many rainy August nights spent searching for a pyjama-clad eight-year-old, my parents changed their open-door policy, and put as many obstacles as possible in my path, to keep me inside at night.

My adult nocturnal rambles were quite different. In the treatment centre, during hour after expensive hour with psychiatrists and therapists and counsellors, they kept returning to the one question I couldn't answer – from the first session on.

'And, Joe, was there one single *recent* event that might have set this off?'

'I've been under a lot of stress lately – the new appointment – as bishop.' I thought I'd focus on this. 'You see I'm quite young for the job. There were others – with expectations – ahead of me in the queue, if you understand.'

The psychiatrist nodded vehemently. Clearly, he did.

'And then of course you had that dreadful tragedy in your family abroad. Malta, wasn't it?'

'Sicily.'

The psychiatry intern raised her fingers in the expectation of keying something juicy into the iPad.

'Yes, it was a terrible tragedy, a terrible loss for the family.' I had to draw the line at ending with '*God works in mysterious ways*' but I was tempted.

The intern seemed disappointed.

The psychiatrist moved on.

'Joe, in your sleepwalking bouts of recent weeks, you were walking naked. Do you think there might be any sexual reason for that?'

Of course, there was some sort of sexual reason for it: this whole story revolves around sex! But I'm a bishop, so I'd better not tell them that.

'No, not at all. Maybe I undressed, thinking I was going for a shower – I don't know. I was in an unconscious state.'

'You must have found it . . . very difficult . . . to be discovered like that, asleep in a park.'

'It wasn't my most glorious moment.' I can still see the

tabloid headline: '*Bishop NIPS out for a nap!*'

'It seems to me . . .' The psychiatrist had to pause for an involuntary fit of coughing. 'Sorry about that. Where was I? Oh, yes. The stressor which provoked the renewed sleepwalking did not accompany you to the Centre. You have had no episodes of night disturbance or attempted breakouts since residing here. Correct?'

'None.'

'Good. Then obviously your problem relates directly to your work environment.' The psychiatrist smiled, removed his glasses and put them on the table.

Genius! How many years of study did it take to conclude that? 'I told you as much.'

'Well, Joe, might I suggest that you tackle head-on the source of your anxiety and confront it?' At this, he narrowed his glassless eyes and focussed intently on me. 'Only *you* really know what the conflict is. Just because you haven't shared it, doesn't mean that you are ignorant of it.'

I smiled back weakly. Maybe there was something in that training after all.

The source of my conflict was a centuries-old dilemma – in a nutshell, the Seal of the Confessional. Knowledge of a secret can be a burden at any time, but knowledge of a cover-up where you know all involved is inconceivable. No wonder I had gone stark raving mad.

His disclosure happened in a most unorthodox way. It was late March, with a hint of mildness in the air and we were both out exercising. I had taken the bike for an ambitiously long spin – the first challenging one of spring – and was finding the going difficult. I spotted him coming towards me on the road, walking briskly. Any excuse to stop and give myself a chance to recover.

I dismounted. 'How're you doing! What has you over this way?'

'Same as yourself. I fancied a change of scenery and took a spin over to the lake, and then thought I'd get in a bit of exercise, to shift some of the winter weight. I like your gear, by the way – very trendy.'

'Is it too flash? I tried to get a more conservative strip but they don't do understated Lycra. Something to do with high-viz colours, even for men of the cloth.'

'Well, you're probably better off being a fluorescent bishop than a dead bishop. Speaking of dead, do you have a minute?' His face had a pinched look, the glow of his exercising suddenly gone. 'Can we sit down?' He began walking towards a low wall. Without warning, as he perched uncomfortably on a stone wall somewhere in the diocese of Killaloe, he made his disclosure. I heard the words, and the rationale, and the excuses, but I found it hard to assimilate what was being offered to me. When he

35

begged me to keep it to myself, I knew I was in trouble. I tried to reconstruct our conversation into a formal confession setting. I offered to say a prayer with him, to which he agreed. My mind was racing through all the protocol of the confessional and how to protect us both. I began absolution, but he interrupted me.

'I can't.'

'Let me. It's important. I'm going to offer you absolution for your – *omission* – and then I will bless you.'

But he shook his head. 'How can I? I'd have to be truly sorry for how I acted and make retribution, and I can do neither.' With that, he stood up and half-jogged, half-walked back in the direction from which he had come.

And that, Doctor Psychiatrist, is why I was found stark naked at 4am in a public park.

One of the other newspapers even featured this as its headline: '*STARKERS!*' – probably with an additional two or three exclamation marks.

If I am sensitive on the subject of media presence at my nephew's second wedding, then he and his bride will have to forgive me, but it's precisely the memory of such past intrusion into my life that has informed my decision about officiating.

That, and other things.

Chapter 4

Tamsin

Dublin City Centre, Ireland

I have arranged to meet my mother for lunch in Brown Thomas. We still have to agree the final items for inclusion on the list, before popping next door to have the wedding shop people put it online. As she's already twenty minutes late, I leave my post at the Alessi counter and go into Bottom Drawer to double-check a brand of bed-linen I am not entirely sure about, whilst keeping half an eye on the escalator for Mother incoming. Everybody says the classic Frette range is the best, but it seems a little dull to me. I quite fancy Roberto Cavalli Home designs but Mother isn't keen on pattern – so plain and dull is obviously superior.

A tap on the shoulder alerts me to her arrival.

'There you are! I thought we said at Alessi?'

'We did, but you were late.' We kiss each other on the cheek. 'Look, what do you think of this Roberto Cavalli stuff? I quite like it.'

'You'd tire of the busyness of all that gaudy colour very quickly. Better stick with white.'

'But it's so *boring!*'

'Now, no one said setting up home was all fun and games – there are drudgery bits to be got through as well.'

'Thanks for reminding me.'

'Oh, that's not the attitude! Come on, let's eat and you'll feel cheerier after. What time is your dress fitting at?'

'Four o'clock.'

'Plenty of time to digest your lunch, so! I'll even treat you to a glass of wine.'

'Go mad why don't you, and we'll have two.'

'Liquid sugar. You can't. Not if you want to fit into that dress.'

'Did you hear the latest? Rob wants to come to the fitting.'

'*What?* Under no circumstances.'

'I sort of put him off' – the waitress arrives with our bottles of mineral water – 'but you know how insistent he can be.'

'It's out of the question. If he shows up, leave him to me.'

'He means no harm, it's just – well, he likes to take an interest.'

'Take an interest, or take control? I've warned you. You need to nip that in the bud.'

'I don't know why you say that. Isn't it good he's in touch with his feminine side?'

The wine having arrived, my mother does her annoying

Cin Cin thing – a recent holiday in Sorrento and she has gone native – and clinks my glass over-enthusiastically. Emboldened by an extra-large gulp, she returns to the subject of my appearance.

'Now – *and don't take this the wrong way* – but do you not think you've changed your style of dressing since you and Rob got together?'

'Well, I am a *better* dresser now. Less arty. I mean, I'm older and soon to be married. I can't be running around in micro-minis.'

'Says who?'

'Says me. I don't think it's appropriate anymore.'

'*Why?* Have your legs suddenly tripled in size? Will your arse not fit into your skirts?'

'No, it will. But Rob's not keen on minis.'

'"*Ay there's the rub.*" Or the Rob, if the Bard will give me licence.'

'*What* are you on about?'

'A literary allusion, darling. Forget it.'

The arrival of the crab salad (me) and the *linguine con pesto* (the mother) proves a welcome distraction from Rob's shortcomings and I take advantage.

'Have you had any feedback about the invitations? Most of ours should have received them by now. I didn't mention it to Rob but I sent them out in two batches – our side of the family first! Makes sense. They're the ones who know me best and most likely to fork out for a decent present.'

'Tamsin Roche! How very mercenary of you! And, yes,

I had Aunt Charlotte on the phone first thing Monday morning.'

'And?'

'Thought the actual invitation very *grand* – though, having praised everything, she then went on to criticise the thickness of the card, saying she had managed to cut her hand on it! I swear she does it deliberately.'

'Well, I had some reservations about the weight of the paper too, but Tara convinced me it would look more solid.'

'And *then* – Charlotte couldn't resist – "*Isn't this Rob the same Rob the rugby player who lost his wife tragically on their honeymoon a year ago?*" Nosey old bitch.'

'I get that all the time. People just won't let it go.'

'And how do you react to their comments?'

'I pay no attention at all. Give the pat answer: everybody is entitled to a second chance, to have some happiness in their life after such a sad loss etc, etc.'

'You don't sound as if you mean it.'

'I couldn't care less really. This is *my* time. *And* I hope you informed Aunt Charlotte that it's nearly *three* years ago, not one.'

My mother stares hard at me while wrangling some *linguine* onto her fork, then escapes conversationally to the safety of the food. 'This is tasty. How's the crab?'

'Not one-hundred-per-cent crab – I'd say a touch of old *pomme de terre* swelling its ranks – and before you say it, yes, I *am* thinking of the calories!'

'Have we time for a coffee after?'

'Not here. We might go somewhere else for one after the fitting.'

'With Rob, you mean?'

'*Ha*, very funny. No, I want to split after this – I've a few things to pick up – and Mum, if you wouldn't mind liaising with the wedding list people – I've marked what's to be deleted. Get a printout of the final version – then I'll run around and do the other bits, and we can meet at four at Kathy's.'

'Sounds good. I want to try some make-up downstairs anyway.'

'Right, see you later.'

Although it may have sounded callous, it *was* true what I said to Mother: I don't dwell on Rob's past. I can't. We will have no future as a couple if I keep thinking of it. And, in a way, it's worse for me, since I was a witness to that first marriage. Not a witness in any official capacity but, as the photographer, recording every single gesture and touch and smile between them, not just on the wedding day but in the weeks leading up to it when I spent time with both, or each separately, trying to get a feel for what exactly they were like and what style would best sum up their personalities.

In fact, I was surprised to land the gig in the first place. I was still relatively new at the weddings then, but the *Morning Glory* photography contributor had given me a rave review and forwarded my contact to Vanessa. When I think of the state of me at our initial meeting! She had phoned towards the end of the previous August, with a view to seeing my portfolio and we'd set a date to meet ten days later, before Rob's travelling season kicked off. I had forgotten that it was the week after Electric Picnic, and having partied long and hard for three days and three nights, I had a major recovery job on my hands, which by the following Tuesday was still very much a work in progress.

I arrived into the front lounge of the Shelbourne Hotel, Dublin, wearing a leather mini-skirt, tartan tights, mud-encrusted ankle boots, all topped with a hand-knit poncho in rainbow shades, belonging to one of my flatmates – which one I wasn't certain – I had just grabbed it from the coat rail on the way out. My hair, although washed several times since EP, still smelt of smoke and various other substances. I was a mess.

The golden couple were reclining languidly on an elegant sofa: Vanessa, *chic* and immaculately groomed, was wearing a shift dress in a shade of emerald green which set off her long brown hair perfectly; Rob was smart-casual in the uniform of 'off duty' sportsmen – chinos and an expensive shirt. It was only when I observed the relatively summery dress of my prospective clients, did I register how bizarre and unseasonal my own outfit was. That's what three nights sleeping in a tent in the rain will do to your internal thermostat.

From the beginning, I thought they were a little mismatched. Rob wasn't sufficiently attractive for his beautiful fiancée. I thought he was a bit stumpy, had a fat neck and a childish face. In fact, he appeared to me much younger than Vanessa – and he wasn't. I had checked their profiles in preparing my pitch. I remember thinking: 'He's the sort of guy *I* go for' – I know my limitations, no point in overreaching.

Vanessa, with her image background from fashion and the media, conducted the meeting and, happy with what I had shown her, offered me the job.

That first glimpse – *live* as it were – of who unwittingly would become my future husband, is still vivid in my mind, as was his reaction to me in my odd 'boho' outfit. If it had been left to him to make the decision, I would never have been hired. Rob places a lot of importance on appearance and The Mother hit a nerve earlier when she commented on the increasingly conservative nature of my wardrobe.

As I make my way to the dress-fitting, I smile as I catch a glimpse of myself in a passing window on this July day. I'm wearing a monochrome shift dress and low-heeled pumps. It is almost a Vanessa-dress.

———

It's 3.55 and we are sitting patiently in the ante-room to 'Kathy's – Wedding-dress Designer *Extraordinaire*.' I am – to my mother's disapproval – sipping a glass of the complimentary Prosecco, as is she but that doesn't count. There is no sign of Rob.

'Kathy will be with you in a minute.' A minion has been sent out to pacify us and top up the fizz. 'The dress is here – and might I say – it's FAB! I'm just going to get you some trial shoes for adjusting the length. You are so petite that you need a bit of height, but we can see what size heel you're most comfortable with.'

Later in the inner sanctum, I am down to my undies as Kathy is pinning and marking the alterations of the dress I have just removed. My mother is on her third Prosecco. I have long since stopped – *water from now on* – since Kathy declared an increase of three inches on my hips and two on my waist. Mother opens her eyes wide in surprise. Tipsy, she mouths at me 'Too much sex!' and giggles like a bold schoolgirl. I return a complicit nod and a half-grimace smile. If only. Chance would be a fine thing.

When Kathy and her assistant leave the room, Mother persists: 'Tamsin! You're gaining weight being on the Pill. You'll have to look into an alternative.'

I debate whether to tell her that there is no need for the Pill. This is not a conversation I should be having with my mother, but I suppose the myth of the rampant sexuality of rugby-players has made her presume. When I say there has been *no* sex, I do not mean it in the way that old American president Bill Clinton declared '*I did not have sexual relations with that woman*'. His definition of 'no sexual relations' would have made Rob and me seem positively promiscuous.

When I say no sex, I mean *no* sex. *Nada.* Apparently, we are waiting.

It would have been nice to be told – (or even asked?) that this was the plan until we are married – and not to have discovered it by finding a heap of leaflets among Rob's things. The whole notion is completely bizarre! I mean, Rob has been married *before*! '*True Love Waits*' the brochures declare, emblazoned across a soft-focus picture of a couple – (young) – holding hands and looking longingly at each other. Much Googling later, I discover that no, it wasn't an old Radiohead tune, or even a promo for the title hit of the last Coronas' album, but instead an American organisation which promotes abstinence in Christian relationships prior to marriage. It began way back in the 1980s as a college sex education programme funded and backed by a stream of American presidents – Reagan, Bushes Senior & Junior all endorsed 'the purity plan'.

But back in the last century is where it should stay. When questioned, Rob declared that its philosophy has had a resurgence since the pandemic, about which he is very happy since it endorses his staunch Catholic views about the demeaning nature of 'casual sex' in non-committed relationships. Discussion over. We are where we are.

Kathy's acolyte is back with a pair of mid-heeled satin shoes. 'Try these. Though I can't understand why you don't just practise with the higher heels between now and' – she checks her clipboard – 'the 4th week of August. You need the additional few inches to show off that dress at its best.'

I clamber back into the pinned dress and try on the shoes.

'Tamsin, she's right – *sorry*, what did you say your name was again?'

'Lyndel.'

'Lyndel is right.' My mother is swaying towards me and a couple of drops from her topped-up Prosecco splash onto the flowing skirt. 'You won't be able to "sashay" down the aisle in sensible shoes!'

'These are fine. It'll be one less thing to worry about – being able to walk.'

Conceding, the assistant places her kneeling cushion on the wooden floor, opens her box of pins and sets to work on my hem.

And worried I *am* – the height of my shoe heel being the least of it. Despite me pushing the issue several times, Rob has been reluctant to expand on why he is adhering to the abstinence philosophy. I knew from my earliest contact with him that he was a very committed Catholic (the uncle a bishop and all that) but he's thirty-three now – not a high-school kid. It's not as if he has his virginity to lose! With only a couple of months to go from making serious vows to each other, he needs to relax his attitude. Although there doesn't seem to be any likelihood of that happening any time soon, I'm determined to persist. After all, it's my relationship too!

———

'Turn around.' Lyndel is fluffing out the back of my dress. 'I've hitched it up in the front so you don't tread on the skirt. Do you want to go for a twirl?'

'Wait! Wait till I get my phone.' Needing both her hands, my mother throws back the remainder of the fizz and taps away.

———

With four-fifths of a bottle of Prosecco inside her, our post-fitting coffee is essential. No sooner have I installed her at a counter in Butler's imbibing a badly needed double espresso than my phone rings. It is of course my fiancé, sounding for once a little flustered.

'We've lost the bishop!' He's almost crying down the line. 'Uncle Joe has bailed on me.' And trying to resume control, he adds feebly: 'Do you think your mother might know any priests out her way willing to do the job?'

I look at my half-cut mother, ignoring her coffee and chatting up a Spanish student about one third her age.

'Realistically? Not a chance. Sorry, Rob, this one's most definitely yours.'

'Joe did say he'd help find someone, though I'd prefer

not to go that route if I can. But, as you say, it's my responsibility now. How did the dress-fitting go?'

'Good. No – better than good. The dress is traditional and elegant.'

'Just what I wanted to hear. Will you be much longer? We could meet for a drink about six?'

'I'll have the mother in tow —'

'So? I never have a problem with mothers. I look forward to seeing Finnuala again. The Westbury?'

'Fine. See you then.'

'Love you, Tam.'

'And you.'

Chapter 5

Davey

Old habits die hard. Even though it's a short enough run-out today, I am topping up the water reservoir and adding windscreen wash, as I always do before embarking on any journey longer than my daily commute. *I* am ready, just waiting for Karen.

Through the open window of what used to be a cloakroom and is now grandiosely referred to as the 'office', I can hear her singing along with some geriatric Italian pop star as she prints off Dad's figures. I slam down the bonnet of the car.

'Come on! Are you nearly ready? We said we'd be down by lunchtime.'

'Stop fussing. We've plenty of time. It's a two-hour drive. Tops.'

She's right. I tend to forget that the road from the foothills of the Dublin Mountains to my old family home has changed dramatically over the years. It's motorway all the way now, as far as the exit for our town, and thereafter a good national road until the turn- off for the townlands surrounding the farm. A very far cry from the poorly lit, pockmarked surface of the 'main' road to Limerick of my student days when, as a novice driver, I had to negotiate it every third or so weekend on my obligatory visit from college in Dublin. Then, you could add on an hour and some, if it were raining or foggy.

But, bad and all as the road was, the journey wasn't so arduous that I couldn't have made it every weekend. It had been a deliberate decision on my part to force Dad to cope alone with his new single status. It was probably a bit mean of me, but I dreaded the thought of being trapped – of it being expected of me to rock up every Friday night and alleviate the gloom and loneliness of his week. I felt for poor little Vanessa, being passed from one aunt to another after school, while Dad tried to make even more of a mess of the farm, rejecting offers of help with the livestock and working long hours alone.

Selfishly, I had decided to claim my own life and had begun to enjoy the newness of the city and the freedom of anonymity that a big place brings, a pleasurable emotion that in the year of my mother's death I had doubted I would ever feel again.

It's funny the way age changes you. Now, I quite like the obligation of dropping down to see how the old man is getting on. Back then, my 18-year-old fresher self rationed the affection I slow-drip-fed him, as if by doing so it would make him appreciate me more.

'Should I bring some wine for Johnny?' Karen appears with a straw basket over her arm, incongruously packed with manila folders, plastic buckets of nectarines and grapes, and what could be a cake in a cardboard box. She has one of the good reds in her hand.

'Not that one. He won't appreciate it. Take a Montepulciano.'

'Are you ever off duty?' But she giggles as she puts the basket into the back of the car, and goes back inside to swap the bottle.

It's not just meanness on my part about the wine; my dad isn't a connoisseur. My mother on the other hand had enjoyed a good glass, though I was too young to pay much attention to what particular kind apart from its colour. It had been the source of great hilarity to Johnny when she joined a 'Wine Appreciation Circle' which met on the second Wednesday of every month in a rather toney country house hotel, a good distance from our place. The circumnavigating mini-bus would pull up outside on the road, and my mother would tip-toe nervously over the gravel, praying that no young animal had strayed onto the good driveway to relieve itself.

When I was in my final year at school, she passed away – a young woman snatched unexpectedly by the silent ravages of pancreatic cancer. We were stunned by the speed of it all – one minute she was just there, being Mam, not feeling great – the next she was in hospital, on the futile merry-go-round of tests, biopsies, diagnoses, bloods, scans, more tests, forever shrinking and diminishing before our eyes, a skull on a pillow, until the death knell was pronounced: inoperable.

It was left to my Aunt Kitty to tell me. She came to the boarding school and told me I was going home for a couple of weeks. Dad wasn't able for the job. He had gone into a silent black gloom and was encamped in the hospital. Once back, I tried as best as I could to keep a normal routine going – making dreadful doorstep sandwiches for Nessa's school lunch and putting whichever casserole had been delivered into the oven for dinner – but Dad would return, eat nothing, and sit up all night in the armchair, fearing I suppose the chill space in his bed upstairs.

'Now! Does this meet with *signor's* approval?' Karen flashed the label past my nose. 'What's wrong – no damning riposte?'

'Sorry. I was miles away.'

'And have been all morning. Do you want *me* to drive and you can tell me on the way what's bothering you?'

'No, having to concentrate will do me good. But I'll tell you what's on my mind, before we hit Allenbeg.'

———

'And he just came out with it like that, propping up the bar of the rugby club?' Karen turned the volume down on the car radio.

'Yeah! Well, you know Rob, he wasn't exactly *ensconced* at the bar – not his comfort zone. I'd say he'd just come straight from the showers – his hair was wet and stuck to his head. But he was ordering a quick orange juice when he spotted me, and straight away began enthusing about the academy's summer camp and the kids with potential and how much they were paying him for his day as a visiting "celebrity" coach, and next he announces that the bishop had gone "A.W.O.L." – talk about a *non-sequitur*.'

'Do you think – well, you know – like the last time, that the man has had some sort of breakdown?'

'At first, that's exactly what I thought, but Rob seemed so wound up – *indignant* almost, that I knew it couldn't be ill-health. I mean, he could hardly be angry with his uncle if he's back in the residential centre.'

'So, what's – *watch that truck, he's trying to change lane to get off at our exit as well* – what's the bishop's problem?'

'Leading some retreat in Rome according to Rob but, given the future groom's reaction, I'd say he just doesn't want to do it.'

'They don't have to use the uncle again. Any celebrant would do. What's Rob's fixation on the bishop?'

'Haven't a clue. Though I do recall Vanessa saying, Joe was kind-of a stand-in dad when his own father left.'

'Maybe that's it. And did he ask if *we* were able to make it?'

'No. That's the embarrassing bit. He just assumed we would. Actually asked if he could rope me in as one of the ushers – again.'

'*Again*? Oh God. How's your father going to take that?'

'We'll find out soon enough.' I indicate and pull across the road into the popular Mountain View Inn. 'Looks like Dad's here already.'

Karen peers around the car park and sees Johnny alighting from the passenger seat of a brown jeep. 'I thought we were supposed to run down to pick him up at the house?'

'He phoned earlier to say he'd grab a lift with Michael. His stomach must have become distrustful at the thought of no food.'

'Are we that late?'

'No, but hunger pangs at a quarter to two in the afternoon is tantamount to the return of the Great Famine for Dad. He's spotted us.'

Karen winds down the window. 'Hiya, Johnny! You beat us to it, I see.'

'There you are. This place gets busy on Saturdays. I just thought I'd try and grab a table and wait for you inside.'

'Good thinking. Here, I'll come in with you and let Dave find a parking space.'

'Grand. Good girl.'

I know my father's motive for being early. He wants to commandeer a table in the service section. While we might arrange to meet for lunch, it always ends up being dinner. In the Mountain View, despite it being a Saturday in summer, the fare on the set menu is robust, and he has no intention of queueing and slithering his tray slowly along the metal bars – to only come away with soup and sandwiches. Besides, like all elderly people who live alone, cooking a full dinner is a dispiriting chore and he seizes the opportunity to have his main meal of the day in company.

———

'That's a nice bit of beef. I hear they've changed butcher.' Johnny reaches for his accompanying Guinness and takes a sip. His greying moustache attracts the cream froth; the mousse settles in nicely.

Karen smiles at this affectionately. She gives me the pre-arranged signal to start The Wedding Discussion.

'Dad, what do you want to do about Rob's wedding? It's not too long before the RSVP date.'

'And we're off on holidays the last week in July,' – Karen interjects – 'so ours definitely needs to go – either response – before we travel.'

'Where are you off to?' Johnny, eyes lowered, battles with an unexpected piece of gristle in his meat. 'Italy, I suppose.'

'No. France. Just south of Perpignan.'

'That'll be nice. Won't it be very hot at the beginning of August?'

Karen smiles. 'That's the whole point, Johnny! Get a bit of heat into these poor old bones!'

'Give over, girl! Old bones. Wait till you're my age, you'll know all about old bones!'

'Dad, can we get back to the subject of the wedding? What are you thinking?'

'To be honest, I'm trying not to think about it at all.' He suddenly tires of his dinner, places the knife and fork in the closed position, and leans back into the chair, drink in hand.

'Well, does that mean you want to *avoid* going?'

'I don't know what I want! Stop going on about it.' He plonks his glass down with force and a skelp of liquid leaps out onto the table.

Karen automatically mops it with her paper napkin. 'You don't have to decide now, not if it's upsetting you this much.' She covers Dad's hand with hers and strokes it reassuringly. 'Why don't we just agree that it'll be a unanimous decision – either we all go, or nobody goes?'

I open my mouth to protest, because this is really not what we had discussed, but Dad seems relieved by Karen's words, so I keep my thoughts to myself. A commotion at the bar provides a welcome distraction as a group of Dutch cyclists follow a tour leader in to place lunch orders. Their levity as they banter with each other is in stark contrast to our sombre party.

'I bet that takes you back! Sicily 2005!' Karen's words are out before she remembers the association.

I flinch as Dad practically regurgitates his Guinness. 'That's a long time ago,' I say. 'Anybody want another drink?'

Karen nods encouragingly but Dad puts his hand over his pint glass.

'I'll see if I can find out where the cyclists are headed, when I'm up at the bar.'

I am not happy with Karen over her Three Musketeers' promise to Dad. After all, ex-brother-in-law or whatever he will become on the day, he and I know each other a long time – the Old Boy supporters' network for the Munster schools' rugby – albeit, given our age difference and abilities (I was useless), we never played together. I wouldn't exactly consider him a close friend, but he is still well connected and has a lot of useful business contacts in his circle. From a work point of view, I don't think I can afford to turn down the invitation.

Besides, I did half-agree to be an usher and Tamsin is apparently already on to designing the wedding booklets. I don't want to be there in print and not in person. Deep down, I guess I had always envisaged going alone and leaving Karen to entertain Dad elsewhere, if he refused to go.

'The Cliffs of Moher,' I put the drinks on the table.

'Sorry?' Karen looks disapprovingly at the label on the small white-wine bottle.

'That's where the cyclists are *en route*. Tour of the Burren, staying in a hostel.'

'Probably safer there, than in Sicily so.' Dad looks up from under his bushy eyebrows at me.

Karen registers the slight. 'I apologise, Johnny. That was thoughtless of me earlier.'

'Ah, we can't whitewash a whole island out of the conversation just because of one incident. Even if it was a pretty big incident.'

The noise from the outside decking is becoming raucous, where the hardy cyclists are braving the Irish summer whilst imbibing a couple of beers, in strict counterpoint to the palpable lull in our conversation inside. Karen takes a folder from her basket.

We both address Dad at the same time.

'Do you want a look at these now?'

'Here's something that will interest you.'

Karen puts the folder down and smiles. 'You go! It has to be more interesting than these!'

'I was just going to fill Dad in about the bishop doing a runner!'

'What do you mean "a runner"?' Johnny rotates his glass trying to resurrect life into the dregs of his pint.

'He won't do the wedding for Rob.'

'Is that so?'

'Yeah. Apparently, a mission or something in Rome, clashing with the date.'

'But'– Karen sips the white wine, pulls a face and puts her glass down – 'Davey doesn't believe a word of it. Thinks Uncle Joe is making it up.'

'Rob even asked *me* if I knew any *padres* over that direction. Can you imagine! He must be stuck.'

'So, Bishop Joseph will not be rubber-stamping the union?'

'Seems not.'

'Is it my turn now?' Karen opens the folder and is waving the first page under Dad's nose.

'What? The VAT returns. Ah, I'll look at those at home later – put them away, like a good girl.' And then, altogether more cheerfully, he stands up, points to my empty glass and says: 'Will you have another, son – what was that – ginger ale, and, Karen, a white wine?'

'No, Johnny, I couldn't stomach it. It was putrid. I'll have a coffee, please.'

'Right you are.'

And with that, Dad strides purposefully to the bar, head held high, his shoulders no longer slumped in that old man defeatist manner. Karen notices it too and visibly relaxes after her cycling gaffe.

'He brightened when you told him about Joe planning to avoid the wedding.'

'Yes, he does seem to have got over his "wedding" meltdown.'

———

He's back and sets my drink down. 'One ginger ale. The pint and the coffee are on their way.'

'Thanks.'

'Remind me again, what date exactly is this wedding supposed to be?'

Karen shoots me a startled look before answering: 'Last Saturday in August – the 27th, I think.'

'Typical bloody rugby player. And I bet he chose that date long before they rejigged the Gaelic calendar for the business end of the football and hurling championships!'

I have no idea why he brings this up, so I probe further. 'Why, Dad? When are the finals going to be held this year?'

'This month. *Imagine*, in July. Did you ever hear anything so ridiculous! Though I guess it frees up the last weekend in August. Normally, that would be one or other of the semis.'

'Does that mean—?'

The barman places a fresh pint and the coffee on the table.

'Johnny?' Karen drops a sugar lump into her cup.

And, with that, Dad settles into his chair and takes a long, satisfying draught of his drink.

'I'm thinking about it.'

Part 2

SUMMER 2019

Chapter 6

Rob

I have never been much good at giving speeches. Even when I captained the school's Senior Cup Team – and we won, two years in a row – I dreaded the few words I was expected to deliver to the ecstatic, roaring kids in the stands. There won't exactly be cheering fans at the Allen Castle next month but, nonetheless, I'm bricking it.

With the rugby season officially over for a couple of months, I have a break from the squad, and have ear-marked this entire weekend to put my wedding speech to bed. I have to write it sometime and, with Vanessa away doing her pre-wedding girly thing, it's ideal. I can concentrate better when she's not gushing in my ear. That's the thing about Vanessa – lovely girl – but she does go on so. The only woman in my house growing up was my mother, and she wouldn't break a sweat to get excited about anything. Vanessa and her various enthusiasms came as a culture shock.

In her absence, I am holed up in my family's apartment in Dublin where I can concentrate. It's not like I don't have good things to say about her: I do. *Ha! 'I do.'* A premonition of The Big Day. Why *do* women insist on calling their wedding 'The Big Day' – as if after the wedding, there will be no other days of equal significance? No pressure on the groom, then.

So far, I have:

'When I first saw Vanessa, I couldn't believe my luck.' Better when I first *met* Vanessa. After all, I must have seen her several times before, presenting on television and being interviewed for lifestyle and fashion programmes. *'When I first* met *Vanessa, I couldn't believe my luck. She was the most beautiful, elegant creature I had ever laid eyes on.'* Not *creature.* Makes her sound like a giraffe or something, and given the disparity in our height, I don't want to be focussing on that. *'She was the most elegant girl I had ever met.'* Will the girl bit upset the feminists in the audience? – *'the most elegant woman'* – Christ, this is a minefield! I should have taken Terry up on his offer to write it for me when he originally offered. I mean, he has to do his best man's few words anyway, and he was always a dab hand at knocking out debating speeches in school and for the Hist or one of those other abbreviated Trinity societies. I turned down his offer even so. I thought it would be a bit disloyal to Vee. Not personal enough – and she'd spot the fluent English a mile off. She doesn't love me for my eloquence. Right. Back to this speech.

'When I first met Vanessa, I couldn't believe my luck. She was the most beautiful, elegant woman I had ever seen. She was everything I longed for in a partner: funny, considerate, calm. I need calm. Spending your working life with your head wedged between two 120-kilo men, you need your personal life to be calm. Vanessa brings this serenity into my life, and I am the better for it.'

Actually, that's not really true. Vanessa is not at all serene. If the truth be known, she's a bit giddy. I've had to ask her to 'calm down' several times, but I think we are beginning to understand each other. She has even dialled the flirting down a notch or two. Not being one of life's natural flirts, I guess that's why I find it hard to handle.

'She and I share the same family values and I am particularly proud of the loyalty she has shown to her father – Johnny over there –' (pause for applause) – *'They supported each other with strength and –* (what's that word – fortitude?) – *fortitude ever since the premature passing of Brenda/Breda'* – (I must check with Davey what exactly the mother's name was) – *'and I know full well I will always only be the second-choice bench player where her affection is concerned.'* (I like that bit – the team will enjoy that.) *'An accomplished businesswoman, some of you here today also know of her work with the Simon Community, but I am happy to say that since we got together she is fundraising with me for some of my Christian charities.'*

I'd like to expand on this last bit, but people can be funny about religious stuff. Particularly the rugby lot. It doesn't fit their idea of what a Munster hooker should be. Which, come to think of it, is what exactly? An over-confident ex-private-school boy, used to women flinging themselves at him? A hard drinker when not playing and sometimes even when? A magnet for all kinds of sexual attention, once a bit of social media digging reveals he's available? A man who takes advantage of the no-strings-attached sex on offer: repeatedly.

Not for me, any of this. I bear no resemblance to the stereotype and yet I haven't the balls to acknowledge it. My match programme note *should* read: 'Serious, committed Catholic, Irish representative on the board of True Love Waits, whose hobbies include fundraising for charity, cross-country and classical music.' Instead, they print the usual drivel: 'Captain of winning SCT team '09, '10, U-19 & U-20 Irish Squad; enjoys golf, athletics and socialising.'

I dread socialising. I even hate the word, which is just a synonym for heavy drinking, and my bladder can't cope with hour upon hour of fizzy water. Yet, with the team, I have to go. It's all about 'bonding' and 'camaraderie', so I have to plaster a bemused grin on my face, sip my water and look like an embedded teammate enjoying himself.

The night I met Vanessa, I had only gone to the Park Hotel because I was more or less ordered to. Earlier in training I'd lost my cool with two of our jumpers repeatedly making a bollocks of the lineout. The forwards' coach gave me an ear-bashing, said I owed them a couple of drinks, so I didn't have a choice. I didn't mind so much, as the Park is more low-key than the team's usual haunts.

That's where I first spotted her: a tall, classy woman in a pink dress – (she insists on calling it *'fuchsia'*) – holding

66

court with a group of younger girls in a corner of the bar. A smartly dressed guy with a bow-tie seemed to be interviewing the young women in turn, jotting down stuff on his clipboard. My eye was drawn to Vanessa, because she was wearing clothes which actually covered *more* than a quarter of her body. Most of the younger ones looked like they had been parachuted in from a tropical island in glittery swimwear, so scant were the dresses.

After the guy with the clipboard was finished, it wasn't long before we were besieged by the shiny girls. (Our team are easily recognised when out – at least the media darling backs are.) But the lady in pink, who looked familiar from somewhere, just smiled and didn't join in the fawning.

Clutching my glass, I had wandered over. 'Hello, there!' I ventured. 'You either have a huge family of female siblings, or this is some sort of works outing? Am I warm?'

'Luke.'

'Rob, actually. Luke's the flashy little scrumhalf. Can I get you a drink?'

She tossed her long, brown hair over her shoulder and grinned. 'Aren't you the wit, Rob Cunningham. And yes, a glass of Prosecco would go down nicely, now that the business of the evening has concluded.'

I was taken aback that she knew me. She didn't look like the usual rugby 'groupie'. 'And what business would that be, now that I gather the girls are not all your sisters?'

'Inquisitive *and* comedic! I feel like I'm compiling character notes before interviewing you!'

And that's when I realised where I recognised her from! Early morning TV. She presented a magazine programme on the commercial channel two days a week.

'Vanessa!'

'Last time I checked. Tell me, has prohibition been introduced in Limerick, or am I likely to get a drink this side of Easter?'

I scurried to the bar, my dopey recognition of who she was finally sinking in. Vanessa Walshe of *Morning Glory* fame! I thought she might have been a model for a while and if I wasn't mistaken, I'd heard my mother talk about visiting her clothes shop in Dublin.

The barman had to go in to the storeroom – (there had been a run on the Prosecco – all those shiny girls) – to fetch a few bottles. I remember waving over at her – miming the popping of a cork – I was such an asshole at the beginning!

'Only one glass?' Vanessa grinned as the bottle in its ice-bucket was placed on the table.

'OJ.' I poured my Britvic 55. 'Back in camp from tomorrow.'

'Very dedicated. Can't say your teammates are abstaining.'

She was right. The sedate bar of the Park now had a boisterous alcove, from which rowdy conversation and the occasional rugby chant was escaping.

'*Cheers!*'

We clinked glasses.

'I'm glad this gig is over.' She took a sip. 'A tricky Miss

Ireland heat. They amalgamated two geographical regions into tonight's round. Some of the girls were a bit put out.'

'Is that for Miss World?'

'Well, it could be, eventually. Long way to go. I'm one of the judges of the preliminary rounds.'

'Thought beauty contests were frowned upon by you feminists!'

'They've come a long way in recent times. Some of these girls have PhDs!'

'They didn't look like they did.'

'*Jud-gey!*'

She was right to call me that. Between the Prosecco and Miss Ireland, I had begun to vacillate. I could visualise how well she'd look on my arm, and anticipate how my street cred would soar . . . but these frivolous aspects of her personality were not the match I sought.

That was, until she said: 'You don't remember me, do you?'

'Isn't that an oldies song?'

'*Sorry?* Last Christmas. On the Simon soup run.'

She was referring of course to the Simon Community – the amazing charity that looks after people who find themselves without a home. In an effort to promote the caring side of the squad, our team Communications guy had assigned each of us to different charities to do 'walk-arounds' in the busy pre-Christmas period. I had nearly been excused as I was off injured – in Dublin receiving surgery on my shoulder.

But then he got the bright idea that more coverage might be got from featuring the dedication of the *rival* province's hooker, nursing his strapped arm as he helped out on the streets of the capital. Vanessa was right: I had in fact trailed around with Simon volunteers on a misty December evening, distributing soup and sandwiches to their regular clients – most of whom were greeted like friends by the charity's team.

'*You* were there, Vanessa – the night I went out with Simon?'

'You mean your celebrity drive-by?'

'A bit harsh. I did help – even with one functioning arm.'

'Rob, regular, dedicated workers who do the beat two and three nights a week *hate* seeing guys like you rock up, with a snapper in tow. For starters, you're usually dressed all wrong and make the clients feel uncomfortable.'

'But we weren't allowed take photos with the homeless guys – I remember that quite clearly. They were quite insistent.'

'Proper order.'

'Anyway, tell me about your nights "on the beat" as you call it: is it very depressing?'

And as she talked earnestly, compassion lighting her face when she described Bill or Matt and their back-story, and how they'd ended up homeless – I saw the goodness in her. She became less frivolous by the minute and I decided the lady in the pink dress might be a fit after all.

I think I'll include that dress in my speech – the *fuchsia* dress – and the way she ignored me at first. My dim-witted, slow recognition of who she was. *Where did I leave off?* Oh yeah, the Christian charities bit. I had better go on about her career. Business owner, TV presenter. A discreet and hard-working campaigner for a homeless charity. Vanessa Walshe. My Vanessa. Soon to become Vanessa Cunningham. (I haven't checked if she is going to take my name. I just assume she is. I quite expect her to.)

Let's see what this bit sounds like:

Imagine the reaction I got at training when I said I was dating a former model and Miss Ireland judge – kudos or what? – and me only a lumpy front row! Apart from being bowled over by her looks, it was obvious from her business interests and her natural charm and intelligence on television, that my Vanessa was one smart operator. She also happens to be the first girl I have ever dated who turned me down for a day-trip to London, because "she had to go to Mass with her father".

(Pause for laughter here. There shouldn't be – but I know there will. *I* like the fact that she's a committed Catholic – I was even more impressed later when I learned it was her mother's anniversary, but I'm not comfortable sharing that.)

In fact, I'm not comfortable sharing a lot of this stuff, but the speech *is* supposed to be personal. God knows I

71

should be able draft it in my sleep, given the number I have had to sit through at teammates' weddings over the last year. (Is there anyone *left* on the regular first team who is not coupled up?) It was great having Vanessa by my side at the final two functions: instead of my usual panicky scramble to find any old date for the day as my Plus One.

Because no matter how close you think you are, some friends still ridicule you and look for a chance to criticise. My reputedly 'loner' status has always set me apart and even in the comfort of these boozy brothers-in-arms, I have been among them but still felt very much the outsider.

That's who I am – the outsider. I hate it. I try hard to 'belong' – but with every year and every new team addition, I still feel the same scrutiny and subtle dismissal of my teenage years. Don't get me wrong: they don't hate me or anything. I'm fine and I'm functional, but I'll never be anyone's 'bestie'.

Whereas, I thought I *had* a 'bestie' in Terry, my sane non-rugby-playing mate, someone with an inkling of what made me tick. The same Terry, responsible for my recent stag trip, which as middle-class professionals we are not supposed to call 'a stag' anymore for it smacks of vulgarity and naked, tarred and feathered butts bundled into the back of a van going God knows where! Instead, our plan involved capitalising on the end of season charity match against Northampton which most of the team had signed up for, overnighting there after the dinner, and taking my 'bachelor' jaunt on a mystery tour the following day for some civilised activity, dinner, drinks and a club.

It helped that we had scored an emphatic victory in Franklin's Gardens, our opposition's home grounds and, buoyed up by the win – there is no such thing as a 'friendly' in professional rugby – most of the team boarded the smaller 'bachelor' bus the following morning, joined by a handful of non-rugby friends invited by the best man. As long as they stuck to the plan, I wasn't bothered.

I had no idea where the bus was heading, but became enthusiastic when I noticed road signs for Silverstone, home of the British Grand Prix, and wondered if they allowed amateurs whizz around the circuit for a prenuptial thrill. I watched in disappointment as the final road sign and exit for Silverstone receded and we ploughed on, joining the motorway heading south. For one crazy moment, I thought we were going as far as London, but not even Terry would be that stupid, to waste so much time travelling. When we peeled back off the motorway, I cheered up on seeing directional signs for Oxford.

I'd never been to Oxford before – well, not in person. I had spent a lot of time there as a nerdy teenager, when I devoured hour upon hour of reruns of the TV series *Inspector Morse* with my father, on the rare weekends I got to stay with him. It was one of the few things we had left in common.

As we drove across Oxford from the Holiday Inn on one side to the Premier on the other to drop off two smaller groups of the guys, the buildings all seemed so familiar. Our final stop was the Randolph. When the bus pulled in at the steps of the iconic hotel, I began to wonder if I had ever let slip to Terry my embarrassing television viewing all those years ago. As a lonely, hormonal youth, my affection for the crotchety old opera-loving detective definitely was not something I was ever going to share consciously with my peers – I was already odd enough.

The Randolph contingent – coach, Captain Gaz, Davey, Terry and I – had a quick lunchtime cocktail and sandwich in the appropriately named Morse Bar. I spent most of the time wandering around looking at the various stills on the wall from the film set. I was beginning to relax about my afternoon jaunt, when the porter called Terry out and pointed him in the direction of a clothes rail on which a set of costumes were hanging. Apparently, whatever we were doing, we were doing it in fancy dress!

I don't know whether you've ever been punting, but it's a fairly benign, gentle kind of way to travel along a waterway. Unless, that is, you're in medieval dress and accompanied by twenty pumped-up rugger-buggers. The guy at the Magdalen Bridge boathouse, looked unsure as he hired us out four smaller punts. We could have had two large ones with a chauffeur, but what would have been the fun in that? The plan was to wreak havoc on the peaceful June day, with a noisy, rambunctious race along the Cherwell.

The singing started once we passed the playing grounds and the mood of a few romantic twosomes in small punts was seriously interrupted by the more robust lyrics of our chanting. Several post-exam student punters joined in, and even when I was inevitably dunked overboard into the shallows, the atmosphere remained jovial.

Unlike later that evening.

———

None of what later came to pass could possibly appear in a wedding speech: neither the one I am attempting to complete, nor the supposedly jocose section of the best man's few words. Terry is acutely aware of the consequences of including any sly reference to what became the nadir of the evening.

According to the sticker on the custom-made Munster crest antlers I was expected to wear, our evening venue was The White Horse, a pub I quickly found on Google Maps, very close to the Randolph, near that famous bookshop. Despite the snack picnic provided on the punts, I had been too wet and uncomfortable to eat much of it, and was ravenous. Just as I was about to slip around the corner to a fast-food joint I had spotted earlier, Terry knocked on the door.

'Are you right? The bus will be picking us up in ten.'

'Bus? The pub's only around the corner. I'm going to grab a burger first.'

'Plenty of time for that later. We have a private-room with four-course dinner booked.'

I was half-dragged, half-pushed out the door and down the corridor. Terry pressed the button for the ancient pokey lift and stuck the antlers firmly on my head. The bus bit was still bothering me.

———

We did indeed convene at *a* White Horse Inn but not at the sedate little pub I had been anticipating. After a forty-minute drive, the bus pulled into the car-park of a scruffy-looking white building. Not a horse in sight. The illuminated signage flashed in rotation the wares on offer. I saw the dreaded words: *Adult Entertainment*.

Once inside, we were ushered to a function room by a Slavic-looking doorman, and to my surprise, a long, dining table was tastefully decorated and set for supper. Scantily clothed girls circulated with trays of champagne and a couple of token orange juices. I was made sit at the head of the table and the rest of the group piled onto seats, ordering their choice of mains from the small printed menus scattered the length of the table. I tucked into my meal when it arrived. Wine and beer flowed, and although loud and a bit raucous at times, the banter was fairly innocuous and good-humoured.

Until I was called away from the table by the same guy

we had met on arrival, whose job description seemed to include *maître d'* as well as bouncer. The manager needed a word about the credit card Terry had given him for security. On the other side of the door, there was no manager, nor any semblance of a place that could be considered an office. Instead, I found myself in a plush velvet-walled boudoir, with swathes of flimsy gold shimmering material wafting from the ceiling and draped around imitation pillars.

A woman reclined on a gaudy chintz sofa, encased in a long, Greek-style tunic. Her head was half-covered by a length of gold-and-white fabric.

'Hello! Welcome!' She extended a slim white arm out from the tunic and offered me her hand. 'Come. Sit beside me.'

I froze. If this was a private lap-dance organised for my benefit, I was going to kill Terry.

'You have been misled – I – I don't require any of your services.'

'Your friend said you were shy,' she lisped in a Hispanic accent. 'Just sit here beside me for a while.'

Tentatively, I sat at the other end of the sofa, and without warning, the white tunic fell from the woman's body, revealing a sequinned all-in-one piece of underwear. Her head remained under wraps and it made it difficult to engage face to face with her.

'I'm sorry – madam – eh – please put your robe back on.'

The woman began to touch me. 'My name,' she said, 'is

Vanessa.' (She pronounced the 'V' as a 'B'.) And with that, she pulled away her head wrap, revealing long dark brown hair, styled identically to Vee's.

I jumped up from the sofa in shock and stumbled. In the dim light of the seduction booth, I caught my foot on the claw of a large wrought-iron chair and sat heavily into it. For one crazy moment, despite the phoney accent, I thought they had flown Vanessa over, such was the resemblance. 'Vanessa' seized upon my astonishment, and lithe as a cheetah sprang across the room after me, cuffing one wrist to the frame of the chair before I realised what was happening. She attempted to attach my second arm but I pulled it away. She was astride me in a flash and was disturbingly hard to dislodge.

'*Stop! Please stop this!*' I managed to half-stand up, dragging the heavy chair with me and she slithered to the ground.

'Why you resist so much? Just enjoy it.'

The volume of the background music increased and the woman clambered up, swaying and removing her complicated sparkly bra top, in time to its rhythm.

'Think of *your* Vanessa, as I give you pleasure.'

The mention of Vanessa in such a demeaning context enraged me. I could hear my breath become faster and shallower until I was rasping and struggling to breathe at all. '*Take – this – fucking – handcuff – off me!*' I made a lunge at the dancer, still impeded by the chair, and she backed off, looking scared. Whether fake Vanessa hit a panic button or not, the Slavic guy burst through the velvet wall, and yanked the cuff roughly from my wrist.

'*You! Crazy stag. Not normal. Go. Get out.*' He threw the discarded tunic at the dancer and she wrapped herself protectively in it.

———

Back among 'my friends', still gasping for breath, I made for Terry, and would have hit him, had the coach not intervened.

'Take it easy, mate. It was only a bit of innocent fun.'

'*Yeah, but, Robser, she really was a ringer for Vee, wasn't she? Got you going there!*' one of the younger squad members called out.

'That's enough,' Davey intervened. 'You can see he's upset. Drop it.'

I pulled Davey aside. 'How did he know what she looked like?'

He lowered his eyes and pointed to the wall, where an oversized gilt mirror was in fact a screen, relaying everything in the velvet boudoir to those clients of a voyeuristic nature. My humiliation was complete.

———

It's hard to dismiss that feeling of being deliberately set up by so-called friends, most of whom will attend our wedding in three weeks' time. Something altered that night in my relationship with Terry, a friend I thought I would have for life. He doesn't 'get me' anymore. If he had, he would never have asked that stripper to dress up in a Vanessa wig, or to assume her name.

It's too late and too embarrassing to sack him as best man – (what would I say to Vanessa?) but on my wedding day, in the conclusion of my speech, he'll be in no doubt that he has been demoted. Something like this:

I stand before you all today, family, teammates and friends of many years, on this my wedding day, and I am delighted to present Mrs Vanessa Cunningham, the latest addition to our family. My beautiful, pure, kind and generous wife. My love, my life, and my best friend. And from this day forward, the only best friend I shall ever need.'

Chapter 7

Bishop Joe

Father Tom has opened all the windows in the east-facing reception room which I use as an office, but there still isn't a breath of air. Unusual for County Clare even in the month of June. Late June, to be precise, the week before my nephew's wedding, and I have left the fine-tuning of my notes as celebrant till the eleventh hour. In fact, only the arrival in yesterday morning's post of the booklet for the wedding service prompted me to allocate this afternoon to concentrate solely on the imminent happy occasion.

It seems a very long two months since Rob and Vanessa called to see me and suggested the readings and music that I find laid out before me. Some of Vanessa's original music choices had been quite unsuitable – too secular – and Rob, more sensitive to the requirements of a Catholic church wedding, had persuaded his fiancée to omit them in favour of traditional repertoire. They had argued the toss back and forth and, although she seemed put out, she eventually accepted that some of the lyrics might not have been appropriate for a church. The final version of that compromise is a tasteful selection of classical stalwarts that will add dignity to the ceremony.

Although I haven't always been a fan of families producing their own leaflets for weddings or funerals, this time I am quite grateful to have a neat framework of the proceedings to hand. I can't recall when I last officiated at a wedding – it's not a bishop's usual role – but, when it's for a family member and particularly for such a sincere young couple like Rob and Vanessa, it is exciting and I'm delighted to have been asked to do it. I am also greatly relieved that Rob has chosen to marry such a personable yet grounded girl as the one he had the good fortune to meet. Vanessa – or Nessa as he sometimes calls her – is not a rugby WAG type. She doesn't fawn all over him nor make his career her sole purpose in life. Her public profile is greater than his through her media interests. She even appears on the rival television channel from the one which covers the provincial rugby. That's the sort of female role model he needs in his life, given that he never had such guidance from his own family. An only child, he was idolised by both parents, until my brother – shame on him – decided to add a fourth member to the family – his younger mistress. The taking of this lover was so Gallic and smooth that nobody even knew of her existence for over six years, until the inevitable happened as she approached her late thirties and began demanding a baby before her biological window of opportunity expired. Frank – my boring, older brother – came home from work one Friday evening and announced that he was leaving, to be with his new family. He had his already packed bags in the boot of the car, a task which must have been some days in the preparation.

Lilian, Rob's mother, went to pieces on every front – domestic, emotional, professional – and particularly maternal, with her affection for Rob fluctuating between a suffocating closeness to replace the male attention she had finally lost, to a cool indifference towards the constant reminder of his wayward father. This was so unlike her, having been the alpha partner in the family since they married. The confidence of coming from moneyed stock will do that to you – and that made Lilian's talk of pulling Rob out of Rockwell where he boarded seem all the more unfathomable. It wasn't for financial reasons – just her dread of being home alone during the week. After Frank left, henceforth Lilian was absent although physically present, polishing and perfecting her star role as victim. I felt I had to intervene and have a word with the principal at the college, because taking yet another familiar thing away from Rob would have been a disaster. The boss had a discreet chat with the Head of Physical Education, who persuaded the lonely mother that her son had a great talent and was almost certainly guaranteed a future as a professional rugby player, if he continued to progress and improve. Lilian relinquished her plan to bring him home, but I still went a step further by suggesting she set up a direct debit for the payment of the school fees – just in case.

Rugby saved Rob. Had it not been for the eagle-eye of the under-14s coach at school encouraging him to consider a front-row position, he would have fallen by the wayside. Frank only had interest in his son's success as a glamorous fly-half and, prior to his flit, had put in many hours out in the paddocks feeding balls and supervising place-kicking. He had even persuaded the fencing contractors they used for the stud farm to custom-make a set of goalposts for Rob's practice area.

But twin girls are very time-consuming and, once they arrived, Frank gave up on transforming his rather podgy twelve-year-old into a nimble kicking-machine. Plus, there was his bi-location issue – he had returned to work for an accountancy firm in Dublin and was living in the family apartment that he had encouraged Lilian to buy for Rob's university years. Rob felt doubly abandoned – by his father and his personal coach, all at the same time.

I suppose my tacit support of Rob and his subsequent successful career has been one of the reasons why we are closer than a religious uncle and his nephew would usually be. Yet, despite the relative physical closeness of our locations now that he's with Munster full-time, we have grown apart. Something bothers me about adult Rob – a remoteness in his dealings with people.

Take for example, our 'pre-marriage' chat in April. Although not somebody who usually administers the official course, I felt it was a simple matter to run through the topics and exercises recommended and to save the couple another lost weekend, as they were already coming to visit me in Ennis to discuss the details of the ceremony.

It was a Saturday and despite it being his day off, Father Tom had opted to help out and have the morning-room prepared. He had the table arranged for the business part of proceedings and a trolley set with items for a late breakfast, given my visitors weren't local. He was on hand to cook whatever needed cooking – (where would I be without him?) – and at precisely nine-thirty, he ushered Vanessa into the room. Alone.

'Good morning, Vanessa.' I shook my future relative's hand warmly. 'You're very punctual – and for a Saturday! Where's Rob?'

'Oh, we're travelling separately. I was with Dad last night. Rob is nearer to you – I thought he'd be here first.'

'Coffee? Father Dillon – Tom – is on commission from the pharmaceutical company that manufactures statins – he'll be force-feeding us a cholesterol-bomb fry when we're all assembled, but while you're waiting?'

'Coffee would be great.' Vanessa looked around her awkwardly, as if wondering where she should sit.

'Please, settle yourself on the sofa, while I go and chase this coffee.'

But Father Tom must have the office bugged, because ever-efficient and on cue, he arrived with a *cafetière* and pastries. The bell went at the same time. My secretary set the tray down and made to go for the door.

'I'll get that,' I said. 'You look after Vanessa.'

When I returned with Rob, Father Tom was leaning against the radiator, sipping a coffee and laughing heartily with Vanessa who, now more at ease, was relaxing back into the comfy sofa cushions, her long legs stretched out in front of her.

I thought it was my imagination, but I could have sworn I heard Rob suck in his breath in a startled kind of way. Instead of greeting his fiancée, he stood stock-still in the middle of the room, no trace of any emotion on his face. Oblivious, Vanessa beamed an enthusiastic smile in his direction and jumped up to greet him with a clumsy half-hug, forgetting the coffee cup still in her hand, which dribbled the residue of its brown contents down the front of her dress.

'Oh, poor you – your lovely dress!' said Father Tom as he sprang forward, looking for something to mitigate the worst of the coffee stain. As he came closer to our latest visitor, their eyes met, but Tom turned away and focussed again on Vanessa. 'I'll get a cloth.'

'Thanks, Father Tom.' Vanessa was all smiles.

Rob's eyes followed my secretary out of the room. He

crossed to the wing-backed armchair and sat down. 'So, Ness, no problems finding the Palace – obviously?'

'No, it was well signposted. But what kept *you*?'

'I told you – I was staying with Mum last night – impossible to make a quick exit.'

When Father Tom returned, a damp towel in hand, he approached the sofa and I feared he might attend to the mopping of the visitor's dress himself.

But Rob jumped up suddenly from his chair and closed his hand over the cloth Tom held, staring directly into his face as he did so. 'I'll manage this.'

Tom released his grip and headed for the door.

'That guy – what did you say his name was again?' Rob looked from me to Vanessa.

'My new secretary? Tom Dillon. Why? Do you think you've met him before?'

Rob reacted. 'How could I? I thought you just said he was new.'

'No, but you two are of an age – I thought you might have run into him at college . . . or even out in Dublin. That's where he's come from.' I knew I was making a mess of this. And the tenser Rob became, the more Vanessa looked quizzically from me to him. 'Of course, silly me. How could you? Wrong university.'

'Right. Let's get this show on the road, *Bishop*. What do you want to do – the pre-marriage stuff first and then the liturgy, or vice versa?'

'We'll do the chat first, then have the breakfast I

promised Vanessa. We can go through the liturgy afterwards. Does that suit?'

'Fine by me. Nessa?'

'Great. I'm looking forward to Tom's breakfast already.'

Rob shot her a look and abandoned the armchair for the sofa beside her.

'Actually, we probably need to gather around the table,' I said. 'There's form-filling and questionnaires to be completed.'

The future groom fished a pen out from the inside pocket of his jacket. 'Fantastic.'

'OK. This is all fairly standard stuff. I am going to ask each of you to jot down three things which appealed to you about the other when you first met.' I laughed. 'You can remember back that far, can't you?'

Rob and Vanessa looked at each other, like two camera-shy celebrities on *Mr & Mrs*.

Vanessa was first in with a response. 'Of *course!* It was only last year.'

Rob was less enthusiastic. 'Christ, this is like being back in school – no offence.'

'None taken. The "three best things" go on the blank page at the front and when you're done with that, fill in the questionnaire that follows. I'll give you a bit of time.'

I probably shouldn't have left them as they're not supposed to compare notes, but I was cognisant of Rob's 'school' comment, and they were adults who had voluntarily given up their free time, so I popped down to the kitchen to see how the chef was getting on.

When I returned sometime later, Tom accompanied me, and I collected the paperwork as he set the table. A quick glance at the questionnaires showed me there had been very little collusion, as most of the answers were different.

We tucked into our breakfast. Tom refused to join us and scurried back to the kitchen, obviously uncomfortable around Rob, whatever the problem was.

'He's a good cook, this secretary of yours!' Vanessa laughed, waving her fork with a piece of rasher dangling on the end. 'This bacon is just like my dad likes it – a little bit crisp on the rind but the meat still tender.'

'And how do you like your bacon, Rob?' I was trying to warm him up a bit. He still seemed off with me since my suggestion that he and Father Tom might have crossed paths before.

'Never usually touch the stuff.'

'No, Rob's strictly a muesli or porridge kind of guy,' Vanessa said. 'Not that I make his breakfast too often.'

Heads down, Rob and Vanessa concentrated on their plates. I thought it would be no harm to tease out casually some of the views I had seen in their questionnaires.

'No, of course. You're currently not living together. That's unusual, these days.'

'Why so?' Rob eye-balled me.

'Most couples of your age – late twenties – usually co-habit, if nothing else but to save on the extortionate rent.'

'We are not "most couples".'

'Clearly not.'

'And, besides, I'm not full-time in Dublin, so the family apartment – rent-free – suits me when I am.'

'You're lucky to have that option. One of Frank's better ideas.'

Vanessa shifted in her chair. 'We are closing on a house very soon – in Newbridge. Hopefully, the middle of June. I can't wait to take delivery of some of the furniture I've ordered.'

'But we're not moving in until we come back from our honeymoon in Sicily.'

'Well, *I* might.' Vanessa placed a crumpled napkin on her empty breakfast plate. 'I'm not paying out Dublin rent *and* half the mortgage on our place. Besides, it makes more sense. Newbridge is nearly halfway home to Dad.'

'You leave the mortgage to me.' Rob almost puffed up his chest as he said this.

'Ah, it's not the 1960s, love. I'll pay my way.' Vanessa poured herself more coffee. 'Besides, Jenny O'Dwyer – my flatmate – is one messy mare. I don't think I could stick her chaos in the run-up to the wedding.'

'I'd prefer if you didn't move into the house on your own.' Rob put his hand over his coffee cup as Vanessa tried to pour.

'Ah, he's all worried about me!'

'Your safety is not a laughing matter. Anyway, I thought you were keen on spending your last few weeks as a free agent with your father.'

"'*As a free agent!*'" Do you hear that, Bishop Joe! You're a witness! I'm going to be a chattel, post this wedding!' Vanessa bounced up out of her chair, ruffled Rob's hair, and kissed the top of his head. 'Rob Cunningham, I do love you, but sometimes you sound as if you belong to a different era! Bishop Joe, where's the bathroom?'

'Joe – please – and sorry, Vanessa. I should have pointed it out earlier. Down the corridor towards the kitchen, on your right.'

'Thanks.'

When it was just the two of us, I thought I'd tackle Rob about some of the discrepancies in their respective questionnaires, particularly the divergent view on the role of sex within a relationship. It wasn't an easy conversation to have – in fact, it was made more awkward by virtue of the fact that he was my nephew. I would have tackled the subject with greater ease with any other prenuptial candidate.

Rob was – as I had expected – reticent.

'Yes, I did state that I saw no role for sex before marriage, and that within marriage it was primarily for procreation. What's wrong with that?'

'Well, not a lot in a strictly doctrinaire sense, but very outmoded in today's real world where a majority of very committed Roman Catholics interpret that in a more relaxed fashion. I mean, have you considered if that's also Vanessa's view?'

'She knows I'm not interested in having sex before marriage.'

'And what about sex *after* marriage? Sorry, I have to ask.'

'What *exactly* are you trying to imply?'

'Nothing. *Nothing.* Just Vanessa's answers are quite different. Here. Take a look.'

Rob snatched one of the pages from my hand. His face became visibly disenchanted as he read – a kind of vacant stare that I had seen only too often in his mother's eyes invaded his. He was just about to respond when Vanessa came back into the room.

'That Father Tom is a treasure. He's down there, scrubbing the kitchen floor, and he has a couple of cakes of brown soda in the oven. He's going to give us one to take home.'

'What were you doing in the kitchen?' Rob snapped. 'I thought you were going to the loo?'

'I couldn't resist having a little peek. It's a lovely kitchen – an Aga just like ours at my dad's in Allenbeg.'

'Do you do a lot of cooking for your father – Johnny, isn't it?'

'Yes, well, as much as my schedule in Dublin will allow. I batch-cook for him when I'm around, and freeze the meals, but he's typical of his generation – the freezer and he are not great friends. Prefers "fresh".'

'And when you two set up home, who'll do most of the cooking?'

'That would be me!' squealed Vanessa. 'There are only so many boiled eggs a girl can eat.'

'Unlike Father *Tom*,' said Rob, 'who no doubt could do

you *cordon bleu* every other evening.'

'You have your special talents too, Rob. Cooking just doesn't happen to be one of them.'

Before things became fractious, I decided to move the conversation away from the contentious subject of Rob's culinary deficits.

'Right. We'll exchange your questionnaires now and you two can chat about any differences in your respective answers. I think you'll find it an interesting exercise. I'm just going to fetch my liturgy folder before we tackle what you are thinking of using for the marriage ceremony.'

Rob looked calmer and fetched a sheaf of pages from a document wallet he had left under the armchair. 'Fine. I have some ideas here.'

———

If the groom lost the Battle of the Questionnaires on that April weekend, he won with a bonus point the Crusade of the Marriage Ceremony. In fact, as I look today at this printed booklet, I recall that he probably argued more vehemently than necessary for the inclusion of his selection. Unable to beat Vanessa with his views on sex and his lack of prowess in the kitchen, he was determined he would use his superior knowledge of the Catholic liturgy, to beat her into submission in the realm of Church doctrine.

Which is why his odd behaviour around Father Tom bothered me. Their ages suggested that they might have bumped into each other during my nephew's aborted four-week stint of study at Maynooth, when Rob – either to annoy his father or because he really believed he had a vocation – decided he'd study to become a priest. When Frank finally wheedled their son's intention out of Lilian, he had driven to Maynooth and physically removed Rob from his accommodation, imploring him to take up his deferred place in Business at Trinity. Rob's haughty demeanour when I made my gaffe on the day of the pre-marriage course, would seem to suggest he has never shared this with Vanessa.

But what concerns me most as the imminent celebrant of Vanessa and Rob's union, is that Father Tom – the past acquaintance he may have deliberately chosen to forget – is most definitely a very happy, gay man.

Chapter 8

Johnny

I pull yesterday's date off the calendar on the kitchen counter, scrunch it up and throw the paper in the bin. It's one of those flip-over ones that has a small detachable page for each day – the old-fashioned kind with a quotation and a piece of historical information on it. Breda had loved them, and Vanessa – God only knows where she continues to find them – always puts one in my Christmas stocking. Today is July 4th – a big day if you're an American, an ominous date if you're a father preparing for your only daughter's wedding in less than forty-eight hours. The gem of wisdom designed to help me through all this Americana strangely enough doesn't come from a US source but from Germany, courtesy of the composer Beethoven: *'To play a wrong note is insignificant, but to play without passion is unforgiveable.'*

Right. That's going to be a lot of fuckin' use to me since I was never a musician, not even much of a singer. And besides, wasn't Beethoven deaf? What would he know about it?

But what I *do* know about, is passion – about doing something you love with passion. For a very long time, that for me was hurling at a high level, then football as a reasonably good player in the days when very few Gaelic team members switched from one game to the other. Later, I became a trainer of the underage football teams – (the former hurlers had the hurling coaching all sewn up.) Too old for all that now, I suppose my current passion is farming. You certainly have to have something driving you, to keep going these days with the slim financial pickings to be had.

Or, you can do something great *for* someone whom you feel passionate about. Take my Vanessa. I would go to the ends of the earth to make her happy. (I know that's only an expression, but I often wonder where exactly are 'the ends of the earth'?)

Anyways, what I *do* know is what she means to me. According to my Father of the Bride address, she's a compilation of clichés: 'the light of my life', 'the centre of my universe', 'the sunshine in every day'. God, I wish I had more meaningful words to describe her. These weak, ridiculous phrases were all I could come up with when I was making notes – a speech might I add, that I do not want to give, but on the other hand I can't *not* talk about her. I'm not letting the Cunningham side take to the field unopposed and me just sitting there like a dumb stooge. I owe it to Breda.

I am still pushing my bits of paper around the table when I hear the creak in the middle step down to the kitchen. Nessa floats in, wearing just her nightdress.

'Is it my imagination or is it *hot* already?' She picks up an old *Farmer's Journal* and starts fanning herself. 'Not half eight yet. What'll it be like this afternoon?'

'True, there's not a puff of air. I had to put on that new-fangled air-con thing Michael made me buy, out in the milking parlour. The poor girls were sweating. *And* Saturday is to hit 25°C. We'll be passing out in those old monkey suits.'

'I might ask the sacristan at St James's to leave the doors open, once we're all in.'

'Is that wise? The church's very near the road – you'll get traffic noise.'

'Better than having guests fainting from the heat!'

'Now isn't this gas, Ness! I never thought excessive heat was going to be our weather problem!'

Vanessa just smiled at me. 'Are you excited about the day, Daddy? I mean, apart from the threat of fainting aunties, are you looking forward to it?'

'Of course I am. Doesn't stop me being terrified though.'

'What's there to be afraid of?'

'The changes. My world as I know it, changing. You not in it.'

'*What*? And how will I *not be in it*? Don't talk rubbish.'

'Oh, you can laugh all you like, but once you sign that

register next Saturday, you no longer belong to me: you'll be Rob's.'

'I'll be neither of yours, thank you very much! I'll be myself – as always.'

'But you won't, child. You'll lose my name, for starters.'

'No. Not going to happen. Not changing from Walshe.'

I couldn't help emitting a snort at this piece of information.

Her antennae were primed. 'What was *that* about?'

'Just picturing Rob's face when you *share* that. Isn't that what *you* young people call telling a bit of news – sharing?'

'He already knows. Well, when I say he already *knows*, I've hinted at it oodles of times. And when we had lunch with Margery recently, she specifically asked would she do up a release with a change of name for *Morning Glory* when it returns after the summer. I told her absolutely not.'

'Maybe he wasn't paying much attention. You know he doesn't like your agent.'

'No, he was being perfectly pleasant that day. Didn't react at all when I said it.'

'Apart from the surname issue, legally he'll be your primary family – the first port of call if, God forbid, you had an accident or anything. I mean, whose name do you use now as next of kin? On your passport? Or your kidney donor card?'

'Yours.'

'Exactly. All that will have to be changed.'

'Nonsense. You can nominate whoever you want as your "next of kin".'

'Well, I'd like to be there when you explain that to Rob!'

She didn't reply, just stood mooching in front of the fridge, holding the door wide open to visibly well-stocked shelves but, in spite of that, pronounced *'There's never anything I can eat in this house!'* Irritated with me, she flounced off up the steps to the hallway. 'I'm going to get dressed.'

I have a flashback of her – about fifteen – her hair even longer than she is wearing it now, braided roughly from the night before, loose strands falling into her sleepy eyes and the longer escaped strands determined to dip into the cereal bowl. She is wearing pink fluffy pyjamas with white hearts and those ridiculous slippers that come with an entire soft-toy animal on each foot. That year's model, if I recall correctly, had a cream-and-tan puppy.

'*I can't eat this!*' she is whining. 'It's full of refined sugars. Do you *want* me to become obese?'

'You always liked it before.'

'That was *before*. Before I realised all the shit that was in it. Is there no granola or anything?'

'Gran-Ula?'

'Gran-*Ola!*' Honestly, Daddy, you're hopeless. There's never *anything* I can eat in this house.'

But I wasn't always hopeless. Fifteen was just our sticky patch. On the shelf over the Aga, there's a photo from much earlier, Vanessa holding the team shield that she had won in the junior girls' league. She had been the captain and I was their trainer. I had my arm firmly around her, and she snuggled in to me, her straight white teeth dazzling with the beam of her smile. That was taken five years following Breda's death.

Last night I had wanted to bring out the old albums of when she was even younger and her mother still alive, but I thought it might upset her. The only formal photo on display in the kitchen which pre-dates our dreadful loss, is Vanessa's First Communion one. It hangs on the wall beside the pantry door, half-hidden by old aprons and a grease-stained oven glove dangling from a hook. Her seven-year-old face has a serious expression, not greatly relieved by the grimace she had offered the photographer. Her new front teeth with a pronounced gap between them had not met with her approval, and she passed their early years with her lips firmly sealed. Her aunts on Breda's side teased her relentlessly, even going as far as to call her 'vain'. (And then I was surprised when she took up modelling later as an adult?)

I haven't thought as much about my late wife for a long time, as I have done in the past few weeks. It's inevitable, I suppose, when I consider how much she would have enjoyed all the wedding planning and preparation. If I am feeling her absence this strongly, no doubt poor Nessa is too. Maybe I was a little harsh earlier – I could have been kinder about Rob and the name-change business. After all, I'm not the one who's marrying him! I should be satisfied that *she* is happy with her choice.

'Daddy? Jenny rang. The girls have arrived *already*! They are at the Allen Castle. Do you want to put on something smart and we'll go down and join them for a coffee?'

Vanessa, all shiny-haired and glowing skin, is back, dressed in a plain blue dress, and a pair of flat ballet shoes.

'Do you not want to go on your own, love? I am sure you have lots of details to go through with Jenny and Laura.'

'I have, but come with me. Please. You don't know Laura. You really should meet both bridesmaids before the rehearsal tomorrow evening.'

'Alright. I'll go and change.' And knowing my daughter as I do, for devilment I shout back over my shoulder, 'I'll just throw on my check shirt and those khaki combats. Sure, they're grand and clean.'

I could hear her shrieking, as I made my way up the stairs.

'You *will not*! I'll be up in a minute to pick out an outfit for you.'

In the manicured grounds of the Allen Castle, two young women are lolling on a swinging-seat under the shade of a red-and-white striped canopy. One looks vaguely familiar – Vanessa's flatmate Jenny who I have met before – and a curly-headed blonde.

Nessa leans over and hugs Jenny. 'You remember Dad, don't you, Jenny?'

'*Yo*, Mr Walshe – looking very sharp in your linen shirt!'

'Johnny – please. How's Jenny?'

'Great. This is Laura, by the way.'

The curly-headed girl leans forward and shakes my hand. 'So pleased to finally meet you, though I feel I know you for years, the way Vanessa chats about you!'

'Now, I'm worried!'

'Don't be. All good.'

Introductions completed, I sit into an old-fashioned upright deck-chair – the type with two stretches of canvas and wooden arm rests. Vanessa chooses the wrought-iron bench.

'You are *so* lucky with this fab weather, Vee. That halterneck dress will be *just* the thing.' Jenny pushes her feet into the worn grass under the seat, to propel the swing more forcefully, surprising Laura.

'How are your rooms – or did they let you check in yet? It's a bit early.' Vanessa pulls that big phone yoke out of her handbag and swipes her finger back and forth over it. 'Let me check again which ones I booked for you.'

'I just don't get this technology, girls. What's wrong with an oul' paper diary?'

'You're bound to forget it, Mr Walshe. It'll always be where you are not, whereas with our phones and such, we never stir too far without them.' Laura smiles indulgently at me as if I have just waded in off the Ark.

'Would have to be surgically amputated from this one!' Jenny stretches out her leg and gives Nessa a good-humoured kick on the knee. 'All the better to track Rob with!'

There was a low '*shush*' from Vanessa – almost imperceptible – but I heard it, followed by that toss of her head which she gives when she's cross.

'And tell me, ladies, does the groom need "tracking" from time to time?' I look from one bridesmaid to the other, deliberately avoiding Nessa's gaze.

'Ah, Rob is harmless enough,' says Laura, 'though if my mother were here, she'd be advocating keeping a precautionary eye, in case he goes "offside".'

'I'm not sure, madam, that I'm keen on my two-days-away husband being described as "harmless"!' Vanessa stands up, waving the menu in order to attract the attention of the wandering bar-girl.

'Sorry, Vee. That sounded unsympathetic. And he's not. Rob, that is.'

Jenny concurred. 'Yeah. He's just – *different* – from the usual rugger-bugger type. Like, he has real *old-fashioned* manners – opening doors, standing up when you come into a room. All that sort of thing. I mean – he's not a player. Well, he *is* obviously – for a living – but not a *player* in the traditional sense.'

'Shut up, Jenny,' said Vanessa. 'You're giving me a headache.'

The girls laugh.

Vanessa's wild gesticulation at the ambulant waitress finally pays off, as a young monochrome-clad girl makes her way towards us.

'What does anyone want? A pot of coffee? Tea, Dad? I'll get some scones to tide us over.'

'I suppose it's too early for a gin and tonic?' Jenny has done something with that swing-seat and now leans back horizontal, her legs stuck out straight in front of her in a movement that any seven-year-old would be proud of.

'It most certainly is, Maid of Honour. I have a list of things that need doing *sober*.'

'Kill-joy.'

Later, as I cut through the fields alone on my way home from the hotel, I couldn't get the girls' banter out of my head. If Rob were that much of a goody-goody, why would Vanessa feel a need to keep tabs on him? I *know* they're not sleeping together – a piece of information I didn't seek from my daughter. She had volunteered it, one cold February afternoon as we stood freezing on the concrete steps of the South Terrace in Thomond Park – the only tickets she could get at the turnstile as the match was unexpectedly popular. She didn't have her usual Stand tickets because she told Rob she would be working in Dublin that particular Saturday, but turned up unexpectedly at mine, suggesting we head down to see him play. I may only have the one daughter, but for many years I had a wife, and Vanessa's actions struck me as a woman checking up on her other half.

I said as much: 'Do you . . . *worry* when Rob is on tour . . . or has away matches and you are unable to join him? I mean . . . do you think he'd *sleep around?*'

She had laughed at my turn of phrase. 'Too much *Ellen* in the morning, Dad! Well, if he *is* sleeping around, he's breaking his self-professed vow of abstinence, cos he sure as hell isn't sleeping with me!'

It was out there. I didn't reply, just focussed on the pitch, where at least Rob *was* scoring.

From then on, I watched them together. It was hard not to. I found myself constantly observing who touched whom more, who initiated the kisses (usually Vanessa), the hugs (always Rob). I pried shamelessly when they travelled on a recce to Edinburgh or Saracens' games that were in a different pool but likely to come up as Munster opposition, if both progressed. They always shared a room, but that apparently made no difference. Such willpower! I'm thinking back to Breda and me all those decades ago, both of us barely twenty, and how hard we tried to escape detection, doing it in barns, in the cabs of tractors, anywhere we thought we'd go unobserved. Here we are, over forty years later with easy access to contraception, and my daughter is going to walk up the aisle with a man without ever having had sex with him! It made no sense to me at all.

———

If I'd been making heavy weather of completing my 'Father of the Bride' speech, well, my ruminations on this glorious 4th of July have thoroughly quashed my enthusiasm to continue with it.

My scraps of paper still lie in disarray where I left them on the scrubbed kitchen table, the red date on the calendar mocking me with its cheerfulness. I look closer at the Beethoven quotation and think of its meaning – the fruitlessness of a life lived without passion.

I think of my beautiful only daughter. And I feel a cold hand creep round my heart.

Chapter 9

Davey

The sun beat down relentlessly the whole way to Allenbeg. I couldn't even take off the roof, because the boot was stuffed to capacity with all our wedding paraphernalia. As we passed the Curragh racecourse on the motorway, the thermometer hit 30°C. The air-con was going full blast, but it was never quite as efficient in the soft-top. Too much hot air leaking in and a lot of the recycled cool escaping through the canvas.

'We really should have taken the two cars,' moaned Karen. 'At least that way, I could have left early this morning with most of the luggage, and you wouldn't be tackling the Friday afternoon traffic in this suffocating heat. Or at least if you were, you could have let the roof down.'

'Well, it was your idea – *brilliant* if I may say so – to drop the other car out to the Long Term at the airport for our return from Catania. That way, we can just drive Dad

107

straight home on Sunday week and this old jalopy will be waiting for us on the farm.'

'I think the flight's in quite late, Dave. We'll probably need to overnight at Johnny's.'

'That's no harm, is it? *Idiot!* Did you see that? A two-lane manoeuvre with not an indicator in sight!'

I didn't know if Karen would remember the silly refrain an old friend of ours from Palermo – the scariest driving city in Europe – would chant when I'd mention Sicilians' aversion to indicators but, on hearing the prompt, she had, and we chorused it together!

'Because indicators are like fairy lights – just for Christmas!'

'Imagine our *innocence* that first holiday year, picking up the hired car at the airport, not realising it was west of the city and we'd have to negotiate the rush-hour traffic.'

'And nobody *anywhere* indicating where they were going! No wonder Gianni cracked up laughing at our white faces when we eventually made it to Cefalù.'

'But we survived!'

'That we did!'

Karen and I executed our silly version of a high-five – adapted for when we're in the car. It involves kissing the fingers of your own (preferably free) hand and then touching all five with your neighbour's – less easy for the driver in the manual – but a cinch in the ancient automatic Saab in which we are travelling today. I don't know when we started it, or where it came from, but I suspect it was an idiosyncrasy of the elderly Swiss couple with whom Karen used do homestays and who, by her account, were still madly in love after forty years of marriage.

'*Ah, les beaux jours!*' Karen smiled, obviously remembering the Swiss couple too. 'I love you, Mr Walshe.'

'I love you too, Ms Waldron.'

'Even after twelve years of marriage?'

'Even *more* after twelve years.'

'We're a soppy pair.' She grinned. 'Enough! You *do* know we're expected to make this rehearsal? Are we alright on time?'

'We should be. Once the motorway splits, the volume of traffic will lessen. What time is it at?'

'Seven,' she said. 'I hope I don't have to run through my reading.'

'Doubt it. I think it's just the immediate wedding party, so we can all clock eyes on each other before tomorrow.'

'*And* don't forget – meet Bishop Joe, Rob's uncle!' She pulled a face. 'I don't know *what* he's doing marrying them. Allenbeg's not even in his diocese, sure it isn't?'

'Wouldn't have a clue – you know me and Catholic Church stuff. Rob's family wanted him. Well, the mother anyway.'

'Is he *her* brother?'

'No, don't think so. Isn't he a Cunningham? You have the leaflets in your bag.'

'Hang on . . . Yep, you're right. Cunningham. So, did he choose this St James's?'

'No, Vanessa liked it. The town church is a big echoey

barn of a place. Besides, the parish priest has his nose out of joint according to Dad, over her "importing" the big guns! It'll be far more intimate in the little white church.'

'Do you remember *our* intimate wedding?'

'Ah stop! I thought I was supposed to be concentrating on the driving and making excellent time. And *then* she distracts me with our nuptials!'

'Trinity College Chapel. And the downpour we came out to, after the ceremony! Everyone soaked. Despite that, I still wanted the day to last forever.'

'It did, in a way. We're still as happy as we were then.'

'I wonder will this pair survive the pace?'

I didn't respond. Karen picked up on it immediately. Nearly two decades together, there's not much she misses.

'Why the silent grimace, Dave?'

'Ah stuff. I might fill you in later. Let's just see how this evening goes.'

'You have me worried.'

'No, nothing cataclysmic. Just protective older brother stuff.'

Despite it probably commanding penalty points, Karen didn't care as she laced her fingers through my hand as it rested on the steering wheel. We passed the fork in the road for the M8 and sped onwards towards my old home and my baby sister, who the following day was about to embark on her new adult life.

Once off the motorway, the journey took on a more leisurely pace, not necessarily a pace of our making. We were compelled to slow down behind agricultural vehicles taking full advantage of the dry spell to save hay, and only just about winding their way home after a long day in the fields.

"I'm ravenous! Aren't you hungry?' I was rummaging in the central console in the hope of finding a stray cereal bar I'd forgotten about.

'Yeah, I could do with eating, but Vanessa texted earlier to say she has a table booked at Hugo's for the immediate wedding party after the rehearsal. Can you hang on till then?'

'Of course, if she's gone to the trouble of arranging it.'

'Here! There's the signpost for St James's Church.'

Suddenly, the sun-soaked small white church sprang up before our eyes, and I nearly missed the sloping entrance into the car park.

'Oh, look! It's really beautiful.' Karen was impressed.

There were only three cars in the gravelled parking area, which surprised me, but people might have been dropped off earlier by a shuttle-bus which I knew the couple had hired to whizz guests between the key locations. Small knots of people clustered against the raised-bed wall outside the chapel, enjoying the evening sun.

Vanessa, looking taller and more svelte than ever, was hovering at the side door, chatting with two women. The plump dark-haired one held a basket of flowers, so she was obviously preparing the church for the following day. Her red-haired companion had her arms crossed defensively over a music case clutched to her chest. When my sister spotted the car, she abandoned both women and ran across the gravel, hugging Karen through the open car window.

'Oh, am I so glad to see you guys! I expected you *hours* ago!'

I laughed, and turned to Karen. 'Do you see? Only one week a lady of leisure out of the big smoke, and she forgets about the M7 on a Friday evening! Good to see you, kid. Are you nearly ready to begin inside?'

'*I'm* not personally, but I see Bishop Joe eyeing his watch. I think he has to get back to Clare tonight. I know he's not joining us for the meal afterwards.'

'Well, let's not hold him up. Oh, there's Rob!' Karen was waving energetically but he didn't seem to see her.

He consulted first his watch, then his uncle, and began ushering the clusters of nattering guests inside.

The rehearsal was informal and speedy and we were all back out in the car park within forty minutes. Out of the corner of my eye, I noticed an odd scene develop between Dad and Bishop Joe. The bishop was saying his goodbyes when my father put a hand on his arm as if to ask him something, but the clergyman shook him off, nodding towards his car. Out of character for my father – given that he was dealing with a senior man of the cloth – Dad persisted and caught a firm hold of the bishop's sleeve. Bishop Joe reacted, snatching his arm away and half-pushing Dad in the chest. Pale and looking a little stressed, Dad instinctively raised both fists and was dancing from foot to foot as if spoiling for a fight. *What on earth* was going on between these two? The bishop kept moving briskly towards his car and I sprinted after my father, to dilute the situation. Was it the burden of sole responsibility for the following day's proceedings that was resting heavily on Dad's shoulders, or just the heat of a long day? No doubt, like me, he was missing Mam dreadfully.

'*Davey!*'

I could see she was in organisation mode when Vanessa strode purposefully towards us. All she was missing was a clipboard and a lanyard!

'The table is booked for eight out in Hugo's, so I'm trying to herd people in that general direction. Can you and Karen take two in your car?'

'Maybe just one?' Karen laughed. 'I have my overflow wardrobe on the back seat!'

'Great. Then you could take Tom – the young priest? He's staying over to set up tomorrow. Bishop Joe has some charity garden party in Killaloe that he has to show his face at before the wedding.'

After the odd interaction between Dad and Rob's uncle, I had noticed a young dark-bearded man in knee-length Bermuda shorts unload a cardboard box from the back seat of the bishop's car. That must be Tom. They had a few words, then he waved his boss off and returned to the church, where he stopped to chat to Rob. The two had stood laughing and joking for a few minutes, long enough in fact for the man with the beard to place the evidently heavy box on the ground beside him.

As commanded, we offered Tom a lift and he began to worry about the dress-code chez-Hugo. *('What possessed me to wear these Bermudas?')* Hugo's is owned and managed by a French chef who settled in the area about five years previously. He has converted an old schoolhouse into a contemporary yet cosy restaurant, which offers European and fusion cuisine. There's even been a rumour of a Michelin star – which might account for why it wasn't a place particularly popular with the local townspeople. Diners travel to it from all over the county, and it features on a popular tour-guide site, so anytime I've eaten there Hugo is always entertaining foreign tourists – the odd one even in Bermuda shorts. (I tried to reassure Tom.) It was an ideal choice of Vanessa's for her visiting guests, as the only other decent place to eat is the Allen Castle Hotel where they'd be the next day anyway for the reception. I imagine that once the smaller table configurations are amalgamated to seat the Walshe party, we'll probably have the place to ourselves.

I spotted my father hovering on the threshold of the restaurant and escorted him inside where he was installed beside Karen.

As always, she began to charm him. 'Johnny! How are you holding up? Is the pressure getting to you yet?'

'What do you mean *pressure*?' he snapped. Most unlike him where Karen's concerned.

'Will I get you a whiskey, Dad? You look like you could do with one. What was that business earlier with the bishop? I thought there were going to be fisticuffs!'

He didn't answer but, with an odd arching of his eyebrow, he beckoned me out into the covered courtyard where the odd stubborn smoker puffed on the perimeter of the awning.

'What's wrong?' I asked.

'Nothing, nothing. I'm just worried about that *girleen* inside.' He studied the odd stray fag-end that had infiltrated the paved area of the courtyard, pushed a few butts around with the toe of his right shoe, and then looked back up at me. 'Do you think she's doing the right thing marrying that yoke over there?'

I followed the incline of his head and, when I raised my eyes, I could see through the archway into the restaurant that Rob was in further animated conversation with Father Tom.

'Well, yes. *She* seems to think so.'

'*Hmph!*

'You're not so convinced?'

'No, I *am not*. Haven't been for a good while now.'

'Dad, maybe you should have said something to me – *to her* – a little earlier?'

'Ah, you know Nessa – she'd snap the head off you. Her own woman and all that.'

'And I wonder where she gets *that* from?'

He didn't respond, just flicked stray, wind-blown ash from his good jacket, before continuing. 'They're not having . . . *relations*. Did you know?'

'I'd heard a rumour . . .'

'And you didn't think fit to share it with me?'

'It's their own business. A lot of couples wait nowadays. There's a whole new trend towards abstinence.'

'If you ask me, it's not normal – a *stunner* like Vanessa, and that fellow with no interest.' Dad ground the offending butts forcefully into the patio tiles with the heel of his shoe. 'We should be going back in. It's not polite to leave Karen on her own.'

Silently, he led the way back into the restaurant and, for once, I was left speechless.

Back in our room at Allen Castle, I joined Karen out on the garden patio.

'I had the most bizarre conversation with Dad earlier and, ironically, it links into that episode I didn't tell you about earlier in the car.'

'Oh yeah? Spill.'

'No, Karen, this isn't idle gossip. It's kind of serious. Do you remember when I went to Oxford for Rob's bachelor do after the Northampton Charity challenge?'

She nodded.

'Well, we ended up in this grotty club where the lads had set him up for a private lap dance. Pretty standard stuff for a stag, but he freaked out – had a full-blown panic attack, couldn't breathe or anything. Practically assaulted the dancer, who unfortunately had been costumed to look like Vanessa, long wig, the works. He was furious with his best man, threatened to sack him on the spot, and spoke to nobody on the return leg of the journey.'

'So, he's shy. Doesn't like that sort of low-grade entertainment. Probably right, too.'

'But Dad has just confirmed what I suspected – that they haven't slept together yet. Do you not think it's a bit off?'

'I think you're all gone quite mad! It's not so long ago since parents were running around hounding their offspring to hold off until they were married and not to "give it away" to random suitors. Our parents managed to marry *virgo intacta* and went on to have long, happy – and I might add – very fertile marriages. And now, because one couple out of hundreds chooses to wait, you are worrying that there is something sinister – an underlying problem! He's very religious – maybe that's your answer. And Nessa's more traditional than you or I.'

'Maybe.'

'Try not to worry. Vanessa's not some naïve ingénue. She's had her fair share of adventures.'

'That's my point. Why hold off now, with the person she is committing herself to for life?'

'You're over-thinking this, Dave. And it's a problem that will probably be resolved in –' Karen held her watch up to the patio light '– a little over twenty-six hours from now!'

Maybe my wife *was* right. But she hadn't seen the disgust on Rob's face when that sexy woman in the English club had straddled him. Nor had she witnessed the violence he had used to dislodge her.

Something was not right.

Chapter 10

Vanessa

Birds singing – chirping, chirping, chirping. Can't stand it. Shut up shut up shut up SHUT-UP! Can't sleep must sleep – sleep, sleep, sleep! Bride with black eyes big eyes big black circles under eyes. Not good no good. Bad look bad luck. Can't sleep must sleep – sleep, sleep, sleep! Pillow over my head under my head off the bed under the bed under my head. Eye mask blackout hide eyes big black eyes from night light short night strong light. Bells, bells, church bells! Two bells three bells long bells short bell – three bells! THREE BELLS – three and *a half* bells – *for fuck's sake* – half past three. Can't sleep must sleep need sleep have to sleep. Forget about sleep don't try don't lie trying too hard to sleep, sleep, sleep.

Make list. First things first. Have bath do nails wait, wait, wait for girls. Girls laugh make me laugh. Champagne pops, pops, pops! Poor Pops. Alone here on his own no

Ness at home. Poor lone soul alone at home. Sorry, *no* sole. Not nice fish changed dish no fish. I said NO FISH. Next dish please. Good? *What do you think?* Rob likes fish wants dish fish dish. Wants silver dish for fish. Silverfish sliver and dodge. Hate them hate them *hate* them. *Excuse me*, w*here's the dish the silver dish?* Rob on the rob. He wouldn't he shouldn't wouldn't couldn't shouldn't. (But does he?) Screw it won't do it won't screw can't screw you and you and you. Screw you, Rob on the rob! Waiter back. *Where's the dish the silver dish the fish dish?* Sorry, lad. No can do. Down my shoe as you do won't fit in my sock, souvenir of the 'do'.

Big Day. My day. My Big Day. Tomorrow and tomorrow and all the morrows. Sorrow? No, no, no! Put on a happy face no sorrow in the morrow smile though your heart is breaking aching breaking achy-breaky-heart. Fart. He *does* fart. Not nice. Hells bells!

More bells four bells? For Belle the flower girl a bracelet with a heart, will that do? *What do you think?* Are you listening to me? Do you hear me are you near me? Do you care do you share things care about things caring and sharing and sparing some time for each other, spare me a minute a minute of your time. *Buddy, can you spare a dime?* And you do lots of time lots of dimes. A good man a kind man a goody-goody man. Doesn't smoke doesn't drink doesn't stink – well, maybe just a little. Doesn't think. HE DOESN'T THINK. Think about me. My needs my wants my loves my Pops. *No, no, no! Unthinkable. Not happening. Can't come. Leave him home, home alone.* Just a week a little week a little peek at a far-off land. Please, please, please, please! On my knees. Well nearly.

Light bright full light not night. Ah, not light already! Want sleep must sleep have to sleep. A little sleep. To sleep to dream. A little dream a little sleep a little peek at a far-off land. All together. Together forever. Forever together. Till death do us part. Will you take and make and break Vanessa? Will you love her hug her cuddle her smother her forever and ever and ever?

I will.

Will you Nessa take and cherish and nourish this lonely man as your only man your one and only ever after lonely only man?

No.

What?

I can't take him as my one and only lonely man for ever and ever because I have another no mother one brother another old man to cherish and nourish and care for all the days of his life.

Will you care and share with Vanessa the care of her old man?

I don't know if I can really. I'm a man who's lost too much had to share too much had to watch as my old man mauled and pawed another not my mother my lovely mother. 'Go bother someone else,' she said, and he did as he slid disgusting git into the slit of another not my mother not his wife ruined her life for that incubator of twins. Win win. So good he named them twice.

But Rob, where does that leave us – leave *me*? (*Leave* me! Please leave me.) Leave me at the church gate! Too late to

121

change the date. No object of hate. Just go, go, GO!

Not so. I have waited and waited. I have been good. Tomorrow's my Big Day too.

(Tomorrow and tomorrow and tomorrow: what am I talking about *tomorrow* for?)

Bells. Birds screeching. Sun blasting eye-mask failing light shining no sleep. Have a peep anyway. Beautiful day. Big Day. My big beautiful day.

Today.

Up. *Carpe Diem.* Up. Time to get up. Time to get *it* up. Not long now. How long are you going to keep this up? This jealousy, this petty jealousy? My clothes (too short) my hair (too long) my legs (too bare) my friends (too loud) my camera-man (too handsy) my agent (too drunk). Please Rob, let it go. LET – IT – GO.

Oh, I can keep this up for as long as it takes.

(But can you Rob, can you *really* keep it up?)

Quiet house silent house not a creature stirring not even a mouse. Brutus the cat sees to that. Wash dress nails or was it wash nails dress? Where's my list the grooming list the list of lists, there are so many goddamn lists. A grooming list and a list for a groom. To groom a pony good; to groom a child bad. A groom can groom as well – or try to (hair, clothes, legs, friends, camera-men, agent).

Church list, camera list catering list, speeches list, no grooming list. Birds full throttle, pop of a cork from a bottle, *yes!* Yes, I *am* alone drinking on my own bad habit but Brutus the cat no taste for that no taste for bubbles unless you mean Bubbles, late deceased female tabby.

More bells. Six? Lost track forgot to count. Five-thirty? No matter. Want to hear water splatter. Run bath. Shush! Shush! Quiet house silent house not a creature stirring not even a mouse. Let's keep it that way: Daddy an early riser.

More bubbles. In the water, in the glass. Tears flowing. No, no, no! Blotchy nose. Red nose. Eyes stinging. Heaving chest sobbing. (Would Rob sob at no-show?) Snuffy nose, hoarse voice.

Beautiful satin dress hanging in the corner. Satin-covered shoes with rosebud flowers. Low kitten heels. (He won.) Mother-of-pearl boxy clutch. (Fits nothing.) Mother's *actual* pearls on the dressing table.

Nails done no need of help. Good at this. Eyes bloodshot. Hair a mess. Phyllis due later. Hair up. Another victory for the groom. (But have *I* room for the groom?)

Fully awake now, creaking floorboards, Daddy moving around. Must check nose eyes cheeks in mirror for signs of blubbing. Can't cover with make-up: too early.

———

Rattling exhaust pipe racket from down below in farmyard. *What the hell?* Lilac old-fashioned VW Beetle bumps in over dried mud and manure. Official visiting cars use gravel driveway to the front.

But it's cool, unpredictable Tammie, my bohemian photographer, not bothered by a bit of agricultural poo, as she shoves black-and-yellow spotty wellingtons onto her feet before alighting from the car. She was my find and far too unorthodox to ever have passed Rob's scrutiny. If I chose to, I could send her away right now, on this beautiful heat-hazed morning.

I watch from my bedroom window, terrified that her arrival so early and the unloading of copious amounts of camera gear from the front trunk suggest she's going for the frank 'before' and 'after' folio. I panic. I touch my blotchy face. This is really happening.

I hear the back-kitchen door open and lots of exclamation – Daddy has it. I stretch my long, tanned ring-less hands in front of me and admire the painted nails. They are definitely dry. It's safe now to do the one thing I have been wanting to do.

I cross to the dressing table and open the clasp of my mother's drop pearls. I hold them to my neck. The large gold locket hangs just above the sternum and the single strand of substantially-sized pearls supports it perfectly. My fingers seek out the catch and I slide back the receiver, tilting my head as I pull the clasp around to the side to observe better what I am doing in the mirror. Once the necklace is secure, I open the locket.

To the left is a faded headshot of Mam with Davey peeping over her shoulder. To the right, a picture of a young Dad, holding the pudgy baby that I was in his arms. Leaving the locket on, I wrap my new Ted Baker robe around me tightly and go down to face the music.

Part 3

A Walshe Wedding

Chapter 11

When Vanessa enters the Allenbeg kitchen dressed in a silk robe and with the lightest coat of powder concealing her red face, she finds Johnny and Tammie sitting at the table, sharing a pot of tea. The strong morning sunlight casts dusty beams flecked with God knows what across the room. They glance off Tammie's recently coloured hair, the blackness of which shines violet in the bright light.

'*Here comes the bride—*'

Vanessa frowns. Her photographer's attempts at singing leave a lot to be desired. Even Johnny winces.

'Ah, there you are, love. Tammie here was just walking me through all the shots she plans to take. Tea?'

'Not yet. I'll eat something in a while. Any word from Rob?'

'Were you expecting to hear from him?'

'Not particularly but—'

Tammie slaps her mug down onto the worn wooden table. 'Vanessa! Don't go messing with tradition! You're not supposed to have any contact *The Day Of.*'

'Stupid superstition, Tam. Did anyone see my charger? The battery's dead.'

'Here. Use mine. Same model. Are you sure you *really* want to ring him – now – the actual morning of your wedding?'

'Unavoidable. There's something I have to tell him.'

And with the borrowed phone charger in hand, Vanessa heads back upstairs.

Johnny didn't respond to Tammie's offer of fresh tea. After catching his first glimpse of the day of Vanessa, he felt decidedly uneasy. There was definitely something 'off' in his daughter's demeanour.

'Will I, Mr Walshe?'

'Sorry, Tammie. What was that?'

'Make another pot?'

'Ah, I thought the bridesmaids were supposed to be providing us with something a little fancier than tea!'

'It's still early. I'm sure they'll be here soon.'

Within minutes, the excited rise and fall of female voices floated in from the upper hallway.

'Hiya, Johnny! Only us!' Karen had brought Jenny and

Laura and used Davey's key to let them all in at the front door.

She appeared, carrying a tray of croissants, pastries, and interesting-looking bread.

The two bridesmaids brought up the rear, each anchored by a couple of bottles of champagne.

'Morning, Mr Walshe.' Laura set her charges down on the dresser.

Jenny did the same, then crossed to the table and gave Vanessa's father a hug. 'How's Daddy holding up? And you must be the photographer – Tammie, isn't it? Jenny. Chief Bridesmaid and part-time sommelier!'

'Pleased to meet you.' Tammie gave a little salute. 'I could do with your help later to marshal the troops into the various family combos—'

'I'm your woman! Love a bit of "marshalling".' She looked around her for the fridge. 'I'll put one of these bottles in to cool.'

'Or maybe there's an ice bucket?' Laura's head was swivelling around, scanning Johnny's kitchen dubiously.

'Not here. Probably upstairs. I'll go.' Karen headed back up to the seldom-used formal room.

'Never mind the ice-*bucket*. Where's the ice-maiden herself this morning?' Jenny took a croissant from the tray and looked from Johnny to Tammie for an update.

'Had an urgent need to speak to husband-to-be.' Tammie pointed to the ceiling. 'Gone to her room to phone him. Could be a while.'

129

'Oh, that's not on! Doesn't she know the rules?' Jenny began to stack the pastries and croissants on some decent-looking pottery plates she took down from the dresser.

Karen returned with a tray of crystal glasses she had found in the dining-room 'No ice-bucket to be found. What's up?' She began to give the glasses a polish.

'Vanessa. Phoning Rob. Something urgent she has to tell him.'

Karen put down the linen napkin she was using as a glass-cloth and caught her father-in-law's eye. Johnny read her signal.

'Eh, ladies, I suppose I'd better excuse myself. I need to go and check with Michael how morning milking went and run through the arrangements for this evening.'

'I'll come out with you for a breather.' Karen had the door open already. 'It's so warm – it's not even half nine.' And when out of earshot of the others: 'Anything I should be worried about, Johnny?'

'Haven't a clue. But she was acting strangely earlier. Still in the dressing gown – well, the new fancy one you bought her. And wearing Breda's locket with it!'

Karen pulled her phone from her pocket and started messaging.

'Who are you ringing now?'

'I'm just texting Davey, to see if Rob's around. God, Johnny, you don't think we have a problem, like a *real* problem?'

'Like what?'

'Like a *Runaway Bride* scenario?'

'A *what*? But where would she run to? And, anyway, why?'

Jenny was at the door, almost hissing at them: '*She's back! I'm afraid to open the bubbly until I know we have a wedding to go to at all!*'

The satisfying pop of a good cork leaving an even better bottle made everyone relax and have faith that the day was back on track. Laura had dragged a faded and slightly wobbly parasol over to the plastic garden table and the breakfast decamped outside.

'And what was so *urgent,* pray tell, that you had to go ringing Rob at this hour?' Karen, lumbered with having to drive, had a very orangey Buck's Fizz in front of her and wasn't as jovial as the others.

'I did something that Rob wouldn't approve of. I felt he needed to know, before the ceremony.'

Karen shook her drink ferociously, trying to encourage the little alcohol that *was* in it to infuse and help her out. 'Oh? Do you want to talk about it?'

'You'll all know soon enough. I mean, it'll be self-evident at the church.'

Jenny was hovering with the Veuve Clicquot and Karen signalled for an unadulterated glass: how many checkpoints could there realistically be at 10.30 on a Saturday morning on the backroad over to the hotel?

'Can you not put us out of our misery and tell us now?'
Laura held her glass out for the top-up.

'Oh, alright. It's about Frank, Rob's Dad. It was agreed
that we'd invite him, even though Lilian was kicking up a
fuss about it – thanks, Jenny – that's lovely. No, no
croissant, I'm fine. I mean, they still have a *tenuous*
relationship, not great, but not *nothing*. When he RSVPed in
the negative, I lied to Rob and told him he'd be delighted
to come and wrote Frank a second note, asking him to
reconsider.' Vanessa paused to draw in a slurp of
champagne. 'Only he wasn't a bit happy about the status of
his original invitation – it was just him, you see. No
mistress, no kids. This was Lilian's stipulation, and I
suppose you could kind of see her point—'

Tammie, who had been clearing away any non-
photogenic matter from the front hall-door area, came
crunching through the gravel around to the back sitting
area and couldn't resist focussing her camera.

'Look at you all, engrossed in conversation – that's it –
just continue chatting! I want the relaxed nature of our day
– "the-bride-with-no-nerves" kind of theme. Lovely! And
another. That's it. Karen, hold up your crystal – *smile*! Fan-
TASTIC. I'll be back in a while to torment you when you're
dressed. I just need to fetch the tripod and another bag I
need from the hotel. Laters!'

Jenny checked her watch. 'Is Miss Snappy not cutting it
a bit fine – going back over to the hotel?'

'Not really. It won't take her long.' Karen refocussed her

attention on Vanessa. 'So go on – Rob's dad was refusing to attend if he couldn't bring his entourage – Nessa, *please* tell me you didn't!'

'I had to. I just made an executive decision. If Rob was to have his father present, he'd have to invite Guinevere and the twins. They *are* his half-sisters – I mean, what age would they be now, seventeen, eighteen? It's time he got over himself.'

Laura spluttered her drink. 'You *are* joking. Her name isn't *really* Guinevere?'

'Well, it's something French-sounding and it begins with 'G'.' I don't know! It's not important. I just put "and partner" on the revised invitation. And stuck in a second one for Molly and Milly who, according to the card Frank sent with his present, have bought new outfits and are looking forward to it.' She sighed. 'I just thought I'd better warn Rob before they show up.'

'Too right.' Karen made an impromptu fan out of the branch of an adjacent *grisilinia* shrub. Was it the stress, or (Christ, please no – an early menopause?) – but she was seriously overheating.

'I hate to interrupt – but Phyllis is here. For the hair?' Laura, ever-solicitous, was holding a jug of iced water, which she obviously believed was needed.

'Good. Great! Right, Nessa. Off you go and get beautified. We'll clear up this lot.' Karen gave her sister-in-law a tight hug. 'And I better get back and do something with me. Don't want to be *too* shabby come two o'clock.'

'Love you.'

'Go. Knock 'em dead!'

Johnny thought the house was eerily quiet when all the girls had left. For the previous couple of hours, every room he tried had been occupied. If it wasn't the make-up woman, it was the hairdresser. Because the unused bedrooms had long since fallen into disrepair, none were really comfortable apart from Vanessa's own. She'd asked Johnny if he'd mind the bridesmaids setting up camp in the dining-room, which of course he didn't as it was never used any more anyway. One of the make-up girls from the TV station had offered to come and do the honours, and had spread all her kit and caboodle down the length of the mahogany table. In turn once they were finished in the bathroom, Jenny and Laura had decided to head downstairs to dress and have their faces done. Tammie – (nice girl and all that, but she was a bloody nuisance) – had followed Johnny around, recording his every move. He thought he could do with her now, though. Old-fashioned bow ties were a nightmare to fasten on your own! There was always still Vanessa if he got stuck, but since she seemed much happier after the girls' champagne breakfast, he wanted to give her a bit of space.

Still struggling with the bow tie – he had fastened it, but it was a bit lopsided – Johnny checked his watch. She should be dressed by now: she'd been in her room *ages*. Jenny had volunteered to stay behind and let Laura take the flower girl in the first car, but Vanessa had waved her off, saying she wanted it to be just herself and her old dad in the vintage car that would take them to St James's.

As he watched his daughter descend the stairs ever so carefully, the long, satin train of the dress cascading in her wake, Johnny began to cry. It was her beauty – *it was his loss* – that prompted the tears and, although he knew he shouldn't upset her, he felt as if somebody was about to rip the heart out of his chest.

Since time immemorial, he knew fathers have had to suffer this: letting go of their daughters and entrusting them to God knows whom. People scoffed at dowries and arranged marriages and the like but, at least in those societies, there was some degree of knowledge of the opposite family the girl was about to inherit – the 'pedigree' of the intended, the financial viability of the set-up she was about to join.

Not that Johnny hadn't done his own checks and balances on the Cunninghams. Apart from the philandering father, he had come up with nothing dodgy. But he knew there were never any guarantees; people hold deep and dark secrets hidden even from the omnipresent spotlight of Google and Facebook. More tech-savvy 21st century people than himself might fool themselves into believing that if there was anything untoward about the future intended, then the imminent father-in-law could google it out of him.

Johnny wasn't so sure.

'Daddy? I'm ready.'

Johnny hesitated uncertainly in the hallway.

Tammie sprang into action and was out through the door in a jiffy. Her light-meter reading what she needed, she was ready to shoot as Vanessa emerged onto the gravel driveway of Allenbeg.

The chauffeur, his jacket off and temporarily hanging on the wing mirror of the burgundy Austin, was busy cleaning bird droppings off the left side of the bonnet.

'Would you look at that? Feckin' seagulls in a landlocked county in the middle of Ireland!'

Johnny couldn't have cared less about the seagulls, but the tears that continued to leak down his cheeks had him nonplussed. He couldn't handle raw emotion. He needed a distraction. His daughter – knowing how his mind worked – gave it to him.

'Dad, does Mam's locket look alright, or is it a bit odd with this halter-neck?'

'*Odd?* Why would it be odd to wear your entire family around your neck? It's beautiful. *You're* beautiful.'

'Don't. You'll make me cry – *again*! Des? Are we good to go?'

'Ready when you are.' The driver put his jacket back on.

'Let's sort the skirt of this dress out first.'

As the chauffeur carefully – and evidently with much practice – accordion-pleated the long train into the car after Vanessa, Johnny stood alongside Tammie and watched helplessly.

'Sir, are you with us?'

'Of course.'

And with that, Johnny pulled nervously at his bow tie, tucked his tails under his backside and squeezed into the red leather car seat beside his daughter.

Chapter 12

The bridesmaids and groomsmen mingled in the little courtyard in front of the white church. Davey had been drafted in as a late replacement for one of the original ushers who had suffered a broken leg at the hands of a Clermont prop forward and, although the injured guest was still present, he had voluntarily resigned his role as he didn't feel it appropriate to be hopping around on crutches as he distributed wedding booklets. Terry, the best man, was playing a low-key role. In his place, Jenny had taken to her sergeant-major role like a duck to water – putting paid to the notion that nursing is a caring, sharing profession. The Maid of Honour spent her days kicking ass in a tough inner-city hospital, and was ideally suited for bossy bridesmaid duties.

'*Here they come! Places, everyone!*'

Rob, Terry and the groomsmen scurried into the church

as the car slowly climbed the incline into the church grounds. First the driver, then Johnny, helped Vanessa to clamber out. Jenny and Laura assisted, holding the long skirt off the ground. In the porch they settled the dress and teased out the train. They held their own bouquets and handed the bride hers.

Tammie — now smart in a mint-green short-sleeved trouser suit, the spotty wellies discarded — was buzzing around, insinuating herself into every conceivable angle that might yield an interesting shot.

Music queued within, the authoritative sound of Clarke's *Trumpet Voluntary* resonating around the small, high-vaulted church, as father and daughter took off.

———

Johnny had been dreading it — the handover at the top of the aisle — but with his recent worries about Rob, he released his daughter's arm slowly and reluctantly. She kissed him thoughtfully on the cheek, her eyes never leaving his, as she mouthed, 'Thanks for everything, Dad,' before he backed away, ceding position to Rob, who had a peck on the cheek of his own for Vanessa, breaking out into a goofy grin — a kind of sympathetic smile that Johnny had never seen him give before.

———

Vanessa turned to lay down her bouquet. Jenny took it and carefully placed it beside her own kneeler. Rob fidgeted and smiled, a gulf of literal and metaphorical space between him and Terry who was offset to his right. The altar microphone made a static noise as Bishop Joe leaned closer.

'Dearly beloved, you are all very welcome to the church of St James in Allenbeg, for the celebration of the marriage of Rob and Vanessa.'

The bishop was dressed in simple but celebratory garb, not as flamboyant as his usual episcopal regalia, and was flanked on one side by Tom, the curate, and on the other by an older disgruntled-looking local priest with grey hair.

Joe smiled as he surveyed the gathering. 'Wasn't that entrance music very invigorating? It sets the pace for this afternoon's proceedings, brisk but reflective. We are enjoying an unusually warm, sunny spell and I know you're all eager to get back out into the sunlight to join the bride and groom and their families for the more relaxed part of the day. Now, first of all, I call upon the representative of each family to come forward and light the two candles, which represent the different, individual upbringing and traditions of Vanessa and Rob before us.'

There was the obligatory shuffling and clambering as Rob's mother came from her seat to light a candle. Davey did the honours for the Walshe family.

'As Lilian and David have demonstrated, each party here before us —'

The side-door swung open a little too energetically and

banged against the wall. A heavy-set man with grey hair, followed by two willowy fair-haired girls in matching dresses in different colours, took their seats in the side aisle.

'Eh, the parties here before us are individuals, unique as they commit to form one union in God.'

Karen, observing the new arrivals, gave Davey a sharp dig in the ribs. 'That must be Frank.'

'Who? Can't hear you.'

'*Frank*, Rob's father,' Karen repeated, loud enough this time to attract annoyed glances.

On Rob's side of the church, his mother in the front pew looked like she was having a seizure. A woman beside her patted her arm, half-soothingly, half in restraint.

'And, now, I'd like to invite the readers to join us up on the altar for the couple's chosen liturgy.'

'You're up.'

'What?'

'Karen – your reading! *Go*.'

'Christ, where's my leaflet with all the markings?'

'Take mine.'

The readers made their way onto the altar, delivered their piece, stood back and waited until the responsorial psalm was sung, before returning to the congregation.

Bishop Joe adjusted the mike back to his own height and prepared to read the gospel. The rather shrill soprano launched into an Alleluia.

'*Phew*, I'm glad that's over,' Karen muttered as she

fanned herself with the leaflet. 'I can follow the ceremony in earnest, now that I'm done.'

'You were fine. Oh, she's off again, the screechy soprano.' Davey checked the singer's name on the back of the booklet as she launched into a less strident rendition of the *Ave Maria*.

The musical interlude gave everyone a chance to relax, whilst Vanessa and Rob took their positions on the steps for the Rite of Marriage.

'Bet they use the Honour and Obey version.' Karen giggled.

'Can't see my sister going for that.'

'That's what I mean. It'll be in Rob's vow!'

But it wasn't, both of them having written a personalised and uncontroversial Church-approved set of their own. The promises to each other were simple but sincere and by the end even Johnny was smiling as the congregation prepared for the exchange of rings. Rob began to rummage in his pockets for the box Vanessa had given him at the rehearsal. She had been quite adamant that she wanted to use her late mother's wedding band, rather than the shiny new one that paired with Rob's own.

As the groom opened the box to extract the ring, he dropped it, and it rolled across the red carpet to the side of the altar. Father Tom descended the two steps swiftly and bent to retrieve it, before taking a long stride and placing it into Rob's shaking hands.

On the front row mahogany bench, Johnny was

outraged, audibly tut-tutting. '*Did you see that?*' he hissed. '*The fool! And what's the best man up there for – a bit of decoration? Isn't he supposed to look after rings and the such-like?*'

'They've had a bit of a row,' Davey whispered.

'Who has?'

'I'll tell you later.'

'*Who's* had the row?'

'*Sssh*, Dad. You're disturbing people. *Rob* and the best man.'

'*Well, that's only great*,' Johnny continued to hiss. '*He's supposed to be giving me the heads-up at the speeches later.*'

By the time the soothing strains of *On Eagle's Wings* reverberated around the high-ceilinged church and Johnny had filed out to receive Communion, he was in a happier place. The ceremony drew to a conclusion, the couple went off to sign documents and the onlookers were entertained by even more string quartet music, as they awaited their return.

———

To the wolf-whistles of the rugby teammates and the more sedate applause of the media set, Rob and Vanessa glided out into the sunlight and were immediately surrounded by friends and well-wishers. A photographer from *VIP* magazine had made it to Tipperary, as had two more who covered the social and personal columns of the Sundays. The guy from the *Indo* asked for a more formal family photo, but Rob wasn't keen. Dithering what to do with his mother, Frank and the willowy twins, he offered him Bishop Joe with himself and Vanessa. As one of the youngest bishops ever to be appointed in the country, he was already well-known in his own right and had garnered a lot of publicity on his consecration. This suggestion seemed to satisfy the press photographer. Tammie, never one to lose a buckshee opportunity, shadowed the other pros and tried to improve on their angles, knowing that most of her contracted work would be done later in the relatively calmer surroundings of Allen Castle's beautiful parkland.

The champagne reception enticed the guests to linger in the sunshine far longer than the schedule had anticipated. Some of the non-rugby guests were awe-struck at being up close and personal with guys they normally only saw on television and hovered for selfies or an old-fashioned autograph. Even other hotel clients unconnected to the wedding, had drifted out to the grounds in the hope of catching a glimpse of their province's heroes. Tammie was driven to distraction trying to isolate her important photographic groupings without the infiltrators, as Maid of Honour Jenny was not proving to be quite so reliable at herding activities with half a bottle of champagne inside her. Recognisable rugby pundits and the occasional sports' journalist present were being coaxed to pose for images that would bounce around social media within the hour.

———

Vanessa had already instructed the semi-redundant best man that once the guests were seated at their tables they should kick off with the speeches. Her dad would go first after Terry's brief introduction, followed by Rob, then the best man himself, the toasts, and a quick run-through of any messages or congratulations that had come their way. She had studied this order, wondering where she should fit in her own few words. A full speech had sent Rob into a tailspin, but she was reluctant to allow only male voices be heard. After that, over and out and let people enjoy their evening.

Terry opened the order of business in a confident manner. There were mutterings and a few groans from the guests when they heard the speeches would take place *before* the meal. As the first one up, Johnny bore the brunt of the restlessness, but they warmed to him when he began with: 'I'll be brief, because I know you're all hungry.' Laughter and applause followed. 'Thank you for coming to share our day –' he lifted his prepared speech and read – '*to bear witness to Rob and Vanessa's vows to each other. A lot of promises are made in the first flush of love and romance. It's the promises that are kept and continue to be respected through the years that matter. I welcome Rob into our family as an honorary Walshe and am entrusting him with the most precious thing in my life – my beloved*

Nessa.' He paused and looked at Rob. 'Don't mess up, Rob. Or you'll have me to answer to.'

The guests laughed, uneasily. There was something steely in the way Johnny delivered the warning.

'*When Breda, my late wife, was dying, I gave her my word that I would be father and mother to that little girl. That I would make her the centre of my universe – and I don't think I have done too bad a job. She is still the axis around which my life spins, and you, Rob, are not taking over that responsibility – just helping me share the task.*' He paused again. 'Just remember that.'

Davey nudged Karen, worrying that the tone of the speech was inappropriate, and in the gesture implored her to intervene as his dad was standing to the left of her chair.

But he needn't have worried, as Johnny, scanning his page of notes, turned it face down, mumbled 'Thank you' and sat down abruptly.

Terry, thrown by the shift in emotion, called for a toast out of sequence: '*To absent friends – remembering Breda!*'

With their glasses raised, the guests complied.

'*To absent friends! To Breda!*'

Terry resumed his MC role: 'I give you the groom: Rob Cunningham.'

Rob stood up, looking less self-assured. He took a sip from his water, and replaced the glass on the white linen tablecloth. Then he picked up his script and began to read.

'*When I first met Vanessa, I couldn't believe my luck. She was the most beautiful, elegant woman I had ever seen. She was everything I longed for in a partner: funny, considerate, calm. I need calm.*

146

Spending your working life with your head wedged between two 120-kilo men, you need your personal life to be calm. Vanessa brings this serenity into my life, and I am the better for it.'

(Lots of titters from the rugby crowd.)

'She and I share the same family values and I am particularly proud of the loyalty she has shown to her father – Johnny, who you have just heard. They supported each other with strength and fortitude on the premature passing of Breda and I know full well I will always only be the second-choice bench player where her affection is concerned.' Rob glanced pointedly at his new father-in-law. *'Imagine the reaction I got at training when I said I was dating a former model and Miss Ireland judge – kudos or what? – and me only a lumpy front row!'*

(A supportive ripple of applause from the guests.)

'Apart from being bowled over by her looks, it was obvious from her business interests, and her natural charm and ability on television, that my Vanessa was one smart operator. She also happens to be the first girl I've ever dated who turned me down for a day trip to London because "she had to go to Mass with her father".'

(Uncertain laughter.)

'As an accomplished businesswoman, some of you here today also know of her work with the Simon Community, but I'm happy to add that since we got together she has agreed to back some of my Christian charities.'

(Lighter applause now, boredom setting in.)

Deviating from his script, Rob looked at Terry and continued: 'As our schedule in the garden overran this afternoon and we are quite a bit behind, in the interest of your stomachs and the kitchen staff, there will be no best man's speech. Davey Walshe, my new brother-in-law, will take charge of the other toasts after dessert and read out any greetings.'

(The guests looked at each other in bemusement.)

Rob turned to the last page of his speech.

'Finally, can I ask you to please charge your glasses. I stand before you all today, family, teammates and friends of many years, on this my wedding day and I am delighted to present Mrs Vanessa Cunningham, my beautiful, pure, kind and generous wife. My love, my life, and without doubt my best friend. Vanessa Cunningham, ladies and gentlemen!'

'Vanessa!'

'Vanessa Cunningham!'

Vanessa sat by his side and tried to acknowledge the toast and the applause, but the smile never reached her eyes. As her husband sat down, he leaned in to kiss her but she was already getting to her feet.

'Thanks, everyone. That was a lovely round of applause. Let me start by introducing my husband – Rob Walshe – the artist formerly known to you as Tea-Leaf Cunningham!'

(The crowd laughed – the guys wolf-whistled.)

'Rob, welcome to my family! As my dad said, you're now an honorary Walshe and I think, as such, you can take my name! It has a certain snappy appeal to it, hasn't it, boys?'

Vanessa was smiling but Rob downed more water, looking puzzled.

'In my family, we have a lot of traditions and quirky habits that I'm sure Rob will get used to as he gets used to us. And, yes, one of them does include me going to Mass with my dad, if I happen to be in Allenbeg for a weekend. Perhaps Rob might sidestep the occasional Sunday match and join us the next time!'

'*Don't even think of it, Tea-Leaf!*' Gaz the coach shouted.

(Whoops of laughter, a bit of foot-stamping.)

'We had a lovely thoughtful toast to my late mam earlier – thank you, Terry. Now, I would like you to raise your glasses for the man who raised me – Johnny Walshe – the best, the kindest and most considerate dad a girl could have. *To Johnny!*'

'*To Johnny!*'

'*Yo, Mr Walshe! Cheers!*'

'*Johnny Walshe, sound man!*'

With all this talk of dads, Rob looked anxiously around the function room for the 'waifs and strays' table at which his father and half-sisters had been placed. The girls were hard to miss in their vibrant micro-dresses – Milly in yellow, Molly in cobalt blue. He hadn't spoken to them at the church – too many paparazzi hanging around – but the unstructured nature of the garden champagne reception had made it impossible to avoid them drifting over for a chat.

In the end, it had been the twins who made the first move. 'Congratulations, Rob – isn't that what you're supposed to say?' Molly twirled the stem of her flute nervously. 'You look cool – real clothes suit you!'

'Because,' Milly chimed, 'normally when we see you you're in kit, covered with muck and/or blood!'

'Do you come to my matches?'

'Only if you're playing Leinster.' Molly pointed to her dress. 'See! I'm even loyal to my colours today!'

'*He* forces us to watch you, if the match is on TV.' Milly inclined her head towards the circular rose bed, where her father, Frank, was happily seated on a bench chatting to a group of people.

'*Ye-ah!* Every single bloody one! He records them and everything.' Molly tried and failed to catch the eye of the girl with the champagne bottle. 'You should invite him along to an *actual* match someday – and then he wouldn't be tormenting us at home. That champagne girl is ignoring me – I'm going to split and hunt her down! Are you coming, Mill?'

'In a minute.'

When there was only one of them, Rob felt awkward. He knew very little about his half-sisters, his mother having insisted contact be kept at a minimum – and, besides, the irregular nature of his father's second family still bothered his conservative, religious beliefs. He couldn't help it – that was the way he felt, even if it made him seem like a fossil in the 21st century.

After some silence and smiling, Milly broke the ice.

'Let's walk and talk a bit.'

'Sure.'

They strolled off.

'Are you still at school, Milly?'

'In college. Just finished first year Law in UCD – with Spanish. I think I nearly enjoy the language module best.'

'That's great. And Molly?'

'She took the year out. Repeated a couple of subjects in June – didn't get the points first time round. Too much socialising and too many boys.'

'Takes after Frank then.'

Purposely, Milly had steered their walk directly towards the rose bed and their dad.

Rob watched as his father stood up from the white bench, excused himself from the other guests and took two strides towards them.

'Now, it's about time you two talked to each other like adults,' Milly said. 'I'm off to find Moll.'

'Hello, son. Congratulations. This is a great wedding.'

'Thanks. Not that you'd know much about them – since you don't do weddings.'

'Can you not just let that go, even today?'

'I suppose.'

'It was kind of Vanessa to invite us – eventually.'

Rob remained silent.

'She's a fabulous girl. Will be a great asset to you.'

'What's that supposed to mean? She's not an investment portfolio!'

'Is she not? Look, Rob, this is what you need if you're to be considered for the national squad. It's not just the rugby – which by the way, has really improved – it's the whole media-friendly, social-profile rubbish as well. Look at the current team: their celebrity status, their sponsorship deals. You've always been – a bit lacking – on that front.'

'Thanks.'

'But that's all changed now! Consider the journos and coverage here today! You're made, boy. Just add a couple of bonny babies to the package, and you'll be a Lion in three years!'

Rob looked away, then he said, 'I hear from the twins you've been following all my games.'

'Why wouldn't I? I'm proud of you. Vanessa is exactly what you need – focus on her and your new family – and less on – well, other things. Your rugby career and Vanessa go hand in hand. For Christ's sake, Rob, don't fuck it up.'

'And there it is! Setting me up to fail. You just can't help yourself.'

'Son! Don't walk away. I didn't mean—'

───

Later, in the Allen Castle Garden room as the decibel level increased and the first course of the wedding banquet was served, Rob reflected on his wife's toast and wondered what made Vanessa love her father so much and he love his own dad so little. Perhaps if he followed Frank's advice – *for once* – things might improve between them.

Just how he was going to effect a complete personality change in such a short time, he really wasn't sure.

Part 4

Sicily

Chapter 13

Honeymoon, Day 1

The wedding party was comatose on the early morning flight into Catania. Even Karen had to admit that the scheduling wasn't the best, but Sicily was hard to reach so they had gone with her recommendation to opt for the direct high-season charter. The honeymoon couple had a separate deal made directly with the travel agent, which included their accommodation in the panoramic hilltop hotel in Taormina, a private limo transfer with champagne on ice to soothe them on the journey from the airport, and premium seats up the front of the plane from Dublin that the rest of the family were booked on. Karen had just purchased the flights and booked a taxi transfer to their hotels independently.

Having observed how emotional her father-in-law had been the previous day, she questioned whether it was prudent to have agreed to his request for a separate hotel quite a distance away from herself and Davey. Although only sixty-four, Johnny hadn't travelled a lot, and she thought he looked completely wiped out as he slept open-mouthed in the window seat next to his son.

She was also feeling a bit miffed by the groom's grumbling over the early start. His dissatisfaction had been palpable in the dewy dawn light at Allen Castle, as they boarded their minibus to the airport. Vanessa hadn't complained, smiling contentedly as she oversaw the loading of the luggage.

'Davey?' Karen elbowed her husband. 'Are you really asleep or just resting your eyes?'

'Well, I'm not now, that's for sure. What time is it?'

'Nearly eleven. Irish time.'

'Add an hour. We shouldn't be too long.'

Within the cabin there was very little activity. The crew was taking a break in the galley, their dividing curtain temporarily closed before the final push to clean up the aircraft in advance of landing.

When she stood up to store her jacket in the overhead locker, Karen could just about see Row 2 on the opposite side of the aisle, where Vanessa and Rob were sitting. No heads were visible which was a good sign, as it suggested they were inclined towards each other and, with any luck, asleep. She hoped Rob would be more positive after a bit of rest. That was the problem with recommending somewhere *you* love to other people: you always ran the risk of them absolutely hating it, and then feeling doubly responsible for having suggested it in the first place and ruining their holiday if they were disappointed.

And this was Rob's *honeymoon*, not just any old holiday, despite what Vanessa might have argued in the days when she was trying to persuade him that it would be great to have everybody in Taormina at the same time. Although Karen was loath to say it to Davey, she thought Vanessa was being bossy and inconsiderate in imposing her entire family on her new husband for the first week of their stay, on the grounds that she wanted her father to enjoy a little holiday in Sicily too. Karen had tried to talk her out of it, even suggesting that she and Davey take Johnny on a break later in the summer, but Vanessa had bounced back with the riposte that if she had opted for the travel agent's package which *included* a wedding ceremony in Taormina, would the rest of the family have been expected to fly home the following day? Of course not! There really was no answer to that, so Karen had gone ahead with their separate bookings. Still, at least she and Davey would be on hand to entertain Johnny and give the newlyweds the space and privacy they should have on honeymoon.

As for the location, it *was* Taormina: surely not even *Rob* could find fault with it? He was used to all that celebrity fluff and to frequenting five-star locales for fundraisers and charity balls through his job. This was an opportunity to embrace the glamour of the place and to kick-start their romantic break, by parading his stunning wife on the obligatory nightly *passeggiata* through the flower-filled

157

piazzas and the winding bougainvillea-draped lanes in search of an authentic *trattoria* in which to dine.

For a moment, Karen pondered if she were attributing to Rob and Vanessa what *she* would take pleasure in doing. They might have a completely different interpretation of how to enjoy themselves on the island. Perhaps Rob was less adventurous than Dave. Maybe he'd prefer to stay within the confines of predictability on the main tourist drag. She found this a depressing thought, but to each his own. She didn't have the monopoly on the attractions of Sicily.

Earlier that morning in Dublin Airport, a quick scan of their fellow passengers at the gate seemed to confirm that all human life was present. Karen hadn't expected quite so many young people: there were three or four groups of friends in their late teens and early twenties. She hoped they wouldn't find Sicily too sedate – not that the younger backpackers were going to have the budget to hang out in the sophistication of Mazzarò or up in Taormina itself, but even less salubrious places offered quiet and refined nightlife, with very few 'open-all-hours' clubs apart from in the main cities of Palermo and Catania. Hersonissos it wasn't.

The numerous small children surprised her – some of whom were still excitedly vocal three hours later – demonstrating more stamina than the adults on board, sleep evidently being for old people and wimps. She hoped the families were headed to one of the rare sandy beaches dotted along the coastline, it being a spectacularly rocky island. Hotel pools were fine and dandy, but in July? In the arid heat of 32°C? She wished them well.

The final identifiable group were those who marketers describe as delivering 'the grey euro'. If she and Davey had misgivings about 64-year-old Johnny being able to stick the pace, then the tour operator who sold seat upon seat to this destination had no such qualms. They had sticks. They had limps. They had hearing-aids. (What Karen wouldn't give for a hearing-aid right now! The luxury of being able to turn the volume down on those screaming children!) Several of the elderly passengers had availed of the Personal Assistance service and had been whizzed right up to the gate in wheelchairs, whereupon they stood upright, produced a collapsible walking-stick that they would later stow in the overhead bin.

Some of the other mobile ones had sidled down the air-bridge ahead of them and Karen had noted the volume of walking-aids that were seized by a steward at the final bend to travel in the hold. Had no-one warned these elderly passengers about the ubiquitous steps all over the island? As for those ride-on mobility scooters that they might find to hire in other resorts, well, not a chance of that in Sicily! They'd only get stuck in cobblestones or capsize into potholes of gravel, should they ever find an outlet offering this service.

But despite the walking-apparatus and their infirmities,

they were cheerful, they were chatty. They beamed at fellow passengers and greeted the steward civilly, unlike Rob whose mood still hadn't improved and who had practically growled ungallantly at the air hostess when she pointed out that he was filing into the wrong side of Row 2.

———

Suddenly the grey privacy curtain at the top of the plane was swept back and two air hostesses and a steward burst forth, brandishing white plastic bags. The lead party strode purposefully to the rear and the third demanded rubbish with menace from the long-legged people in the front rows.

Davey grinned at Karen, pleased to see the crew on the move because he knew the plane's descent couldn't be far off and, besides, he needed to use the toilet.

'Great. Action stations. Can I climb out over you, before she gets going with the rubbish trolley?'

'Sorry. I was daydreaming! Wait. I'll step out.'

Davey made a break for it, just as Cabin Crew Miriam, clad in turquoise-blue, launched her clean-up truck. Pausing at 2D, she was persistent. 'You're *sure* you have nothing to dispose of? What about that newspaper in the seat pocket? Will I take it?'

The passenger clutched his paper in defiance and Cabin Crew turned to her right.

Still standing, Karen waved up at Vanessa who was out in the aisle, allowing the window-seat passenger back in, while Rob gathered up an armful of snack wrappers, an empty Prosecco bottle, plastic beakers, a fashion mag and the weekend supplements for the bin, before resuming his seat. The hostess rewarded him with a wide smile – he really *was* the best boy in the class – and then she recognised him as a Munster rugby player.

'Oh *hel-lo!* I didn't realise you were on board. I'm from Cork. *Mad* into Munster. You should have made yourself known to me at the beginning. Never do that again!' And, in a flirtatious manner more suited to a seventeen-year-old, she lilted: 'Are you still alright for everything – I could get you a beer or – a Prosecco for – *Vanessa Walshe*! Your lovely girlfriend.'

'Wife actually. As of yesterday.'

'Oh, congratula*t*ions!'

Davey, making his way back down the aisle, got tangled up in the gushing but, despite Vanessa's attempts to introduce him, the captain's authoritative voice over the Tannoy brought the jollity to an end.

'*Good morning, ladies and gentlemen, and thank you for choosing this flight, operated by Aer Lingus on behalf of several tour operators. We are currently commencing our descent into Fontanarossa Airport, Catania, and expect to land in a little over fifteen minutes. The weather in Sicily is a comfortable 28 degrees centigrade – they had a couple of light showers there this morning – and a small amount of residual haze is still lingering. Hopefully, that won't obscure your view of Mount Etna, which passengers seated on the right-hand side of the aircraft should particularly enjoy as we make our final approach. Cabin crew, checks for landing, please.*'

The chatty air hostess skipped through the galley and pushed the security code into the pilot's cabin.

A couple of minutes later he was back: '*Eh . . . I have just been informed that we have the pleasure of carrying on board with us today Munster rugby team-member Rob Cunningham and his lovely wife, TV presenter Vanessa Walshe, who will be honeymooning on the island. A round of applause for Rob and Vanessa and congratulations to you both!*'

The passengers who heard the message clearly gave a few polite claps. Those not interested in either rugby or minor TV celebrities, murmured '*Who? Who did he say was on board?*' as they began rummaging in hand-luggage for passports and documents to pick up hire-cars or collect their transfers.

'That was nice of him.' Karen located the two passports in her handbag and put them in an accessible front pouch. 'Do you have Johnny's?'

'Karen! He's not an unaccompanied minor. No, I don't!'

'But you did take the folder with all the hotel reservations, didn't you?'

'Yeah, they're in the laptop bag. I hope Vanessa and Rob don't mind all and sundry knowing where they're spending their honeymoon. That was a bit indiscreet.'

'It'll be in the gossip mags before the end of the week anyway. A lot of people had already recognised them.' Karen took off her jumper and squashed it into her tote. 'I often think that the Walshe family don't realise how big a deal Rob is. I mean, you and your dad kind of sneer at his pedantic ways.'

162

'We don't *sneer*. Maybe tease him a bit. He can take himself very seriously sometimes. And, Ms Waldron, are you *excluding* yourself from the Walshe family in this attitude?'

'Not exactly, but I get a totally different impression of him when I hear my brothers and their friends talking. They absolutely *revere* him, both on and off the pitch.'

'I suppose we just know him too well.'

An outbreak of squealing and '*oohs*' and '*aahs*' from the passengers, confirmed that Mount Etna was indeed visible despite the low cloud, but the glimpse was fleeting as the plane did a loop out over the ocean and, shortly afterwards, bounced onto the tarmac at Catania airport.

Johnny awoke with a jolt when it touched down. 'I cannot believe I slept through the landing! I'm not usually that relaxed.'

'You're exhausted. We've been up all night.' Davey patted his father's arm.

'Go on! Rub it in, why don't you!' Karen rolled her travelling socks down over her ankles and took them off. 'I *know* it was an awful itinerary. I'll apologise to everyone later. The first cocktail tonight is on me.'

'Sure, we had to travel at the time the plane was going, girl. It's not your fault.'

'Thanks for the vote of confidence, Johnny, but it *was* a tough haul after the long day and excitement of the wedding yesterday. Speaking of which, *they* seemed to have cheered up.'

Rob and Vanessa were standing in the aisle beside their seats, waiting to file out – rather pointlessly – given the hatch still had not been opened. She had turned back towards him and had her arms laced around his neck as she intermittently planted silly kisses on his lips and nose. It looked affectionate and fun. Rob was whispering into her ear and, to an outsider looking on, they appeared rapt in their own private world.

'Given that they *are* on honeymoon, don't you think we should just make that dinner for three tonight?' Davey grinned at his dad.

'And leave them to strike while the iron is hot, you mean?'

Father and son exchanged glances. Karen ignored Johnny's crudeness, as she gathered her hand-luggage and followed the other passengers off the plane and into the terminal.

Once through to the Arrivals Hall of the airport, Vanessa headed confidently towards a line of men brandishing name-cards of passengers they were meeting. She zoned in on a white-shirted driver holding an iPad with 'Walshe' emblazoned on its screen.

'Hello!' She smiled at him. 'I'm one of the Walshe party.'

Rob, steering the heavily laden trolley, caught up with her. 'No, love, that's probably the transfer Karen booked for the rest of them. Our limo driver is probably over there, with the guys holding agency boards.'

'Oh, did I not tell you? I cancelled the limo for this leg. A total waste of money – and fuel if we're being eco-conscious – since we're all going to the same place'

Rob reached out to take Vanessa's carry-on case and add it to the luggage trolley, as he shook his head. 'Well, I hope it's a mini-bus. We've a lot of luggage between us all.'

'We'll be fine. I emailed Karen's hotel with the updated passenger numbers.'

The private Taormina transfer stopped first at La Villa where Rob and Vanessa would stay. It was an unobtrusive boutique hotel tucked away in its own terraced gardens, in a narrow, mainly residential street. The taxi driver negotiated the tight approach road with aplomb, weaving in and out between tourists walking distractedly on both sides, and squeezing the cumbersome 9-seater people-carrier between bins, bollards and abandoned motorbikes. Every so often there was a flash of the azure blue sea below in the gaps between buildings, and the three Sicilian novices swivelled their heads in unison. Karen, more sensitive to the celebrity of her in-laws, thought they would be unlikely to run into any tourists from home in this type of hotel, as despite it being included in the travel agent's brochure, it attracted mainly Italian clients, or occasionally artists performing at the Teatro Antico, the Greek Amphitheatre a ten-minute uphill walk away. She and Davey had enjoyed many lunches in its pretty garden terrace.

But the overwhelming deciding factor in recommending the choice of this particular spot was the spectacular unobstructed view from the hotel's high position – an infinity view straight ahead to the horizonless blue of the bay, and to the right where the land curved eastwards, the skyline was dominated by the magnificent brooding backdrop of Mount Etna, puffing and poised for action at any given time.

Vanessa gasped in delight when the car stopped at a narrow, pillared entrance into the pretty courtyard of La Villa. Even Rob, who had initially quibbled at the price of the rooms, seemed impressed by the beautiful terracotta house, its dainty wrought-iron window-boxes full of scarlet geraniums. The attentive bell-boy was with them in a flash, his brass flat-bed trolley clattering over the original cobblestones. He waited for the rear doors to be opened so he could seize the relevant luggage before bumping back the way he had come, towards the hotel door.

A member of the reception team came across the courtyard to the parked taxi at the gate and shook Vanessa's hand. '*Benvenuta, signora, signore.*' He extended his hand to Rob. 'Welcome to La Villa!'

'Well, I don't think we'll see them again tonight!' Davey chuckled, as the people-carrier continued on its journey down the narrow one-way street.

'That was some fine house, wasn't it?' Johnny, refreshed from his three-hour nap on the flight, was full of enthusiasm for his new surroundings.

Karen smiled. She really enjoyed seeing her father-in-law embrace the novelty of his new environment. She explained to the driver in Italian that their next stop would be the Hotel Giorgio up in Castelmola, some five kilometres away from everyone else, up a precipitous, winding road high above Taormina.

'*Bravo, signori! Bella Castelmola. Meno caos!*' The driver, pleased with their decision to escape the built-up tourist town, put the car into first gear and his moccasin on the gas.

After the vertiginous bends, they arrived at the stone and timber-clad hotel, which had a Swiss-chalet look about it. While Davey helped the driver select the luggage from the boot, Karen accompanied Johnny inside.

The reception at the Hotel Giorgio was unoccupied. Instead of a smiling face, they were greeted by the sight of two large bundles of bed-linen each tied into an outer sheet and lying in their path in front of the high wooden counter.

'This doesn't look good.' Karen looked anxiously at Johnny and rang the old-fashioned brass bell.

'*Sì, signori?*' A young blonde girl, clutching a novel which she had obviously been reading, appeared out from behind a screen.

'*Buongiorno!*' Karen smiled at her. '*Signor Walshe – per il check-in.*'

The rumbling sound of suitcase wheels on a tiled floor announced Davey's arrival.

'*É troppo presto – zu früh.*'

'What's she saying?' Johnny took a swig of water from his plastic bottle.

'Check-in is not open yet.' Returning her attention to the teenager behind the desk, Karen continued: '*Signorina, per favore. Facciamo il check-in, lasciamo i bagagli, e potrà avere accesso alla sua camera più tardi. Siamo irlandesi. Lui parla inglese.*'

'Karen, tell me what's happening!'

But just as he'd begun to feel anxious, the young hotel employee approached Johnny with a beaming smile.

'Hello, Irish! You are very welcome. I am Elke from Bern in Switzerland. I take the classes in Dublin for English last year.'

'Thank God for that!' said Johnny. 'Now, missy, can I get rid of that case – and have a look around?'

'I will myself take you to the *piscina* bar for the welcome *limoncello. Komm.*'

And with that, Johnny linked arms with young Elke and shouted back over his shoulder to Karen and Davey, '*Talk to you later!*'

Back in the taxi, the third and final stop was Hotel Giulia on the pedestrianised Corso Umberto in the centre of

Taormina. Karen had told the proprietors about the wedding and she knew they were disappointed that the extended family hadn't decided to accompany herself and Davey and all stay together in their regular haunt. Giulia had finally accepted Davey's explanation that, with separate living arrangements, everyone retained their independence but yet had easy transport in place for meeting up: Italians they were not.

'I hope that hotel works out.' Karen heard her phone 'ping' as the taxi made its final descent into the town. 'I might have to eat humble pie with Giulia and move Johnny back down to us if it doesn't. Oh, it's Rob – of all people – suggesting we all meet for dinner. He says I owe him a mocktail after the horrendous early start!'

'Interesting. So, we *will* be having the pleasure of the honeymooners' company tonight after all!'

'I'll pick somewhere central to eat – near the taxi stand for Johnny. You might have to go up for him, Dave.'

'Not a problem. Let's leave all that till later.'

Vanessa and Rob strolled hand in hand into the Piazza, every bit the picture of love's young dream. The bride was still sporting her pre-wedding tan and the lemon sleeveless dress she was wearing complemented her tanned limbs. Rob's face was more ruddy than usual, but he looked relaxed and happy. They stopped at various shop windows on their way, adopting the non-purposeful pace of the locals at this hour.

A couple of teenage boys ran past and whistled, calling out: '*Che bella signora!*'

Rob laughed and kissed her on the cheek. 'You see! You're even turning Sicilian heads!'

Outside La Badia, Davey and Karen had already claimed a drinks' table and were surprised when Johnny appeared on foot, dressed in a very colourful short-sleeved shirt.

'Hi, Dad! Where did the taxi drop you?'

'I didn't bother with one, Davey. The manager showed me the bus-stop. Right outside the hotel there's a set of steps – steep enough, mind – but they bring you up to the main square of Castelmola where the buses turn. A huge big blue yoke of a thing that I thought would never be able to take those hairpin bends – but it did. Flew down in jig-time.'

'Good for you! Live like the locals, that's what I say!' Karen laughed. 'How did you get on with your room and all, after we left?'

'No problems. When little Elfie gave me a couple of the complimentary shots, I calmed down a bit. And the manager himself – nice lad, Fred – brought my bags up and asked if everything with the room was to my satisfaction. Once he threw open the shutters and all I could see was land and open space, I was happy.'

'That's great, Johnny. Oh, here's the other pair, all smiles!'

'*Buonasera!*' Vanessa slid into the chair beside her father. 'You liked the shirt, then?'

'Yes, good and cheerful. A lovely surprise, thank you. How's your room in the Villa?'

'Oh, it's a *suite* – not just a plain old room! Very *grand*. It has a terrace with olive and lemon trees on the land off to the side. There's a bit of a garden – well, a patch of bumpy, baldy grass that ends at a low post and rail fence. And Rob went out for a ramble and found the cable-car, so we're planning to head down for a seawater swim first thing tomorrow.'

Johnny frowned. 'And did *you* not fancy the walk?'

'Are you having a laugh?' Vanessa giggled. 'I lay down on the bed to try it and was out cold in five minutes! Rob had to put a throw over me before he left. The air-con is fairly powerful – and, it has to be said, very noisy.'

'I'm off to these Alien Islands tomorrow,' Johnny volunteered. 'Big notice at Reception about it, so I booked the tour going straight from the hotel. You can all do your own thing without me slowing you down.'

'Aeo*l*ian islands!' Vanessa teased. 'We want to visit them as well, but maybe not tomorrow? Though I don't like to think of you going on your own.'

'I think our dinner table is ready,' said Davey.

The waiter was signalling impatiently at him.

'And on the subject of trips, we're going up Etna on

Wednesday. Any takers? I'd need to book that tomorrow. It's always oversubscribed.'

'Count us in,' Rob said.

'Me too,' said Johnny. 'I'm getting quite fond of oul' Etna – looking at her from out my bedroom window up there in Castlemoley. And she's puffing away good-oh all the time.'

'Fit to explode, is she?' Rob hopped up briskly from his seat, carrying his unfinished mocktail. 'I'd say you can identify with that, Johnny!'

Karen looked at Davey in puzzlement at Rob's throwaway remark, but the table move diluted any possible tension as they claimed their new post nearer the restaurant door. Once settled, however, Vanessa – who had sidled in beside Johnny with Rob across the table from her – returned to the 'exploding' comment, while everybody studied the extensive menu which ran to many pages, although they were chiefly interested in pizza which was reputed to be excellent here.

'Why would you think Dad was "fit to explode", Rob? That was an odd thing to say!'

'Huh? I was talking about the volcano exploding.'

'But you compared it to him!'

'Ah, maybe I was just thinking about Johnny's reputation on the football field back in the day – his short fuse.' Rob grinned half-apologetically across the table at his new father-in-law. 'Isn't it true, Johnny? You were known to have a bit of an explosive temper!'

'Well, you're not far off there. I was a bit of a hothead on the pitch.' Turning to Vanessa, Johnny ran his finger down the menu. 'Which of these is the one you usually get me in Mario's in town?'

'I'd say the nearest to it is . . . the Capricciosa.'

'How apt!' It was out of Karen's mouth before she could stop herself. She glanced surreptitiously at Johnny, hoping he hadn't realised she was comparing his choice of pizza with his own unpredictable, sometimes mischievous temperament. She thought she had got away with it, but Rob turned to her at the top of the table and winked. She didn't know he had any Italian.

The orders having been dispatched and beer instead of wine delivered to the table since they had all opted for pizza, Johnny voluntarily returned to the subject of his football-playing days.

'Ah yes, I was a terrible man for losing me rag during a match – particularly if we were winning and there was a poor call – like a kickable free for the opposition.' He took a sip of his Moretti beer. 'I'm sure you've had similar experiences, Rob, with bad refs.'

'Don't talk. But it's beaten into us – from when we're young players – to accept *even* unjust decisions without reacting.'

'Hard to do, though,' Davey piped up. 'I mean, do you remember that Munster Schools Senior Cup final, when Rockwell were two points clear and the game was in like the 84th minute or something – and the ref blew up for a penalty, which they converted. Were you at it, Rob?'

'Of course I was! If you give me a minute, I'll tell you the year!'

'And I remember I nearly throttled the guy beside me – with his gloating and jeering when the final whistle sounded!'

'Goodness!' –Vanessa paused to remove the decorative umbrella from the remainder of her cocktail. 'I didn't realise I was surrounded by such a short-tempered family! I'll have to watch my step!'

As the Piazza continued to buzz with exquisitely dressed strollers enjoying the cooler evening air, already the sliver of a crescent moon hung over the Campanile of the Chiesa Santa Caterina.

The Walshe family table was strewn with the detritus of their meal and, as the waiter cleared, he pushed dessert or more drinks on them.

Johnny checked the bus-timetable that the hotel manager had photocopied. 'I've time for a small beer – nothing more.'

'Dessert? Rob, Vanessa?' Karen couldn't make up her mind between a pannacotta or a semifreddo.

'Nothing for me.' Vanessa smiled across the table at Rob.

'Nor me.' Rob excused himself and went inside the restaurant.

The waiter added a semifreddo and a cannolo for Davey onto the order, and brought Johnny a small bottle of Moretti.

'Right.' Rob reappeared and walked around to the back

of Vanessa's chair, where he put his hands on her shoulders. 'That's us. We're going to head back to our hotel now. Enjoy your day tomorrow and your trip, Johnny. Davey, Karen, talk soon.'

'Wait!' Vanessa said. 'Are we not making arrangements to meet up?'

'No need, Nessa.' Karen wiggled her phone. 'Just message when you're in the mood for company again!'

Having hugged everybody and told her father to be careful on his islands trip, Vanessa re-joined her new husband, and they followed the sloping cobblestoned lane past the darkened windows of closed ceramic and baby clothes shops on the route back uphill to La Villa.

Chapter 14

Honeymoon, Day 2

The minibus called at Hotel Giorgio in Castelmola at 6.30am. Had Johnny known the tour was going to kick off quite so early, he might have been less enthusiastic. He wasn't the only Giorgio guest to travel – a Swiss couple and their teenage daughter greeted him as he got into the middle-row seat. They were waiting for two Frenchwomen who Johnny had noticed at the early buffet breakfast the hotel had laid on for those heading to the islands.

'*Mesdames, dépêchez-vous! Le car à Taormina n'attendra pas.*' The driver was now revving the engine as the two clambered aboard.

'*Désolées, monsieur!*' And scanning the other passengers, the shorter of the two women added, 'Sorry, *tout le monde.*'

Johnny was impressed by how everybody seemed to speak several languages. The driver was definitely local – yet he slipped happily into French to chivvy the late guests.

It had been the same the previous evening down in the pizzeria – as the waiter floated easily from German to English depending on the nationality of the diners.

He felt a bit ashamed of his own monolingual status, unless you considered belting out the National Anthem in Irish at Croke Park on final days. It amused him to imagine Tadhg, the Allenbeg bus driver, greeting the passengers in various tongues as they alighted the local service vehicle. In fact, if any language other than English was likely to be heard, it would be Polish, since there was now a second driver on the route – Marek, a nice lad – who would happily chat away to his compatriots as he drove. The private bus company had responded to the large numbers of Polish speakers living in the area and now carried written information in that language on the window and the printed timetable and fares leaflet.

But the Walshe family were no linguists. Davey and Vanessa were as bad as their father – which in his son's case Johnny found strange, since he was back and forth to Italy for work. Karen had pushed him into taking evening classes to try and improve, but once he grasped the essentials sufficient to get around, he had lost interest. Thank God for Karen and her brilliant Italian – the way she had sorted out little Elfie up at the hotel when they arrived the previous day was truly impressive. Otherwise, God knows when he'd have been able to check in and have a little sit down after the gruelling journey.

'*Signori, siamo qui.*' The driver positioned his minibus in such a way as to prevent the coach pulling off without the Giorgio passengers. 'Here we are. *Il Pullman di colore argento, con SAT in rosso.* Big silver bus with red S-A-T. Remember – many, many coach in Milazzo.'

The two Frenchwomen consulted each other as to who had the reservation printout – and the grey-haired one smiled at Johnny as they queued to get on.

'*Bonjour!* Do you think you take the bath *thermique* in Vulcano? My friend, she says the sulphur – we smell bad after!'

'Never even knew there were sulphur baths! Though I have my togs for a swim.' Johnny patted his bulging knapsack.

'Oh, much better to swim in the sea at Lipari – the first island.'

'Are we only visiting the two? I should have read the information leaflet properly! The manager pushed me into this Alien Islands' tour, when I arrived yesterday morning.'

The grey-haired lady smiled. 'How long do you stay?'

'Just this week.'

'*Quel dommage!* It is too short. We have fourteen days – we move to another place for the second week.'

He didn't wish to be rude but, once he had passed the driver, Johnny scurried down to the end of the bus and claimed a window seat in a heavily occupied section of the bus. An Italian man and his blonde wife sat opposite him across the aisle so, as there were no more vacant seats nearby, he reckoned he had shaken off the two Frenchwomen. He settled himself, pulled back the window curtain and took out the tour itinerary to see how long it would take the coach to reach the port of Milazzo and their ferry to the islands.

On the breakfast terrace of La Villa, the guests were beating off wasps who fancied the delicious pastries and jams just as much as they did. Each table carried an old-fashioned trap – a large kiln jar filled with water, its inside rim coated with jam, the attached lid dangling to the side. The occasional juvenile insect gorged on the jam and once satiated, dropped innocently into his watery grave, but most of the vespid population on the panoramic tree-shaded seating area were not fooled.

'Wasps. A bloody nuisance. As bad as their namesake.' Rob flicked the breakfast menu at yet another.

'*What*? Oh, those Wasps. Are you ever *not* thinking about rugby?'

Rob grinned. 'Rarely. Did I tell you I heard a rumour that the province was trying to recruit Gopperth?'

'Are they? I thought he was the Wasps kicker. Don't you already have Joey?'

'Yeah, but Gopperth plays at centre as well. Though he's been crocked most of the season – makes no sense why they'd go after him this year.'

'I never see the point of bringing in outside players – I mean they'll be of no use when it comes to playing for the national team.'

'Different purpose – develops the individual clubs.'

'Gopperth is a Kiwi too, isn't he? Like Joey.'

'I wouldn't let Joey hear you say that! Joey's family are all from Kildare. He was just born in New Zealand, but he's been living here since he was a kid.'

'Which is why he plays for Ireland. Of course, I'd forgotten that. Anyway, enough about rugby. What'll we do for the day? I fancy heading to a beach. Karen never warned us there was no pool here.'

'I hate pools. Too much like training. Besides, you know I've been down already for an early morning dip.'

'Yeah, you sneak! You should have waited for me – I'd have gone with you.'

'You just looked so peaceful. Our travelling day was long and exhausting – I thought I'd leave you be.'

'*Actually*, that's not what you said.'

'No?'

'You said you needed "a bit of space".'

'Did I? Well, you have me all to yourself now for the day!' A particularly bold wasp landed on the front of Rob's hand as he drank his juice. He felt the scratch of the insect's antennae just in time, before it released a sting. 'Ah, this is ridiculous! We can't be expected to eat breakfast out here. Is there no indoor dining room?'

'There is. In the Orangerie. But it was full – and a bit stuffy.'

'Right. That's decided it. I'll order room-service breakfast from now on. This is far from relaxing.'

'Yeah, you have a point. So, apart from the beach, what do you want to do?'

'Did I say we'd go to the beach? I really want to visit the Bellini house in Catania – and what with all these tours Davey has us booked on, we mightn't get a chance later.'

'Don't exaggerate! We're only going to Mount Etna. And *you* were the one mad keen to do that trip. Why don't we leave the Bellini place till next week—'

'I'd prefer not to. You know classical music is my thing – and – this is Sicily – they could go on strike or close it for renovation or something without warning. Please?'

Vanessa crumpled her linen napkin into a ball and set it down beside the plate of half-finished bread and croissants. Alert wasps read the gesture as positive: at least three had alighted on the unfinished breakfast by the time she had stood up and shaken crumbs from her skirt.

'OK so.'

'You're the best.' Rob put his arm around her. 'Now, let's go to Reception and sort out breakfast for the remainder of our stay. They might also have info on transport to Catania.'

The minibus driver hadn't been exaggerating. When the SAT coach pulled into the lay-by opposite the entrance to the port of Milazzo, there were at least fourteen tour buses already parked and disgorging their passengers. Johnny looked at the brochure the guide had given him, to see what was so exciting about the islands that they were attracting all these people. The guide blew into the microphone before addressing them.

'*Signore, signori*, we are now taking the ferry. There are as you see, several. Ours is the big blue-and-white one – *Siremar*. It leaves exactly at nine o'clock, so if you can walk to the sign, I will distribute the tickets for embarkation.'

Johnny slung the small backpack that Vanessa had bought him especially for the holiday over his shoulder, and stood up to file out of his seat. The blonde lady opposite had the same idea, and first she, then he, hesitated, unsure who should proceed.

'Please, you go first,' she said in a distinct Irish accent. 'There are two of us.'

'Eh, thanks.'

As they made slow progress up the aisle, Johnny became aware of the couple chatting behind him – in English with the occasional Italian sentence thrown in. They were laughing heartily at something, but he couldn't catch the conversation. Earlier, during the journey up from Taormina, he had occasionally glanced over at them – it was hard not to when he had no-one to talk to – and he had thought to himself how in love they seemed, so wrapped up in each other. The Italian man was staring adoringly into the woman's eyes. Intermittently, he would place his hand on her cheek or caress the back of her neck, running his hand through her curly hair. Johnny found it hard to stop staring, comparing as he was a lack of similar spontaneous affection between his daughter and new son-in-law.

'*Prego, signore, signori.* Before I lose you, I forgot to say the ferry, he makes one first stop at Vulcano. Do not get off then, if you want to see Lipari. The group will visit first the white island – Lipari – and then, meet again to take the ferry back to Vulcano after lunch, where you spend the rest of the afternoon, before we return later to Milazzo. *Grazie.*'

'*That's very confusing!*' a thin bald man called out. '*Do you have the times of the ferries written down anywhere?*'

'No, they change the times very often. Just listen to the announcement on board.'

Johnny was glad someone else had voiced his thoughts. He was beginning to regret coming on his own. Then he spotted the two Frenchwomen joining the queue of exiting bus passengers.

'*Ça va ? Pas de mal de transports?*'

'Sorry*?*'

'She means no "travel-sickness",' the other woman translated.

'No, I'm a good traveller. And you two? Will ye be OK with the sea crossing?'

'Oh, it is very calm today. I think so.'

'Did you follow all that about the boat stops? I don't blame yer man asking. I can't see it anywhere on the leaflet—'

'I think she will give us some detail with the ticket. Stay with us, if you like. We have done this trip many times.'

'OK. Thanks.' Although Johnny agreed, he really didn't want to be stuck with his two fellow hotel guests all day. Yet he was afraid of messing up the ferry changes, and thought it might be useful to tag along with them – at least until they were on *terra firma* on the right island.

⸻

As the ferry manoeuvred out of the port of Milazzo, the receding view was dominated by the sturdy bastion of Federico II's five-towered castle and so impressed was Johnny, that he had a go at photographing it on his phone.

'It is impressive, *non*?' One of his French companions was standing beside him.

'It is that. We have a lot of castles in the part of Ireland I come from.' Johnny kept his head down, concentrating on closing down the camera function on his handset.

'*Dis-donc!* Séverine was right. You *are* Irish. I thought, maybe *gallois* – from the Wales? You have a strong accent.'

'A rural accent – country. I'm not from Dublin.'

'We were in Dublin once. My wife's niece did an Erasmus year in the university there. We went to visit her at the Easter holiday.'

'Oh, did you?' Johnny put his phone away. 'And did you enjoy . . . the holiday?'

'Very much. We must return.'

Once out on the open sea and with the wind in his hair, Johnny felt a lot less tense about the day. The news which Élodie, the older of the two French ladies had imparted, also made him relax. Hadn't the world really changed, he thought. He would never have twigged that they were a couple – let alone that they were married to each other. He had them down as two friends – maybe widows – or spinsters who teamed up for holidays, sharing the room for a bit of company and to save on costs.

Yet he remembered hearing them fuss to Elfie at Reception that their bed wasn't the four-poster one they had booked and they wanted to change room. He had just thought they were being picky French, but now it made sense. And to think, he used scoff at Christine, Breda's sister the actor, when she swore she would *never* double up in a hotel room on tour, no matter how miserable the fee, because she didn't want to be considered a lesbian!

Irrespective of his sister-in-law's feelings on the subject, Johnny was mighty relieved about this particular pair of lesbians. For some vain reason, he had got it into his head that the one who spoke little English fancied him. Secure in the knowledge that he was off the hook, he saw no harm in joining them for a gander at Lipari and maybe even a spot of lunch.

In the end, there wasn't time for the swim on Lipari that Johnny had promised himself. The Frenchwomen were determined to get value out of their four hours on the biggest island, and from the instant the ferry docked at the quayside fronted by pretty white and pink buildings, they had established a brisk pace uphill to the walled citadel which housed all that was important in the ancient settlement. Johnny fancied a look inside the cathedral, but was strongly encouraged to visit the archaeological museum first, which Élodie insisted would reveal the story of the incessant invasions from other conquerors and cultures that Sicily had undergone down the centuries. That way, she assured him, he would spot the different influences in the art and architecture he encountered during the rest of his holiday. Johnny wasn't quite so sure about this, but the cooler temperature inside the museum swung it in the end, and he bought a ticket.

When the cultural part of the visit had concluded, they split up and wandered independently through the narrow streets. Élodie had nominated a time and place to rendezvous for lunch – an easy-to-find small square with a water font in the centre. When they reconvened, Johnny noticed the women had lots of bags – obviously having used the time efficiently to plunder the local wares.

As they studied the menus to decide which *trattoria* to choose for lunch, the low purr of an electric scooter was followed by a couple of cheery *ciaos*. All three turned to see a helmeted couple on a sizeable Piaggio bike which was creeping slowly through the pedestrians. Johnny thought the pillion passenger looked like the blonde woman from their tour bus, but it was hard to be sure with the helmet. When the bike came to a stop and she removed her head protection, his instinct was proved right.

'Hello!' she said.

'*Giorno, tutti!*' said her companion.

Then she addressed herself particularly to Johnny. 'How's it going?'

'Fine. Just waiting for white smoke on the lunch venue.' He nodded towards his French companions. 'It'll be a bit of a rush wherever we go, if we've to meet your woman at the quay at 2.15.'

'That's why we stopped. Rico' – she inclined her head towards her partner – 'is reliving his teenage years on the scooter and wants to ride around the island, visit the white beach for a swim — so we're not bothering with Vulcano. Just in case the guide asks about us.'

'Why *would* she, *gioia*? Once they get here, people do their own thing. Now maybe in *Milazzo* . . . she will count who is on the bus—'

'Well, now somebody *else* knows, OK? Enjoy the rest of your day!' The woman replaced her helmet and the moped weaved its way back up the street.

The quayside wall offered no shade against the searing sun. Johnny had bought himself one of those white hats with the black ribbon around it – a Panama hat – at a small souvenir shop on the way back down from the castle. His new French friends had been horrified that he had none: they were predicting heatstroke if he tackled smelly Vulcano with a bare head. Already, even on Lipari, he was glad of it, though a slight breeze had got up, and he debated if he'd be better removing it once on board and taking his chances rather than lose it to a gust of wind.

As a blue-and-white *Siremar* ferry made its final approach into the port, spewing unhealthy black fumes in its wake, people squinted in anticipation. A crew member looped a rope around one of the concrete bollards on the quay and lowered the gangplank across the narrow gap. The people near the front rushed forward, much to the annoyance of the sailor.

'*Piano, piano! Con calma!*'

A second uniformed official began checking the tickets of the queueing passengers. Nearly every second person was turned back, creating more confusion as unwittingly they were heading for Naples via Stromboli, instead of Vulcano or the Sicilian mainland. Hearing disgruntled mutterings of 'Napoli' from those rejected, Johnny and the women stepped out of the queue.

'Well, you'd think they'd put a board up on the side of the deck with the destination of the ferry, wouldn't you, Melody?'

'And ruin the surprise?' Élodie opened the *Siremar* timetable that Séverine had handed her. 'The Stromboli-Naples one leaves ten minutes earlier than ours.'

'*Et en plus, le nôtre, c'est beaucoup plus petit*. Here, it arrive now.'

Séverine was right. Standing off, was a much smaller version of a passenger ferry.

'That really *is* confusing. What if you didn't speak Italian – like me? I'd be happily winging my way to old *Napoli*, as innocent as a new-born babe!'

'You worry too much, Monsieur Johnny! We'll have to make you relax in the bath *thermique* on Vulcano!'

'I thought you said they were too smelly?' Johnny removed his Panama hat and put on his sunglasses.

'Oh, we can all be smelly together on the bus home! *N'est-ce pas, Séverine?*'

As the Taormina tourists waited outside their red-and-silver SAT bus at Milazzo harbour, it was easy to tell who had been slathering in volcanic mud and who hadn't. The distinct smell of rotten eggs clung to their skin and hung on the evening air among the clusters of queueing passengers. The driver, having finished his cigarette, boarded the bus alone, whereupon he activated the air-conditioning at its highest setting.

Johnny had never smelt so bad. Not even in the aftermath of Breda's death when he was hitting the whiskey hard and had fallen several times into the ripe and pungent manure on his way to or from the milking parlour, did he stink like he did following nearly an hour in the mud baths on Vulcano.

There was something primal, he thought, about wallowing in unguent muck, but on this volcanic outcrop it wasn't the type of mud he had anticipated. It was more liquid mud; a bit like taking a hot bath in dirty water. As he had watched the other tourists emerge newly slimed – their lovely swimsuits destroyed – it reawakened memories of his teenage hurling games, when in winter he had trained – and rolled – in boggy, mud-ridden fields and his mother would exclaim in despair at the filthy clothes he came home in. Today's bagged-up togs in his knapsack would have to be ditched: a new pair of trunks were on Johnny's shopping list, once he got back to Taormina.

'Hello again! Did you enjoy your day – oh, and the mud bath?' The blonde Irish woman, linking her partner, stopped at Johnny's place in the bus queue and then took a couple of steps backwards.

'Well, it was different anyways – sorry about the smell.' Johnny thought he should introduce the Frenchwomen. 'Eh, this is Melody and Ceptarine – from France.'

'Isabelle – and Rico.'

'Élodie and SEVerine. *Enchantées.*'

'And I'm Johnny. How was your spin around Lipari?'

The couple looked from one to the other and gave a smirk. The man eventually answered. 'It was marvellous – we had a great time, thank you. We are – particularly fond – of Lipari.'

'Don't mind him,' Isabelle laughed. 'It's just when we first met, I was staying in a villa called *Lipari*. He's being silly. Oh, I think we're on the move. He's opened both doors and here's the guide with her list.'

'I hope the driver makes good time.' Rico checked his watch. 'Remember, *gioia*, I have that meeting at La Villa when we get back?'

'We'll be fine. It's a late dinner.'

'Oh!' said Johnny. 'My daughter and her husband are staying at La Villa. They're on honeymoon.'

'How nice! If you'll excuse us—' The Italian put his hand firmly in the small of his partner's back and steered her down the side of the bus where they both got on at the midway door.

Johnny thought it better not to follow them this time – it was no doubt the smell thing. He recalled Melody saying they could all sit together on the way back. Although he had only known her less than twenty-four hours, he had the impression that when the Frenchwoman made a comment like that it was to be taken as an instruction. He took a sip from his water bottle and followed them up the steps to the front section of the bus.

Chapter 15

Honeymoon, Day 3

When Vanessa awoke, she found Rob missing – again. This was the second morning in succession that he had done this. She was annoyed at what now appeared to be a self-determined morning routine: leaving the marital bed and the hotel without her, for his solo funicular trip down to the sea at Mazzarò where he plunged into the salty water – alone.

Well, at least she *presumed* he went swimming alone. He certainly didn't want to go swimming with her. When questioned the previous morning when he had at least alerted her to his intentions, he had been calm but crystal clear that he didn't want her to tag along. He hadn't been cross in making the point, just gently hinted that he needed his own space. He justified his decision by trying to make out he was thinking of her. 'And, besides, you always say that the salt water is too harsh on your beautiful hair!', he had quipped, as his lips had brushed hers momentarily with the flutter of a butterfly alighting and then immediately flitting off. With that, he had grabbed his beach bag and was gone.

This was not the way she had imagined her honeymoon beginning. Everything about the setting was idyllic: the luxurious room, the romantic location, the fabulous weather. The staff had obviously allocated them the slightly more remote suite in a wing away from the main house to protect their privacy. But they needn't have bothered, because any activity they were indulging in could safely be witnessed from outdoors without any other resident being embarrassed.

It wasn't that he hadn't tried to initiate sex – *proper sex* – not the usual immature petting that she had become accustomed to – but normal relations, that would finally result in the blissful consummation of their marriage. But, although he had been amorous enough on their first night after the speedy pizza with her family, his overtures had petered out, before either of them had got going.

Even the previous evening – despite their futile trip to Catania (the Bellini house was closed for restoration), he had been attentive and very affectionate – and she had convinced herself that the Rubicon would finally be crossed – but, at the last minute, he had apologised, as he failed to perform.

Rob's distance was puzzling. Moreover, it was embarrassing. As the rest of the family were obviously being discreet in leaving them to their own devices on their first days in Taormina, Vanessa still had to field juvenile innuendos on the phone about 'being tired' and 'not getting any sleep', as if she and her new husband were doing it every hour on the hour hanging upside down from a chandelier! Davey's behaviour was just plain silly, as was to be expected from brothers, but she was more taken aback by Karen suggesting she should become a complete vamp in the bedroom. The brass neck of her! *What did her sister-in-law think she was doing – going to bed in a winceyette nightie buttoned up to her ears?* Why wouldn't they all just let it go? Sex wasn't everything.

Vanessa had known from early on in their relationship that Rob had strict views. She had even found them refreshing, after all the users she had encountered along the way. But *married* sex, she knew that this to him was *everything*. This was a man who trailed briefcases of proselytising leaflets for the True Love Waits movement around school's sex-education programmes. The course co-ordinators loved him, because he was exactly the non-geek type of role model the more right-wing Catholic schools welcomed, and because of his sportsman status they knew the students might listen to him. Vanessa had found herself arguing futilely about the rights and wrongs of the influence he might wield, but he had repeatedly dismissed her views, in an affectionate, paternalistic way.

She supposed she should have pursued with more vigour the implications of his views on their future life together, but she had noted how impatient and uptight he had become with her when they had read each other's questionnaire answers at that pre-marriage chat with Bishop Joe. That had been a couple of months before the wedding, and Vanessa still felt optimistic that the rigid elements of Rob's doctrine would relax even before she had the ring on her finger. It had seemed to her crazy – and mortifyingly embarrassing which is why she had told nobody except her dad – that in the 21st century, she appeared to be the only woman with a fiancé who wouldn't have sex. As the weeks hurtled towards their wedding and his refusal to cave persisted, she had reluctantly acquiesced rather than antagonise him.

This was out of character for her – she knew that – she was used to asserting herself both personally and professionally. In a strange way, the manner in which she had begun to 'tiptoe' around Rob on the subject of sex was reminiscent of how she had tiptoed around her father following her mother's death, as if at eleven she were the one responsible for her dad's broken heart and it was her duty to try and mend it.

But Vanessa was no longer eleven and had her own mature philosophy of living and loving. Rob's views were *his* and his alone; they wouldn't become or alter hers.

———

Still dressed in her strappy nightdress, Vanessa walked into the living room and popped a coffee capsule into the

Espresso machine. She opened the French windows onto the terrace. Maybe she should give it another go when he came back from his swim – though she thought Rob had booked their room-service breakfast for half nine, around the time he had returned yesterday, which might be a little awkward!

On the hotel side of the terrace, the sun was already drenching the seating area, so she took her coffee out to the lounger. She closed her eyes, leaned her head back and felt the taut muscles in her forehead relax as the heat massaged away the tension from her brow. The sharp crack of a branch underfoot alerted her to someone's presence, and she opened her eyes expecting to see Rob, but instead saw two individuals staring at her from the lemon grove to her left.

'*Scusi, signora.*' A well-dressed man came through the side gate. 'I am sorry, *signora*. We thought you were not here. Let me introduce myself. I am Marcello Orlando, the *geometra* – the surveyor – working on expansion project for the hotel. Is it OK if we make some measurements?'

'Hello. Measurements of what?'

'Just the land and garden here.'

'Go ahead. It's not a problem. I'm going in now anyway.'

'We will at some time need to measure inside. Maybe tomorrow, when I do not disturb you?'

'Of course.'

As Vanessa came into the lounge area, Rob opened the front door to the suite. His hair was wet and tousled and his ruddy tan had developed even more. Damn the bloody workmen, Vanessa thought – this would have been an ideal moment to make a move.

'Still not dressed?'

'Firing on all cylinders today, Rob! Do I *look* dressed?'

'Hard to know sometimes, with the flimsy sundresses you've had on over the last day or two!' Suddenly he spotted the movement of something white outside. 'There's somebody on our terrace!'

'I know. It's the hotel's architect or somebody. Come to measure up for an extension. Gave me quite a start. I was lying on the lounger.'

'And he saw you in your nightdress?'

'I'm perfectly decent!'

Rob shook his head and went out the back door, carrying his wet towel.

A thin man in a white short-sleeved shirt and khaki shorts was slowly rolling a trundle-wheel across the width of the terrace. He stopped, made a record in his notebook and then said something to his colleague in Italian.

Rob draped the wet towel over the back of one of the loungers.

'*Buongiorno, signore.* I hope we do not disturb you. A few minutes and we finish.'

'I don't see why you have to work at all when we are in residence.'

'*Mi dispiace.* As I said to the lady, we thought there was no one in. I need the measurements urgently for a meeting

. . . in – *Dio mio, in una mezz'ora.*' With that, he set aside the measuring wheel, growled something at the labourer who produced a manual measuring tape from his combat shorts. The surveyor took the extending end and marched down the sloping ground to the fence. In an effort to include Rob in the activity, he turned to explain. 'The ground – too – *come si dice*' – he made a wavy motion with his hand – '*irregolare* for the other instrument.'

But Rob had no interest in regular or irregular ground levels and turned his back on the intruders. Despite the hot day, he shut the French doors firmly behind him when he went inside.

———

Following her shower, Vanessa stood wrapped in a towel and studied the contents of the bathroom cabinet. Things were not where she remembered putting them. She hoped the chambermaid hadn't been into it – she really had no need to open the cupboard at all. Rob's freckled face appeared in the wall-mounted make-up mirror. He was standing behind her.

'Looking for something?'

'Well, yes. Everything is disturbed – and there's stuff missing. I had a little pouch with pharmacy stuff and it's missing. I'm going to speak to the cleaner— or complain at Reception.'

'No need. I was looking for painkillers. I must have put your bag back in the wrong place.'

'Oh? Painkillers for what?'

'I had a thumping headache last night.'

'You never said.'

'Didn't want to ruin the mood.'

'Is that why . . . you know . . . nothing happened? You should have said you weren't well.'

'It's embarrassing. It's meant to be our honeymoon.'

'Maybe it was the late hour. What if . . . we go back to bed now—'

'I'm hungry. We haven't even had our breakfast yet!'

On cue, the front door bell rang and a chirpy waitress called out: '*Room Service!*'

Rob opened the door and the girl came in and set the breakfast tray on the living-room table. He pressed a €5 note into her hand as she left.

'*Grazie, signore. Molto gentile. Buona giornata!*'

Vanessa half-heartedly played with the almond croissant on her plate, while opposite Rob peeled a banana, added it and a selection of nuts and raisins to his breakfast muesli, chose a non-sweetened yoghurt from the selection and poured it over his concoction.

'What's wrong with you, Rob?' Vanessa sipped the bitter coffee. 'Have you . . . sunstroke, or something? You've been behaving oddly.'

'There's nothing wrong with me. Orange juice? Or did

you order grapefruit – where's the docket?'

'Will you stop with the breakfast order! Tell me. Have I done something to upset you?'

'No. Not really. Just . . . you could cover up a bit more, when there are people around. Those goons in the garden. You're *my wife*. I don't really want every randy Italian copping an eyeful.'

'I didn't expect anyone to be out there. Come on, hurry up and finish your breakfast and we'll go back to bed!'

'And they say it's *men* who think about sex every seven seconds!'

'We're on our honeymoon – starting a life together. Of *course* I want us to have lots and lots of sex!'

'But with no consequences.'

'What do you mean – *consequences?*'

'Don't be naïve. I couldn't help noticing your little pink and white packet of smarties in the bathroom bag when I was looking for headache tablets.'

'Rob, of course I'm on the pill – we don't want to be a cliché having a honeymoon baby!'

'Why not?'

'Oh love, we haven't even discussed children.' Vanessa broke another piece off the croissant and tried to eat it. 'It's a huge decision – and we're not in a rush, are we?' She smiled at him – residual croissant flakes caught between her teeth.

'You're not getting any younger. All the experts say it's best to have babies as soon as.'

'I'm not even thirty! I think we're alright for a while yet.' Vanessa covered his hand with hers as it rested on the table. 'Though, we could always put in a bit of practice!'

'Now? I wouldn't feel comfortable with those guys just outside the window.'

'They're probably gone. Will I check?'

'No! Besides, it's the best part of the day. I want to go out . . . and *do* something!'

'OK. You're right. We haven't done anything "touristy" yet – just us two.'

'We went to Catania yesterday.'

'And *that* was a disaster! The Bellini Museum was closed for restoration and the others were either on a half-day or having a long siesta when we wanted to escape in out of the heat!'

'Well, I said we should have gone by train, instead of with the rambling bus. We'd have arrived much earlier.'

'Let's not squabble. It was six of one and half a dozen of the other, by the time we would have got down to the railway station. Let's stay local today.'

'Where did you have in mind?'

'I thought we could pop up to Castelmola and check out Dad's hotel? And visit the little village, of course. There are a few interesting things worth seeing.'

Rob stacked the breakfast things back onto the tray and took it over to the entrance door. 'Are you sure you don't want to salvage anything before I leave it outside? You ate hardly anything.'

'I'm fine. We'll have lunch in Castelmola. I'll just clean my teeth and get dressed. I won't be long.'

———

Vanessa rubbed protection sun-cream into her face and down onto her neck. She took eye-make-up out of the bathroom cupboard but rejected most of her usual products. Two days of 30°C heat had taught her that it just melted away. She settled for a fine slick of eye-pencil and a smidgen of mascara, tissued off any residue and flicked the foot-pedal on the bin to drop in the paper hanky.

The first thing she noticed was her medicine bag on the shelf under the sink. As she bent to retrieve it, she felt a sharp pain in her side and an urge to go to the toilet – again. She had just been. She hoped she wasn't coming down with something. She wouldn't be a bit surprised if she were – weddings were so exhausting. She was probably run-down.

She could hear Rob singing out in the lounge area. As she replaced the gold rings on her left hand, Vanessa felt an anxious knot form in her stomach. What if even their new marital status was not enough to rid his head of that fanatical dogma about 'committed sex only' and these physical problems persisted? This was something she had worried about but pushed to the back of her mind.

As she came out of the bathroom, a smartly dressed Rob – still singing – was busy packing a day-bag with bottles of water from the minibar and fruit from the bowl. He seemed much happier.

Banishing an inexplicable feeling of disappointment, Vanessa tried to sound upbeat. 'So, Castelmola, here we come!'

Chapter 16

Honeymoon, Day 4

The trip up Mount Etna which Davey had arranged was the first outing that saw all five of the family back together since the night at Badia Pizzeria. Vanessa felt strangely relieved by the company of the full group and felt less tense around Rob. It hadn't been a very early start — they had to join the tour down at the bus terminus, which was lower down the same road as the cable-car station.

As their minibus whizzed past the blue-and-white Funivia entrance, Rob sighed at the lost opportunity of his morning swim as his usual path to freedom receded behind him.

Once on the coach, Vanessa deliberately sat in beside her father in the third row. The tour wasn't full so Davey and Karen followed Rob down the bus, filing into the seats across the aisle from where he had chosen to sit. On the empty seat adjacent to his, Rob had placed his camera bag and was rummaging inside for something.

'Going to document the day then?' Davey nodded at the complicated-looking camera.

'Something like that.' Rob pushed objects around in the bag. 'And, I fancy a bit of peace and quiet.'

'Sorry. We'll move.' Davey stood up. 'There's two seats up near Dad.'

'No, man, I didn't mean—'

'You're fine. Karen will want to reminisce anyway as we travel. That's if I can extract the ear-buds from her and break up this relationship with Eros Ramazzotti!'

The coach whizzed along the Autostrada towards Catania. Mount Etna dominated its progress, looming larger and more distinct as the minutes passed. The volcano was in benign mood, emitting only a gentle plume of silver-white smoke.

Johnny was conflicted.

'Ness, do you think we should go up to the craters, if it's smoking away like that all the time?'

'Apparently that's normal. According to this' – she consulted the guidebook on her lap – 'it's a "constant gentle release". It *is* Europe's most active volcano, after all.'

'That doesn't really reassure me, sweetheart.'

———

Rob was pleased to be alone. Nobody had warned him how hard it would be to find himself closeted with the one person twenty-four hours a day. Over the years, he had

205

developed strategies to avoid the enforced proximity demanded of him on tour with his teammates. But for some reason, he had anticipated that being with Vanessa – being with just one, attractive woman full-time – would be easy. It wasn't. She was everywhere. Her slight figure seemed to expand and fill every available space and her voice resounded constantly in his head, even when she wasn't present. While here in Sicily, he was fine once they were *doing* something: visiting a village or a church. Even yesterday up in Castelmola when they had accidentally stumbled into Bar Turrisi and discovered phallus upon phallus venerated in the form of lampstands, sculptures, wall imagery – *even forming the arms of the chairs* – they had taken their drinks back outside and laughed and laughed at some of the truly gigantic specimens. Despite the ridiculous dimensions, he had found the sculptures strangely arousing and would have suggested a bit of 'al fresco' sex if he could have found somewhere suitable.

But Vanessa had ruined the mood, by insisting that once they had finished with lunch, they should take the steps down to Hotel Giorgio to check out where her father was staying.

In the planning stages of the honeymoon, Rob had been astounded by the suggestion that the other three Walshes would come on holiday at the same time! But, following his sense of claustrophobia over the previous days, his feelings were now more ambiguous. This bus journey – even being able to *sit on his own* – had only been made possible by their presence, as Vanessa was happy to catch up with her dad and leave him to plan his photographic exploits.

Would it always be like this, he wondered? Did Vanessa expect them to be like Karen and Davey, so wrapped up in each other even now nearly twenty years into their relationship, as they travelled literally and metaphorically down Memory Lane on today's journey?

Yet coupledom with Vanessa was what Rob had sought – what he had been striving for – for nearly eighteen months. And now that he had it, he wondered if he could carry it off – become that popular team-member with the beautiful TV-presenter wife, a national squad place awaiting him in the not-too-distant future. He would restore his father's faith in him; he would make him proud. He might even make him a grandfather – though not if his performance in the bedroom didn't improve. Last night had been much better: he kept having flashbacks of the enormous appendages in Bar Turrisi, and it had spurred him on.

But if he didn't – what was the official Catholic Church word for doing the biz? – *consummate* – this marriage fast, Vanessa would have grounds to complain.

She'd also probably spill her guts to Karen – and even Davey might coax it out of her – and his sexual prowess would be in question. They were a nosey lot, the Walshes.

He couldn't understand what all the fuss was about. Sex was just sex. Sometimes it was great and sometimes it

207

wasn't, but because of his self-determined abstinence with Vanessa before their marriage, he couldn't really offer an opinion on that.

He dreaded to think how many partners – *proper* sexual partners – she had had. He wasn't talking about 'boyfriends'; everybody had a past. He had even had a few romances himself – but in the sixteen or so months that he had been seeing her, it worried him the ease with which her flatmate Jenny seemed to drag men home to their shared apartment – on a weekend basis if his observations were anything to go by. She regularly teased Vanessa about the fact that Rob rarely stayed over. Why would he – when Jenny's dubious morals made the place feel like an unofficial brothel, with different men hanging out around the breakfast table every Sunday morning? The only thing that had sustained him through the previous months of anxiety was the nickname Jenny persisted in using for Vanessa: the Ice Maiden. He took that as a hopeful sign.

The coach began to slow down, changed into the right-hand lane to follow the exit for Zafferana. Vanessa checked her map.

'I think this is the approach we take up onto Etna.'

'What?' Johnny had fallen asleep, and was leaning against her shoulder.

'Daddy, wake up. You're missing all the scenery.

Zafferana. It's the southern route up the volcano.'

The road began to twist and climb steadily, flanked on either side by a mixture of olive terraces and fruit groves.

Vanessa was surprised. 'Look at all the orange trees! Funny, I had always visualised volcanic landscape as black and barren. These must be the fertile lava slopes.' She glanced at the map again. 'I suppose we are still low enough down on the mountain.'

In the mid-section of the bus, Rob spotted a photo-opportunity and stood up out of his seat. He crossed to the opposite side, where the lemon groves to the left of the road were more bountiful.

The tour guide who had been silent up until this point of the journey, plugged in the mike and began her spiel.

'*Signore, signori*, we have just passed through Zafferana and are now on the steep climb towards Rifugio Sapienza, where we will leave our bus. I would ask you from now on to refrain from moving about, as the road is perilous, and the driver does not need any sudden displacement of weight when we are taking the hairpin bends. *Grazie*.'

Davey leaned out into the aisle, turning to gesture at his brother-in-law, to suggest the guide meant business and he should sit down, but Rob either didn't see him or just ignored him, continuing to click away.

'Do you think that pair have had a row already?' Karen asked.

'Hard to tell. He did say he needed "peace and quiet".'

'And Vanessa hasn't seen much of Johnny the last few

days, what with his islands trip and their jaunt to Catania. Maybe they agreed that she should sit with her dad.'

'She would anyway, particularly if she's upset.'

'What's she upset about?'

'You know Nessa. Could be anything.'

'I don't understand.'

'Well – I don't know – say if she and Rob have had words, Dad's her emotional default setting – she'd go running to him – the one man who will never let her down *or* find fault in her.'

'Not the healthiest position to hold, if you're just newly married!'

'And Dad's the same! Didn't you hear his speech at the wedding? *"You mess with my dah-ter – you end up dead!"* Christ, he was really preparing for his trip to Sicily. I'd say Rob's afraid he'll wake up to a horse's head in the bed!'

'Lovely way to talk about your sister.'

'Ah, you're on *fire* today, Ms Waldron!' Davey pounced on Karen and began tickling her.

There was a sound of static as the microphone re-engaged and contravening her own counsel, the guide half-perched on the driver's window ledge, her thin brown legs barely touching the floor.

'*Signore, signori*, as we pull into Rifugio Sapienza, just a few practical details. If you want to buy snacks or drinks for the climb, there are a few shops here. Then we'll head to the cable-car station, where you can purchase your ticket. When you get off the cable car, your choice is to climb on foot to Piano del Lago, or go in a 4 X 4. As only accredited Etna guides may take tours on the volcano, at that point I will hand you over to Sandro. You should be off the mountain by two-thirty and lunch is booked in the blue-and-white-fronted restaurant over there, for three. Any questions?'

Rob tuned out, as the various predictable questions were asked and answered and since the bus was stationary, he wondered if he should head up and talk to Vanessa and Johnny before they disembarked. He wanted to clear the air. This trip to Etna had been planned as the highlight of their honeymoon and he wanted her to enjoy it. She had seemed upset this morning when they were leaving the hotel. He didn't really know why, though it might have been about him asking her to change out of her tiny shorts, into something more substantial. That was only for her own sake: it would be cold higher up.

He knew she resented his comments about 'dressing appropriately', but he worked in an all-male environment where the guys frequently made vile remarks about girls 'being up for it', based on their scant clothing. He didn't want *his* wife subjected to that sort of abuse. Take yesterday when he had come back to find her still in her *nightdress*, while that surveyor was walking around with drawings and his hodometer measuring the distance from the terrace to the fence and over and back to the lemon trees. I mean, what did they know about him? Nothing. So what if he worked for the hotel? He could be any kind of

211

deviant. *And* it appeared the guy intended to come back on a regular basis, if the message Rob found in their cubbyhole at Reception last evening was anything to go by! A message from him – from *Marcello* – requesting a convenient time to come to the suite to test the internal boundary wall that was due for demolition. It really wasn't on – all this intrusion – given the shekels he was forking out for the stay. He had told the receptionist as much and insisted that if the surveyor really had to get into the room, then he should do so when they were up on the mountain.

Inside the cold and noisy cable-car station, lengthy queues had begun to form in front of the cash desks. The official Etna guide distributed their tickets and joined the car in which the Walshe family was sitting. Sandro was a low-sized man with an electively bald head, beautifully tanned from the long Sicilian summer months. Slowly, the cable began to rotate and they moved off on their ascent.

Once clear of the station, the red cabs were suspended mid-wire over the grey slopes. They seemed to be travelling far too slowly for Karen's liking, who despite her confidence in all things Sicilian, was not good with heights. She squeezed Davey's hand.

With a terrifying winching noise, their cable car shuddered to a halt. A dilapidated blue-and-white sign announced their destination as the *Rifugio Montagnola*.

Underneath the larger sign, a myriad of hand-painted notices offered padded jackets, mountain boots, wet-gear, walking poles and even umbrellas for hire.

Sandro, now in a pair of serious mountain boots, held an orange flag with a number on it and assembled his group.

Vanessa and Rob, who had been in a different cab, joined the rest of the family.

'Did you enjoy that?' Vanessa thought Karen looked a bit pale.

'Nah, can't say that I did. Not keen on them.'

The diminutive guide cleared his throat.

'*Signore, signori, if I could have your attention, please?' First of all, I would like to welcome you to the real ascent of Mongibello. Yes, you thought you were on Mount Etna, but we Sicilians refer to our beloved volcano by this name, meaning Mountain of Mountains – monte and djebel – taken from the Italian and Arabic for mountain. Those of you who want to ascend by jeep, I suggest you go to the relevant point at the cable-car terminus and group yourselves accordingly. Remember, the 4x4s are only allowed to go up to a certain height on Piano del Lago. I will join you in a few minutes to make sure there are no difficulties, but since the majority of the group has expressed an interest in proceeding on foot, I will be guiding the climbing group.'*

Vanessa checked with Johnny. 'Well, Dad, jeep or shank's mare? It says here it's about two kilometres.'

'Oh, on foot, what else?'

Sandro was back. '*I also want to caution you that this is not a trip for flimsy footwear. If you have any openings in your shoes, please*

213

hire some boots and socks at the relevant desk. Volcanic soil is dirty and gritty and will make walking very uncomfortable if it gets on your feet.'

Karen ran around and pretended to check their footwear. 'All present, and correct?'

'Yes, Mammy.'

'Shit. I deserved that. Sorry, am I being a pain?'

'No more than usual.' Vanessa gave her sister-in-law a friendly thump on the arm. 'Why don't you tag along with me? Steve McCurry over there is stuck to his camera, and Davey can stay with Dad for a while.'

'Great. We can set our own pace.'

The guide went around the smaller groups of walkers and repeated exactly what Karen had already done – checked the footwear.

'Could I have your attention again, before we get separated? I nearly forgot to mention the subject of geysers or hot springs. Every so often you will come across these natural phenomena. While it is interesting to go up close, feel the heat of the steam and take a photo or two, I must advise you that they can be very hot, so do not burn yourselves. So, if everyone is ready, we will begin. I will stop every so often with information of interest to you. Avanti!'

'Avanti!' Karen, finally recovered from the cable-car, studied Vanessa. 'Are you alright?'

'I think I could do with the toilet before we head off.'

'Oh, quick then. Go back to the station. I saw a sign. I'll wait here.'

Sandro was waving his orange flag. '*Signori, Signore, un attimo, prego. You will see ahead of us an old fissure or side vent. In modern times, most of Mongibello's eruptions occur not through the central summit craters, but through these side-vents. A previous eruption occurred here, but now the fissure is practically closed. We are currently at a height of 2,650 metres. The total height of the volcano is estimated to be about 3,342 metres, depending on volcanic activity. Are we all good to begin walking?*'

Karen looked around for Vanessa, who was running up the black soil to rejoin them.

'Are you OK? You look a bit upset.'

'I am having pain – you know – when peeing. Most uncomfortable.'

'Honeymoon cystitis! Poor you.'

'Well, maybe.'

'Have you taken anything?'

'I had a couple of over-the-counter sachets with me, but they haven't helped. Plus, they've run out now.'

'I suppose it's just the shock to the body from abstinence to full-blown action!'

Vanessa shot Karen a look. 'How did you know about that? Have you all been laughing at me behind my back?'

Karen shifted uncomfortably. 'No, of course not. Just Davey mentioned – anyway, don't get at *me* – the social media accounts for that American organisation he supports, have him listed as endorsing their philosophy. We just presumed—'

'Great. So now I'm a joke among my friends and family as well.'

'You know that's not true. But none of this is new – is something more recent bothering you?'

'Well, if it *is* a urinary tract infection – it's a bit, how do I phrase this – pre-emptive!'

'Not following.'

'We still haven't had – *proper* sex.'

'You have explained to him that this abstinence lark isn't supposed to go on *after* you're married?'

'Oh, it's not that he isn't *trying – I shouldn't be talking to you about this –* it's private.'

'But he can't "perform"?'

Vanessa nodded.

'Look, he could be tired. Give it a day or two—'

'*Ladies and Gentlemen.*' Sandro temporarily planted his flag in the black soil. '*From this vantage point you can see one of the secondary cones created from an eruption back in 1983. This was the first eruption that man was able to control, diverting the lava emissions, preventing them from reaching Nicolosi, the town farther down the slopes to our west. Repeated eruptions continued through the nineteen eighties—*'

'But what if this cystitis gets worse? I'm pushing him for sex and then I'll be uncomfortable. Plus, he made a funny comment when he found my pills.'

'Found?'

'Well, they were in my medicine bag.'

'What was he doing riffling through your private things?'

'*Shhhh!*' An irate tourist turned and hissed, as she strained to hear the guide.

'*Mi dispiace,*' Karen apologised. 'Go on,' she said quietly to Vanessa.

'He wasn't. Riffling, that is. He was looking for paracetamol. But once he found the packet, he commented that I was mad for sex since it would have no "consequences".'

'You've lost me.'

'Babies. Sex being an activity primarily for the purpose of making babies.'

'Christ. He's really taking the conservative interpretation of his faith the whole way, isn't he?'

'*Shhhh!*' A second cranky tourist poked Karen in the back with his guidebook.

'Sor-*ry!*

'*And* I'm worried if he gets his – *performance* – issues sorted and I have to get antibiotics for this UTI, they might interfere with the Pill. I don't trust any contraception that I'm not in control of! Imagine! A honeymoon baby – the embarrassment of it!'

Karen fell silent. She didn't want to offend Vanessa, but she really couldn't see what would be so awful about that. She and Davey had wanted nothing more when, after years together, they finally got married and felt their relationship was in a place where a baby would have been lovingly welcomed.

Yet they hadn't been lucky. Nor in the ten years since, despite many expensive medical interventions, had their luck improved. She didn't know how Vanessa could be so insensitive as to not remember all their troubles.

'Still, Ness, you should try to get something for the cystitis.'

'Would they give me antibiotics over the counter in a pharmacy?'

'Doubtful without a prescription, but we could try a clinic. There's bound to be one in Taormina, since it's such a busy tourist town.'

'Thanks.'

'Don't worry. You'll work it out – I mean, the other problem. In the meantime, we'll find you a clinic in Taormina.'

When the group finally reached the stone bearing the name *Piano del Lago*, there was a collective sense of achievement. Davey borrowed the good camera and took a photo of Johnny and Rob either side of the marker. Johnny dug the walking poles he had hired into the unrelenting black rock, whilst Rob couldn't decide whether to keep his sunglasses on or off and kept flicking them up and down onto his head, which bothered the photographer. The deepest blue sky silhouetted them and, apart from it, there was nothing else visible beyond. Karen and Vanessa caught up and piled in for the final shot.

'*Signore, signori.*' The pride in Sandro's voice was audible. '*You have achieved something great today – arriving at the craters of Piano del Lago. One thing you need to remember about volcanoes – they are unpredictable. Sicilians have a love-hate relationship with their powerful friend Mongibello. On the one hand, they have benefited from the rich soil its lava deposits provide for the surrounding land, and the subsequent wealth it has brought the local people through their abundant citrus fruit and olive production.*

Yet they live in peril of it turning on them – its powerful, burning emissions destroying their homes and maybe even their lives – at any given moment. Like it has done from antiquity to the present day. My advice? Respect the power of fire. Handle with care.'

Chapter 17

Honeymoon, Day 5

V anessa lay awake in the pre-dawn dark, her back towards Rob. She had hardly slept a wink and, when she had found herself beginning to drift off, she had roused herself deliberately, afraid to let her guard down or to fall into a deep sleep and miss the opportunity of carrying out her plan to try and find out what Rob was up to.

Matters had taken a mysterious turn the previous evening, after their Etna trip. When the tour bus arrived back into Taormina, it was forced to wait for an empty bay to disembark its passengers at the coach park. During this time, Rob had advanced up the aisle, gear bag in hand. Just as he was about to jump out, his phone pinged and he checked it.

Then, as the group meandered in single file up the narrow footpath of Via Pirandello, he had excused himself from Vanessa, muttered something about his missed sea swim, ducked speedily across the road, and sprinted in the direction of the steps down to the Funivia.

His rapid departure did not go unnoticed by Johnny or the rest of the family.

'Where's he off to?' Johnny asked Davey, who shrugged but didn't reply.

'Ah, I think he's just overpowered by the gang of us — he needs his space.' Karen tried to lighten the mood. 'Typical only child! I felt like that in the beginning, but I've just got used to putting up with you all!'

'Oh, have you now?' Vanessa gave a half-hearted smile and fell into step with her sister-in-law as the footpath widened. 'And anyway, *you're* not an only child!'

'I *know*! So can you imagine how the poor guy feels!'

They linked arms. Karen was keen to keep Vanessa and her unreliable watery eyes away from Johnny. The mood the new bride was in, she might collapse into tears and tell him every intimate detail. Not good. Although he had mellowed since, Johnny's short temper during his playing years had been legendary. Him punching Rob's lights out if he perceived a 'slight' towards his beloved daughter was not the way to go, Karen thought. She sought a suitable distraction for them all.

'Why don't we call in to that sinful *gelateria* near the San Domenico and indulge? The lunch up on the mountain was a bit spartan.'

'*Spartan*?' chimed her husband. 'It was *dire*. Talk about taking advantage of a captive audience!'

The four of them – now in single file again – made slow progress up the Corso through the sea of tourists beginning their evening *passeggiata* or returning from similar excursions as theirs. The exertion of the long day was beginning to catch up, and all eyes were focussed on a sign for the famous ice-cream spot as a sugar-fix and a sit-down were badly needed.

Just as they reached the tiny lane, Vanessa noticed the illuminated green cross of a pharmacy. She waited for Karen to catch up and pulled her aside.

'Would you come in with me and translate? See if we can't persuade some meds out of her?'

'Sure. Davey, we're just popping in here. See you at Fanaberia in a couple of minutes.'

But Karen had been correct in her assertion that the pharmacist would stick to the law and not dispense to a stranger, given she didn't know the patient's full medical history. Instead, she suggested a packet of the calming sachet drinks and Vanessa made her way to the counter to pay. Karen availed of the lull to enquire of the pharmacist about the nearest women's clinic. The helpful woman handed her a couple of business cards, pointing out that their hours were a bit odd – some didn't open till five in the evening. She put an X in blue biro on the one she considered the best.

With the sachet drinks in her knapsack and a leisurely ice-cream consumed, Vanessa strolled the short distance to La Villa and somehow made it back ahead of Rob. He must have been having a very long swim.

As she unpacked her day-bag, she heard a shuffling noise under the window, followed by a knock at the outside door. Vanessa presumed Rob hadn't taken his key, but when she opened it, Marcello the surveyor was standing there, with various small instruments sitting atop his clipboard.

'*Buonasera, signora*, again I am sorry to disturb you. We asked the permission of your husband to come and inspect the walls – is it OK to do it now?'

Hesitantly, Vanessa let him in – not because she felt any degree of threat from Marcello – but conscious that Rob wasn't there.

'Yes, come in. My husband is five minutes behind me, if you need to talk to him.'

'No need. I will be finished by then! Just a very quick measurement from this big wall.'

The external wall in question ran the full depth of the suite, bordering as it did the small entrance hall that led straight into the bedroom, then continuing on into the lounge area. Marcello was tapping and taking a reading of the living-room section when Rob returned. His cheerful expression dissipated when he saw Marcello.

'What the fuck are you doing here?'

'Apologies, *signore*, but I left a message to ask if I come today?'

'And *I* left a message back to say "yes", but when *we* were *not* here – like all day up until four or five this afternoon? And what do you do? You wait until this late

223

hour when my wife is here on her own, and then you come sneaking in when my back is turned.'

'*Mi dispiace, signore*, but seven in the evening for us *is* still work time – because of the heat.'

'Rob, he's fine, he's just finished.' Vanessa put a restraining hand on her husband's arm.

But Rob shook off her hand, lifted the clipboard, the tape-measure and a small instrument from the table, shoved them all into the surveyor's arms and bundled him out through the bedroom to the hall-door.

'*Yes, he is finished and he's not coming back without prior notice and only when I am here!*'

'OK, OK, I am gone!'

Vanessa ran her hands through her hair. 'Rob! Did you *have* to be so ill-mannered? He's a professional working for the hotel! What's got *into* you?'

'What's got into *me?* Every time I leave you alone, I come back and find that slime-bag in the fucking place!'

'Rob, you're losing the plot. Honestly, I think the sun is getting to you.'

'*The sun? The sun is getting to me?* You and your fucking family drag me off to this expensive hotel on *my* honeymoon – for which I am paying in total by the way – and then, instead of having a bit of private time with my wife, I am forced to go on excursions, all five of us jammed into a people-carrier like the bloody Waltons!'

'Well, at least you got to go up Walton's Mountain today.' Vanessa half-laughed at her wit, but he just scowled.

'And it's not accurate to say we've been all cooped up together. The Etna trip was our first outing as a group. As for the people-carrier – the tour organisers always use small vehicles to gather up guests, because the streets are so narrow. There were other people with us from this hotel – it wasn't *just* my family!'

Rob crossed to the fruit bowl and selected a mandarin, which he began to peel.

Vanessa persisted. 'Look, we've hardly seen the others, and we'll have all of next week, just us. Come here.' She went and tried to put her arms around his neck but he removed them gently.

'Not now.' His attention seemed elsewhere. He pulled the sweaty T-shirt over his wet hair and strolled over to the wardrobe, where he chose a fresh shirt and long pants, and carried both off into the bathroom with him. After a couple of minutes, he poked his head back around the door and said: 'Oh, I met some Cork lads down at the sea who recognised me. I've arranged to meet up with them later for something to eat. You don't mind if I fly solo, do you? You'd be bored out of your mind.'

Freshly spruced up, Rob had then gone out, leaving Vanessa deeply perturbed. To think, it was less than a week since they had married and embarked on what she had expected would be a relaxed, fun-filled holiday. Instead, they had spent a very strange – even tense – few days, circling around each other. Obviously, not having lived together properly before the wedding was making the adjustment period more difficult.

Had she not been so exhausted after the Mount Etna trip, Vanessa could have followed her family up to Castelmola for dinner. But even that would have been stressful, as she would have had to explain away Rob's absence.

Instead, she had gone over to the terrace and eaten dinner alone and heard nothing from her husband until she became aware of him slithering into the bed beside her in the early hours of the morning.

In what seemed less than an hour after his return, dawn broke, evident from the weak shafts of sunlight which pushed through the slats of the shutters and played on her half-shut eyes. Vanessa listened to Rob's heavy breathing and doubted he'd be able to stir himself to follow his usual swim schedule. That suited her plan, because if he waited for breakfast, she fully intended to surprise him at the beach. She had been passive for far too long. She needed to make him see she wasn't happy to be abandoned like this on her honeymoon.

First, she would message Karen and push back their arrangement to visit the women's clinic until its evening surgery. She hoped the doctor could sort her out as she was increasingly uncomfortable.

As for the timing of any future babies, she would sit

Rob down calmly and talk it through, when he wasn't wandering around bare-headed under 32 degrees of Sicilian sun.

———

Her packed beach bag sat snugly under the teak terrace table as she finished her breakfast. The rest of their order awaited Rob in the lounge, as by ten o'clock he still hadn't shown his face.

Eventually, the French door creaked as he pushed it fully open. 'Oh, you're out here,' he said, smiling at her. 'What's today's update on the wasp population?'

Vanessa grinned back, surprised by how crisp and attractive her husband looked in his pristine white T-shirt and multi-coloured surfer shorts, despite his lack of sleep. 'Good evening, last night?'

'Middling. Sorry about leaving you on your own but I just—'

'—needed space. I've heard it before, Rob. Maybe you should join a monastery and be done with it.'

'*What* do you mean by that?'

'Nice and quiet in a monastery.'

'But I wasn't on my own. I told you, I met those Cork lads.' Rob twisted the lid off the miniature pot of honey and poured it on top of his cereal. 'I could be tempting fate with this!' He laughed and looked around him. 'And, by coincidence, when I was chatting to the receptionist about

227

the Marcello issue yesterday, he suggested we should head out towards Letojanni to the beach bars some night. Livelier. And cheaper.'

'Only you forgot to bring me.'

'Next time.'

Vanessa got up and went inside to put on another espresso.

'That's where we ended up. The guys were staying there. Had a few beers. Let my hair down. Honestly, Letojanni was far more relaxing. Taormina . . . is a bit too Karen – a bit *rarefied*.'

'*Oooh!* Fancy word for a front row!'

'Vanessa, don't undermine me.'

'Whatever. Well, I'm off now to meet "rarefied" Karen for some shopping. Enjoy your swim. Isola Bella, is it?'

'Shopping – this early?

'*I* wasn't out half the night. I'll message you when I'm done.'

———

Vanessa browsed the endless coral pieces in the display window of a small jewellery outlet near Porta Messina. As the church bell chimed eleven o'clock, she saw Rob approaching down the final stretch of the Corso. She ducked into the shop, waited for him to pass, gave him a head-start, then stepped out onto the street. She walked swiftly under the ancient stone archway and onto Via Pirandello.

She could see him ahead – his colourful shorts weaving

and bobbing between oncoming tourists – and she had him in sight the entire time as he descended the steps on the side of the cable-car station marked *Ingresso – Entrance*. She accelerated her pace, feeling in her dress pocket for some coins to purchase a ticket, hoping there was a machine and not a big queue at a sales hatch.

Through the glass door, she could see the incoming white cable pods advancing up the overhead wire. Unlike the elaborate and heavy multi-cab cable system from the previous day on Mount Etna, this was just a funicular, designed for the short and frequent hop up from Mazzarò at sea-level to Taormina town.

She passed the toilets on her right and pushed her ticket into the turnstile where she was admitted into a holding area, dense with waiting people as it was a popular descent time. A uniformed female official controlled the next barrier, keeping it firmly shut until the ascending passengers had disembarked and were exiting the station.

Vanessa could see no sign of Rob. She thought this strange, as a cable-car was only just arriving – so he couldn't have caught the previous descending one. As the four empty cabs slid into place on the rotating platform, the official opened the barrier and the crowd surged forward to select their seats. A quick glance over her shoulder revealed to Vanessa the next set of people queueing for the turnstile: she was going down, whether she liked it or not.

Once out of the Mazzarò station, she stopped to read a timetable on the noticeboard, keeping an eye out for Rob in case he had by some chance got into the pods behind hers. But he was nowhere to be seen.

She followed the crowd. The younger ones were equipped with sun-umbrellas, beach-mats and cooler bags heading for the free public beach; the foreign tourists like herself had just their beach bags, planning to head for one of the private concessions and a comfortable sun-bed.

When she finally glimpsed the pretty curve of the bay from the top of what seemed like hundreds of steep and perilous stone steps, Vanessa's heart missed a beat. She was overwhelmed by the beauty of the protected nature-reserve area below – its pretty island – the Isola Bella of the name – which wasn't a true island, being accessible at low tide by a narrow stretch of raised land. While she processed the magnificent vista below, Vanessa's thoughts turned to anger. To think, it was Thursday. They had been here since Sunday and this beauty had been within a half-hour's reach of their hotel – yet Rob had selfishly chosen to keep it to himself – more than that, he had deliberately excluded her from his outings, chanting his Marlene Dietrich-esque mantra of 'I want to be alone'.

How dare he! Push her aside, keep her in a little 'box', his trophy jewel to trot out in public when *he* felt like it! Where had the nice man she had dated and spent time with over the previous sixteen months *gone* to?

Well, wherever it was, it wasn't the beach at Isola Bella. Having descended the hundreds of steps, as the sun reached its midday zenith Vanessa traipsed across the large

– and uncomfortable – rounded pebbles of the rocky shoreline, passing claustrophobic row after row of various coloured sunbeds and parasols, as one concession merged into another. The clients were Italian, German, French, middle-aged couples or well-heeled young professionals with small babies cocooned in the shade of their mini-tents. This was not Rob's sort of place. She couldn't imagine him frequenting it on a daily basis, even just for a swim.

Her sundress sticking to her, Vanessa sat down heavily on one of the vacant sun-loungers and began to strip off to get into the sea.

'*Prego, signora. Lettino?*' A blue-T-shirted beach boy with a money belt had stopped at her feet.

'Sorry, I don't speak Italian.'

'You want the bed . . . you take ticket at *Cassa*. OK? Here, I save for you. *Ombrellone?*'

'*Si*. Yes, please.' Why not, Vanessa thought. She wasn't going to let Rob ruin her day. 'The *Cassa*, where is it?'

'Go to the restaurant and you can pay there. *D'accordo?*'

'Thank you.' As Vanessa spread her towel out on the sunbed, the blonde woman on the lounger very close to hers spoke.

'And get yourself a large bottle of water while you're at it – before the busy lunch trade starts. You look like you could do with it.'

'Thanks!' Cheered by the stranger's thoughtfulness – and someone who spoke to her in English – Vanessa returned the favour. 'Can I fetch anything for you when I am up there?'

'No, thanks. I'll be ordering lunch later. They bring it down on a tray – it's less chaotic than at the counter.' The stranger stared hard at her. 'Hey, don't I recognise you from La Villa? I think I saw you dining on the terrace last night?'

'Yes, that's where we're staying.'

'Oh, I thought you were travelling "sola".'

'No, I'm on honeymoon – just doing our own thing today – sorry, I'd better go and sort out—' Vanessa waved her purse at her neighbour and moved away brusquely.

Why did she *do* this, she thought. Feel compelled to tell everybody her business? Probably not helped by the fact that the blonde lady was obviously Irish as well – a nation with gold medals in the art of the direct question.

———

Vanessa floated on the salty buoyant sea and stared at the cerulean blue of the afternoon sky. This was her third swim – it was really too hot to stay sitting on land for any length of time. She felt her limbs relax and her thoughts float in the water beside her. For the first time since they had come to Sicily, she wasn't thinking of Rob. She and Isabelle – that was her sunbed neighbour's name – had chatted over lunch and shared a carafe of wine, delivered to them at the water's edge. It had been great to talk to a stranger, who, obviously not a fan of breakfast TV, hadn't recognised her. Vanessa realised how much she had begun to miss this – just presenting herself to the world as an independent entity – not part of a couple. Perhaps she had more in common with Rob than she thought.

When she came out of the water, Isabelle was back in her street clothes, her bag packed.

'I have to head off now. My partner is conducting a concert at the Teatro Antico tonight. He's always a bit jittery before performance, so I'll have to go and "minister" to him – camomile tea and the like. You and your husband should come. It's popular opera arias and duets – nothing too heavy.'

'Would we get tickets at such short notice?'

'Ah yes, it's open air. They just sell a section and squash you in! Stone steps. Bring a cushion – hard on the bum!'

'Thanks. We'll think about it.'

'Do. It's a magnificent setting. We stop off at the Mediterraneo Caffè for a drink on the way back to the hotel afterwards. If you go, see you there.'

Vanessa checked her watch and realised that the re-arranged appointment with Karen was imminent. She would need a good forty minutes to get up into the heart of Taormina. She also realised that she hadn't bothered to turn her phone back on all day, or contacted Rob as promised. Karen might be interested in the concert as well; she'd mention it to her. It would be nice to organise a night out with her brother and his wife.

For the first day since her honeymoon had begun, Vanessa felt like she was on holiday.

Chapter 18

Honeymoon, Day 5, Evening

When Vanessa arrived at the doctor's clinic, Karen was sitting outside on a stone bollard, under the white-and-red cross sign. The ancient mahogany door behind her was firmly shut.

'No joy? Did we get the times of the surgery wrong?' Vanessa dropped her beach bag with the damp and now heavy towel at her feet.

'Hiya. Not according to this.' Karen waved the small business card that the pharmacist had given her. '*Clinica serale martedì e giovedì.* That's Tuesdays and Thursdays – and today's Thursday. From five to seven. I've rung the buzzer several times – nothing.'

'Also, there's no-one else waiting. Not a good sign. What are the times tomorrow morning?'

'Nine-thirty to eleven. Early. They don't make it easy, do they?' Karen looked around to see if there was a small shop or tobacconist at which she could make enquiries. 'Look there's a bar over there – fancy an *aperitivo*?'

'Sure. Though it's a bit back-street – could we not go somewhere nicer?'

'I was only thinking of you. They might know about the comings and goings at the doctor's, since they are practically opposite.'

'Good idea.'

Karen's hunch bore fruit. The girl serving their table was indeed up to speed with why the *clinica* was shut. The doctor who took the evening surgeries had herself had a family emergency in Siracusa, and had to go home at short notice to look after her mother. The morning clinics were taken by another female medic who lived in Castiglione di Sicilia – a hilltop village not too far from Taormina. Both of that doctor's parents were deceased, the waitress assured them, so there shouldn't be a problem.

'So, I guess it'll be "up before my breakfast" tomorrow morning?' Vanessa sipped her Martini.

'What?'

'The early surgery coincides with the arrival of my room-service breakfast at La Villa!'

'Why room service? Rob keeping you all to himself?' Karen called the girl back for some extra ice.

'No. Wasps – the terrace is inundated with them. Tomorrow, I'd prefer to be here by ten o'clock, in case there's a lot of people. Is that too early for you?'

'No. We have breakfast about eight-thirty. On the

rooftop. Not a wasp in sight – no plants. You must have joined Rob at the beach today – your hair is all wavy. It's nice.'

'I *was* down in Isola Bella all day – but – what's that expression they use here for "on your own"?'

'*Da sola.*'

'*Da sola.* Well, not completely. I fell into company with a woman staying at our hotel – Irish. She's involved with some music man – in fact, she was trying to encourage us to go to his concert at the amphitheatre tonight. Where would you get tickets?'

'Probably at the Box Office on the road up to the Teatro Antico. Is it the operatic concert? I saw the poster – we were thinking of going.'

'I hoped you might say that – just, with us having gone our separate ways for the day, it might be easier to persuade Rob if I had already arranged it with you.'

'How did you end up going to different beaches?'

'Oh, we just missed each other – at the cable-car thing. No harm done.'

'Eh, hel-*lo!* 21st century modern technology – called a mobile!'

'I accidentally left mine behind,' Vanessa lied. 'Will we chance this ticket office place?'

'They don't usually open till six-thirty or seven on the evening of a performance. But we should be able to book online and pick up the tickets later. That's what I've done in the past. Here, I'll log on. I think my TicketOne site is still active.'

'I'll give Dad a ring. He might enjoy it.'

'I thought you said you'd forgotten your phone?'

Vanessa blushed. 'I . . . detoured to the hotel on my way here to collect it.'

'I doubt Johnny will come. We had him down in Giardini Naxos this morning – at a beach club we used go to when we stayed in an apartment nearby. He was fairly whacked after a morning's swimming and a leisurely, boozy lunch!'

'Gone straight to voicemail.'

'Actually, I remember the reason now he wanted to head back to Castelmola early . . . something about seeing two Frenchwomen before they left? Honestly, Vanessa, your dad has been the success story of this trip! The way he has adapted, gone on tours on his own, made friends. Even taking that bus up and down to Castelmola rather than forcing us to get taxis to collect him.'

'Yeah, he's a feisty old lad. Hats off to him.'

'Oh, and have you *seen* the Panama hat? Anthony Hopkins isn't in it!'

'I have seen very little of him all week. I kind of wish he'd stayed at La Villa with us.'

'*Nessa!* You know you couldn't have done that! Rob is grumpy enough about him being here in the first place—'

'Rob is grumpy. Period. And it's not all about Rob, Karen. Remember, it's my holiday too. Have you those tickets booked yet? I'll go and pay for our drinks.'

The front windows of the suite at La Villa were shuttered against the early evening sun. Vanessa used her key, calling out as she came through the short hallway. '*Rob? Are you in?*'

She pushed open the door to the bedroom. A pair of shorts and one of his T-shirts were bundled up on the wicker chair – she thought it was the outfit he had been wearing that morning. The ensuite bathroom door was open, so he wasn't in there. Through the arch into the living area, she could see the hotel beach towel and one of his flowery surfer swimming shorts drying outside on the miniature pull-out line. The patio area was in shade, only the lower reaches of the sloping garden were catching the western rays.

Stuck under the fruit bowl on the dark wooden table was a page torn from the hotel's notepad. Rob never left written notes, so she wondered what had prompted this.

'*4.20 pm. Vanessa! Since you've decided to turn off your phone for the day – don't know why – I can only guess you've gone to spend time with Daddy Dearest. I'm heading up to Castelmola now. If you're reading this, well, we've crossed. Just ring me. I'm starting to worry.*'

'*Daddy Dearest*'! That's a bit sarcastic, she thought. Why on earth had Rob gone to Castelmola? He was going to make them late for the concert – which, in fairness, he knew nothing about. She scrolled to his name, registering the four WhatsApp messages sent earlier and the three incoming missed calls.

But as she hit the call icon, she could hear his ringtone – coming from the hallway.

'You're back! I was just ringing you.'

'Never! After – let me see – what time again did you go "shopping" with Karen – ten-fifteen this morning?'

'I went to the beach – afterwards. Thought I'd surprise you. But you weren't there.'

'Which beach?'

'Down at Mazzarò – Isola Bella?'

'You must have misheard. I said Mazz*eo*.'

'No, you didn't! I specifically asked you. Anyway, it doesn't matter, *I* enjoyed Isola Bella and my day.'

'On your own?'

'Yes. *Da sola!*'

'And you didn't think to invite Daddy Dearest with you?'

'Rob! Stop calling him that – it's actually quite insulting. No. I was under the illusion that I was joining *you*. Once I got down all those hundreds of steps, I decided to stay put.'

'So, like a fool, when there was no sign of you all afternoon, *I* take a taxi up to Castelmola to Hotel Giorgio and what do I find?'

'No idea.'

'*Johnny* – in a pair of tight swimming trunks, lolling on a lounger flanked by two old women in bikinis! A sight I don't think I'll recover from. Get this – he *even* asked me if I'd like a set of his spare togs to have a dip in the hotel's pool! Jesus wept!'

Vanessa couldn't help herself. She just burst out laughing

at the image forming in her head: Rob, in his cool shorts, his well-toned muscles bulging from a crisp short-sleeved T-shirt, inadvertently sucked into the vortex of encroaching old age embodied in the exposed flesh of her sixty-something dad in too-revealing Speedos and his scantily clad companions, who she took to be the French friends.

'And were you not tempted to take him up on his offer – you who are such a water baby?'

Rob stared hard at her, then crossed to the fridge where he pulled out a can of Coke.

'Well,' Vanessa ventured, 'apart from the beach, I had a busy day arranging things – outings and such – and managed to get hold of tickets for a concert at the amphitheatre – you know, the famous Greek one we can see from the terrace? For tonight.'

'Tonight? Thanks for the notice.'

'The concert's only on tonight, but it starts late, nine-fifteen according to the website.'

'Do we *have* to go? When will we get time to eat? I'm starving!'

'Yes, we *do* have to go! Karen has paid for all the tickets and will pick them up. We can always grab something snacky on the way.'

'Doesn't suit me at all.'

'You'll change your mind when you see the programme. It's all operatic stuff – duets and solos and orchestra bits. Your kind of music. The conductor is staying here – in this hotel.'

'Oh?'

'Yeah, I bumped into his wife or girlfriend or whatever she is, down at Isola Bella. That's how I heard about it. In fact, she mentioned some café they go to after. We could try that to eat before?'

'You have it all worked out, haven't you?'

Vanessa ruffled Rob's hair affectionately, as he sat sipping his drink. 'I have. And now, I'm going to have a quick shower and get ready. Have a scout around for any spare cushions – apparently, it's a good idea to bring your own to sit on the stone steps!'

⸻

Once they had taken their places in the Teatro Antico, it was obvious to the Walshe family why the event organisers waited until dusk for the concerts to begin. The spectacular elevated amphitheatre with its onstage lighting was further enhanced by the natural backdrop of the amazing vista out over the curve of the bay below, the twinkling lights onshore hugging the coastline. In the distance, the cone of Mount Etna was visible, and Davey swore he had seen some of her orange fireworks spurt high into the sky during the course of the evening.

⸻

The music seemed to have cheered Rob up. Karen, who was sitting beside him, had heard him sing along to many of the popular tunes. The orchestra were seated on the stage – and the conductor had a good rapport with both the audience and his soloists, who he introduced in several languages and gave a short overview of what their aria or duet was about before they began singing. Every so often, the musicians would just play on their own without a soloist. Rob was less keen on this.

'Lollipops,' he muttered to Vanessa.

'*What?*'

'Short orchestral pieces – fillers, to use up time and give the singers a rest.'

'But I know all those tunes!' Vanessa checked the order on the printed programme. '*And* I knew that lovely aria about the baby.'

'Which?'

'This one.' Vanessa pointed at the last soprano solo they had just heard. '*O Mio Bambino Caro.*'

'That's about her father! *BABBino,*' Rob corrected. 'I thought you'd like that!'

'No, it's not! Why would she *say* "she'd throw herself off the bridge" – that's what the conductor said in his intro – it has to be about her baby that died or she gave up or something.'

'Vanessa, I *know* this. Stop contradicting me. It was one of Frank's favourites.'

'We'll ask Karen when the concert's over. She'll understand the Italian.'

Onstage, a chorus of singers had joined the orchestra and soloists and had begun singing very softly the beautiful

'*Va, pensiero*' from *Nabucco*, the piece more popularly known in English as the 'Chorus of the Hebrew Slaves'. The conductor turned around and was encouraging the audience. The hush of the amphitheatre was broken by spontaneous, melodic singing of the much-loved chorus.

The summer tourists, some of whom had travelled long distances to share the joy of attending a musical spectacle in the magnificent open-air setting, were on their feet and beginning the slow, tedious descent down the stone steps to exit the arena through the ancient structure's original arches. Rob had chivalrously given his cushion to Karen to sit on, and now took it back from her to carry. All around them were the happy sounds of people satisfied with the entertainment they had just heard – chattering and joking with each other.

Vanessa wouldn't let it go.

'Karen, you know that last song the soprano did – "Mio bambino" something or other—'

Rob and Karen responded in unison: '*Babb*ino.'

Rob persisted: 'Karen, please inform my wife that *babbino* is a pet name for "dad".'

'Oh,' Vanessa said, 'I always thought it was "bambino". I've heard it on the radio loads of times.'

'You and countless thousands!' Karen tried to make light of Vanessa's misinterpretation, as it seemed to be bugging Rob, judging by his tone of voice.

Stuck together as they were in the long queue, all he could do was comment: 'So, Daddy Dearest after all.'

———

There was palpable relief among all four when they finally reached the avenue that would take them outside the confines of the amphitheatre and back onto the town's streets. Karen and Davey were both familiar with the Mediterraneo Caffè, the rendezvous spot Isabelle had suggested to Vanessa for a post-concert drink. It was a regular haunt of theirs, which they had frequented from its opening days and the proprietor greeted them enthusiastically, as they descended the small steps from Via Teatro Greco to the open-air seating.

'*Buonasera! Ben tornati!*'

'*Grazie! Possibilità di un tavolo?* Goodness, you're really full!'

'*Fuori?* Not for one hour. It is the concert – they all come after.'

But Vanessa hadn't worked in television for three years without picking up a trick or two about using 'celebrity' status. She sidled up to Karen and the café owner and took control.

'Hi there! We had arranged to meet the orchestral conductor from the concert and his partner after the show. Perhaps they are here already?'

'*O sì!* Wait. I will ask Gianandrea – he sometimes puts aside a table. You are four?'

'Yes.'

'Mrs VIP, turning on the charm!' Karen laughed. 'Maybe the musos made a reservation.'

'I hate to break up the party, but I'm bloody starving. Could we not just go somewhere else?' Rob was kicking his shoes on the cobblestones, trying to dislodge imaginary dust. 'All I had to eat was a *panino* from a van on the way to the concert.'

Cecilia, the proprietor, was back. '*Sì*, the *maestro* has pre-ordered some food, which they will have inside. But Gianandrea has only reserved a table for two. However, we can give you a table nearby, where you can chat while they have their meal.'

Karen wondered if this was a bit intrusive. 'Nessa, maybe we should leave it – just wait and say "hello, well done" and, as Rob says, go somewhere else before last orders?'

'No, I don't think so. When you three were off doing your own thing all day, this lady was kind enough to keep me company on the beach and invited us to meet up.'

'For fuck's sake, it's nearly' – Rob checked his watch under the street light – 'eleven o'clock! We're never going to get anything to eat at this rate!'

A ripple of applause and a bit of commotion from tables on the Via Teatro Greco side of the café announced the arrival of the celebrity maestro and his blonde companion. She left him signing concert programmes and came around to the entrance, where she waved at Cecilia.

'Sorry we're so late. He was spending some time with the orchestra since it's the last concert.'

'No problem! I have your table ready. Your friends are already here.' She pointed to the two couples on the pavement.

Isabelle swung around and recognised Vanessa in the middle of the group. '*Ciao*! You made it after all!'

'Yes, it was great! Really something. We're just waiting . . . for a table.'

'Oh, join us. I'm sure he can stick another one on. Inside is not so popular with tourists.'

Rob, who was scrolling through his phone for the closing hours of the pizzeria at which they had eaten on the first night, tuned in.

'In*side*? In this heat. You're joking!'

Vanessa caught his arm and made the introductions. 'Rob, this is Isabelle, who I met at the beach club today. They're staying at our hotel too.'

'Well, not for long. We're off tomorrow. Pleased to meet you, Rob. Oh, here he is, *finally*! You're holding everyone up, Rico!'

'*Mi dispiace,* but it's not polite to rush people, when they have just paid your fee for the night! And now, we are to have more company?'

'I've asked Vanessa and Rob from Ireland and their friends to join us inside, as there are no tables free.'

Rico shook the linen jacket from his shoulders and silently went indoors to the corner table, where a discreet, white *Riservato* sign held centre stage in front of the candle.

By a quarter to midnight and with platters of bruschetta of various kinds devoured, dishes of comforting lasagne polished off and plates of cheese and fruit dotted across the three adjoining tables, the mood of everybody inside the Mediterraneo Caffè had mellowed. Once his hunger and thirst were satiated, even Rob was enjoying the good-natured banter with the chef and co-owner Gianandrea, who was recommending places to visit a bit beyond the walled confines of Taormina.

'Are all the beaches around here stony?' Vanessa asked. 'I didn't have the little shoes today, and it was quite uncomfortable.'

'It's sandy out around Letojanni – do you have a car?' Gianandrea asked.

Rob shook his head.

Cecilia appeared with a tray of flaming Sambucas on the house – in homage to the Sicilian village of the same name, and to toast the maestro whose concert had sent so many customers their way. She extinguished the blue flame from the *digestivo* and passed the little glasses around.

'Isn't that where your admirer is from – Sambuca?' The conductor put his arm around his girlfriend. 'You know, it is good we leave tomorrow – Isabelle here seems to have caught the eye of the hotel *geometra* Marcello! They have become best buddies!'

'Oh, we've encountered that Marcello as well,' Rob interjected. 'Haven't we, Vanessa?'

Vanessa grabbed the small *digestivo* glass and took a mouthful.

'*Piano, piano* . . . the glass is still hot,' Cecilia cautioned. 'You know, you can take the bus to Letojanni if it's sand you want. It's not far.'

'Or towards Capo dei Greci – there are some nice little coves out there,' Gianandrea concurred.

Cecilia laughed. 'Well, maybe stick to the hotel resort . . . you don't want any surprises!'

'Surprises?' Vanessa didn't follow.

'Let's say – there mightn't be much to appeal to couples like you – the sandy coves attract another clientele! Now, if you'll excuse me, some of *my* clientele want to pay.'

Karen observed that most of the outside tables were vacated. A couple of stragglers remained nursing a drink, but the food menus had been removed. 'Come on, guys. These people need to clear. And some of us have an early start in the morning.' She smiled at Vanessa.

The conductor and Isabelle were already at the counter, saying their goodbyes to the owners. At the table, Rob had his card in his hand, ready to pay. Cecilia dropped the bill and the card machine over to him and went back to hug Isabelle, before she waved them off. '*Alla prossima!*'

'*Speriamo*! Let's hope so, Cecilia. I love Taormina.'

'And it loves you two right back!'

'*Grazie per tutto*, Cecilia, Gianandrea.' Rico put his hand in the small of Isabelle's back and ushered her into the white taxi which had pulled up in the narrow street. 'Till next year.'

———

Vanessa linked Rob on the downhill walk back to La Villa. 'Strange that, getting a taxi for such a short trip.'

'Who? Oh, maestro and the mott.'

'Rob! You're so disrespectful.'

'Well, his wife she certainly ain't.'

'Who cares, these days?'

'You know I do.'

'You shouldn't be so judgemental. Live and let live.'

'Do you think so? Maybe that's exactly what I'll do. Live a little.'

'Do. And I might have a surprise of my own for you tomorrow.'

'I can't wait.'

Chapter 19

Honeymoon, Day 6

Whether it was the romance of the operatic concert, or the tranquilising effect of his favourite music, but Rob was most definitely in the mood for intimacy when he and Vanessa had returned late to La Villa the previous night. He was positively jovial, humming bars from some of the arias as they got ready for bed. Vanessa felt herself relax – it was so nice to experience the return of his affection, instead of the fluctuating prickly moods she'd had to endure all week.

When their usual non-penetrative lovemaking showed signs of continuing on to a normal, consensual conclusion, Rob paused, as if he were distracted by something.

'What's wrong?'

'I wonder – should I use something as well – since you're so determined not to get pregnant!'

'Rob!' But then she thought, why not? Just in case the clinic doctor put her on some weird antibiotic that upset her stomach and interfered with her pill. 'There's some in the bedside locker. Let me.'

'Well, you can *try*, but I don't hold out much hope for you.'

Vanessa observed the flaccid, 'no-longer-in-the-mood' penis and felt a strange mixture of relief and disappointment as Rob rolled away.

———

It was therefore a pleasant surprise, when despite things not working out the previous night, Rob was up and about very early – still singing. Maybe, Vanessa reasoned, this was all still part of the difficult adjustment period – not having lived together in any consistent way he found people – including her – in his space 24/7 very difficult.

So, when he began preparing his beach-bag, instead of badgering to accompany him, Vanessa encouraged him. 'An invigorating dip in the sea will do you the world of good. Enjoy!'

He pecked her on the cheek and left, now whistling the same aria as earlier, and strode down the path from the suite with a particular spring in his step.

Her encouragement was a trifle disingenuous. Without awaiting the nine-thirty delivery of her room service breakfast, she had thrown her phone and wallet into a cross-body bag, grabbed a bottle of water from the fridge and a banana from the fruit bowl, and headed out in hot pursuit of her husband.

This time she knew the route he took down to the Funivia but, when wandering around with Karen, she had learned a quicker route through the Naumachia lanes, avoiding the congested Corso Umberto. She had decided to lurk in one of the tacky souvenir shops directly opposite and hope she had made it ahead of him.

She saw him go down the steps of the cable-car station, his beach bag slung over his shoulder. He was wearing his particularly nice new surfer shorts that they had bought together before travelling. Even though she was spying on him, Vanessa thought he looked very attractive – more so than usual.

Already in possession of a booklet of tickets, she was able to bypass the sales hatch, and watched as Rob went through into the security holding area and waited for the incoming cable-car.

Vanessa held back until the last conceivable moment, then jabbed her ticket in the turnstile and followed the not-so-busy nine o'clock crowd into the waiting space. As before, the official opened the barrier, and the travellers rushed to seize their preferred pod.

Rob was in the second. Vanessa waited and climbed into the last. A family of Sicilians with inflatable toys – already inflated – were occupying a lot of space, the children high on excitement at the anticipation of the beach.

Once out into the car park of Mazzarò station, Vanessa knew the direction he should take. She could see his stripey T-shirt ahead of her but, unlike all the other early passengers, he turned left, away from the direction of Isola Bella beach. He checked his phone, and waited at a bus-stop.

Vanessa didn't know where to go. There wasn't much coverage on the busy, traffic-ridden Via Nazionale. She thought about popping into a coffee bar, but doubted she could see the stop from inside. Instead, she went into a beach shop and purchased a large straw sunhat, tucked her hair up under it and donned her sunglasses. She hoped she was practically unidentifiable.

Sitting on a bench a short distance down the road from the bus stop, Vanessa didn't have long to wait. The red tourist bus which travelled on a continuous loop serving the beaches arrived. By this time, there were five or six other people at the stop with Rob. As he boarded and paid the driver for his ticket, Vanessa watched as the destinations rolled in rotation in a LED display on its side. The now familiar names of Spisone, Mazzeo, Letojanni – and Capo dei Greci repeated. The bus pulled out, and headed on its journey.

Vanessa felt strange. She wondered about Rob's morning cheerfulness and his eagerness to be on his way. There was a lot of sea far nearer, if a swim was what you were after. No need to board a bus and travel – presumably kilometres – out the road.

Her phone diary reminder beeped. Ten o'clock was the

time she had agreed to meet Karen at the Medical Centre. It was now nine-forty.

She made her way to the Funivia which in ascending direction at this hour was quiet, and she was back in Taormina by five to ten, sitting on the same bollard as Karen had done the previous evening. Thankfully, the door to the *Clinica* was open this time, and patients were coming and going, though there was no sign of Karen.

It wasn't long before the inevitable message pinged. **'Sorry. Disorganised. Be with you soon – latest 10.20.'**

Rather than sit on the hard stone for a full twenty minutes, Vanessa had noticed that the small travel agency nearby where she had booked the tickets for a surprise yacht trip for Rob and herself, was already open. Since her initial visit, the agent had put a new poster in the window advertising the trip: a soft-focus backlit sunset with an indeterminate couple scoffing champagne.

Surprisingly, the travel agent remembered her when she pushed through the door, and with a wry smile he presented her with the tickets in a wallet wrapped in a colourful brochure, and wished her a lovely trip.

Back on her bollard, Vanessa studied the brochure. Although she couldn't understand all the Italian text, the word *'privacy'* in inverted commas in English caught her attention, as did the fact that as she browsed the different images most of the couples featured seemed to be male.

Had she inadvertently booked a trip to a gay beach? It wouldn't bother her – she loved her gay friends and colleagues – but might Rob be quite so relaxed about it? She dropped the envelope with the tickets into her bag as she noticed Karen sprinting up the side street towards her.

'Sorry, sorry! Davey has a bit of a gippy tummy this morning. Don't ask.'

'I hope it wasn't anything he ate at the café last night?'

'Doubt it. We've eaten there hundreds of times; it's a very reputable place – and sure neither you nor Rob are sick, are you?'

'No.'

'Will we go straight in, since I'm so late?'

'Probably best.'

The visit to the clinic was fast and efficient and having pee-ed on a stick, it was declared that yes, she did indeed have a UTI. The doctor wrote a prescription and they headed back to the pharmacy on the Corso to pick it up.

Vanessa completed her purchase and accompanied Karen to Nino's for her missed breakfast.

'Well, I'm all sorted. Hopefully it'll calm down soon.'

'I'm sure it will. You don't look in any way sick. You look very smart, by the way – I love those linen city-shorts on you *and* you're wearing your mam's locket. I haven't seen it on you till today.'

'Yeah. It's been in the safety deposit box all week – actually, the clasp was acting up on the day of the wedding

– it kept opening – but that was probably on account of the halter-neck of my dress. Then I thought – what the heck – it needs to be worn! I wondered was it too much – with this scarf? But I just felt like dressing up a bit this morning.'

'Good for you. And Rob? How's the form?'

'Fine. Good actually. Went off singing this morning for his swim!' Vanessa was still niggled by the sight of him boarding the bus, but Karen had no need to know this.

'So we have Happy Rob today! Nessa, has that fella had a bang on the head recently?'

Vanessa laughed.

'No, seriously. Could he be concussed? He seems to have undergone a bit of a personality change in the last couple of weeks.'

'Well, he *did* have about three HIAs during the Spring season, but the "return to play" protocol is very strict. They wouldn't let him back if he hadn't passed them.'

'I mean . . . he was always a bit . . . earnest – the Christian thing, even the abstinence business – but he was also good fun, particularly on the rugby scene. Now, he just seems . . . distracted – almost unhappy most of the time.'

'Maybe he's stopped trying to please everybody. Perhaps he was on his best behaviour before – and now because we're married, he's relaxed enough to be himself.'

'Secure in the knowledge that he *has* you? That's worse!'

Vanessa felt downhearted. She thought of her early morning sleuthing and tried to recall some of the less familiar names from the side of the bus. She took out her phone and pulled up the local map, swiping along the coast to see would any ring a bell.

'What are you engrossed in now?' Karen licked cappuccino froth from her lip.

'Do you remember last night – when the owner of the café made a joke about some resort – the one with the coves? "Capo" something or other?'

'Capo dei Greci. Yes.'

'Have you and Davey ever been there?'

'Only once. To the resort hotel of the same name, which is lovely. It's a bit out of the way.'

'Is it a gay beach?'

'Well, it's not a beach per se. There are small beach inlets all around there, quite a few. I had heard that area was popular with the gay community – men in particular.'

Vanessa reached into her handbag. 'Brilliant. One of those secluded coves is the swim stop-off for the yacht-trip I've organised! Here, look at the brochure.'

The window poster imagery was replicated on the ticket coupon. Two bronzed males gazed at the ocean. One had his arm draped languidly across his mate's shoulder.

'Just tell the skipper you want to stay on board.'

'And have Rob sulk with no beach time? You know how obsessed he's become with his solo swim.'

Once she heard herself say it out loud, the dominoes clattered one by one down the steps. Vanessa looked at Karen, whose averted eyes told her she was thinking the very same thing.

When they parted, Vanessa half-ran, half-fell through the maze of streets near the medical centre. Her heart was thumping hard, not precipitated by the steep incline or any lack of fitness on her part, but by an uncomfortable feeling that she had stumbled upon something she did not want to.

Could he be? Was this the explanation for the lack of interest in sex throughout their relationship? Or was she reading too much into it? Perhaps he was just what he professed – a right-wing, committed Catholic who took his religion more seriously than she did.

But then she thought of his impatient desire to have children and his sarcasm at her being on the Pill. What if he thought that by fathering a child or two, he had the ultimate, tangible confirmation of his heteronormative status, something that now as she began to think about it seemed very important to him? Since he hadn't shown much interest in the carnal enjoyment of *her* body, perhaps he wanted to have minimal sex with her, but with maximal opportunity to become a dad!

Vanessa felt sick. She needed to talk to someone. What she really needed was her father. She longed to be a teenager again when she could just run into the shabby sitting-room in Allenbeg, fling herself on him in his armchair and bawl crying like she had done dozens of times, with the wail: 'It's not fair. It's *just not fair.*' He would act all embarrassed and complain that he couldn't see the match on the telly, but what he really wanted was to stem the heart-breaking flow of her tears, to hold her and hug the pain away, to banish the suffering and protect her forever from the hurt and torment that the world might throw at her.

Because he loved her. He loved her more than any man would ever do. He was her ally, he was her confidant, he was her tease, he was her back-up. He was her coach, he was her adviser. He was her best friend.

And he wasn't there.

She pulled the phone out of her bag and scrolled down to 'D'. It rang and rang but he didn't pick up. Finally, it switched to voicemail: 'Hello Johnny Walshe – that's – *I'm* Johnny Walshe – *ah, feck it* – you know what I mean. Leave a message.' Karen's voice could be heard admonishing in the background: '*You can't say that! Do it again.*'

'Daddy,' Vanessa's voice broke into sobs, 'I need you. Can you come down to the Villa? Quickly. It's Rob . . . I'm afraid—' But as she passed under the arch of the Porta Catania, the signal dropped and the call cut off.

She hadn't really worked out yet what she was going to say to Rob – or how she was going to broach the subject, but she thought she should talk to her father first and get his input. It wasn't likely that Rob would be back already, given his journey. She really wanted to have the place to herself when her dad arrived.

When she opened the door to the room, all was quiet. The chambermaid had been and the place was immaculate, scented with the lovely lemon spray she used. Vanessa went into the lounge, turned on the stereo pre-set at some easy-listening Italian music station and filled the miniature kettle to make tea for her father. She took her phone out of her bag to check if he'd left a message. Nothing yet. She was sure he'd be on his way soon. She began to calm down. She added water to the Espresso machine and, as she was firing it up, she noticed Marcello and the gardener in the adjacent plot. Still embarrassed by Rob's rudeness on the surveyor's last visit, she went out onto the terrace phone in hand, and called over to them.

'*Buongiorno!*'

''*Giorno, signora.*'

'Marcello, could I have a word, please?'

'Of course!' He muttered in Italian to his colleague, swung his leg over the railing and walked onto the terrace.

'I just wanted to apologise for the behaviour of my husband the other evening. He was a bit impolite.'

'*Non c'è problema, signora.* But, how are *you*? He is very *geloso* – how do you say it – jullus?'

'*Jeal*ous. No, it's not that really. He's just a bit over-protective. How's the work going?'

'Come over to the boundary and I will show you.'

'I was just making a coffee. Would you like one?'

'*Sì!* That would be good.'

'I'll just—' Vanessa nodded towards the French doors and went in to prepare another capsule for the machine.

When she emerged a few minutes later with the coffees on a platter, Marcello had spread a drawing out on the larger of the terrace tables.

'Would you like to see the plans? Here, your room will be part of the new building. It will go over to now where is the lemon grove.'

'Ah, not the lemon trees, Marcello! You're not going to cut them down!'

'Not all will be affected. We will move the two large and replant some smaller ones in their place. The big ones – they will go back in this garden where is now the bad grass.'

'That's a good idea – it's really too bumpy for grass. Plus they'll hide that fence which has seen better days. And what about that olive?' Vanessa pointed to a mature tree to the left of the terrace.

'*Peccato,* that has to go. It is right where will be the new building.' Marcello turned over the first A2 page, then the second. '*Che strano!* I had an illustration of a new olive grove to go out the front. Perhaps I left the paper inside when I measure the wall. *Permesso?*'

Marcello gesticulated towards the French doors.

'Of course.'

As the surveyor looked around for his missing drawing, Vanessa tried to imagine the new extension.

Marcello re-appeared at the door.

'*Scusi, signora.* Can I possibly use the bathroom?'

'Of course. You know where it is.'

Marcello put his phone on the sideboard and went through the bedroom to the ensuite.

The draught of air rushing through the room caused the hall door to slam loudly behind whoever had just come in. Marcello came back out of the bathroom to be confronted by Rob.

Chapter 20

Honeymoon, Day 6

'Well, would you look who it is! *What* are you doing in our bathroom?'

'Washing my hands –'

'I thought I *warned* you the other evening, but you don't seem to learn that fast.' Rob grabbed Marcello by the shirt – then thought better of it – and let him go.

Vanessa, hearing raised voices, folded the two large drawings, tucked them under her arm and hurried into the sitting area. Through the arch she saw Rob and could tell by his stance that he was angry.

'Oh hi. I didn't hear you come in. Did you have a nice morning?' She offered the papers to the surveyor. 'Did you find the other drawing you were looking for? Rob, Marcello was just showing me the plans for the new development and where they're going to replant the lemon trees. It will really enhance the façade of the hotel. You should have a look.'

'*What do I care about the fucking façade of the hotel? With a bit of luck, I'll never see this dive again!*'

'Why don't we all go outside?' said Vanessa. 'I'll make some coffee.'

Marcello didn't have to be asked twice. He strode past Vanessa, picking up the third drawing as he went. 'No coffee for me, *signora. Grazie.*'

'Rob? Are you sure you wouldn't like a quick look at the plans?'

'*No, I would not!*'

He strode out after Marcello.

'*And if you've finished doing whatever it was you were doing – would you get the fuck off the property I am paying extortionate money for! And take that other cretin with you!*'

The shocked gardener was avoiding the aggression from the safety of the lemon trees. Both men scarpered out the side gate.

Vanessa left the shady terrace and walked down onto the uneven ground. The scorched, hay-like grass was bathed in sunshine. She stared out at the view and toyed nervously with her necklace.

Rob followed. 'I'm sorry. That guy just winds me up. *And* I'm not the only one! Didn't you hear that conductor man – Rocco – say the same thing?'

'*Rico.* And no, he was only teasing his girlfriend about flirting with Marcello. It was completely good-humoured.'

'Whereas?'

'Whereas your reaction to him is completely over-the-top. Possessive. Aggressive, even! Rob, I'm tired of it. Tired of your moodiness. I can talk to whoever I want.'

'But you're my wife.'

'Yes, who can still talk to other people! And, anyway, you haven't been treating me . . . much like a wife.'

'Ah, not this bloody sex thing again!'

'Not just that, Rob. You keep *vanishing* on me! And if you mention "space" one more time!'

Rob exhaled hard and strode to the terrace, lifting the two light canvas deckchairs and carrying them back down to the bumpy grass where he set them up in the sun.

Hesitatingly, Vanessa sat. The chair didn't seem too stable on the grass.

Rob remained on his feet.

She looked up at him. Her breath was coming fast.

'Look, Rob . . .' She almost lost courage. 'Look, this isn't an easy conversation to have – but I think I might . . . understand . . . why you've been . . . *strange* about having sex with me.'

'What are you talking about now?'

She forced herself to say it.

'You prefer men, don't you?'

Rob raised his eyebrows in astonishment and lowered his head towards Vanessa in the chair.

'*What?* Have you been drinking, Mrs Cunningham?'

'*Stop.* I'm being serious. *Is* it true? Am I right?'

Rob flinched and rubbed his chin anxiously. 'Now *you're* the one sounding like you've been out in the sun too long! Why on earth would you – *imagine* – this?'

265

'If it's true, you can't keep living a lie.'

'*Who's* living a *lie*? What rubbish is this? *I am not gay!* Haven't I just married you, for Christ's sake?'

'Was that – oh, I feel sick even *saying* this – was that part of your plan – to deflect attention from your true inclination?'

'I can't listen to this!' Rob kicked the deckchair he had yet to sit on, and it fell over on its side. He gave it a couple of additional boots and it did a 360-degree roll a metre or two towards the boundary marker. He began pacing back and forth. Vanessa stood up – her sudden movement causing the light chair to tip backwards – and went after him.

'Rob. I followed you. This morning. And yesterday. And neither day did you go for a quick dip to Isola Bella beach.'

'You've been *spying* on me! This gets worse!'

'The first morning I genuinely wanted to surprise you, but you lied about where you were going.'

'You misheard.'

'You know full well I didn't. But this morning, you headed off on that bus . . . the one that serves all those beaches. Including Letojanni – and the infamous Capo dei Greci.'

'Your point being?'

'I don't know . . . maybe to link up with one of the Cork lads? Or some anonymous Sicilian in the coves off Capo dei Greci.'

'You've lost the plot entirely!' Rob turned away from her and focussed on the sea.

Vanessa waited a couple of minutes, then followed him

to the boundary. 'But *have I*, Rob? *Look at me. Look into my eyes. Tell* me the truth. I deserve that at least.'

Rob made a fist and thumped the bleached, grey timber of the fence.

'Stop that! You'll break a bone in your hand. God, I feel like thumping you myself! How *could* you do this to me? String me along – let me go through the – the public *humiliation* of a fancy, media wedding – all for nothing – I don't know – just to be in the spotlight for a while? To convince people you're heterosexual? What *were* you thinking of?'

For the first time since the awkward conversation began, Rob looked worried. His ruddy glow had deserted him and his usual glib ripostes just did not come. He exhaled heavily. 'I thought I could carry it off.' He hung his head, leaned against the fence, turning his back on the view.

'*Carry it off?* You're not acting a part in a play! This is my *life!*'

'I'm sorry.'

'Sorry doesn't cut it.'

'You wouldn't understand. I . . . I want to live my life like all the other guys on the team – to fit in.'

'By pretending you're not gay? That's crazy! And, besides, nobody has an issue anymore with people being gay.'

'You *think?*'

'Society has moved on. People don't care about sexual orientation.'

267

'Maybe in fashion or media! Try sport and see how well it fits.'

'Oh, you're wrecking my head with all this! Surely there are gay rugby players? In fact, I think I've even interviewed one.'

'*One*. Think about that. And I – *know* I could be a great player – for my country even – but I'm not popular.'

'There are different ways to be popular.'

'Well, I'm not "media-friendly" or even "photogenic" enough to secure a sponsorship deal – or to be plastered all over the newspapers—'

'So you're using *me* to attract a potential sponsor – this gets worse! *Please stop, Rob!*'

Vanessa could feel the tears coming. She wanted to be anywhere but in the sticky heat of this hotel garden with nobody she knew nearby to console her. Then she remembered the panicky voicemail she had left for her father. What on earth would he make of this, when she told him?

'Vee, please. Don't tell anyone. Let's just continue as we are.' Rob caught her gently by both arms. 'We get on . . . most of the time, don't we? We're good friends, *and* I don't find the thought of sex with you repulsive. Why would I? You're lovely!'

Vanessa sighed, and momentarily relaxed, leaning her head against his shoulder. 'I can't, Rob. I couldn't share your sexuality with someone else – because that would be what you'd be asking of me.'

'Please. Try.' He ran the hand-painted scarf she was wearing through his hands as he spoke. 'Look! Do you remember when we bought this?'

'Yes. In that little hilltop village outside Nice.'

'Saint Paul de Vence – full of artists. I was so pissed off after we'd been knocked out by Racing that the last place I wanted to go in my first weekend off in months was France. Yet it turned out to be a great trip. *You* did that: you made me forget the disappointment.'

'That was early in our relationship. I knew hardly anything about you.'

'But don't you see? We were fine together – happy even!'

'That was then. Things have moved on. I can't pretend to *not* know what I know now. It would end up killing us both. Even this week – you've been out of sorts, *so* unhappy stuck with me all the time in your new role as husband. If you're like this after – less than a week – what would you be like after six months, a year?'

'Because it's been hard for me and a bit claustrophobic with your family watching our every move!'

'Don't lay it on them! We've hardly seen them at all. And you have found ways to escape – to find . . . solace . . . elsewhere, haven't you?' She pulled out of his arms and took a step backwards. 'I'm not a fool, Rob. There's plenty of places to swim – nearer here.'

His eyes began to water. 'I'm sorry.'

'And I am sorry for you, that you don't feel able to be honest. But this isn't what I signed up for! You've made a complete fool of me. You're not the only one with a public image. Did you ever consider that? The harm to *my* reputation?'

'Please, Vee. Don't publicly turn your back on our marriage and humiliate me. Have you – told anyone – of your – suspicions?'

'Not yet. Though Karen might have an inkling.'

'Great! Then that's Davey and all that lot! Thanks a bunch!'

'Hey, don't go putting this on me! You're the one living a double life! Look, I'm willing to try and dissolve the marriage privately – maybe get an annulment on the grounds that it was never consummated. I'm sure Uncle Joe could help you with that. Then you might have to consider coming out and being who you *really* are.'

'Can't you see? That's the whole point! I don't *want* to be who I am! I want to be a popular, hetero guy – a *family* guy! I don't want to be "out and proud". I don't want to be "out" at all. Just because there are rainbow flags hanging from the rafters, doesn't mean I want one draped around my neck!'

'That, Rob, I can't help you with.'

Rob began to pace. 'And if you start to talk about this publicly, I'll deny it. *Who* do you think is going to believe you? After all the shared rooms on trips away, the hundreds of photos in the public domain with our bodies wrapped so tightly around each other you couldn't squeeze a ten-cent coin between us!'

'We could make a formal statement later on about the split – "irreconcilable differences" or something like that.'

'That always means sex! Which would point the finger firmly back at *me* and my sexual prowess! No, that's not happening. I can't allow it.'

Vanessa watched as Rob's pacing increased. He began to do some exercises – a couple of squats, then some stretches. His face was contorted in tension and anxiety. He finished his mini-workout by giving the boundary fence a couple of punches.

'Rob! Enough. You really will hurt your hand!'

'I need to think. I think better when I'm exercising.'

'Well, I'm going inside. I'm thirsty.'

'Wait. I'll just deny it. I'll say that it was *your* fault – the lack of sex thing. That you and that tramp, Jenny, were practically running a knocking shop in the apartment you shared and I was afraid I'd catch something nasty from you. Remember, there are two careers on the line here!'

'You're being ridiculous now.'

'Ridiculous, is it? You'd humiliate me and let the whole rugby world think I was gay – and it's *me* who's being ridiculous?'

'Now, Rob, I've given you a reasonable way out, so grasp it with both hands. Or I'll do what I have to. Let me pass.'

'*What if I don't?*'

'There's no need for aggression.' Vanessa clasped the locket around her throat for reassurance. She was beginning to feel nervous. 'We can sort this out – amicably.'

271

'You always think you're right, don't you? You and your smug, perfect family!'

Rob's face flushed red with temper as he grabbed both sides of the flimsy scarf Vanessa was wearing, crossing it over on itself to encase her neck. Without warning, he pulled at the ends of the scarf, tightening it on her throat.

Stunned by his action, Vanessa beat at him with her fists.

'Rob! What are you doing! Stop! You'll choke me!'

Johnny had tried the doorbell four times with no success. There was music playing inside. He thought he heard the sound of voices somewhere in the not too far distance. The unlocked side-gate gave a loud squeak as it swung on its hinges. He'd try going around to the back through those lemon trees.

As he crossed onto the terrace, he saw Vanessa and Rob standing close together, the upturned deckchairs strewn on the grass near them. There was something about the clinch of the couple that looked to him far from romantic. In her phone message, Vanessa had said she was afraid . . .

He saw Rob's hands near her throat . . .

He sprinted across the paved area and accelerated his pace over the bumpy grass, hurling his body at Rob with all the strength and momentum he could summon.

'Noooooooooo!'

As Johnny thudded into Rob's side like a man possessed, his startled son-in-law let go of his grip on Vanessa, and both men fell to the ground. The impact of their collision flung Vanessa clear forcefully, where she crashed backwards into the low boundary fence. Despite windmilling her arms to try and save herself, the momentum carried her over, letting her fall, fall, fall screaming down the steep slope to the rocky scrubland below.

Chapter 21

Honeymoon, Day 6

In the works office Marcello reached into the pocket of his combat shorts for his phone, but it wasn't there. In an instant, he could visualise it – still sitting where he had left it – on the sideboard in the living room of the honeymoon suite. The honeymoon suite of all places – where that paranoid, jealous man was staying!

He was not going back for it alone, but he needed the phone urgently, as many of the contractors only had that number and he was expecting call-backs from several. This was one for the hotel manager, who had already heard of his altercations with Signor Cunningham.

Taking the key, the manager agreed it was wiser to accompany his colleague and they crossed the courtyard to the side wing.

As Marcello believed the residents were still in, both men waited patiently as they knocked on the front door.

No-one answered. Italian music was playing from inside – Radio Margherita that the *signora* had been listening to earlier. The manager knocked more authoritatively a second time.

'Maybe they can't hear with the music,' suggested the surveyor. 'Will I go around the side way through the lemon grove?'

'Not you. *I'll* go. I'm reluctant to use the key, if you are so convinced that they are at home.'

Before the manager could move, a high-pitched scream cut through the ambient noise.

'*Dio mio!* What was that?'

Both men ran around the side of the building, where they found Signor Cunningham and another older man whom Marcello had not seen before, standing at the boundary fence. The grey-haired man had one foot on the lower rung and was swinging his leg over the timber divider.

'Will – you – ring – a fuckin' ambulance – *now!*' he said as he jumped down on the other side.

'My wife!' gasped Signor Cunningham to the manager. 'She's fallen down the cliff!'

At this, the manager went into professional mode, dialling and barking information in Italian.

Marcello hopped up onto the fence and over it. Still holding on to the fence rail, he leaned down, grabbed Johnny's arm and tried to pull him back up the metre or so he had managed to descend.

'*Vieni, è pericoloso! It's too dangerous! You also will fall!*'

275

'My daughter . . . my baby!'

Rob had his mobile out, frantically jabbing at the emergency call. He then tried to follow the other two over the fence, but the manager put a restraining hand on his arm. Rob could see no sign of Vanessa. Immediately below, there was nothing visible but rock-face, punctuated every so often with overgrown scrub and broom and other plants able to survive the barren ground. If he leaned over further, he could make out more dense vegetation lower down – hopefully, that was obscuring the spot where she was lying.

Pulling and persuading, Marcello managed to get Johnny back over the fence.

As more hotel staff piled into the small garden, Rob decided to take control. 'Please, we need to do something before this ambulance arrives. Do you have a rope or climbing equipment in the hotel?'

A man ran and returned with a sturdy rope.

As Rob liaised with Marcello about something solid to fix it to, the manager was trying to dissuade him, saying the fire brigade had also been called and they had better equipment. He checked his watch and said he should really go out onto the road to flag them down.

A woman with a first-aid kit stood redundantly beside a doctor with an old-fashioned leather bag.

Without warning, Rob turned on Johnny. *'You fool! You bloody jealous, interfering fool'* And with that, he swung at his father-in-law with a clumsy right hook.

But one of Johnny's other juvenile sports had been

boxing and he was too quick for his assailant. His fists were raised immediately in defensive position, Rob's one and only weak blow his sole contact. Johnny struck out at his son-in-law, hitting him in the face several times.

'*Now!* Look what *you're* responsible for, you *gobshite!*'

'*Signori, calmatevi!*' cried Marcello.

The first-aid woman hovered expectantly as blood gushed from Rob's nose. '*Permesso?*' She advanced with some cotton wool and antiseptic, cleaned the nose and produced a wodge of cotton to stem the flow, as blood persisted in dripping onto Rob's T-shirt.

'I just can't stand here doing nothing!' Rob, now with a wad of cotton stuck up his nose, was calling out down the slope. '*Nessa! Nessa!*' He turned to nobody in particular. 'Have you got a megaphone or something, just so she might hear us and know help is coming?'

A waiter scuttled across the terrace towards the building in search of one.

Then, piercing the sound of birdsong and the distant thrum of ordinary traffic, was the unmistakeable whine of emergency vehicles. It was the fire brigade. Firemen raced around the side of the suite, secured their tether and one officer in a harness was lowered down the rock-face.

Johnny, now weakened by the fisticuffs and his emotional distress, sat on the end of a teak lounger, the hotel's first-aid officer trying to ply him with something to drink.

Rob stood at the fence, surprised by the speed at which the fireman abseiled down the rocky slope.

Radio communication from the abseiler to the fire captain said that he had reached Vanessa, but he didn't think it wise to move her. The manager relayed the information to Rob. She seemed to have had a double fall – tumbling down through the scrub initially where she went over at the steepest part. Then it appeared she might have tried to grab hold of a bush to break her further descent – an uprooted broom suggested this – but the shallow-rooted plant hadn't held – and she fell further, landing on a stone ledge, where her inert body now lay. It was the second fall that appeared to have done the damage.

Then the fireman relayed a further message and the manager updated Rob.

Johnny left his seat and approached, sensing a development. '*In the name of God, is there any news?*'

The fire captain looked to the hotel manager, knowing his English wasn't up to the job.

'*Signori*, yes, the ambulance knows the precise location of the lady and has decided it would be better to approach through the residential streets below, where the paramedics can climb up and assess her on the ground. If necessary, they have the use of the helipad in the Palace hotel and the helicopter is on standby if she has to be air-lifted out.'

'*She's bad, isn't she?*' Johnny pulled distractedly at his hair. '*Would one of you tell me?*'

Rob turned away and began walking towards the terrace and indoors.

'*Signor Cunningham!*' The manager ran after Rob. 'I will

take you to the lower road in my car. And the other gentleman?'

'He can make his own way.'

When Johnny was left behind at La Villa, he became audibly distraught, searching the terrace and the garden for his bum-bag, which must have fallen off in the earlier spat with Rob.

The doctor tried to calm him down and work out where he fitted into the picture.

'*Calmati, calmati, signore!* What are we looking for?'

'My phone. It's in that bum-bag yoke. I need to call . . . my family.'

'Are you related to the poor *signora?*'

'I'm her daddy.' And with that Johnny sat heavily into one of the now up-righted deckchairs and began to cry.

The Sicilian doctor needed no more information as to the importance of this quest and waved at one of the remaining staff members to help him. The young waiter found an iPhone with a sparkly cover on the terrace table, but when he presented it to Johnny his eyes filled up as he declared it was his daughter's. Minutes later, the nylon waist-bag, its plastic clasp broken, was retrieved in the high grass pushing through the fence at the end of the garden.

With trembling fingers, Johnny pulled out the phone and tried unsuccessfully to find his saved numbers. The doctor took the phone from him and asked who he should be looking for.

———

Karen was the first to get the news. She was initially puzzled – and then worried – by the foreign accent purporting to be Johnny, and when that voice announced ominously '*There's been an accident*', her sense of foreboding centred on Johnny himself. She was thrown a minute later when her father-in-law's tearful voice came on the line.

'*It's Nessa,*' he croaked. '*Something bad has happened.*'

Her gut reaction was that the bad thing related to Rob. Did she follow him out to the beach to see *which* particular stretch he frequented and had he turned nasty? Or had she been foolish enough to accuse him outright of being gay or bisexual or whatever he was – because in the world of Rob such an idea would be deemed an *accusation*. In fact, the thing that concerned Karen as she waited for Johnny to stop crying and expand, was how she could conjure up several scenarios in which 'bad things' might happen to Vanessa, all with Rob centre-stage.

'Oh Karen, she fell down the rocky slope – the bit at the back of their hotel. The ambulance is trying to locate her from where she's ended up. There's a road nearer to her lower down. It's gone for her now.'

'Oh my God! Is she badly hurt? And what do you mean the ambulance is "*gone for her*"? Where are *you*?'

'Still at the hotel – *I'll be with you in a minute, thanks –* they're going to drive me to the access point.'

'Johnny, can you put on one of the Italian staff? I'm very confused!'

'*What are you confused about? She fell over the fuckin' boundary fence, bounced down the cliff and is lying flat out on a concrete ledge, unconscious. Are you clear now? I'm off.*'

Karen held on tightly to the phone. The line was still not disconnected. She had moved to close it when she heard her father-in-law's gruff voice: 'Tell Davey.' And then Johnny's name disappeared from the screen.

Tell Davey. But tell Davey what? 'Your sister has had a fall' – *How? Where?* – 'Sorry, don't know. Your dad is on the way to her now, to meet the ambulance' – *Where?* – 'Sorry, don't know.' – *How bad is she?* – 'Bad.'

In all of this, there had been no mention of Rob. Was he with her when she fell? Or had they had another row and he'd gone back down to that infernal beach?

When Karen heard the church bells chime, it occurred to her that the surprise yacht trip Vanessa had planned was for *this* afternoon. In an hour's time, they should have been sailing out of the Bay of Mazzarò along the picturesque coastline and on their way to a champagne picnic in a secluded cove near the Capo dei Greci.

Hospital San Pietro, 22.10

Johnny, Karen and Davey sat in stunned silence in the relatives' room at the hospital. Rob had been taken away by a nurse, to formally identify the deceased.

Vanessa Walshe had died at 21.34, July 12th.

It wasn't surprising that the family sat in silence nor that the silence could be described as 'stunned'. What else could it be, given the speed and traumatic circumstances of losing their beautiful daughter, wife, sister – and friend – in a flash – in an unfortunate fall. There one minute, bronzed and glowing, emanating life and energy – gone the next, stretched out an unforgiving slab of concrete, white and listless.

Rob, an ashen pallor invading his ruddy complexion, returned with the consultant.

'*Signori*, you are the family of the late Vanessa Walshe?'

'Cunningham. Vanessa *Cunningham,*' Rob insisted in the tone of a man who had repeated this quite a few times over the previous eight hours.

'I am Professor Garafano. Firstly, my condolences at your tragic loss.'

Karen cried into a hanky, tears and snot mingling to the degree that she had to finish it off with a nose-blow, and dispose of the disgusting thing.

'As you know, the *signora* took a bad fall from a height. She suffered a traumatic brain injury – basically, she fractured her skull when she banged it on the concrete.'

Now it was Johnny's turn: tears rolled prolifically down his cheeks. He wished he could stick his fingers in his ears

282

in order to avoid hearing medical terminology used to describe parts of his daughter.

'Normally, when a patient has had a fall, we would not be too worried about early unconsciousness – it is bleeding we have to be aware of.' The doctor checked his notes. 'On her first and second CT scan – still unconscious – the patient showed some swelling, but no evidence of a bleed. However, as the afternoon wore on, a further MRI showed a serious epidural haematoma had developed and we were forced to perform an emergency cranial intervention to try and relieve the pressure. When we opened her – *insomma* – it was too far advanced and although we tried very hard, we could not stop the bleeding. *Mi dispiace.* I am sorry.'

The silence was punctuated by snuffles and sobs.

Rob looked shell-shocked but remained dry-eyed. 'Why didn't you intervene earlier? You said you didn't open her up till late in the afternoon.'

'That is correct, but the procedure itself is highly invasive and risky. When she was showing no signs of cranial bleeding, it would not have been the thing to do.'

'And now – she is dead!' Rob tilted his head in derision.

'I know you need answers. The hospital will carry out a post-mortem, to see if there was perhaps any other underlying condition of Signora Walshe.'

Johnny didn't like the idea of them cutting Vanessa again. 'And this post-mortem, do you *have* to do it?'

'I am afraid so. Also, the *Carabinieri* will request the PM findings from us to support any investigation they may need to do. Don't worry. If it is all clear, the body will be released back to you in a few days. Again, my sympathies.'

The door closed behind the consultant. Johnny stood up from his chair. 'I'm going – to sit with her a while.' He raised his hand in a stop gesture. 'Just me.'

Karen looked around for her handbag. 'I'd better ring the hotel.' And, more gently, she addressed Rob. 'Can I call anyone for you – your mother, Frank?'

Rob held his head in his hands and didn't answer. Karen left the room to make her call.

'Ah, man, this is awful. Just *awful.*' Davey scratched his already blotchy nose.

The door opened.

Karen sat into the chair beside Rob. 'The police have cordoned off the terrace and the rear of . . . your suite. So you'll have to move to another room – or hotel – if you'd prefer. Would you like me to ask Giulia if there's availability down at ours?'

'What about our things – *her* things – all her lovely things—' Rob balled his whitened knuckles into his eyes, as tears finally came.

Karen hunkered down beside him and put a comforting hand on his arm.

'I'm sure the staff will pack for you – that's if you want them to.'

Rob dropped his hands and looked at her in despair.

And for the first time since they had come to Sicily, Karen saw his vulnerability return and felt sorry for him.

Chapter 22

Honeymoon, Day 7

L a Villa had a visit from both the town *Polizia* and the more serious crimes *Carabinieri*. The honeymoon suite with its private terrace and garden was now the focus of attention for uniformed officers, its patio area and side access cordoned off with ticker-tape. Contrary to Karen's belief that the chambermaids might pack Rob and Vanessa's things, a white-gloved female *carabiniere* was conducting a very close examination of the entire suite's contents and was not admitting any staff.

On arrival at La Villa, Davey was worried by the prominent police presence. He hadn't been able to get a clear picture from anybody as to how exactly his sister had ended up on a rocky ledge with a fractured skull, halfway down an inaccessible rocky outcrop. He was disinclined to push it with his dad, given his age and obvious emotional state, and he was taken aback by how Rob seemed genuinely in shock.

The hotel manager had been tipped off by the taxi driver that the family were finally on their way back from the hospital, having observed an overnight vigil by Vanessa's side. When the Walshes arrived, he was already out in the courtyard to greet the people-carrier.

'*Signora, signori*, my sincere condolences. What a dreadful, dreadful accident! Please come inside to my office for a refreshment.'

The normally dapper group looked like they had slept for two nights under the footbridge at the railway station. Their clothes were creased and some had coffee and tea stains on them. Rob had somehow managed a speedy change somewhere; his distracted state might have accounted for the odd combination he was wearing – a formal linen shirt with gaudy surfer shorts. He was normally 'just so'. Johnny was still in his 'fighting' shirt and trousers – Rob's nosebleed blood clearly visible among the splodges and stains. Davey didn't look too dirty – just strange. He had been on a cycling trip the previous morning and in the process of stripping out of his clothes to hop into the shower when the first call from Karen came through. His discarded top already lay on the bathroom floor and he thought he'd have a quick wash and jump into his clean clothes before calling her back. But when her insistent second call came, he had dragged on the nearest cotton shirt over his cycling shorts and left.

Karen still looked like Karen, but the stained, sweaty little top that she was wearing had been pristine less than two days previously, bought as a gift by her now dead sister-in-law. She rubbed the cotton between her fingers, as if it were a genie's lamp that could magic Vanessa back to life.

The ordeal had taken its toll on the Walshes. They were oblivious to their appearance, but it was so at variance with the sharp-jacketed cut of the hotel manager that an onlooker might be forgiven for thinking La Villa had entered into a benevolent programme for housing refugees, and this was one of the first parties to arrive.

Once inside, the manager cut to the chase. He was very sorry, he said, about the dreadful accident that befell Signora Walshe. Obviously, the hotel was very distressed at the death of such a lovely client. However, the poor *signora* fell to her death on common land outside the boundary of the hotel, over a clearly marked barrier fence that warned not to go there in three languages – *Pericolo! Danger! Achtung!* At this, the manager took a breather – fanned himself with a convenient brochure from his desk – and said: '*Madonna*, the poor lady, what *was* she trying to do?'

———

That was also a question which would interest the *carabinieri* who came later in the afternoon to take their statements. True to his promise of offering any assistance he could, the hotel manager had given the family access to a suite for the day, so at least when they faced the police, they would do so clean. The interview was scheduled for three o'clock.

Johnny really needed to get a change of clothes and, somewhat out of character – particularly after their fraught altercation the previous day – it was Rob first in with the offer to accompany him in a taxi up to the Castelmola hotel. That gave Karen and Davey plenty of time to go down to their own central hotel and sort themselves out.

But not before Davey had diverted to the side wing and appealed to the better nature of the young policeman on sentry duty outside the suite, to allow him see the spot from which his sister had taken her final plunge. The policeman checked with the *carabiniere* inside and she agreed, provided he accompany Davey and Karen.

There was something angry about the obviously pretty little terrace. Aggressive ticker-tape zig-zagged from the lemon grove railing on the left, across the flagstones of the patio to the right, finally looping through the handles of the French doors of the rear entrance. It looked like urban Hallowe'en decoration run amok.

The teak lounger which Vanessa had adored was for some reason standing on its side, and the boundary fence now had police crush barriers in front of it. A couple of deckchairs were folded and stacked beside the fateful drop.

Davey approached the fence tentatively. The rugged, unattractive terrain and sheer descent the far side of the timber barrier should have been a deterrent to anyone thinking of climbing over for whatever reason. The manager's information had been accurate. The multilingual warning signs were posted at two-metre intervals on the hotel garden side.

Karen held Davey's hand as she peered down to the road below. She had this worrying suspicion of it all getting too much for Vanessa. But she wasn't the type – surely not?

'*Signora, signore!* Time to go.' The policeman was hovering.

And it was time to go – time for Davey and Karen to head *home* to the comfort of their familiar base – to the sympathy and affection of the hotel staff who after five years were more friends than sycophantic serving staff. Besides, there was the little issue of two fresh outfits required for their afternoon appointment with the police.

———

In the tall-windowed drawing room of La Villa, the Walshe family sat nervously around the polished walnut table, awaiting the arrival of the police.

The *maître d'* – no longer in the habit of serving beverages or anything else to clients due to his senior role – had just this once agreed to demean himself and placed a tray with tea, coffee, water and a plate of small pastries on a cloth in the centre of the table. He distributed place mats and crockery. No sooner had he left than he was back again, ushering in the two *carabinieri*.

The female *carabiniere* led the interview. With a svelte figure not typical of most Sicilian women of her age, the immaculate dark-navy uniform flattered her neat waist. She introduced herself and did her best to put everyone at their ease.

'I am Primo Capitano Graziella Di Francesca, of the *Carabinieri* in Taormina. This is my colleague Sergente Marco Nicolosi.'

Everyone did a noddy-hello thing.

The *maître d'* hovered, mumbling something about coffee. The police captain asked him to serve everybody – and then leave.

Capitano Di Francesca dropped a sugar lump into her coffee, stirred it and began.

'The purpose of my visit today is to take a statement from you all, to record the tragic death of Signora Walshe.'

'Cunningham. Signora *Cunningham*.' Rob was at it again.

'Thank you, Mr. Cunningham. I refer to the record of the hotel arrival, where it is evident that the deceased lady was registered with the passport of one Vanessa Walshe. Therefore, her official name under Italian law is Vanessa Walshe. *Allora.* I understand, that when the dreadful accident took place, two of you were present – Signor Walshe – the father – *mi dispiace* – very sad – and Signor Cunningham, the husband.' She paused. 'As we need to take the statements of those who were present at the incident, I will ask my colleague Sergente Nicolosi to accompany Signor Walshe to the small office next door to give his – if that is OK, Signor Walshe? *Va bene?*'

Johnny – not expecting this – nervously took a sip from his tea and stood up.

'Take your tea – and some pastries – with you, Signor Walshe. We will see you in a few minutes.'

Capitano Di Francesca smiled and her sergeant loaded a small plate with pastries and took a cup of coffee for himself. Dazed, Johnny clutched his china cup and followed the policeman out the door.

'Now, Signor Cunningham. More coffee before you start? No? OK. *Allora*, can you begin by describing what happened before your wife fell?'

'Eh, we had been out on in the garden bit enjoying the sun. Vanessa was looking at the lemon grove – over there.' Rob waved his arm vaguely over his left shoulder to indicate where he thought the lemon grove should be in relation to the drawing room. 'Then, her dad – Johnny – arrived. We were slagging – eh, that means joking, teasing – each other about rugby versus Gaelic – that's Irish football. Johnny is a big fan of the Irish football, whereas I'm a rugby player. Professional.'

'*Che bravo!* Congratulations. And then?'

'Vanessa works – *worked* in television – and did a lot of fashion blogging as well. When we were arguing sport, she was wandering around looking for the ideal location to record some reels – with the lovely view in the background.'

'Where exactly were you and Signor Walshe in the garden?'

'Sitting on the two deckchairs – quite near that bloody – *excuse me* – near that fence.'

'And then what happened?'

'She let out a sort of squeal. It was then that she realised it was missing.'

'What was missing?'

'Her mother's locket. She hadn't worn it since our wedding day – she thought there was something wrong with the catch – it had opened a couple of times by itself on the day. That's why I was surprised to see it around her neck when I came back from my swim earlier on.'

'Was it valuable?'

'Maybe not in monetary terms, but to Vanessa, it was precious – her mother is dead, you see.'

'*Mi dispiace.*'

'So, she began to fret and asked Johnny – Signor Walshe – and me to help her look for it. I went back up to the terrace and into the living room – wondering if she could have taken it off before we went out to sit in the sun – and Johnny tried the side of the garden that borders the lemon grove where she was earlier – she'd been chatting to the surveyor previously about where the trees were going to be transplanted when the extension work began.' At this, Rob became visibly upset. 'Then I heard a whoop of delight. I came out to see Vanessa astride the fence. She jumped down on the bad side and seemed to be reaching for something. "*I think I can see it glistening under a bush!*" she called out – which was quite possible, if the locket had broken when she was over at that part of the fence earlier when doing "her backdrop recce". I began to hurry down the garden.' At this, Rob grabbed his glass of water and took a sip. 'She was poking at the bush – with a broken branch or a stick or something – then she seemed to lose her balance and started to slither . . . *that scream!* I will never forget that high-pitched scream. One minute she was there – the next she just vanished out of sight – and was gone.' Rob continued to clutch the water glass with his two shaking hands.

'Then, what did you do?'

'I ran to the fence but I couldn't see her anywhere.'

'Did you not try to climb down after her?'

'I just froze. Johnny ran over when he heard the scream and tried immediately to go after her. He inched down the first bit of the slope – only a metre or so – but couldn't see her. Then that surveyor climbed over the fence, grabbed Johnny and pulled him back up.'

'Ah yes, Dottore Marcello. We have already taken his statement.'

'Yes, he and the manager had arrived just after she fell.' Rob shot the police captain a nervous look.

'And the locket? Could you see it?'

'After Vanessa fell, it was the least of my priorities.' He paused. 'That's what I remember. It all happened so quickly.'

'*Capisco.* It was very traumatic for you. You have been very helpful. Unfortunately, the hotel's security cameras don't cover that little garden as it is private for the clients, so we need to piece together what happened from those who were present. I am so sorry for your loss. You can leave us now, Signor Cunningham.'

Whilst the interview continued elsewhere with Johnny, Capitano Di Francesca took a shorter statement from Karen and Davey, given that they were elsewhere at the time of the accident. She did however push them a little on the relationship of the deceased and her new husband and how happy they had been together. Karen squirmed when she said that they were mad about each other, and when asked had there been any recent issues about which they had rowed, both she and Davey lied confidently. Given the forensic nature of the policewoman's questioning, Karen had already decided not to mention any imaginary theories about Vanessa's low mood or the nice long drop from the fence over the cliff.

The stressful afternoon concluded with a visit from the hospital family liaison person, who informed Rob that the post-mortem was scheduled for the following Monday.

Pending the results, the body was scheduled to be released later that week.

She gave Karen business cards for the section at the airport which looked after repatriation of bodies, as well as the Irish Consulate in Rome.

———

As the only Italian speaker, Karen knew she was expected to deal with the practicalities of winding down Vanessa's life. She looked at the array of contact numbers spread before her on the polished table and wondered where to begin. Selfishly, she was thankful that it was still the weekend and that gave her a day or so to gather her thoughts.

She glanced over at Davey and saw the dull, vacant set of his face. During the family's hazy sleepless existence of the previous days, they had been distracted from the fact that there was a beautiful, twenty-nine-year-old bride lying cold in the freezer drawer of a hillside hospital, when she should have been oil-slicked and warm, stretched out on a sun-kissed beach.

The period of distraction was well and truly over.

Part 5

Ireland

Chapter 23

Bishop Joe

I can't believe this is happening. That I am sitting in my office in Ennis, studying funeral rites. News has spread like wildfire through the area. How could it not, when you consider the high profile of the deceased – *poor Vanessa* – and her widower – (what a strange, *old* word to describe a 30-year-old man!) – the province's Number 2.

Father Tom has been wonderful, selecting and suggesting liturgy and liaising with a list of musicians and singers that we keep on file, most of whom even if they were previously booked are doing their best to accommodate us given the tragic circumstances. It is common knowledge that it is my nephew who is bereaved.

I suspect I was one of the last to hear the bad news, out as I was with a few from the Spinners' club enjoying the Doolin Loop. When cycling, I tend to keep the phone on mute for my own sanity and the safety of everyone else on the road, so I wasn't aware of the five missed calls from Rob until we took a break at a service station near Garrihy's Cross. *One* call from him on his honeymoon would have been strange, but five? I knew it was bad news.

I suspected the problem was with Johnny, Vanessa's father. Rob hadn't gone into any detail when he finally left a message, only a request to call him, but his voice sounded tearful and I feared the worst. Armed with my cup of tea, I was just about to tackle the return call when Tom rang me.

'Bishop? Are you off the bike?'

'Would I be talking to you otherwise? Yes, what's up?'

'If you have Wi-fi where you are, turn on your newsfeed. I'll drop this call now – to give you a few minutes. And, Bishop, take it easy. It's bad news.'

It was carried on two of the TV channels' 'breaking news' sections and already up on one of the daily nationals. My small screen filled with a wedding shot, with yours truly between the happy couple – Rob and Vanessa. The headlines were shocking. I read in disbelief. '**Tragic Vanessa Dies in Fall**'; '**Rugby Star's Tragedy**'; '**Honeymoon Horror**'. And on and on they went. Vanessa's own TV station opted for: '**Vanessa Walshe: R.I.P**', with a screen grab of her on the set of *Morning Glory*.

'Bishop Joe?' Father Tom was back. 'Are you alright? What a dreadful thing to happen! The poor family. Poor Rob!'

'I – I just can't process it.'

'Do you want me to come out and collect you? You

probably shouldn't be cycling just now.'

'No . . . I mean, yes, I'll tell the others to go ahead. Do come and collect me. I'm better off this bike at the minute. I'm in the garage near the Cross.'

And my kind-hearted curate left the friends he was enjoying a barbeque with, and drove across the county on a gloriously sunny day, to rescue me.

In the intervening days, Rob and Vanessa's family have somehow had the focus to select suitable material for the funeral, and Tom is running off the leaflets here in the office. Although I have spent a good deal of time with my nephew, I haven't been able to get him to open up. I know it's unreasonable to expect him to do a lot of soul-searching so soon, as he is clearly still in shock, but I wish I could fulfil my role in a more constructive manner as both his uncle and the spiritual adviser who will lay his lovely wife to rest.

Rob's restlessness has not been helped by his refusal to choose a permanent base to lay his head since his return from Sicily. He spent the first night at Johnny's where they had all headed directly from the airport. I offered him a room here, but he said it was too far from Allenbeg. The following day he went home to his mother's, which although the right side of Lough Derg for the Walshe homestead, has the disadvantage of having flaky Lilian in residence. He is back there again today, from where I will pick him up later to go to Allenbeg, where Johnny has insisted Vanessa should be waked.

It will be my first time to see her dad since the accident, as Rob and Karen have been the ones organising the funeral. I can honestly say that I am dreading it.

On the journey to Tipperary, I had the luxury of my silent, empty car from Lilian's to Allenbeg, as Rob wanted to have his own transport at Johnny's, intending to stay there till the formalities were over. More familiar with the minor roads to the farm than I, he arrived ahead of me and seemed to be in the throes of a discussion with his father-in-law when Davey let me in.

Johnny's decision to bury Vanessa in the plot with her mother has upset him. I don't think the father is being particularly unreasonable, since Vanessa was only married to Rob for less than a week and not too long together with him before that, but he doesn't see it that way. I stumbled on their row in the kitchen.

'*Why do you always have to take over?*' my nephew was shouting. '*She's my wife, but you still think you have first claim on her!*'

Johnny was sitting unshaven in a shirt and pants that had seen better days. He really didn't look dressed for visitors. The shadows under his eyes bore evidence of a man who had not closed them in a long time.

'It's decided, lad. There's no point arguing or upsetting yourself.' And then the horror of the situation seemed to hit him forcibly. 'The gravediggers are probably opening the ground as we speak.' He got up and walked out of the house to the backyard.

'Rob? Let it go.'

'Ah, Uncle Joe, I didn't realise you'd arrived.'

'Look, what does it matter where she's buried? It's a lovely little cemetery. You are family now, so you'll be here visiting all the time.'

'It matters. It's the token Walshe thing. *I'm* Rob Walshe now. I'm the one who's changed name! Do you know the trouble I had getting *Cunningham* put in the death notice? And he only agreed if we went double-barrelled! But with Walshe first, that pushes the listing right down to the bottom of the column where no-one will find or read it!'

'Rob, you're focussing on trivial, insubstantial things, rather than trying to understand this is all just grief that you're experiencing. Forget about the death notice! It's front-page news – everyone knows anyway! And those who matter, will have sought the arrangement details from elsewhere.'

'Ah, he's my mother all over again! Thinks *he* has the monopoly on loss.' And with that, my nephew marched out the back door and headed in the opposite direction to the one Johnny had earlier taken.

301

Last night, I left the wake to the family, as soon as I deemed it respectable to do so. I prayed with them a short while, and was pleased to see that Rob's faith appeared to have calmed him down. It seems to be the only point on which Johnny and he agree.

This morning, Tom and I left home excessively early, in order to be at the church well ahead of the ceremony, as I felt uneasy that there might be a few hitches. Davey filled me in about some standoff brewing over which guard of honour should take precedence outside the church, but this is really out of my control, and Johnny and Rob will just have to compromise.

When we pull into the car-park of St James's, the small white church is silhouetted against an even deeper blue sky than on the day of the wedding, I am struck by the similarity in setting and weather conditions and it's making me both nostalgic and distressed.

———

Despite my anxiety, I am robed and ready to begin. The priest from Johnny's official town parish church joins us with his curate and we decide that four of us standing out front to receive the remains seems excessive, so the two curates are sent inside to prepare the altar. The funeral cortège is heard arriving before it is seen: a melancholic Gaelic melody wafts through the heat haze of the July day, as a solo traditional piper leads the group. As the hearse climbs the hill up to the turn into the church, the pathetic sight of the family approaching behind the hearse would break a heart of stone. The immediate family and anyone able-bodied enough to do it have walked from the Walshe holding to St James's. To the front are Karen and Davey supporting Johnny – one wing each – and Rob follows close behind, linking his own mother. After that, the crowd intensifies – I can't identify anyone in particular – older aunts, neighbours, the throng goes on and on.

As the acquaintances fall to the back, I recognise the pretty young bridesmaids of last week, their pastel dresses exchanged for sombre shades of grey and navy. One of them is clutching the hand of a poor unfortunate child who is crying non-stop. I suspect she's the little flower-girl.

Out of nowhere, at least twenty young Gaelic players in the purple-and-blue kit of Allenbeg club file in the gate and stand with their backs to the wall on our right. Some are carrying hurleys which they raise in a makeshift arch; several of the girls carry a football. They hold their 'guard of honour' as the piper peels off and stops playing when the hearse pulls into place.

The undertakers slide the coffin out onto the bier and, before they enter the church through the side door, they place an elaborate floral display of red and white roses on the lid. I am completely focussed now and can't believe the silence, despite the church yard teeming with people. The eeriness is finally broken by the loud cooing of a nearby pigeon.

We begin our walk up the centre church aisle, intoning a

psalm as we go and join the pall-bearers as the remains are now in place in front of the altar. Karen is fussing with a framed photo and placing several personal items on a side table.

———

My voice is shaking as I begin. 'Dearly beloved, I hadn't planned on seeing you all so soon. I certainly never thought that it would be in these circumstances. As we come here to pray for Vanessa and her broken-hearted family, it is hard to understand how such a tragic event could be part of God's plan. And I say this as a man of the cloth for thirty or more years. I *should* have words of consolation to give you, but I have none – none anyway that you would find credible or heed. Let us stand and try and take solace in singing the first hymn.'

Once the congregation is upright, the inevitable latecomers creep in. I can't help noticing that it's the younger set, those who have travelled from Dublin or Limerick: Vanessa's media and fashion friends, Rob's rugby mates if the show of club blazers and ties are anything to go by. The repeat appearance of what are obviously friends who were wedding guests, is making the funeral even more poignant and I look to the front pew to see how the recent groom and the lonely father are holding up. Rob stands stoic and white-faced; Johnny cries continuously – slow dignified tears, that he makes no attempt to wipe away, tears that gather momentum as they drip down his face, onto his shirt and his dark suit.

The readings pass in a blur, the music plays, people file out to receive Communion and file back, shuffling into the wrong seats, the women worrying that they should have carried their handbags up to the altar with them. More reflection, more music – (no oration, Johnny has put his foot down) – more prayers, more music. And then the dreadful, final moment of commendation, of farewell. The slow last march to wherever.

I take the thurible and the waft of incense seems inappropriately strong. Father O'Reilly sprinkles holy water to bless the remains.

The undertakers approach the bier and call forward those who had agreed to carry the coffin. Rob and Davey make to carry the front, whilst two of Rob's burly teammates take up the rear. His old schoolfriend and best man Terry puts a hand to the middle and another blazered man moves into position opposite him, when all of a sudden, Johnny leaps out of his seat and elbows Davey from his front berth, lacing his arm over Rob's shoulder.

'Saints of God, come to her aid,
Come to meet her, angels of the Lord
Welcome her soul,
Present her to God, the Most High.'

The older folk in the congregation respond pat without prompting:

'Receive her soul and present her to God the Most High.'

The younger mourners say nothing, just sniffle and sob, as the casket passes them. It's then as we progress slowly down through the church that I spot my brother Frank, at the end of a row. I am glad for Rob's sake. Between incantations, I acknowledge him with a nod.

Once outside in the sunshine and on the short walk to the adjacent cemetery, I take a back seat and let the local parish priest carry the cross. Some of the older neighbours are reciting 'Hail Marys' as they follow the remains to the graveside, where Father O'Reilly will conduct the prayers.

'Thank you, Joe. You are most gracious.'

'Not at all. I need to join my family now.' I look around for Lilian and Rob, and I'm heartened by the sight of his father with his arm around him.

'Frank.'

'Joe.'

'Good to see you here.'

'And *why* wouldn't I be? My poor boy has suffered this tragic loss – where else would I be?'

'With your *real* family,' Lilian pipes up. 'Where are the Olsen twins, anyway?'

Ignoring Lilian, Frank addresses himself to Rob. 'They send their condolences. They're both out of the country. Milly has only started her language course in Salamanca. I think she's sent you a couple of messages. And Molly flew out to the States last Monday. She's working in some seafood restaurant in Montauk for the summer.'

Lillian blows hard and fans herself with the church service leaflet. '*Boo-bloody-hoo.* Who's interested?'

'Sure, they only met Vanessa once – at the wedding.' Rob's voice cracks when he says this.

I spot Father O'Reilly already at the headstone and eager to begin. The Gaelic players are now straddling the graves behind the part-guarded green-grassed one. Several of Rob's teammates, in their formal attire, take up position under the trees on the opposite side.

Out of nowhere, Johnny appears and confronts Rob. '*I said no fuckin' rugby guard of honour. This is Gaelic country! Get rid of them.*'

'It's just out of respect. We always do it if—'

'Dad! Let it go!' Davey says and places a hand on Johnny's arm but, despite his son's calming presence, Johnny manages to give Rob a tentative dig in the arm and shows no sign of retreating, until Frank intervenes.

'Mr Walshe, cool it. This is not appropriate behaviour for consecrated ground. Can't you see the lad is in bits?'

'Yeah, he's heartbroken. You don't know the half of it. Get out of my way.' Johnny marches off and gives the signal to the local priest to begin.

'Is he always this aggressive?' Frank asks Rob.

'He has a bit of a temper alright. Thanks for sticking up for me.'

'No problem, son.'

When the burial is over, we wend our way back out through the car park across the road to a small public house for the traditional refreshments. The annoying sound of cameras can be heard whirring and clicking – press photographers and some TV channels following the sad demise of the popular presenter, who, having respected the request to not cover the funeral, now feel it's fair game to document proceedings once out on the public road.

I am fearing what sort of reaction Rob and Johnny will have to this media intrusion when one of the reporters leaps in front of them both and says: 'My sympathy, Rob – Mr Walshe, but is it true that the Italian police are investigating the death of Vanessa? That it might *not* have been an accident after all?'

As I intervene to stop my nephew throttling the journalist, his photographer clicks away repeatedly, capturing us both. Unperturbed and holding up his phone to record, the journalist holds his ground and says: 'And would I be right in thinking it's *Bishop* Cunningham, not Father? Correct?'

And, like an imbecile, I reply: 'Yes.'

Chapter 24

Davey

The presence of the media at the funeral two days ago has really upset Dad. They are a crew of shameless bastards, turning up like that, capitalising on our private grief. Karen and I nearly had our first row in over ten years about it. She said she could understand their interest. I went mad.

'It was Vanessa's *funeral*, for Christ's sake! My twenty-nine-year-old sister celebrates her wedding one week and then comes back in a box the next and there they are – hovering like vultures, picking at the remains of her flesh, as they snap away, thinking they might get a scoop.'

'Stop, Davey. That's a horrible image.'

'But it's true: they're no better than vultures, preying on the dead.'

'You have to see it from their point of view.'

'*No, I do not!* It was *my* sister. Not yours.'

'Now that *is* unkind. You know how traumatised I am over Vanessa.'

'Facts are facts. You know her *how* long? Fifteen – sixteen years? I've been around her since she was born. I babysat her. I ran behind her holding the seat of her first bike the day we took the stabilisers off. I held her pudgy ten-year-old hand in mine, when we both stood at that same grave and lowered my mother into it. So, forgive me if I am a little bit upset on her behalf!'

Karen was temporarily silenced, but she had to come back with some defence of her feelings.

'Look, I know how protective you are of your sister – of your sister's memory – *and* your family's privacy, but Vanessa *was* well known. She was on television every second day. Rob is a professional rugby player whose team is never out of the newspapers, and both of them courted the media for promotion of themselves and their charity fundraisers. That interest doesn't suddenly stop, just because something bad happens. I'm sorry, love, but that's the way of the world.'

'Well, it's a lousy, shitty world if that's its way!'

I left her and went for a spin in the convertible. I needed a breather. Allenbeg has been like a hothouse since we arrived back from Sicily and I'm not only talking about the soaring temperatures. Too many people constantly calling and staying too long. The uneaten wedding cake being distributed to the mourners. Ould ones that none of us know dropping off casseroles in the only heatwave Ireland has experienced in about eight years.

Everybody wanting a piece of our grief, an insight into the accident, a sliver of privately disclosed information that yes, the accursed press of which Karen is so fond, has not written in their papers. It was interminable.

And all the time, Dad wandering around like a man suffering from dementia – unwashed, unshaven, his hair standing on end – not knowing what day of the week it is or why all these people are in his house.

Rob still hasn't budged. We expected him to stay the night of the informal vigil for Nessa and the actual funeral day but, even after all the ceremonies have concluded, he's still shadowing my father. He is driving him crazy. I wonder just how long he intends to stay.

It's not like he has nowhere else to go. When Bishop Joe suggested a few days' break with him in Ennis, he didn't seem overly keen. His other option is with his mother Lilian but, poor soul, she's on a planet of her own and he would probably end up looking after *her*, which might not necessarily be a bad thing as a form of distraction therapy. Then there's the father, Frank, who turned up this time without any of his new family – twice in two weeks to the arsehole of Tipperary – he must really feel he's living the high life! Though I can't see any invitation for Rob to stay issuing from him – too complicated.

The elephant in the room is, of course, the new house – Rob and Vanessa's house in Newbridge, the purchase of which according to post addressed to Vanessa and awaiting us at Allenbeg on our return, has after a month's delay finally closed and whose keys are available for collection at the auctioneer's. Even I couldn't be that insensitive as to suggest the place in Newbridge but, wherever he decides to go, I wish he'd push off soon, as my father can't relax around him.

On the way home from my 'breather', I decide I'd better get petrol – the car hasn't been filled since before the wedding. I have just engaged the pump when Karen rings.

'Hiya, love, are you OK? Sorry about going all debating society on you earlier. Listen, are you nearby?'

'Not far. At the petrol station. Why?'

'Well, I've had a call from Sicily. From that Capitano what's-her-face – Graziella. Apparently, the prick at the church on Saturday wasn't far off. They *are* conducting a formal investigation into how Vanessa died.'

'Why?'

'She didn't go into any great detail – just said something about it being fairly standard when a foreigner dies. And that the post-mortem had showed up unexplained pressure marks on Vanessa's neck – like a ligature or something – and they just wanted to gather further witness statements, if there were any.'

'Christ! This is all dad needs. *Ligature marks?* I wouldn't have had Rob down for any sort of kinky sex.'

Karen says nothing.

'And when do we get the findings of this investigation?'

'*Ha!* This is the good bit. The police have to inform the public prosecutor within forty-eight hours of a suspected crime – so even if they think it's *only* an accident, they have to file their report fairly pronto, in case it turns out *not* to be an accidental death, which is why I suspect that Graziella woman took our statements the day after Vanessa's fall. Once the public prosecutor receives the report, he then has up to six months to complete his investigation.'

'No pressure, then.'

'She also said that the investigation was necessary in case the family decide to sue for negligence.'

'Sue whom?'

'I don't know. Sue the hotel over the signage – the barrier – the owner of the land? Who knows?'

'*Do* we want to sue?'

'No. But Rob might.'

'As if. He was only with Nessa a wet weekend.'

'But he has rights, as the husband.'

'It would be more likely my father who'd want to sue, if he ever returns to normal.'

'Oh yeah, speaking of which, Johnny is missing. Well not *missing* exactly, but not here. And the jeep is.'

'Karen! Why didn't you say that first! You know the state he's in. Look, I'll just pay for this petrol and have a

313

drive around. If he shows up, message me. See you in a bit. Hopefully.'

'Love you.'

'Love you too.'

I throw fifty euro on the counter and am leaving the garage when I spot one of the tabloids with a picture on the front page of the bishop trying to break up the fisticuffs between Rob and their journalist. I snatch the paper and add some loose change to my note which still lies uncollected.

'*Hold your horses!*' the young one roars after me. '*I need to scan that!*' but I'm already out the door.

I've a fair idea where I'll find Dad. The cemetery is usually very quiet but, when we had suggested a ramble as far as there yesterday afternoon, he had point-blank refused to go. As it was a Sunday, the newly mounded grave with its copious floral tributes to their neighbourhood TV celebrity had attracted the attention of locals and late Mass-goers for a bit of rubber-necking. I suspect he's come back today, when there's no-one around.

He isn't immediately visible but, when I walk towards the grave, I see his feet sticking out from behind the headstone. He's sitting on the plinth of the neighbouring plot, a bottle of Paddy on the ground beside him.

'Dad! What are you doing?'

'I think that's obvious. I'm having a little drink with my Nessa.'

314

'How long have you been out here?' The bottle is half-empty, so I can hazard a guess.

'Not long enough. I'm escaping.'

'Escaping from what?'

'From the whole shaggin' lot of you up at the house. And from that bastard Rob.'

'Why, what's Rob done now?'

'What's he *done*? What's *he* done?' At his dramatic repetition, he waves his hand in the direction of the mound of flowers. '*That's* what he's done. My Nessa.'

This was not the time to fill him in on the news from Sicily.

'Do you think you'll be ready to go home in a while?'

'*Home*? I have no home any more. Only an empty hole of a place with no-one in it.'

'I thought you were complaining a minute ago that the place was overrun!'

'An empty hole with no-one in it that *matters*.'

'Oh, thanks very much! I'll be sure to tell Karen that.'

'You know what I mean.'

'I do. And I bet that you haven't even had your breakfast yet! Why don't we wander back – I've the car with me as it happens – and we'll put on something to eat. Here!'

I reach for my father's hand. He needs a bit of a pull to stand up. He's reluctant to leave, so I roll with it – reading a couple of cards on the wreathes and commenting on who the people are that sent them. Then we walk slowly back through the car park. Just as I think I have him on the move, he doubles back and retrieves his half-drunk bottle.

I open the passenger door and he half-clambers, half-falls unsteadily into the front seat. There is a crumpling noise as he sits on the tabloid.

'Ah feck it, I'm destroying your newspaper. Wait a second.' And he pulls it out from under his bottom. His eye catches the photo of Rob with his hands around the reporter's throat.

'That fellow,' he says, tapping his finger on the paper. 'That fellow is far too quick with his fists.'

Chapter 25

Rob

Newbridge, County Kildare, Ireland

It's now November and four full months have passed since her death. I know the Walshe clan won't believe a word of it, but I miss Vanessa. I really do. I miss having 'another half'. I miss booking two of everything: two cinema tickets, two plane seats, a table for two. I miss having a hand to hold walking through the park or down a busy shopping street if I have a weekend off. I miss all sorts of stupid things – like checking my phone after a hard day's training in camp, for a WhatsApp from her. (There are occasional other messages I check late at night, but those have to be taken in the privacy of my room.)

I miss talking in the plural about things: '*We* are thinking of going to Andalucia on holidays' and watching people's reaction when you use the 'we' word. People take more notice of your opinion – of *you* – because you're somebody who *has* somebody. In my case, it's more than that. The younger guys at the club used almost audibly sigh in relief that I was 'normal'– particularly those who were contracted after my engagement to Vanessa and who knew nothing about us. They had obviously been formulating their own theories, until similar casual references were overheard. Since Vanessa, they became friendlier and more relaxed around me.

But because I have lived my life in a gold-fish bowl for the last few years – or the square-screen equivalent of that bowl – a lot of people recognise me. They know I have passed from a 'we' to a tragic, uncoupled 'I', and their sympathy only makes me acutely aware of my new solitary state.

It was the reason I opted to move into this house. Newbridge had always been Vee's location choice: near enough to work in Dublin for her and on the road home to Daddy Dearest when not. I could just suck up the kilometres I was going to have to drive, she figured – after all, I spent long chunks of time in residential camp in Limerick.

After her death, I wanted nothing to do with the bland semi-d' in a meandering estate off the motorway. I preferred the small apartment in Dublin, where I could hide away if I chose to.

But in the first display of united Stewart-Cunningham parenting for nearly twenty years, Frank called in one evening in late July to discuss what I intended to do with the newly purchased house.

'I've had several phone-calls from Lilian – eh, from your mother – about what's best for you,' he began. 'As she's in the advantageous position – unlike me – of actually having the address and *knowing* where in the town it is, she says it's a good property and would sell quickly if you wanted to go that route.'

'Sorry. I haven't been in touch much – over the last year.'

'No. But that's changed now. You have Vanessa, God love her, to thank for that. Have you even collected the keys yet?'

'Yeah, from the estate agent. She'd been dealing with Vanessa, while I did the mortgage and solicitor side. Their fees statement went to Allenbeg, with confirmation that the vendors had left the keys at the office.'

'And you've checked out the house? I presume you have it insured.' Frank had gone into full-blown accountant mode.

'Yes, Dad. I insured it. I left a spare key with the elderly couple two doors down, because I keep getting phone-calls from furniture delivery people.'

'Was that wise? They could put anyone into it!'

'Oh, don't start, Frank. Lecturing me. I had to make a snap decision. I can't be schlepping up and down to Newbridge for every goddamn armchair Vanessa ordered!'

'Is there any beer in this teetotal apartment?'

'Are you not driving?'

'I'm on the DART. I'm only on my way home from work, if you check the time!'

'Oh. I thought it was much later. There's probably a couple of cans in the cupboard – I keep them in case Terry calls over.'

'Have you been *out* of this apartment at all today? Scratch that hot can of lager! Freshen yourself up and we'll go over to the Odeon. You can have a lemonade – and maybe get something to eat.'

'Not the Odeon. Too many people who might know me.'

'You have to face people sometime. And put on a clean shirt.'

That is how, his persuasiveness enhanced by two pints, my father convinced me that I should decamp to Newbridge. My mother, on a Diazepam sabbatical, was willing to move in for the first month and help me 'transition', as well as triage-ing the wedding gifts and dealing with the furniture deliveries.

It hasn't been the worst idea in the world. If I am going to have the financial hit every month of paying the mortgage which I took out solely in my name, then it might be nice to live anonymously among people who neither recognise nor care about transient rugby players.

I'm hardly here at all. Coach was already on the blower early-August wanting to know if by then I felt able to resume pre-season training. As I took the call, my mother kept interrupting me, faffing around with which wedding presents to redirect elsewhere, and which ones I could use. Without hesitation, I told him 'Yes'.

For the second time in my life, rugby has saved me. It has given me a single-minded purpose to get up each morning. Our working days are long and busy and my teammates are a self-absorbed lot, which is great. They have no time to be checking social media or gossip sites for anybody other than themselves or their girlfriends. Occasionally, one of the pack will wander up, and enquire how I'm doing, but I think the team psychologist probably has them primed for that.

Although I'm playing well, better than I've played in a long time according to Frank, who – miracles will never cease, has stuck to his promise of remaining in touch – I have yet to put in a full eighty minutes on the pitch. If I'm named in the starting fifteen – which is an ego-boost and an affirmation as the theoretical first choice position player – I'm replaced in the third quarter. Sometimes I even get an earlier 'break' – a HIA or some-such in the opening half – which I probably don't need at all. I can see the psychologist has the ear of the Forwards' coach as well.

But the important competitions are kicking off end of November, and even the second tier one will be getting more serious by then, so I decide to put in a phone call to that police captain in Sicily. I should find out if and when I might be needed over there.

It goes like this:

'Hello? Is that the *Carabinieri*? Could you put me through to Captain Di Francesca?'

[. . .]

'I'll wait.'

[. . .]

'She's not? OK. I'll call back. [. . .] In an hour? Fine. Thanks.

'Hello again. I phoned earlier. I'm looking for Captain Di Franc— [. . .] she's not? Not yet? You said in an hour. [. . .] OK. I'll try again in the morning.'

I do. I phone the following morning, afternoon and early evening, but with no luck. Eventually, the day I'm driving back to work in Limerick, she returns my call.

'Signor Cunningham, you were looking for me?'

I am tempted to ask if it's usual to wait four days to ring back, but I decide not to start by aggravating her. 'Yes, I was. Several times. I just want to know how you are getting on . . . with the investigation into my wife Vanessa's death.'

'It is really out of our hands now . . . all of the information is with the office responsible for adjudicating if there is any case to answer.'

'And have you taken statements from *all* the staff members who came upon the scene?'

'I did. In fact, we took additional, more detailed statements from anybody we thought the prosecutor might like to call as witnesses. *Allora*, if there is nothing else?'

'Any indication when the preliminary hearing will be? You may remember, I'm a professional rugby player – in competitions. I need some notice.'

'As soon as we know, I will tell you, *va bene?* And good

luck with your competitions!' She ended the call, quite abruptly.

The police captain's phone call was not the only one I received on that journey. An unrecognisable mobile lit the screen as I approached Junction 24. Hesitantly, I connected – to a woman's voice.

'Hello, Rob?' she began, 'you won't remember me . . . but I'm the photographer that shot your wedding – Tammie.'

'Of course I remember you, Tammie! How could I not? How're you keeping?'

'Fine. Well. I've been trying to contact you for ages . . . about the wedding album.' She stopped talking and then resumed. 'That came out all wrong – firstly, I've been trying to contact you to say how *sorry* I am – about all that happened.'

'Thank you. I changed my mobile – after. It really has been the most horrendous few months.'

'I can well imagine. I finally managed to wheedle this number out of your sister-in-law, Karen. I can't apologise enough for not getting in touch about – the tragedy – but I went off to Ecuador to visit the Galapagos Islands shortly after your wedding. I didn't hear until I got back to Ireland.'

'That sounds very exotic – the Galapagos. Not somewhere I'd associate with holidays.'

'Oh, no. It wasn't a "holiday" in that sense. It was a study trip. I'd very much like to train as a nature and wildlife photographer but there's a lot to learn. Plus, as the islands are both a marine reserve *and* a UNESCO heritage site, visitors are strictly controlled. You can't really stay on the habitable islands for more than a night or two.'

'So, what did you do?'

'It was an organised trip – sixteen photographers – and we lived on board a small cruiser for the islands leg of the trip and went ashore to the locations from there.'

'Sounds amazing. A bit of a change from the Allen Castle gardens!'

'You said it! There are only so many weddings I can take. But speaking of which, I do have to – deliver this album to you. Vanessa paid upfront for her order.'

'That would be Vanessa. Super-organised.'

'Yes. Well, where should I send it then? Your rugby club headquarters, maybe?'

I considered this suggestion. It might close down any lurking rumours among this autumn's fresh intake of players, if they saw the detailed evidence before them in all its glossy glory. (And it *was* a very photogenic wedding, if I say so myself.) Then, something Tammie volunteered decided me.

'I suppose I could have sent yours to Allenbeg as well, but your-father-in-law kept returning his with the courier, so I thought I'd better deal with each album separately.'

'How *many* albums are there?'

'Just the two.'

This annoyed me. Even though she was no longer around, Vanessa persisted in putting me on an equal footing with her father.

'And has he received his yet, the old man?'

'Finally, yes.'

The innocence of me thinking I was *equal* to Johnny; I was still very much inferior. He even got to see the album of my wedding before I did!

'Tell you what, Tammie, I'll text you my new address in Newbridge and you can send it on.'

'Or I might even drop it off to you. I think I've a corporate gig for the National Stud in early October – that's nearby. I'll check my diary.'

'You do that, and give me a ring when you know your dates and I'll check where I am!'

'Will do!'

I was already in the High-Performance Centre parking lot when she ended the call. I saved her number to my new phone, so if she rang again I wouldn't be taken by surprise.

Encouraging shouts and drill-calls drifted from a nearby pitch, as the age-grade teams were put through their paces. I opened the back of the jeep and took out my gear-bags, glad to be back at work.

Chapter 26

Davey

Allenbeg, Tipperary

We are well into the New Year now – not that any of us feels any sense of anything being 'new' or the fresh start that the change in the final digit of the calendar usually brings. Dad has not improved at all. Karen and I are extremely worried. I managed to herd him to the G.P. He has been offered – and refused – Anxicalm medication. In fact, he put the poor doctor in her place for even daring to suggest it: *'You are not turning me into some sort of unfeeling fuckin' zombie.'* I sat in the consulting room behind him and looked at my feet. She knew when to back down and suggested yoga.

I don't know which suggestion enraged him more.

When we arrived home, he thundered down the steps into the kitchen – a blood-pressure glow about his face – and vented. At least he *had* someone to vent to, since we were still in residence, having extended our Christmas visit well beyond the 6th of January.

'*Yoga!* What'll they think of next? Can you imagine – *me* – lying on a mat amongst all those housewives in pink tracksuits! And that's all she had to offer!'

Karen was about to extoll the virtues of Anxicalm as an alternative, but I gave her the 'don't-go-there' look. For once, she acquiesced. She still isn't in my father's good books, and doesn't want to aggravate him any further. In all the years of our marriage, I have been fortunate that Dad and Karen have enjoyed a really warm and relaxed relationship. She genuinely adores him – not in a dutiful 'I must-suck-up-to-my-father-in-law' kind of way, but she *likes* him. Which, as we all know, is so much harder than loving him. They are allies. They are buddies. They are conspirators when I'm acting the fool and do they gang up on me or what!

But even buddies can hit the rocks occasionally, and Karen truly ran aground last weekend when she attempted to make a start on clearing out some of Vanessa's personal things from her Allenbeg bedroom. Dad saw the light on from the yard below and dashed into the kitchen where I was preparing dinner, as if we were being besieged.

'*There's someone in Nessa's room! Quick! Come up with me.*' He took a hurley from the boot room and braced himself.

I knew it was Karen – she had earlier carted boxes and a suitcase in from the car – but I followed him up the stairs all the same.

He was only short of bringing the hurley down on whatever intruder he expected to find such was his anger, and it didn't abate much when he discovered Karen on her knees, folding T-shirts and tops into the suitcase.

'What do you think you're doing, lady?'

'Johnny, we need to make a start – on her lovely things. You know Vanessa would want them to go to charity.'

'And who gave *you* permission to come in here at all?'

I could see Karen was taken aback.

'I thought I'd save you a job. It's not something you would enjoy tackling.'

'Put everything back where you found it.'

'But I just thought—'

'*Everything. Back.*'

He stood and supervised as, red-faced, my wife undid her work of the previous hour, unfolding and rehanging skirts and dresses and heavy winter jumpers.

I thought I should offer her some support. 'Dad – we'll have to do it sometime. Why not let Karen sort the clothes at least – it's not so emotional for her.'

But this didn't strike the right note either.

Karen turned on me!

'Want to bet?' Tears were welling up now. 'I *remember* the shopping trips when we bought some of this stuff. I can picture Nessa out at functions wearing this or that dress. Or just having a laugh with me after work on a Friday night, in skinny jeans and a fabulous top. *You men* aren't the only ones who are grieving!'

And in an atypical Karen gesture, she flung the jacket she was hanging onto the floor and ran out of the room.

Dad just stood in the middle of the discarded clothes, mesmerised. I picked up the lemon linen jacket, replaced it carefully onto its hanger and went to the wardrobe.

It was full. Packed to capacity with four-seasons' clothes crammed in badly – far too many items to have been just Vanessa's Allenbeg reserve stock. I knew she visited a lot, but what I was looking at seemed to represent every outfit she possessed.

'You have an awful lot of her things here, Dad. I would have thought some of these clothes would have been in the flat in Dublin . . . before . . . being moved out to . . . their new house.'

'They were.'

'But they're not now.'

'No.'

'How come?'

'He just arrived one Saturday before Christmas with a whole lot of bags and dumped them in the hall.'

'Who? Rob?'

'Who else? *The fuckin' cheek of him!*'

'But he probably knew you'd like to have her things back. Where's the harm?'

'It was the way he did it. No warning or anything. Rang to say he was calling in to the graveyard and would I be in for a cup of tea, that he'd swing by after. Then he rolls up in a shiny Jeep – *new*, no less – some endorsement deal with the brand – and brings me one of those red leafy Ponssie plants—'

'Poinsettias.'

'—to "*brighten up the house for Christmas,*" says he – as if I was even going to *have* Christmas with Nessa gone – and then, out of the blue, he goes back to the car and brings in a rake of *black plastic bags* packed to the brim. The insult of it! Black *rubbish* sacks.'

'Well, that was a bit insensitive alright. And does Rob not want to hold on to anything himself?'

'I doubt it. Apparently, the bagged-up stuff came from her flat-share with that lassie—'

'Jenny.'

'Yeah. Nessa had cleared it all out before the wedding, because Jenny needed to get someone else into the room to pay the rent. She stored it in the Cunninghams' apartment, as they didn't yet have the keys to their new house. Now Rob's oul fella wants to let out the place, since me boyo is basing himself in Newbridge more or less full-time.'

'Makes sense.'

'But he couldn't resist a bit of a dig at the amount of clothes Vanessa bought! Called her a "spendthrift". "That apartment was a tight-enough squeeze at the best of times," he says, "without all her clutter." *Clutter!* He's changed his tune. He used love swanning around with her on his arm, and she dolled up in some expensive designer gown. It made him look less dull!'

'I'm sure he's kept one or two mementoes all the same.'

'Sure, are you? You don't know him at all.'

'Dad, let's go downstairs. It's not . . . good for you . . . being up here.'

'I sit in this room all the time. I can still smell her, you know.'

'Yeah, I can get her perfume alright.'

'No. It's not just the perfume – sure she was always changing perfumes! It's *her* smell – a mixture of all the stuff she used. Creams. Deodorant. Even her shampoo. When I'm up here, she's still alive.'

I could see we were not going to get out of the bedroom anytime soon, so I moved a bundle of clothes from the edge of the bed and sat down. Dad wandered over to the window and ran his hand along the white vanity unit that nestled in the recess.

'I could never get it right,' he said. 'The perfume. Each year before Christmas, I'd check this dressing table for whatever bottle she had on the go, write the name down and head off to Limerick to buy it, but when she'd come to stay for Christmas, I'd notice another one altogether on the shelf – another unpronounceable name in fancy writing, in a different-shaped bottle – she'd have moved on to a new one!'

I was thinking anxiously about the half-cooked dinner downstairs. The roast potatoes would be cremated if Karen hadn't recovered from her upset and realised the oven was on.

'Her whole life is in this room.' At this, he reached in to the far left of the wardrobe and pulled out a miniscule school blazer. He rubbed the stiff old wool between his thumb and index finger and smiled.

'God, Dad, I can't *believe* the size of that!' I took the

maroon blazer from his hand. 'Was that her first one? It looks like it'd only fit a toddler!'

'She started school in that. Aged four-and-three-quarters. They were a horrendous price – I remember nearly falling over when Breda came back from town and told me what she'd paid. That's why most parents didn't bother with them when the kids were small and growing like mad. But Breda insisted. If she was going to the private junior school at the convent, then she was going to look the part. There's a whole load of photos taken of her on the front doorstep on her first day – will I get the album?'

I could see where this was heading and I thought it would do him good to focus on something other than Vanessa for an hour or two. 'Maybe not now, Dad. You know, I was halfway through a roast downstairs – that's if Karen has rescued it from incineration. Why don't we go down and see – and we could walk into the village afterwards for a drink? It'll give you a chance to make up the quarrel with Karen. She really didn't mean any harm.'

'I know that. I'm just not ready to let go of Ness.'

'We'll have to, sooner or later. *And* of these things. Otherwise, it's like building a kind of shrine to her . . . and that's a bit weird.'

'I don't see anything weird about a shrine.'

The Riverside Pub was empty apart from three elderly punters sitting at the bar.

Karen made a bee-line for the leather armchairs beside the turf fire.

'A pint, Dad? Karen, what do you want?'

'A hot port.'

The owner was on tonight and had treated us like VIPS since the accident.

'He'll drop them over.' I settled myself into the third armchair.

'I was just saying to Karen,' Dad began, 'that all this delay in hearing back from the Italian police is most unsatisfactory.'

'It's just procedure, Dad. These things take their time.'

'But they said about six months, and it's more than that already.'

'I'll ring that Captain Di Francesca when we're back in Dublin . . . Thanks, Martin, no, I don't take sugar in my hot port . . . their Christmas break must surely be over by now!'

'What I don't understand is the need for an investigation in the first place.' Dad took the cushion out from behind his back and placed it on the fourth empty chair. 'I mean, we have the post-mortem results – the poor child died from a bleed as a result of fracturing her skull when she fell. What do they need to investigate?'

I was inclined to agree, but noticed that Karen had become a little uneasy.

'It might be to rule out any possible involvement of

other people in her death,' she said as she stirred her drink vigorously with the spoon.

'*What* other people?' Now *I'm* confused. 'She *fell*, Karen, for Christ's sake! Are they suggesting that she encountered somebody on the cliff-face who pushed her further down or what?'

'I am only telling you what my brother heard from one of Rob's mates. Apparently, they like to be extra-thorough when it's the death of a foreign tourist.'

'That's the first I've heard of it. Dad, did Rob say anything to you, when he came with the clothes?'

'Not a thing. Apart from – well, he did mention something about suing the hotel for negligence over the fence.'

'I suppose he has a point.' Karen sipped her hot drink. 'It mustn't have been much of a safeguard if she was able to climb over it so easily. Though, in my experience, Sicily is not really a "nanny-state". There are so many drops and dangers everywhere, that they expect people to exercise caution themselves.'

'*Look*, can we stop going over Vanessa's accident? I thought you dragged me out in this freezing bloody fog to take my mind *off* my troubles, not to torment me by going over that horrible, horrible day!'

I had no answer to that – none, at least, that didn't involve the official findings of the police investigation, and that was not something we were going to get on a miserable January evening in the midlands of Ireland.

As usual, Karen tried to see light at the end of this

particular bleak tunnel.

'You know, Johnny, we're entitled to attend the preliminary hearing when the public prosecutor comes back with his report. Would you like to go back to Sicily for that?'

Dad's face clenched, furrowing his brow and forcing his individual bushy eyebrows to meet in one continuous line. 'And *why* would I want to do that? Go back – *go back* to that godforsaken island that robbed me of my peace – that stole my wonderful daughter? And for what? To be told what we already know – that Vanessa died because she fell. She fell because she was only *in* that hotel in the first place because *you* chose it as a location for a holiday – *no*, for a *honeymoon*! She wouldn't have *been* on honeymoon if it hadn't been for marrying Rob. All this – misery – goes back to Rob. I rue the day she ever set eyes on him!'

With that, Dad pushed his half-finished pint across the table, stood up abruptly, took his coat from the back of the chair and marched out the door of the pub.

'That's us told,' said Karen. 'As if I didn't feel bad enough over pushing them into Taormina.'

'It could have happened anywhere.'

'But it didn't. It happened where we sent them. Full stop.'

'Will I go after him?'

'No. Leave him a few minutes. He's probably gone via the graveyard anyway.'

'Should *we* go to the hearing? Whenever that'll be.'

'Well, I think it mightn't be too far off, judging from my last chat with the *carabiniere*. I could re-arrange work, I suppose. And you could probably tie it in with one of your southern Italy visits.'

'It would be good to have someone who can follow what's going on – in Italian, I mean.'

'I don't think my Italian would be up to the legal jargon, but I might get the gist. Anyway, I've a number for an interpreter that the woman at the consulate gave me. I could follow it up with her, if she'll take my call. I hear Johnny's been ringing the consular officer a lot!'

'It's hard on him being left in the dark, particularly when there are gossipy updates in the newspapers every so often with "the latest theory".'

'Speaking of your dad in the dark – I think we should head, Davey. I don't like to think of him walking home alone. Look, he's even left his torch behind.'

'Damn, so he has. Come on. I suppose if Rob is intent on going back to Taormina, that's another reason *we* should go.'

'Messina. The hearing will be in Messina – the regional city.'

'That's nearer the airports on the mainland. I suppose I could combine it with that awkward Calabrian trip.'

'Well, we can look at it in detail once we get a definite date.'

I said goodbye to the landlord and the old lads at the counter, and we headed out into the fog towards Allenbeg cemetery on the road home. We could almost feel the other customers' curious questions bounce off our retreating backs, and I wondered what their topic of conversation would be on our next post-hearing visit.

Chapter 27

Rob

Near Messina, Sicily

I felt strange asking Uncle Joe to accompany me, but I knew it would be an unpleasant trip to make alone. Once I had received the call from Captain Di Francesca in Taormina with the release date of the prosecutor's findings, I got the impression from the additional information they were supplying that they took it as read I would attend. Apart from the Walshe family who I expected to travel as well, I couldn't think of one single friend who would be prepared to trek to Sicily in February, for a very short and probably not at all sweet stay.

This alarmed me slightly. I belong to a provincial rugby squad with over forty players. I consider myself reasonably sociable when we're in camp or on tour. OK, I'm not the most gregarious team-member, but I'm not a complete loner. I've been working on it, ironically, since Vanessa passed away. I am still in touch with guys from my college days – they usually surface when match tickets are in short supply. I thought I had friends in the True Love Waits movement – one or two of the tutors on the education programme – but I haven't heard anything from them all through the winter. There were at least 160 people at our wedding last July – and twice that at Vanessa's funeral.

But, when it came down to it, there wasn't one person who I felt confident enough about asking to give a few days of his time, to get me through the ordeal. I even found myself considering Terry, who has been on the periphery of things lately and repeatedly tries to apologise his way back into my affection, but I stopped short of contacting him, once the date for the hearing was communicated.

For this investigator, whoever he may be, has a strong sense of irony in choosing to make public his deliberations of the so-called 'Honeymoon Death', on February 14th, the internationally recognised annual love-fest. I knew there wasn't a chance in hell that Terry would get a 'pass-out' from his new girlfriend for the three days that critically span St Valentine's Day.

Whereas, at thirty-one-years-of-age, the only Valentine's pass I had to request was of my head coach – forced as I was to declare my unavailability for the week. I find myself back where I started – quite alone – despite having worked really hard at acquiring a wife. Not just 'single' alone – worse! I'm lumbered with the label 'widower', when a widower has always meant to me a man in his seventies or eighties, shuffling around looking like he's carelessly misplaced something and if he tries really hard to remember it will turn up. (It's your wife you've misplaced, poor sod, and she's not going to just 'turn up'.)

Which is why the only travelling companion I could come up with was my uncle the bishop, who will metaphorically hold my hand through whatever comes my way. In agreeing to accompany me – which I know he was hesitant about at first – I suppose he felt his pastoral duty of care was having a temporary extension overseas.

In preparing for the trip, I was like a schoolboy who has never been away for a weekend on his own. I had forgotten what it felt like to have to make your own travel arrangements! Any leisure travel I engaged in over the last two years, was always suggested, arranged and executed by Vanessa, and I just went along with the plan. Apart from my playing trips, I haven't travelled anywhere since Taormina – and I thought I was returning there until Uncle Joe read the email with the court details more carefully. Instead, our presence is requested in Messina; I didn't even know where it was until I checked the map. However, I *am* grateful to Joe that he has spared my ambiguous feelings about Sicilian hotels, by arranging for us to stay with a good clerical friend of his in the village of Scaletta a bit south of the metropolitan city where we'll attend the hearing.

———

Being in a 'clerical' house, is having a strange effect on me.

The younger priest, Padre Bernard, who collected us off the bus from Catania airport, obviously runs the show – manages parish duties, as well as being cook, driver and carer for the two elderly confreres still living here. I haven't quite been able to establish how Uncle Joe and he first met, but as Bernard is Swiss – 'from the shores of Lac Léman,' he proudly told us – I suspect their paths crossed during one of Joe's earlier stints in Rome.

Although he is very pleasant – *and* speaks English fluently – I had to invent an excuse to go out for a walk around Scaletta. There was something in the exaggerated 'niceness' of the interactions between him and us that brought me back to my eighteen-year-old self during my one and only month of study in Maynooth. It set my nerves on edge.

I used the ramble to clear my head and when I spotted a bakery I picked up some cakes for dessert, as Padre Bernard had been just about to embark on preparing dinner when I was leaving the house.

'You took your time!' Joe taps his watch, which is an irritating habit of his.

'I picked up a contribution to the meal.' I put the pastry box on the dining table. 'Hey! Sharp change of clothes! I'd hardly recognise you – is this your Italian wardrobe? Very 007!'

'You need your fine wool polos in Italy in the winter.

341

Don't be fooled by the sunshine.'

'I didn't even bring an overcoat – just my Parka. I don't know what I was thinking of.'

'*Le voilà!*' Padre Bernard carries in a complicated-looking portable grill, which he places on a heat-resistant placemat in the centre of the table. There are individual little pans sitting on the second shelf. On his second trip, he follows up with a tureen of boiled potatoes which he covers with a lid and then a tray with small plates of pickled onions, gherkins and cubes of bacon. I haven't a clue what we're going to eat.

'Did you use the barbeque outside for the cheese?' Joe asks Bernard.

'No, we are only three – I thought each could do his own. And now, I will get my *pièce de résistance – mon fromage.*' The Swiss priest skips back into the kitchen and returns with half a cheese, which he proceeds to cut into large chunks. He lights the grill and fills a carafe with red wine from an open bottle on the sideboard. 'Raclette! In honour of your visit to me. Joe, Rob – *bon appétit!*'

'You *are* joining us, Bernard?'

'Yes, of course. I'll be back in a couple of minutes. I have a different meal to serve the two old boys in the sitting room.'

Joe begins assembling potatoes, gherkins and onions on his plate, and selects a chunk of cheese to melt in his little pan. I follow suit.

'Mind your mouth with the melted cheese – don't burn

yourself.' Joe serves himself some wine. 'Are you sure you won't have a glass?'

'You know I don't drink.'

'A glass of wine won't kill you. It might help you relax.'

'I'm relaxed.'

Uncle Joe shakes his head and removes his little pan from under the grill, scraping the melted cheese over the contents of his plate. 'You seem – preoccupied – since we got here. Are you worrying about tomorrow?'

'Not particularly.' My cheese is bubbling away – and the cubes of bacon I added are burning, so I remove the pan. 'Uncle Joe, I have decided I'm going to try and clear the air with Johnny tomorrow.'

'I didn't realise you'd fallen out.'

'We haven't exactly. Just had – words – over stuff. I'll try anyway. Irrespective of the hearing outcome, I still think he should join me in suing the hotel for negligence.'

'And he won't?'

'Doesn't want to. I mean, we could get a good compensation settlement.'

'Did you *say* that to Johnny?'

'Just pointed it out.'

'No career in the diplomatic corps then, Robert, when you hang up your boots.'

I look around for a bottle of water. Unusually, there's none on the table. 'I'm going to see if I can find some water in the kitchen.'

'No. No water. Not with raclette. You never drink water

343

with melted cheese – fondue or raclette – unless you want to have the mother and father of cramping all night.'

'What am I supposed to drink then?'

Joe just takes my glass and fills it. 'Sip. And don't bring the subject of compensation up tomorrow, if you want to mend fences with Johnny.'

'Unfortunate choice of phrase, Uncle Joe.'

'Thoughtless of me. Sorry. Now, let's do this raclette justice or Bernard will never forgive us.'

Messina, February 14th

At the courthouse, my plan to make peace with my father-in-law backfires; he is nowhere to be seen. Instead, Karen and Davey are in the hallway, chatting to an Italian woman who I suspect is an interpreter.

I walk towards them. Davey averts his eyes and studies a page she is showing him.

'Hiya. It's cold in here, isn't it?' I offer. 'No sunlight getting in.'

Karen smiles. She's always been civil, Karen.

'Hi, Rob, how are you feeling?'

'Let's hear what they have to say, and then we can decide how we feel. No Johnny?'

'Didn't want to come.' Davey finally speaks to me, now that the interpreter has gone to an information hatch. He hastily finishes devouring a flaky pastry and looks around for somewhere to deposit the wrapper. 'Second breakfast! We came over on the ferry from Reggio this morning.'

'Not staying in Messina, then?'

'No. I've a Calabrian liquor plant to visit, so we've taken a few days and hired a car. I'll probably do the call tomorrow.'

The sound of leather soles clipping across the black and white chequered tiles precedes Uncle Joe's arrival.

'Sorry, sorry! Have I missed anything? Karen, Davey. Good morning.'

'What kept you?' I ask.

'Bernard insisted on showing me somewhere nearby to eat afterwards.'

Silvia – that's the interpreter's name – has a word with Davey and we all shuffle after her into this very ordinary small room. At the top, there's a mahogany daïs with a big solid table on it, behind which three people in formal attire sit. We clamber into what for all the world looks to me like school desks. There's a lot of mumbling in Italian from the top table – possibly a prayer? I notice Joe seems to know the words and joins in – and then the man on the right gets to his feet. Even though I don't speak Italian, the rhythm of the speech is repetitious and resembles what you'd hear in English in an opening argument.

Silvia is taking notes and I tune in every time I hear 'Vanessa Walshe' mentioned.

The man in the centre then requests the witness statements to be presented.

'Look!' Karen whispers to me. 'It's the manager from La Villa and two other guys. Do you know who they are?'

'The surveyor and the gardener.'

'Why are *they* here?'

'I'd say as witnesses. They probably had to give a statement as they were in the garden just before the accident and the surveyor was there just after it.' Rob takes a handkerchief from his pocket and blows his nose.

'*Si-lenzio!*'

The first witness is called.

'Dottore Marcello Orlando, I will address you in English for the benefit of the family of the deceased, as I understand you speak English quite well. In your statement, you say that when you left the garden terrace of the honeymoon suite, Signora Walshe was there with her husband who had arrived home from the beach. Is this correct?'

'*Si.* Yes.'

'Did you, Dottore Orlando, have any dealings with the late Signora Walshe, before her unfortunate fall?'

'Well, yes, as the suite in which they were staying is the building we are redeveloping. I had visited to take measurements in the garden a few times. Signora Walshe was particularly interested in the lemon trees and wondering if they would be sacrificed. I was happy to assure her that they would be lifted and replanted after construction.'

'In your statement you say that you left the couple on the terrace, but returned sometime later. The next time you saw Signora Walshe, where was she in the garden?'

'She wasn't. When I came back for my phone with the manager, she was gone. She had already fallen. The men were at the fence. They were distressed and calling for help.'

'You did not therefore, Dottore Orlando witness Signora Walshe climb over the fence in question to the other side?'

'No. I have already said. She was already – *gone* – when we arrived.'

'Thank you. I also see from your written statement that between your first and second visits to the honeymoon suite, you were with the hotel manager in the project office.'

'*Sì*. Yes, this is correct.'

Matters resume in Italian as the next two witnesses read their statements – a short one from the gardener and a lengthy, more formal-sounding one from the hotel manager who is quizzed for what seems a protracted time.

Joe turns to me. '"*Va bene?*" as they'd say. How are you holding up?'

'Fine,' I reply. But I'm far from it. A huddle at the bench with the Villa trio, all speaking in rapid, agitated Italian is making me anxious. Our interpreter is scribbling notes.

Karen, on my other side, has scrunched her face up in the way people sometimes do, when they are straining to hear.

'Can you understand any of that?' I ask.

'Too fast. Just catching: "*aggressivo*", "*molto aggressivo*".

Somebody aggressive – *very* aggressive – towards whom I can't make out.'

'Uncle Joe? Any joy?'

Joe just shakes his head, and puts his finger to closed lips.

The judge gets to his feet and reads a few short sentences.

Then in English, he addresses us: 'Ladies, Gentlemen. We will take a short *pausa* and come back in ten minutes, when I will give my pronouncement.'

Outside in the watery sunshine, we huddle. Davey manages to get four espressos from the vending machine and Silvia sips on a fruit-infused water bottle. I can't comprehend the speed at which proceedings are galloping to a conclusion. I probe the translator for details of the manager's statement.

'He was reiterating that the scrubland did not belong to the hotel. They had placed the warning signage on their side of the boundary, the fence having been fitted a long time before by the previous owner when it was his private house – what is now converted into La Villa.'

'So, is the *fence* not even on hotel grounds?'

'It would appear not. The scrub may – or may not – have been considered part of the Old Villa, but it is not included in the land registry map that shows the plot purchased by the hotel owners.'

'Who owns it now, then?'

Silvia grimaces. 'Oh, it's common land. There is a lot similar in Taormina – because of the gradient of the terrain. Nobody would have an interest in it – it is unusable, because the rock-face is too steep and not suitable to build or grow anything on.'

'No man's land,' Davey says.

'Exactly.'

The court usher is on the steps. It's time to go back in.

I know I'm not going to hear anything I do not know already, yet I'm incredibly nervous waiting for the judge's findings.

'This is it,' says Uncle Joe. 'Poor Vanessa.'

I take my uncle's hand and squeeze it.

'*Signore, signori.* Firstly, I would like to thank you for travelling to join us here in Messina for the findings of this investigation into the death of Signora Vanessa Walshe on the 12th of July 2019. I would like to thank also Dottore Vazzana the prosecutor for the diligent work he has done on this file. Having studied the statements and eye-witness reports of those present or in the area of the hotel on that sad day, I am left with no other conclusion to draw other than the unfortunate lady, in an effort to retrieve a precious possession, voluntarily climbed over the fence and most unfortunately lost her balance, subsequently falling to her death through the common scrubland outside the boundary of Hotel La Villa, 22, viale Matteotti, Taormina. The medical report and post-mortem have attested to the injuries she sustained, and although there were marks on her neck not consistent with that fall, they were not serious enough to indicate strangulation or any life-threatening event. In fact, if you forgive me the personal intrusion, the pathologist offers the suggestion that they are not inconsistent with the natural playfulness of a young beautiful woman and her new husband on honeymoon. Because of all that I have lain before you, I find that there is no culpability to attribute, no persons to try and this hearing will conclude by pronouncing a verdict of accidental death in the case of Vanessa Walshe. Thank you for your attention.'

I am subdued as we put one foot in front of the other and descend the steps from the courthouse out into the glaring midday sunshine.

'So that's it?' Karen says, as she passes me a small bottle of water.

'It would seem so.'

Davey gives his card to Silvia and an envelope with what I presume is her fee, and she shakes his hand and heads off across the Piazza in the direction of an elaborate building.

'The university.' Joe's eyes follow her departing back. 'I wonder does she work there?'

'What? Is that what that building is?' I'm still not fully with it.'

'You need to eat.' My uncle puts a comforting arm around my shoulder. 'Let's try the place Bernard showed me this morning. It's nearby and supposed to be good.'

Although not in any kind of mood to celebrate, we are unanimous in our need for food, and follow Joe up a small street to a trattoria, which is already nearly full with lunchtime trade.

Despite its popularity, Uncle Joe is led to a table with a 'reserved' sign. Padre Bernard has made a reservation for us as a back-up, in case we couldn't find anywhere else at the lunch rush-hour in this professional and university district. I suspect he was fully confident that Uncle Joe would act upon his recommendation and, when we see how busy the restaurant is, we are grateful for his thoughtfulness. Our orders are taken promptly and it is inevitable that the conversation returns to the hearing.

'What I can't understand is all that discussion about someone being aggressive?' Davey automatically pours me a glass of red, then remembers. 'Oh sorry! Can I swap your glass with Bishop Joe's?'

I find myself wrapping my fingers around the stem of the full wine glass, reluctant to let it go. 'No, you're fine. I have the odd glass these days.'

'And it's Joe, please, Davey. I'm off duty.'

'Would it have been the gardener, do you think,' Davey pauses mid wine-pouring, 'they were referring to?'

351

'I doubt it, Dave,' Karen interjects. 'He looked very timid – almost nervous.'

'Then *who* was that architect talking about?' Davey persists. 'Did you catch it – eh, Joe?

'Surveyor,' I cut in. 'He was a surveyor, not an architect.'

My uncle looks at me, but remains silent. I know I'd better redirect the conversation; Karen is sharp. 'He probably meant Johnny. I mean, Marcello saw me with the bloody nose after Johnny landed the few punches when we were both upset and frustrated waiting for the ambulance.' I pick at a few *rigatoni*, the first of our food to arrive. 'In fact, come to think of it, the manager was there as well, for that episode.'

'Oh *no*! That's *not* what we'll report back to Johnny' – Karen reaches out eagerly for her plate of risotto – 'when we give him the verdict. Imagine – being remembered forever for boxing her husband when your daughter is stretched out unconscious at the bottom of a cliff behind you! That would really make him feel better.'

'I'd say you can forget any plan of suing the hotel.' Davey is distracted by the label on the wine bottle. 'This isn't bad. I must photograph the details of the *cantina,* I haven't heard of them before – what was I saying? – oh yeah, Rob, you'd be wasting your time and money taking a civil action. Sure, *who* would you sue?'

I knew he was probably right, but I imagine the optics: I'll appear unfeeling if I don't make some gesture – maybe even release a statement. I might talk to Communications back at the club. Even though it's a personal matter, they might help me draft something.

Uncle Joe polishes off his pasta in record time and then checks his watch and begins to fidget.

'Come on, Robert. We can't dawdle over our meal. Eat up. We've to collect our things at Scaletta and then head to Catania for the evening flight to Rome.'

My uncle hasn't called me 'Robert' since I was a teenager, and then only when he was annoyed with me. I am wondering what has brought this on.

'Is Padre Bernard driving us to the airport?'

'To the coach – not the whole way to Catania. He has work to do, you know!'

I bolt down the remainder of my pasta, knock back the wine which isn't half-bad as it happens and excuse myself, so I can head to the cash-desk and pick up the tab for everybody. It will go some way towards reimbursing Karen and Davey for the interpreter's invoice.

When I get back to the table, Uncle Joe has turned his attention to the travel itinerary of the Walshes.

'When do you go back to Dublin?' he says.

'Sunday,' Davey replies. 'Gives me time to do a quick *liquore al bergamotto* plant visit in the morning – they open Saturdays – then we'll meander back up towards Lamezia, staying Saturday night "en route" somewhere, and catch our Lamezia-Milan connection early Sunday, then on to Dublin later.'

'Flights are very convoluted at this time of year.' Joe reaches for the drinks menu. 'And this *bergamotto* drink, what's it like?'

'A kind of limoncello, only with oranges! Bergamot oranges. It's good. Not as cloying as limoncello.'

'And you'll import it?'

'If the price is right.'

I am at a loss as to what Uncle Joe is doing. Having made me belt down my lunch, he's now stalling with Karen and Davey and has even ordered a *grappa*!

'I thought you were in a hurry!' I say.

'I'll be with you in a minute. Go and see if you can spot a taxi in the Piazza. And when you're passing the cashier on your way out, ask them to bring the bill.'

'It's covered.' Aggravated, I dump the receipt for the table beside Davey, and do as I'm told.

There are two taxis waiting in the square, the drivers standing beside the second one, arguing animatedly as they pore over a pink newspaper spread on the car bonnet.

Uncle Joe catches me up, his coat draped over his shoulders.

'Right, are you ready? *Scaletta, per favore*,' he addresses the drivers and waits at the first car.

When we're out the road from Messina, my uncle turns to face me in the back seat of the car. I'm waiting for the 'Robert', so severe is his look.

'So, what's the story between you and the architect man? Were you trying to – I don't know – *implicate* him in Vanessa's fall?'

'*Surveyor*. I didn't – *implicate* him. And there isn't a story – well, not really. Just that he was always hanging around, flirting with her.'

354

'Flirting is not a crime, if it stops at that.'

'I didn't like him, OK? We'd had a couple of run-ins and I was full sure he was going to point the finger at *me* – say I pushed her over the fence or something, so I thought I'd go on the offensive – make him a bit wary of shooting his mouth off.'

'*That's* why he said you were aggressive! Because of these "run-ins". I thought I heard "*marito*" a couple of times. He wasn't talking about Johnny – he was talking about *you*.'

'Probably.'

'And *did* you?'

'What?'

'Did you push her over the fence, Robert?'

'I'm not going to dignify that with an answer. You know *nothing* about what happened!'

'As of today, the official line is "accidental death". But if it wasn't, Robert – well, let your conscience be your guide. You know what you have to do.'

'Bishop first and uncle second?'

'You profess that your faith is important to you. You don't need me to tell you what to do.'

The taxi pulls into the courtyard of the Scaletta house and Uncle Joe pays the driver. He bounces out of the car, leaving me still inside, and runs up the steps to the door, pushing through into the hallway without a backwards glance.

Chapter 28

Johnny

Allenbeg, Tipperary

My head is throbbing and I am sweating profusely. I can't understand why I'm so hot. I must be running a temperature, or maybe I've left the portable gas heater on all night? Breda was always warning me about that – how unsafe it was – what with the fumes and everything. I seem to be lying on top of the bedcovers and the bolster that's normally wedged at the wrought-iron bed-end is nowhere to be seen.

As I open my eyes fully, I realise I'm not in my own room. There's far too much light, for starters. Mine faces north and is dark, whereas despite it only being spring, confident sunlight is leaking through a gap in the curtains, illuminating the awful squiggly-patterned wallpaper and the modern white dressing table in the bay of the window. There is no bolster at the end of this bed, because there is no wrought-iron bed frame. There are in its place cushions

— lots of cushions, shades of mauve and purple — dislodged from their usual neat position. Several are on the floor, and the bedspread thing that matches that dreadful paper is just about to join them.

I have crashed out on Vanessa's bed.

I reach for the switch on the bedside lamp and discover I am fully clothed. The heavy oiled-wool sweater I was wearing yesterday is stuck to me with sweat. I kick my leg out from under the last stubborn cushion that's clinging to the bed, and am relieved to see no boot on my foot.

I don't know how, but nearly nine months later the bedcovers still smell of my daughter. The fragrance permeates my brain and conjures up a series of fast-moving images of Vanessa — each captured and frozen in a diverse pose like those lads in Pompeii with a bowl in their hand and a spoon raised to their lips as the lava struck. I see her in her favourite red winter coat. I picture her presenting the sponsor's award on the stage of the Miss Ireland final. In another, she's wearing a drab grey sweater and woollen hat, out on the streets serving soup with her Simon Community friends. There she is helping out in mud-splattered dungarees and a checked-shirt, whooshing the girls into the milking-parlour, or more recently, down in the kitchen, wrangling with fiddly bits of coloured marzipan, the petals of flowers for the wedding cake which just would *not* stick on to the icing. Now, at the hall-door in her wedding dress, Breda's locket at her throat. Smiling beside the car as the chauffeur squashes the billowing material of her long train in after her. Then, she's standing at the top of the church. The bishop is waiting to start. But the seat across from hers is empty; there's no groom! He's left Nessa at the altar!

I sit bolt upright on the bed, sweat now pouring down my face. That's it; there's my dream out! That's why I woke feeling so uncomfortable, almost delirious. It's the recurrent one about the wedding day – where the groom is a no-show, and in the end there is no wedding.

When I throw open the curtains, I have a fair idea of what I was doing before I succumbed to sleep. Scattered on the floor are a lot of newish-looking summer clothes – light flimsy stuff the like of which you'd never get any decent wear out of during an Irish summer. Flung across a pile of shorts and tops, are a few smart dresses – a blue one, an emerald green one and a sleeveless lemon yoke with a little jacket to match. They have hardly a crease in them, so new do they look. I'm sure they never saw the inside of a washing machine.

And how could they have? Because I recognise that what I have chucked out of the wardrobe are all the things Vanessa bought especially for her pre-wedding functions and her honeymoon. Karen used refer to them by some fancy French word, which I can't for the life of me remember. I start to bundle the clothes into a heap in the corner and wonder what in my liberated drunken state of the previous night I was planning to do with them. Was I thinking of a bonfire maybe, to wipe out any physical reminders of the outings and events linked to last July? I wish I had a chance to wipe out *more* than just the clothes – preferably, to wipe out that whole period from my memory. Not only Vanessa's tragic death, but – as in my dream – to wind the clock back even further to a time when there was no honeymoon because there was no wedding and – most of all – when there was no Rob.

My whiskey haze begins to clear and I notice a couple of crumpled newspapers under the last of the clothes. All but one is folded open on an inside page, where amidst miscellaneous tales of insurance scams and compensation for slipping on squashed tomatoes in the supermarket, I have marked in red Biro a short column: **Honeymoon Death: Accidental**, with a head and shoulders shot of Vanessa in her wedding dress. No groom here either, interestingly enough.

The remaining two papers feature similar material, with the provincial weekly placing the story on the front page with a bigger headline: **Local Girl's Honeymoon Tragedy: No Case to Answer.**

This, of course, is what must have sent me for the whiskey. How could I – *even for five short minutes* – have forgotten what had me in that state last night, or the states I have been in on each preceding night since February, when Davey phoned with his non-news from Sicily! The whiskey fug is not the only culprit. Since it happened, I have gone over and back in my mind about what I should do. Who should I tell? But tell what? A bit of idle gossip.

An ambiguous voicemail from my now dead daughter. An uncomfortable hunch I've had for some time. Something I *think* I saw but that nobody else can corroborate.

And what would *I* risk in speaking out about something that no longer has any relevance – to my family, anyways – but will only serve to titillate and sell newspapers who would reprint even more pictures of my beautiful daughter, tugging the heart out of me as her eyes might catch me unawares, staring down from the garage shelf when I'd least expect it? Is *that* what I want? I have done the soul-searching and the self-doubt for over nine months: *why* am I only reaching crisis point now?

It might be because the investigation is over and that has made the papers. People are stopping me in the village and commiserating with me. Shaking my hand all over again. *'Wouldn't you think the hotel would compensate you?'* Or worse: *'That poor young husband of hers, I don't know how he's ever going to pick himself back up and get on with life after such a thing.'*

I am in turmoil, more so than ever. Because I'm expected to *react:* to show *more* than just grief. To demand a civil case; to lead a public campaign for mandatory safety measures on private premises. To march on the embassy, to request the Minister for Foreign Affairs to intervene. Even if I had the energy, how could I? How *could* I do any of those things, feeling the guilt that I do? Knowing the truth of what really happened on that scruffy little patch of bumpy grass to the back of La Villa's honeymoon suite?

And strictly speaking, it shouldn't be my job to pursue

any further action; it should be her husband's. If I were to go to the press about my dissatisfaction over the investigation, it might only fuel those – *crazy* – no – those *disgusting* – insinuations he made last July.

It was during one of those nightmarish post-funeral days here on the farm, both of us circling each other like tomcats trying to mark our territory – me nearly feral with the grief – when one sunny morning, out he comes with it *again*: 'Did you not consider,' says he, 'that you were a bit "*over-attached*" to Vanessa?' I had thought – *hoped* – that he had forgotten the nasty insinuation he had already made when we were in Sicily. I had put it down to his shock after the accident, but it seemed, no, he intended to keep stirring the pot.

I began to be hypersensitive about my normal affection for my daughter and ran around the house like a madman, tearing down photos of just her and me, rummaging in the photo box for pictures of all four of us to replace them with!

I drew the line at deleting from my phone one of the last pictures we had taken together – up on Mount Etna, an oul' geyser puffing away in the background. She had her arm around me – which *I* know is just the normal affectionate way we carried on. Yet if these images were to be made public, it might give credence to his crazy, sick theory.

On Vanessa's white dressing table sits the wedding album. It's here, despite my repeated attempts throughout last summer to reject its acceptance and send various delivery vans packing. It was only when that funny old car bumped across the cattle-grid and into the backyard, did I realise that Tammie, the little photographer girl, had brought it in person.

I still wanted nothing to do with it, but I could hardly send her packing straight away, seeing as how she'd driven down from Dublin on what had been an unseasonably hot and sticky September day. Besides, I was curious to hear why *I* was getting the album and not Rob.

She asked for a cold drink and I found some Fanta in the fridge. 'Will we take it outside?' she said, and promptly lifted two glasses and the bottle off the table. (Since when do Irish people now eat and drink outdoors at every conceivable opportunity?) I went along with it, presuming she felt like a bit of air having been cooped up in the car, but not before I doubled back in to the sink to get a damp cloth and one of those cleaner-sprays. There were all kinds of dirt and droppings on the chairs and table – don't ask me where the seat-pads have gone – Karen is a dreadful woman for tidying things away where I can't find them.

As soon as it was safe to sit down, she pulled a grey-and-pink-bound wedding album out of a now familiar Jiffy bag.

'Now, Mr Walshe, I know you've tried your best to keep this out of the house, but let me explain.'

I took a sip of the gassy drink. 'You're right. I want no memories of that cursed wedding.'

'Of course. I can understand that. And let me begin by apologising for not being . . . at the church. Or indeed coming to see you sooner, but I was away . . . travelling.' She ran her hand distractedly across the cover of the album. 'I was – deeply shocked – to hear what happened to Vanessa. There are no words—'

'No. At least we're agreed on that.'

'But . . . in time, you might treasure some of these images . . . the ones of you and her, here at the farmhouse, before you headed to the church.'

Tentatively, I reached out and took the album. I turned to the first page. The early sequences were solo shots of Ness – fixing her dress: putting the finishing touches to her hair, standing in the doorway, flicking her train behind her. The next batch were all of me: straightening my bow-tie; talking to the chauffeur, fussing with the buttonhole.

I remember the exact question I asked Tammie last September: Did the photographer – did *she* – choose the order in which to compile the album? Emphatically, she had assured me 'no', the choice of shots to include and their precise sequence, was all Nessa's work. As soon as she had received the contact sheet, she had instructed Tammie about which to use and which to delete. She must have done that from Sicily if the photographer's memory was to be believed.

Six months later, I'm looking at that same squat block of collated images sitting on her dressing table, and wonder would it be so awful if I ripped out all the later pages. If I just let the story end at the point where we get out of the car at St James's – just her and me – and as in my dream, no Rob appears and there is no wedding.

But what if an outsider should someday flick through the wedding album and find inside – no wedding! Just picture after picture of a loving daughter and her adoring dad? Surely I'd be leaving myself wide open to Rob's sick accusations.

———

I make a quick appraisal of the room. For some reason, Davey's warning against preserving it as a shrine comes into my head. Perhaps it *is* time to make a start. It might even help me to process her loss. That, and talking to someone.

But before I close the door on the mess, I cross to the white dressing-table, open Vanessa's little jewellery box with the pink ballerina that used to go around and around when she'd wind it up – and lift Breda's locket out. I rub the tarnished gold with my thumb and let the two halves of the broken pearl necklace drape over my wrist. It was decent of that Captain Dee Francesca to send it back to me when the police eventually found it in the undergrowth at the back of the hotel.

No matter what the family makes me give away, this stays. I will treasure it and take it back to my two girls when my time comes to join them in the grave.

In the midst of my daily grief, I am consumed by the guilt of my silence. I am strangled by a promise I made and the fear of what might happen to me. I cannot bear it much longer. Someone needs to know.

Chapter 29

Bishop Joe

When I was a young priest, I served as a chaplain to the prison service. I remember being disturbed at how depersonalised the inmates seemed – how when I would meet them in the Visitor's Room – different individuals on different days – there was a 'sameness' about them. They dressed in 'civilian' clothing, but those clothes were not their own from their pre-prison days and, as a result, there was a dull frumpiness – a similarity about the serviceable prison-supplied outfits. Irrespective of the crimes they were admitted for, or the length of sentence they were serving, their chat was invariably repetitious. They focussed on the day-to-day routine of the place – the aspects of the exercise or the work programme they enjoyed. They talked about the day of the week they liked most – usually because of the dinner that was served on that particular day. Only when they were nearing their release date, did I hear anything about their family or loved ones on the outside, and sometimes those thoughts were voiced fearfully, as if their release might not happen, or their people on the outside might not continue to exist in the same way as previously.

Here in the Anima Sana Sanctuary in Dublin where I have been resident for the past three and a half weeks, I observe the same conversations. My fellow inmates stick to the conversational safety of *'What's on the menu for tea?'* or *'Are you going to Mindfulness at four?'* because it's more sociably palatable than to say: *'Hey! Fancy a gander at the forty-seven slash wounds I inflicted on my abdomen, when I was going through my self-harming phase?'* That's why we stick to evaluating chicken chasseur versus vegetarian lasagne, or the Donnybrook Pilates instructor versus the Chinese yoga master.

Who was it said something to the effect that humans can't bear very much reality? It's so absolutely true of this place.

All sorts of people cave and crumble when the reality of their life gets too hard. That's what I've discovered over the past couple of weeks. My cell – sorry – roommate – is a university lecturer who tried to drown his baby son because he wouldn't stop crying for nine hours on the trot – the baby, that is, not the lecturer, though I'd say the latter did his fair share of crying after the event. I am doubtful the lungs of an infant could sustain nine hours but, however, I am just reporting what I was told. And I am

366

inclined to believe him, because there is an unspoken solidarity among inmates, every bit as staunch as anything I saw in Mountjoy as a green novice priest. We take each other's truth at face value; not to further compounds the reason we're in here in the first place.

Mostly, we're here because we have been REFERRED. Let's not fool ourselves with all this PC nonsense of entering 'freely' to solve our problems. That's psychiatrist-talk for 'arm-twistingly encouraged' to come i.e.: *Come or Else!* You don't have an option. Either you agree, or they'll get some well-meaning relative to sign a bit of paper sectioning you. I mean, I don't say to a friend looking for a change of scene for his holidays: 'I'll refer you to the Hotel Belvedere in Lake Garda. You'd love it!' They can play around all they like with language and call our admission a 'check-in', but we are as much inmates as the lads in the bad clobber up in 'The Joy'. We may wear our own clothes, but only a dumbed-down version of our personal wardrobe – clothes that have been checked and scrutinised, every sharp button and decoration removed! Not to mention the belts – even the drawstrings in our sweatpants! The jewellery – not that I have much, but the women filled me in – locked up 'for safe keeping'. *Mon oeil,* as our French friends would say.

And then there is communication with the outside world: discouraged. More than that, made impossible. At least the prisoners are entitled to one phone call a week, but mobiles are seized, bank-cards – *(what's a bank-card?)* – sequestered. No mon, no fun.

Too accessible, this centre, one of the nurses explained. That's why the bank cards are *verboten*. Zip through the car park, leg it through the *perovskia* beds, hop over the wall and Bob's your uncle! Out to Bray on the 145 or if you're daring, run across the road and the city-centre is your oyster.

———

Imagine how I felt when I arrived: the de-frocked bishop – although not officially struck off, still 'just Joe' in plain clothes. Driven here by dear faithful Father Tom, who from the beginning of my derailment has been loyal. He collected me from the police station in Ennis on that dreadful night, mercifully bringing with him a set of clothes, and managing to talk the guards around to dropping the 'public indecency' charge, saying it was a medical condition, this sleep-walking.

And was it? Illness induced? I'm not sure, but I do know that my restlessness had been building and the stress had forced it underground, where it manifested itself in my unconscious body wandering the pavements in the dead of night. Because what *is* a man of the cloth supposed to do, when confronted with a Solomon dilemma – a crisis of conscience concerning his extended family? His only option is to shed that cloth, renege on his episcopal garb and all the responsibility that it carries, and escape back into the anonymity of his primal state. The nakedness was a symbol of my desire to go back to being 'just Joe', a rural King Lear, wandering a county-town street at three in the morning *sans* teeth, *sans* clothes, *sans* everything.

Well, I do still have my teeth, but that's about all, because I certainly don't have my job in Ennis. I received a very sympathetic call from the archbishop two days after I had made my press appearance, suggesting that the trauma of what happened to my nephew's wife the previous year and my obvious closeness to them, had taken its toll on me, and I was being granted permission to take a leave of absence to deal with my condition. 'Post-traumatic-stress-disorder' is what they decided I had – but unlike other frontline warriors, the soldiers in God's unit would never be compensated for it in any court.

Instead, I was sent off on 'garden leave'; in my case, to the pretty gardens of the Anima Sana complex in Dublin. Four weeks to begin with, of therapy and an assigned team of psychiatrists and social workers and counsellors and yoga instructors. There was basket-weaving and art therapy as well, but I intended to avoid them.

Initially irate at being sent away, I slowly resigned myself to the idea, and became appreciative of the intermission. Grateful too, for the anonymity, because either fellow mental-health patients don't follow the news, or they are just too polite to admit to it. Either way, I could be 'just Joe' and forget for a while what I needed to do, or even if I *could* do anything, with the information I had been given back in April.

Sometimes people tell you a secret just to unburden themselves; they have no expectation of you ever using it. In fact, as in my case, they often explicitly *ask* you to 'do nothing' with it, thereby neatly off-loading their guilt onto you.

This was precisely what had happened to me and, in the sanctuary of Anima Sana, I slowly began to accept that. The poor girl was dead. She wasn't coming back. The local police had decided it was just an unfortunate accident. My family were already hurt enough; so were hers. What was there to be gained by unpicking those last five minutes of Vanessa's life?

But try though I did to erase from my memory the imagery that I had been presented with – I couldn't, and coming into constant contact with those involved did not help the progress of my elective amnesia.

This morning, my psychiatrist has given me a release date – they call it a 'discharge' date – but if feels like the former. I rang Father Tom and told him the good news. By chance, he happened to be in Dublin meeting an old friend, so he decided to call out to visit me. I don't think I have ever been so pleased to see anyone. It was as if I was reclaiming my normal life – not experiencing the dead-air artificial calm and false politeness of the centre that passes for life – where your every minute is programmed and accounted for, in case you might sneak off for half an hour on your own to just breathe and do nothing. *Doing nothing* is not espoused. Mental health illnesses abhor a void. If you want a quiet space, then you have to go to a room to 'meditate' or 'reflect' or 'commune with a higher being' – not just sit in the garden and do feck-all.

Tom brought with him both post and news. The accumulated correspondence of over a month quite happily filled two large brown envelopes, and as I was obviously deemed sufficiently in recovery to read a couple of circulars, my secretary was allowed hand them over.

The important communication which I had been hoping for was buried among the fundraisers and the latest encyclicals. I had been successful in my application for a secondment to the college in Rome, where I would begin instructing new seminarians in September. The post would be for a calendar year, after which I would return to Ireland to resume my role as bishop – once a suitable vacancy in a new location presented itself.

Although it's still only June, I am already looking forward to the move, and plan to go earlier than my academic commitments require, to acclimatise and enjoy a bit of the Italian summer. My curate couldn't help but notice my obvious delight when I read the confirmation of the new posting.

'Something has brought a smile back to your face, Bishop.'

I shushed him. '*Joe!* It's Joe in here. Always. It's my secondment to Rome. It's come through.'

'I'm delighted for you. Not so delighted for myself, but however! I don't know if I'll be let stay on with your replacement.'

'Oh, I'm sure they'll find something for you. If not in Ennis, maybe in Dublin? Would you like that?'

'I enjoy the buzz of city life – and my family are here. We'll see. Certainly, I have more friends working in this general area, than in Killaloe diocese. Speaking of friends, I bumped into your nephew – Rob – earlier.'

'I didn't know you considered Rob "a friend".'

'We met in the Choral Society in Trinity when I was doing my Theology degree. Did you know Rob is quite a good singer? We were quite – close – for a while, but we lost touch after he left. It's really through you that we've become friendly again.'

'But of course! I completely forgot that. You were a mature entrant into the seminary at Maynooth. I am just so used to curates going in straight after school.'

'No. A "late vocation". That was me. Saw a bit of life first.'

'And yet Rob blanked you completely when you met at that pre-marriage chat last year in the palace. Why was that?

'Oh, I suppose he was embarrassed – with Vanessa – God rest her. He wasn't – that into girls, when I knew him.'

I felt uncomfortable with Tom sharing this and tried to shift the focus back to the present. 'So what was Rob doing in the middle of the day in the capital?'

'At some fundraising campaign for the Children's

Hospital. There were a couple of other rugby players there as well. He was with that little photographer – the one who did the pictures for the wedding? I presume she was working on it.'

'Did you say you were coming here to visit me?'

'Well, I didn't like to mention it with Tammie there. Should I have?'

'No. He knows where I've been. Not for long more. Thankfully.'

'So next week, back to Ennis – then *Roma!*'

'Yes, life must go on.'

'Rob was just saying that too. Imagine, it's nearly a year since Vanessa died.'

'Not quite. A couple of weeks to go yet.' Something in the way Rob was *anticipating* the first anniversary – almost wishing time would accelerate to the milestone – made me wonder if his reason for being with the photographer was work at all. 'Do you think Rob is seeing this Tammie – I mean going out with her, or whatever is the current expression?'

At this, my curate started to grin. 'I doubt it. I wouldn't think she's really his type.'

'And what *is* his type? I mean, post-Vanessa – it's hard to know.'

'Vanessa was a once-off. I don't think he'd try to repeat the experience.'

'But he *is* likely to start dating again?'

'Put it this way, Bishop, I think he'll look elsewhere in

future. Now, if you're OK to hang on to those envelopes, I'll leave you in peace. I have to meet my mother in half an hour. Let me know exactly when you expect to be out and I'll organise everything.'

I stand under the porch roof and watch him go, zipping through the car-park at speed, heading for the main road and freedom.

I walk around the side of the building and select a bench. I sit with my face raised to the midsummer sun and commit the mortal sin of 'doing nothing', apart from mulling over what my curate had said: that Vanessa was a once-off, an experience that Rob wouldn't try to repeat.

For everyone's sake, let's hope he's right.

Part 6

Autumn 2022

Chapter 30

Rob

Blackrock, County Dublin, August 27th

The view from the attic bedroom that is unofficially mine when I stay at Frank and Genevieve's never fails to lift my spirits. It stretches across the expanse of sea to the peninsula of Howth directly opposite. To my left lies the port of Dublin and its more industrial skyscape watched over by the twin barber-pole chimneys of the now defunct Poolbeg power plant. To the right, the architecture cedes to the residential areas that hug the coastline, culminating in the pincer-protected harbour of Dun Laoghaire, and the backdrop of its town skyline punctuated by church spires and, once again, by construction cranes.

Although not a Dubliner, I love Dublin Bay.

Strangely enough, I also love this house. It's a pre-war semi that's ramshackle and disorganised and, as far as I can see, shows no evidence of either my father or his partner being particularly interested in homogenous décor – or even that keen on tidying up.

But when I think back to the animosity I nurtured for so many years towards Genevieve and my dad's second family, it is a miracle that I am here at all. I didn't hesitate when he suggested spending the night before my wedding to Tamsin under their roof. He has even invited my mother and her new partner, Ronnie, to join us for the brunch which we'll have in about an hour's time.

My half-sisters – the twins – are bridesmaids – one of Tamsin's better moves. It has really endeared her to Genevieve who can be prickly enough in her own way – I don't think she has ever forgiven not being included in the Round 1 invitations to my first wedding – but I have to give her credit for opening her door to Mum today. At least one of them is a grown-up.

⸻

'Robster? Are you decent – can I come in? It's Milly.'

'Well, I'm in my brunch gear – not the full bells and whistles yet – it's too early.'

'Your mom has arrived already – with what's-his-face.'

'Ronnie.'

'And he *has* one – a "Ronnie" – that's what Dad calls a moustache.

'*Très drôle.*'

'Wrong lingo. I study Spanish. Speaking of Spain – I've

378

had bad news on that front.'

'What?'

'Email from the airline. I'm going to have to split early from the wedding – straight after the dinner. They've cancelled Sunday's flight and I really need to be back for Monday. I've re-booked on the late one out tomorrow night.'

'How will you make the airport from Wicklow?'

'Dad's going to drive me to the coach – probably to one of the Dublin stops. It depends on how we're doing on time.'

'That's good of him.'

'Yeah, he's cool about it. Anyway, I was sent to get you – I think *my* mom's a bit uncomfortable with Lily on her own.'

She had no reason to be. Even I am taken aback by my mother's conviviality – and it has to be said, by how glam she looks! Already in her wedding gear – a teal-blue frock with a matching jacket and a very audacious mustard-gold faux corsage – she has also had the presence of mind to throw into her bag a white over-shirt, which she swaps her good jacket for. A messy meal, is brunch.

Molly exclaims out loud when she sees Mum's outfit is the identical shade of blue as her bridesmaid's dress. Tamsin gave each of the officiating bridesmaids a choice from five colours: Milly went for the fuchsia pink – which is disturbing me slightly. The girls look really pretty and have spent the last few hours doing each other's make-up

379

and hair – Molly even dried and crimped mine! We will travel to the church in the limo together. They didn't really feel comfortable about getting dressed at the Roches' – so Tamsin suggested this solution. I love the way she's relaxed about these things: she doesn't get all 'hung-up' on protocol and worry that the world might go into a tailspin if two bridesmaids were seen arriving in the groom's car.

The covered deck to the rear of the house is sufficiently sheltered for us to enjoy our brunch. My mother and Ronnie are silenced when they get their first real glimpse of the magnificent view. When the white car ferry looms below us in the bay, framed by the petrol-blue sea of the late summer day, I see a flicker of distress pass over Mum's face. Is she sad? Or jealous? Or maybe regretful that things with Frank fell apart. It's hard to know, but when she refuses Genevieve's offer of a Buck's Fizz and asks if by any chance she might have a G & T, I am pretty sure Ronnie won't go the distance.

I am now in full dress uniform as specified by Brigadier General Roche: in other words, I'm wearing this silly morning suit. I don't know what to do with the hat – I *could* carry it but I'm definitely not wearing it. Honestly, Finnuala, not your finest hour. Maybe I should just abandon it completely – leave it here at Frank's – because if I don't make a stand over a superfluous felt top-hat, I am straying back into Walshe territory, and I really can't go back there.

For the second time today, there's a tap at my bedroom door – and it's Frank – eh, Dad.

Unlike me, he is enhanced by his morning suit – the black and greys complement his silver-fox hair, whereas with my newly curled locks I look like I'm the MC at a holiday camp talent show.

'Good, you're ready – all trussed up like the proverbial — sorry, I shouldn't say that. You look very smart. Your car is here.'

'I feel like I'm about to go on stage.'

'You are, son. Marriage is mostly about acting a part.'

'Is that what you did with Mum?'

'At first, yes. In the beginning I got away with it. But I was a lousy actor, and couldn't carry off the suspension of disbelief.'

'And with Genevieve, do you still "act"?'

'It's different with Viv. We're not married – so in a way, we *have* to be more honest, because nothing other than love binds us to each other.'

'*Why* is love *so* difficult?'

'Because our expectations of human beings are too high. Maybe we should be forced to do the three-riddle test that Turandot demanded.'

I smile, remembering Frank's lovely, thoughtful gift to

381

me over the bank holiday weekend – a father and son bachelor trip to Verona with tickets for Puccini's *Turandot*.

'But *Turandot* didn't work out too well! The suitor got all the riddles right – but she still didn't want him.'

'*That's* what makes love so difficult. We cannot choose who we fall in love with.'

'Not sure I one hundred per cent agree with you. It's not always a "rush of blood to the head" decision. Sometimes, a kind of love can flourish from a decision made with thought and pragmatism.'

'When did *you* get to be so sensible? I guess all that strategic planning on the rugby pitch has to infiltrate other aspects of your life.'

'I suppose.'

Frank looks at his watch – then at me, with a 'stern dad' face.

'You have to go. One last thing: do you remember our conversation when in Verona?'

'Which one? We had lots.'

'The evening we *weren't* going to the opera and we went for a leisurely dinner in Piazza Bra—'

'To that restaurant with the Irish-sounding name—'

'Yes. Liston's. Do you remember the thing I asked you to do?'

'Vaguely.'

'Don't mess with me, Rob. You remember full well. Ditch this organisation you have got entangled with – this "abstinence" crowd.'

'True Love Waits.'

'It's a load of bollocks. Resign from the board, have nothing more to do with them – it's harming your reputation – in rugby circles – and elsewhere.'

'I don't see what my personal convictions have to do with my professional life.'

'Bullshit! You know full-well it makes you look odd! Tell me, was it Joe who pushed you into their arms?'

'*Uncle* Joe? Not at all. In fact, he's of the same opinion as yourself. Thinks I should cut loose.'

'Well, that's something, at least. Would you not listen to him – and act upon his advice?'

'I'm done with Bishop Joe's *guidance*. Now, haven't you and I got a wedding to go to? We'd better make a move.'

I watch my father adjust his clearly disappointed face, as he leaves the bedroom, calling out for the girls as he goes.

I guess this is it: Robert Jeremiah Cunningham is off to be married again.

Chapter 31

Tamsin

Greystones, Co Wicklow, August 27th

The flowers sit in a huge basket on my side table. The selection is exactly what I would have chosen myself: white lilies – with yellow stamens rather than those devil-spawn staining rusty-red ones; freesia – shades of mauve and lilac – a bit of an indulgence this late in summer, but I'm worth it. The arrangement is padded out with baby white carnations and double chrysanths and the ubiquitous gypsophila filler beloved of florists. I'm less enthusiastic about the chrysanthemums, finding them a bit creepy ever since as a naïve fifteen-year-old I accidentally bought them for the aunt of my then French exchange student, not aware of their Gallic significance. When we arrived to dinner at the aunt's apartment – me bearing the flowers, she promptly burst into tears when I held them out to her, and shut herself up in the bathroom for a good hour. Unknown to me, her husband had passed away three months previously, and chrysanths are only offered in French households at a time of mourning and, even then, rarely brought into the house.

Still, no mourning here. The general look of Rob's basket is thoughtful and expensive. I have him well trained.

When I inherited him after Vanessa's death, he hadn't a clue. He wouldn't have known a dandelion from a daffodil, and I often wondered what she had got as gifts for special occasions – birthdays, Christmas, Valentine's Day. These things don't particularly interest me, but Finnuala is the archetypal south Dublin mummy who sets great store by showy manifestations of affection. I tried to redress Rob's deficit to keep her onside. It's an inter-generational thing: my mother had been well-primed by *her* mother before her to start off a relationship the way you meant to continue. From a teenager, she had schooled me to 'demand'.

But the older and more independent I became, my artistic temperament reacted against my mother's philosophy. Only in those early weeks when I was trying to decide whether a relationship with Rob would be worth the hassle, did I try out a few 'demanding' requests of him, to see how he'd respond. Strangely, he seemed to *like* them and went out of his way to please me. Today's wedding-morning bouquet demonstrates that he continues to do so.

———

'How's it all going?' My relationship tutor has entered the bedroom. 'It's nearly eleven. Nails are here. Do you want to come down or will I send her up?'

'She can come up.'

'Oh, you got Rob's flowers! He's a sweetie, isn't he?'

'An absolute "pet", as you'd say yourself.' Then I notice my mother still looks a bit hungover from whatever she was up to at the golf-club the night before, and suggest: 'Mum, it's not too soon for you to head in the direction of Make-up. You could stay in your dressing-gown, and when Nails are finished with me, I'll get her to do you next – in your room.'

'*Already?* Is it not a bit early?'

'You want to get in ahead of the bridesmaids. I mean, there's five of them. That's a lot of slap.' Then I remember the twins are dressing in Frank's – and only joining us at the church. 'Well, three from here, that is.'

'I still think that was a bit foolish of you – to let those girls do their own thing. What if – *I don't know* – they go with a Goth look, or something awful?'

'They'll be fine. Molly and Milly are young and beautiful – they haven't a lot to worry about.'

'Apart from the mismatched dresses.'

'Just different colours, Mum – they match perfectly.'

'Whatever. I'll just pop down to the kitchen and see that

386

they have the champers on ice – for the girls – and any visitors.'

'You do that.'

I am not insensitive to the fact that today is going to be hard for my mother. I am delighted she has agreed to walk me up the aisle but I know, in asking her to do that, it is going to highlight my dad's absence for those attending who know nothing of our family circumstances. Apart from finding the whole 'giving me away' concept generally a bit offensive, I was *not* going to press-gang a superfluous uncle whom I hardly knew into doing the job, just because he has a penis. Finnuala and I have done fine, just the two of us, since Dad died. Who else would I want to do the handover?

But Rob, I've grown to understand over the last few months, is incredibly conservative when it suits him, and I have had to learn the true meaning of compromise. It was hard enough getting him to accept that a *woman* might give me away; I didn't like to think how he would have reacted if I said I didn't intend to be given away at all.

With no sign of the manicurist, I go down to find out what has happened to her, and find Mother already lined up, awaiting her turn at the table.

'What happened to your make-up? I told you to get in ahead of the bridesmaids.'

'I tried to. But the make-up artist had already started on Anne and, God knows, she needs a lot of time. I thought I'd pop in here and join this queue.'

'Go easy on the sauce, Mum. I don't want you dragging me into a side pew as we walk up the aisle.'

'As if!'

———

Back in my room, I tidy up the bed and try to make the place presentable ahead of the beauticians. I know I'd probably be better off going downstairs to get my nails done, but I am trying to avoid all the fluffy 'brouhaha' that's going on.

For I'm not a 'natural' wedding person. I guess having been around so much *nonsense* when the only photography I did was wedding work, I was 'weddinged-out'. Don't be fooled by the five bridesmaids, three of whom have been handpicked by Finnuala. As an only child, my mother had no option but to rummage through the presentable cousins, eliminating those who were currently in advanced stages of pregnancy. Eventually, she settled on two – in their *forties* – and tracked down a girl I had been friendly with in school. The wedding in its current manifestation is all Finnuala's. And because I know this sort of thing is important to her, I just let her off. If I could have got away with a registry office and a witness, I would have preferred to go that route.

In all this showy drama, my mother has had a staunch ally in Rob who, if anything, was over-enthusiastic in his desire to help. She resisted at first – deemed it 'interference'

— but then began to enjoy his evident glee at the paraphernalia that surrounds wedding-planning, unlike me, who focussed only on the aesthetic elements that might reflect poorly on me professionally after the event, as I am still reliant on some wedding photography for an income.

One recent August evening as we were out walking on a blustery South Beach, Mum informed me she'd be bringing along 'a date' to the wedding. I just love the quaintness of her generations' language! It turns out some fellow who had repeatedly signed up as her partner for the Mixed Foursomes in Delgany had an ulterior motive. I am delighted for her but, as I will only meet him for the first time today, I reserve my judgement. I am attributing the escalation in her excitement about *my* wedding, to her newly found personal happiness.

But that beach walk was significant not only for my mother's disclosure about her new man; she also marked my card as to how our relationship would continue post-marriage.

'I've put in my – nearly thirty years, if you count the pregnancy. Tam, you're a fully fledged adult – and after this wedding, you will be financially secure and my responsibility for you is over. I want my life back.'

'That's lovely, Mum! You're washing your hands of me.'

'I am doing no such thing and well you know it! I am

just – looking forward to not worrying about you. Not feeling you'd be completely alone, if anything happened to me.'

'You're sixty-six, Mum, and going nowhere!'

'OK. But what if *I* want to live a little? Go on a world cruise – sell the house, I don't know. Just break out from being a widowed mother!'

'Mixed-Foursome has really got to you!'

'Maybe he has. But Tamsin, Rob has money behind him – a family – *two* families, really!'

'Yeah, and I'll have two mothers-in-law. Thanks for reminding me!'

'Nonsense! Genevieve will never be your mother-in-law, just Lilian. But you *are* going to have a lot of people in your life in the future. And that pleases me, to know you're not going to continue as "a loner", with just photography and your trips for company. You can continue to do all those things when you need a break from him. But you'll have the security of a home to return to, and that can't be taken from you as his wife. No matter what.'

'You've given this some thought.'

'I have.'

After my mother's confessional sunset walk, I was not as surprised as I might have been when Rob arrived to Greystones one evening shortly after with a large white envelope containing a prenup. Clearly my mother wasn't the only one who was concentrating on the 'business' side of the marriage contract.

Even though I was aware that such a document holds no legal status in Ireland on the breakdown of a marriage, I cast this aside, as reading through the requests and items listed in the agreement, gave me clarity and an insight into Rob's expectations of our union. By considering what was laid out before me, it also gave us an opportunity to discuss the type of relationship we were embarking upon – something we hadn't to date done in any great detail.

On the subject of children – not something we had discussed at all – Rob is really keen to become a dad, and I have agreed to two – if fate and health will co-operate. I have requested a nanny in the event of becoming a mother, as I fully intend to continue with my career – and, as the nature and wildlife side of my portfolio continues to grow, that will necessitate being away from home for quite a considerable time.

If he is to have his children, then my demand is for a better house – somewhere on the Wicklow coastline that I am accustomed to, and not in his soulless estate where I'm tripping over Vanessa's bad taste in furniture every time I turn a corner.

The final – and most difficult aspect – of our hollow contract, concerns my willingness to accept and allow him 'continue as he has always done'. Take what you like out of that but, although it's a concession that pains me, I will agree to it, because I want our partnership to work.

All relationships have bits that are not perfect. I don't necessarily agree with all of Rob's views . . . do I agree with *any* of his views? But I know that I want a nice lifestyle, and he can give me that. I don't want to find myself forty and alone, struggling to survive financially and with the few friends I *do* have all booked up with their significant others at weekends while I sit in alone with a takeaway and a bottle of wine, crying over *Casualty*.

Because it's a slippery slope from Electric Picnic social dynamo to sad 'too-old-to-party' lone person. I refuse to use the word singleton since the damage Bridget Jones did to it.

These things happen incrementally. One minute you're twenty-five and you are out there – skirts up to your arse, a shot in your hand and you think, like Céline sang, that you'll go on for ever. The next, you're thirty-four and the gynaecologists are describing you as 'geriatric.'

Marrying Rob is a rational rather than a romantic decision. I am only doing what generations of women have done before me, in decades when you didn't have to suffer the pressure of being a 'new woman'. Women like my mother married men they hardly knew, and didn't have to defend themselves to the sisterhood who breathe down our necks now, *demanding* a reason for our decision, questioning what *we* are getting out of it and wondering why, oh, why are we capitulating and turning our backs on the feminist ideology by *giving in*.

We give in, because we fear that lonely Saturday night with

the rancid wine and the gelatinous Chinese, and no company other than a box-set of a decades-old medical drama.

There's a light tap on my bedroom door and my mother enters without waiting, carrying a half-empty bottle of Bolly and two glasses. She's been through Make-up, has her dress on and is looking very presentable. Mixed-Foursome is a lucky guy.

'I don't want you to be cross – but I've been on to the woman organising the music.'

'Why?'

'Well, you remember yesterday?'

'Most of it. It was Friday.'

'Now don't go mad – but the Polish violin player at the rehearsal in the church – the one with the allergy to flowers or whatever? I've sacked her.'

'You've done *what?*

'The coughing and spluttering – sure, we couldn't put up with that.'

'But she's critical to the operation! A *Quartet*. You need four of them to make it work.'

'Oh, I'm sure they'll manage grand without her. She'd ruin the recording with all that hacking. Shouldn't you be getting a wiggle on? I don't want to put you under pressure, but it's nearly one.'

'I thought we'd agreed that I'd be fashionably late?'

393

'Yes, but you still need to get dressed. Here. Have a glass – I've some canapés out on the landing. Your hair is very nice, by the way.'

'Thanks.'

'When you're done with the victuals, put your dress on and she can touch-up your face. Will you need help with those fasteners?'

'Probably. I'll give you a shout.'

'And don't dilly-dally. That Rob – he might have his moments, but he's a good catch. You don't want to push your luck!'

A 'good catch'? Poor Mum! Apart from the sexism of her language, even *she* might throw this particular fish back into the water had she read Clause 5 in the prenup!

The work I've had to do to lure him away from that cracked celibacy organisation! I'd say Mum gets more action out of Mixed-Foursome on the 9th Tee, than I do out of Rob on a regular basis.

Before signing the 'document', I give him an ultimatum: either I road-tested the merchandise or there would be no wedding. He didn't like it, not one little bit. He gave me the whole spiel about his faith and beliefs, but I called his bluff and reminded him of Clause 5. He had the good grace to blush deeply and looked quizzically at me as if there was something he wanted to ask – but decided against it.

Later that evening when I wasn't expecting him, he

called in to my place on his way home from a pre-season photocall at rugby HQ. It was most strange: *he* seduced *me* – full-blown seduction. The sex wasn't the best I've ever known but, there you are, we've notched it up on the bedpost and he is technically broken.

'Tamsin? Are you ready, love? It's time.'

My mother – head-to-toe in her favourite colour, lavender – comes out of the sitting room. The blusher on her cheeks has dissipated the Bollinger flush and she looks serene. She is fidgeting with her bag – a fussy diamanté-encrusted clutch – and I look at her and I feel an ache in my chest as I prepare to leave my girlhood home forever.

'Mum? I love you. Thanks for everything.'

'Stop. Don't get maudlin. Sure, you'll be back the first time he comes home steaming drunk, roaring and bawling and demanding conjugals.'

I think of the way Rob looks at Father Tom and I cry.

The cars are waiting. The bridesmaids line up, bouquets in hand. They kiss me and pat me and tell me I look 'amazing' and I know it's all lies: I look averagely attractive, just like I've always looked, and two hours in Hair and Make-up is not really going to change that.

I wave them off in the first car, and steel myself as I get Mum into the limousine on our last sad journey to the church. She spots the mirror on the back of the driver's seat and checks her face. There's a rogue blob of mascara on her left cheek, and she takes a tissue from her clutch to chase it down. The car leaves our road and makes a sharp turn up the hill into St Paul's and I look at her, knowing this is the end of our exclusive mother-daughter partnership. I think my heart might break.

Chapter 32

Davey

South Dublin, August 27th

I am glad we have made the unanimous decision to attend this wedding. Avoiding it would smack of sour grapes, if that's not too trivial a phrase to use about your late sister's widower moving on. It's now over two and a half years since the investigation into Vanessa's death concluded there was no culpability on anyone's part, and that my sister died as 'the result of a tragic, but unfortunate accident'.

Both the protracted legal process and the hearing's outcome took its toll on Dad, plummeting him into a prolonged depression, which despite our best efforts he found hard to shake off. In those gloomy months, the only thing that brought a smile to his face was when the media – both Italian and English-speaking – consistently referred to Vanessa as 'Vanessa Walshe'. Mischievously, he took additional satisfaction out of this minor detail, because he knew how much it must have been irritating Rob.

Because although they had started out good enough buddies at the beginning of his relationship with Vanessa, the esteem in which Dad held him seemed to diminish as that relationship grew. It had further deteriorated well in advance of her untimely death. By the beginning of this year, I suspect my father had more or less written Rob out of his life, which is why his wedding invitation came as such a shock.

There was another contributing factor which accelerated the distance between them – the enforced hiatus years brought about by the public health pandemic, the start of which coincided neatly with the closure of the investigation into Vanessa's death. Although unwelcome, it gave our family respite from outsiders – and, even sometimes, from each other. It certainly was convenient for putting on hold any residual relationship Dad might have been expected to have with his son-in-law. With nobody visiting or travelling much, I suspect my father was relieved to have had nearly eighteen months to breathe and heal out of the public eye.

Perhaps these 'gap' years have been similar for Rob – given him a chance to reclaim his own identity and ditch his 'victim of tragedy' status. Certainly, in the interim, his rugby career has gone from strength to strength. Last autumn, he made the Ireland squad for the international series and he played in two of the matches, one of which I attended. His success continued throughout the spring when he was included for the Six Nations championship and, although he didn't start any match, he came on in the second half against the less onerous opposition. Delighted to be able to attend live matches again, Karen and I went to all the home games, on one occasion with complimentary Stand tickets he sent our way.

In provincial rugby circles, Rob was tipped as the unofficial second choice hooker for the national team's summer tour, and it came as a shock when he failed to be included in the enlarged travelling party. I caught a brief TV interview with him – unfortunately, an interview that Dad saw as well. I hardly recognised him – he has changed his hair dramatically – grown it longer and 'highlighted' it blonde. He must think he's a centre!

When the female sports interviewer asked him if he was disappointed not to be included in the New Zealand tour, he coyly replied: 'A blessing in disguise being left out, according to my fiancée. She has a long list of things that need doing before our late summer wedding.'

Whether it was his enhanced media visibility over the spring or the blasé reference to re-marrying in that June interview that sparked it, but Rob became a renewed topic of conversation in Allenbeg and he was suddenly back in Dad's sights. We have had many worrying conversations at home about his vocal opinions of his former son-in-law.

'Honestly, Dave, Johnny would want to be careful,' Karen said one evening last week when reading the sports supplement of the *Herald*. 'Any more quoted throwaway comments like these, and he'll find himself on the receiving end of a libel writ.'

I tried to defend him. 'I bet that was after an Allenbeg county match. You know what he's like when he's fired up. Loses the run of himself.'

'This is more than just "foot in mouth" disease! It's quite calculated. The journalist was only interested in the GAA game, yet he works in a snide dig. Listen: *"We have real men in Allenbeg's football team, not the overpaid nancy boys that play professional rugby – I should know, sure didn't I have first-hand experience of them when my poor unfortunate daughter linked up with provincial hooker, Rob Cunningham."* I mean, he's mentioning him by name and everything. You'll have to have a word – and before this wedding, in case there's media at it.'

I always do what my wife tells me, so we have invented a rather circuitous route to this afternoon's wedding. Dad will drive from Allenbeg to our house, expected to arrive good and early, where he'll have a snack. Then we'll all travel together to the Greystones church. We want to prep him on the way and make sure he is suitably calm before meeting his nemesis after such an interval. It's important that he sees the reality of present-day Rob in a normal, happy setting – an ordinary, slightly pompous guy who had a bad time a few years ago – but, like everyone else, is entitled to a 'fresh start'.

I know we asked him to be here early, but I am only just out of the shower when I hear the hall doorbell ring.

Karen, ahead in her preparations, opens the door to Dad. I lean over the banister, eavesdropping on their conversation.

'Johnny! You look smart – dressed already! I thought you would have waited until you got here to change into your finery. Where did you park the jeep?'

'Around the corner. Is that OK?'

'Sure, as long as it's not blocking anyone. You know how territorial city folk are about parking. Better run it into our driveway, when there's space.'

'I might go and shift it now, so. I can leave it across your gate for the time being.'

'When you're done, go on in to the conservatory. I've left a tray of sandwiches and a Thermos of tea. I'd better go — finishing touches.'

'Go, girl. Off with you.'

'Davey? Your dad's here!'

That is my cue to appear. I throw on my pants and shirt and head downstairs to relieve Karen.

But when I go into the conservatory expecting to find him tucking into a sandwich, he's still outside on the road, pacing up and down, on his phone in animated conversation with someone. I rap on the living-room window and wave. He gives me the 'thumbs-up' sign but continues chatting.

As I pour two mugs of tea, I hear the hall door slam.

'Finally. Good morning to you! That was a long phone-call. Anybody interesting?'

'Huh? Oh, only Michael. Problem with one of the machines.'

'Not *your* problem anymore, Dad. He's the one making the profit!'

'Profit? Devil a bit of profit in farming these days. What's in the sandwiches?'

'Here. Take a selection and see for yourself.'

Later, when we are all suitably trussed up and finally in the car, I opt to take the scenic route over the mountains to Wicklow – less frenetic. We're hoping the tranquillity might rub off on my father. I kick off with the preliminaries.

'I hear Rob's out injured – not that there's much happening yet – a couple of friendlies. Neck strain, apparently.'

'Hard to believe. Sure, he has some neck, that fellow.'

'Well, it'd be a dangerous injury to play with – considering his position,' Karen says.

'I suppose so.' And then after some reflection, Dad asks. 'What's this Tamsin like, anyways?'

'*Tamsin*? Don't you remember her?'

'How could I remember her when I never met her!'

'But you *have* met her, Johnny, lots of times – for Vanessa's wedding.'

There. It was out. The V-word. Karen had slipped up. We had sworn not to mention Ness if we could help it.

402

Still nothing from the rear.

'Dad, she was the photographer. I think she was calling herself Tammie then.'

'Little Tammie – the girleen with the spotty wellies – and *Rob?*'

I chance a quick glance in the rear-view mirror. He looks displeased.

'She was a nice enough girl,' he says, 'but – I would have thought – a bit *plain* for Rob's tastes.'

'Well, to each his own.'

'*Tamsin* – is *Tammie*. Am I the only thick who didn't make the connection? Why didn't you tell me if you all knew?'

Karen lays a hand on my arm as if to say 'leave it, I've got this'.

'We thought it might upset you, Johnny, since you'd built up a bit of a relationship with her – the wedding album visit and all that.'

I see Dad shake his head in disbelief. Karen turns up the music station and we drive in silence past purple heather and the occasional startled sheep.

***

I'm nearly relieved when we hit the main traffic artery and our exit for Greystones. I follow the directions to the seafront, and suddenly the church springs up on an ordinary residential road, sandwiched between houses. I am surprised it's so big. Its concrete façade is painted in a mellow shade and there are three prominent windows to the front.

For some reason, I had in my mind's eye a Wicklow version of St James's – all white and romantic. Instead, this church is a characterful, urban building with solid intentions.

A guy with a flag is standing at the gate, waving us away: we are obviously too late for a space in the grounds. Dad speaks for the first time since the Tammie revelation.

'Where will you find parking?'

I don't answer, just keep driving towards the beach where I know there's plenty.

'I don't mind a bit of a walk,' he says. 'At least it's dry.'

'But it's windy!' Karen says. 'If this hat takes off, I'm done for! It's a bastard to get on at the right angle.'

'You'll look lovely, anyways.'

'*Thank* you, Johnny!'

I spot a gap between two cars outside the wall of a large house and indicate. 'This will do nicely.'

As we turn into the church gate, I remember my half-promise to be an usher. A hassled-looking guy is standing a few people ahead of us, doling out multi-coloured button holes.

'Is that your man?' Karen says, with one hand still holding her hat. 'I can't remember his name, the fellow Rob demoted from best man?'

'Terry. Back in favour. Or so I hear. Look. He's on his way over.'

'Mr Walshe. Davey.' He nods at Karen.

He offers us our flowers. Dad declines.

'Dave, would you give me a hand with these booklets?' Terry says, pulling out a bundle from under the flowers, and then resumes button-hole duty.

'Sure. I'll be with you in a minute. Now, Dad. Remember what I told you. Just keep smiling, no matter what happens. Don't speak to any fellows with cameras, or phones or anything. You'll probably have to listen to a lot of shite over the next eight hours, but don't react. Just grin and bear it.'

'Why don't I just put a black sack over my head and be done with it?'

'Go on, Davey. We'll be fine.' Karen blows me a kiss.

I don't know why I was enlisted as an usher, because when I follow the best man to the church porch my assigned job has been covered. The leaflets are already out at the end of the seat rows and a bridesmaid is doing the altar kneelers. I go back outside to find Karen and Dad standing chatting to Rob's mother *and* to his father, who has brought the full complement of his other family with him this time, the daughters in different-coloured bridesmaid's dresses.

'Afternoon.' I shuffle in beside Karen. 'Do you remember me?'

'David. Yes, poor Vanessa's brother.' Lilian shakes my

hand and indicates the rest of the party. 'You haven't met Genevieve, Frank's partner – their two girls Molly and Milly, I think you know.'

Karen holds her hand out for one of the leaflets I am carrying.

'You weren't needed for long.'

'All done already.'

'Do you think Tamsin will be on time – or will she do the deliberate stalling thing?' Karen says, addressing no-one in particular.

'Oh, she'll milk it for what it's worth – her *grand* entrance,' volunteers Lilian. 'A bit of a drama queen, though you wouldn't think it to look at her. Not like Ness—apologies. I shouldn't have mentioned—'

'That's alright, Mrs Cunningham,' Dad interjects. 'You can say her name. Nessa.'

'But insensitive of me. And it's *Lilian* – Lilian Stewart. I ditched "Mrs Cunningham" when he ditched me.'

'Well, see you later, Lilian – Frank,' says Karen and taking Johnny's arm she leads him away. As I follow she grins and whispers: 'This surname touchiness obviously runs in the family!'

Dad elbows me in the ribs. "Not the only thing! Like father, like son! Collects wives for a hobby!'

———

As Rob's mother had predicted, it's a quarter past three and there's no sign of Tamsin's car. The groomsmen begin to herd people into the church, and we follow suit.

Photographers snap the famous guests and ignore the rest of us. Dad keeps his head down when one approaches. I put my hand up and mouth, 'Please?' and the guy backs off.

There's an odd-looking middle-aged fellow standing outside the pastoral centre which is attached to the side of the church – obviously not a guest since he's wearing a rather scruffy-looking trench coat and a tweed cap – but Karen notices him as we file in.

'Love, does that bloke not remind you of someone? Apart from the dishevelled look, he's the image of Rob's uncle the bishop. Where did he go to work in the end – Rome or somewhere?'

'Haven't a clue.'

Once within the confines of the large porch, an organ can be heard ululating reflective music to get us in the mood as we queue. I am aiming for a suitable pew a good distance from the altar – to keep Dad as far away as possible from the action and because we're the first wife's family and Tamsin mightn't appreciate us featuring too prominently.

Suddenly, there he is, coming towards us: the groom. He pauses from adjusting the flower in his buttonhole, lifts his head and looks my father straight in the eye.

'Hello, Johnny.'

'Hello, Rob.'

Chapter 33

Rob

I am standing in the garden of the Wicklow Glen. The sun is sinking slowly behind the hills. The sky is streaked with yellow and blue and white and pink bands of striated cloud – a rainbow sunset to match the bridesmaids' dresses! Thus far, it has been a fabulous day. I don't know whether it's a politically correct thing to say, but this wedding has been far more enjoyable than my first.

The Roche family – and by that I mean Finnuala, because she *is* the Roche family – insisted on an old-fashioned receiving line-up, where the guests come and shake our hands. Because of my complicated family status, we kept all the parents out of it. The bride put her foot down and rejected the idea of having a 'gift table', which was popular in the United Kingdom when Finnuala herself had married there all those years ago. If we were strictly observing this 'meet-and-greet' tradition, our guests would have been expected to offload their goodies onto a designated table, with a lockable box discreetly provided for cards that might contain vouchers or even cash.

But this is Ireland, and although we may be as grabby as the next, we are discreetly grabby. We have already fleeced our friends and family for the monetary equivalent of the Glen's most expensive four-course dinner – by two. The guests know it, and we know it, and the wedding-list people at Brown Thomas sure as hell know it.

We have made these transactions simple for them – provided bank-account numbers and recommended outlets whose vouchers we would welcome. I was relieved to get the line-up out of the way before the cocktail reception. It was awkward to say the least – some of these guests had already gifted me substantial amounts a mere three years ago. I do have a conscience, after all.

Despite my quibbles over the wedding-gift heist, I am enjoying the evening. The guests are milling around, taking selfies by the bronze sculpture and the many water features dotted throughout these magnificent landscaped gardens. The champagne is still flowing freely – (I have to say it – not a mean bone in Finnuala's body – she has been very generous). Tamsin looks happy. My mother and father are even talking. There is peace in the valley.

Helped in no uncertain way by two people – my new wife, Tamsin – and my father, who is conciliation personified. Having Frank's renewed support with my rugby career – and the back-up of his advice even if I don't *always* follow it – makes me feel more secure. My life could be good from now on.

I know it's a bummer that I'm out injured, but there have been some advantages. For a start, it made not having most of my teammates present today far easier. Tamsin gave me 'a quota' of rugby players I could invite! I've also been freer to put the final touches to our wedding myself. Finnuala was all up for it, as Tamsin's enthusiasm had begun to wane on the home strait. I imagine having styled and photographed so many weddings over the years, she just ran out of steam for her own.

The *last* time – despite pretending to everybody that we had done everything over a rushed eight-month period, Vanessa and I had been secretly engaged for several months *before* the father knew, and our preparations were well advanced. *Once* he knew, the Walshe clan took over. I was lucky that they allowed me show up on the day, such was their control!

But these last few weeks planning the ceremony with Father Tom and Finnuala have been a total pleasure. I'm glad Uncle Joe wasn't available to marry us, because Tom has been a joy to work with and a far more understanding and sympathetic cleric than Joe would ever have been. I think even Tamsin has enjoyed his company around the place.

Tamsin – dear sweet Tamsin! What can I say? She is so understanding. Unlike Vanessa who monitored my every move, Tamsin is a free spirit – and never puts pressure on me. She allows me the freedom to do my own thing, safe in the knowledge that when I come home, I come home to her oh so willingly. For her part, she demands in return certain standards and attentions of me – and I feel it's only right to deliver.

She even made me reconsider my involvement with True Love Waits and was scathing about the abstinence pledge. Coupled with the pep-talk from Frank in Verona, I began to think they both couldn't be wrong. Maybe it's time I distanced myself and concentrated on matters on the playing field. Tamsin had the balls to follow up her request by giving me an ultimatum: I accepted the challenge, because losing her was not an option.

Unlike Vanessa, Tamsin really is *my* Tamsin. She doesn't belong to *Morning Glory* or the Miss Ireland competition or even the Simon Community. Nor is she enmeshed in the myriad of other fashion and frivolous things that Nessa espoused – *and* from which she made a lucrative living. Tam has her photography – which as her reputation grows is increasingly nature and wildlife and serious field-trip photography – and that's it. No publicity shots at silly o'clock. No cameramen flirting or leching at her while she's still in her pyjamas at 6.00am. I won't have to share Tamsin with anyone, apart from maybe some giant tortoises or a new-born fawn in the Phoenix Park. That suits me just fine.

As for her sharing *me*, well, she has been wonderful about that too. There's a lot to be said for a liberal Trinity education; no uptight nonsense in the shadow of the Silvermine Mountains.

When I think of the Walshes and the year and a half I spent with them! The demands, the constant control and that bloody father forever on my case! They are all here today, but that's PR more than anything. Joanna suggested I embrace the second wedding factor and deal with it head on by including them. She had a point: you don't pay your media adviser that much and ignore her advice. After a lengthy and welcome silence, Johnny Walshe resurfaced as soon as I made the national squad and has been conducting an insidious, damaging campaign to undermine me. I need to nip it in the bud. If I could engineer a photo of them taken with me here at the wedding, that would dilute the impact of any future nasty comments he might come out with. The fact that I would invite them – even make my brother-in-law an usher – would say more about my magnanimity than his petty jibes.

It's funny, but just as our honeymoon – Tamsin's and mine – is about to begin (ten days in an indulgent hotel in Elounda, Crete), I can't help but reflect on the first one – that ill-fated trip to Sicily.

I shudder when I recall how *passive* I was, how I just let Vanessa have her way with everything, because – well, I guess – I felt I owed her.

I remember our first night in Taormina. After nearly thirty-six hours with little or no sleep, I was expected to get washed and dressed and head out into the evening to join the Walshe clan for an indifferent pizza in a mediocre joint. I wouldn't have minded just going for a cocktail, but Vanessa had earlier made me send a ridiculous text from *my* phone, saying I would love to see them all for dinner to make up for my supposed grumpiness on the journey! I had no choice in the matter; I was expected to stick to the plan.

There was fault on my side, too. I probably should have had that Sicilian siesta Vanessa had suggested when we checked in to our hotel, and I wouldn't have been so narky later that night.

But I don't like being told what to do. Didn't then, don't now. And I had turned her down, claiming a desire to go and 'explore', when really, it was a need to get out on my own, to get away from her so I could breathe again.

That sort of enforced proximity will *never* happen with the Roches, because Tamsin's need for individual space is nearly greater than mine, and Finnuala has a life *apart* from Tamsin. Yes, she'll be on our side no matter what is thrown at us, and when the kids come she might help us out occasionally, but she won't always be there – unlike Johnny, always hovering like a bloody drone, watching, waiting, registering if anything goes wrong.

I am being summoned by Terry. They are ready to serve inside and some geezer is banging a gong to clear the garden. One of Finnuala's opera-society friends – dressed in full costume – is standing at the top of the steps into the Sugar Loaf function room. He opens his mouth and bellows a line from *La Traviata*: *'La cena è pronta!'*, which although it sounds a lot posher, is just the Italian equivalent of 'grubs up'!

Our guests begin to troop in. I scan the garden for my wife and spot her sitting with an elderly couple – an aunt and uncle, I think. I make my way across the grass – already dewy in shaded places – and take her hand.

We wait until all the guests are inside, and prepare to make our grand entrance.

Chapter 34

Johnny

We have been summoned into the Sugar Loaf Room for dinner and I'm feeling a bit edgy now. I don't know what to make of the day so far. Karen and Davey seem to be enjoying themselves which is good, because they work so hard and seldom let their hair down. The Champagne reception out in the beautiful gardens has been very civilised and I am beginning to regret my decision not to drink. Mrs Roche, Tammie's mother, seems like a lovely woman and most generous.

I cannot *believe* the change in Rob! I nearly fell over in the church when we bumped into each other. I know he's always been fond of his appearance – the matching outfits and so on – but Christ, this is on a whole different level. He has the hair streaked blonde and is wearing it girly-long; he even has *waves* in it today. Despite not playing because of the injury, he must still be working out hard, because he's definitely dropped pounds, and I'd put money on it that his deep tan came out of a spray-can! The summer hasn't been *that* good. My immediate reaction when I saw him first was that he looked more like Michael Flatley in that first *Riverdance* show than a member of the national rugby squad!

Then in comes the bride, and she too is unrecognisable from the free-spirited, wackily dressed young photographer of three summers past. Poor little Tammie – not the world's prettiest girl – she has gone for a stiff, old-fashioned dress with a big sticky-out skirt – and the girl is short, it doesn't quite work. Whether it's deliberate or not, she has mimicked Vanessa's hair from Number One wedding – an *up-style* – (that's the right name for the hair-do – God knows I had a pain in my face listening to Nessa going on about it). I feel sorry for the poor lass, when I think of what life with Rob could be like.

The church ceremony was very grand, no expense spared. Musicians – *and* opera singers no less! The organist giving it welly for several tunes; even a string quartet according to the leaflet – though one of them was struck down with the lurgy at the last minute, so it ended up being a string trio.

I have a pain in my jaw from the smiling. Davey frightened the shite out of me this morning with talk of writs and solicitors, so I've been the nicest chap in the house since.

At the entrance to the Sugar Loaf room, there's a map

of the tables. I check my phone for a message, before we go in to eat. Karen is scrutinising the guest lists.

'I hate these things,' she says. 'You never know if you're going to end up at the most boring table in the room. There we are – Table 17. Oh, Johnny! They've included your "plus one". I must have forgotten to mention that you were coming on your own!'

'Don't stress, pet. Sure, I can eat the two dinners if I'm up to it.'

Karen laughs, but she looks unsure if maybe I intend to.

I watch and smile as the younger guests – all a bit pissed and skittish at this stage – weave uncertainly through the tables, looking for their number. Oh, to be here just to enjoy yourself! That might be nice. I spot ours – conveniently placed facing the wedding party.

'Davey? This is us.'

Our unknown dinner companions are settling themselves, losing hats and wraps and looking forward to the fun part of the evening, when I notice what Karen had predicted: the place card at the setting to my right reads, *'Guest of Johnny Walshe.'*

I am unsure as to whether it's the done thing to remove my jacket just yet, and as I wait to take my cue from Davey, the chair to my right is pulled out.

'You made it, so.'

As Bishop Joe folds his trench coat in half and drapes it over the back of the seat, the waitress puts two plates – the first course – in front of us.

Karen, talking to a waiter about wines, looks over at me and observes the empty seat filled.

'*Bishop!*'

'Please – Joe.'

'I thought you were tied up abroad somewhere – unable to come?' she says.

'I was unable to *officiate*. I never said I was unable to come.'

'I must have heard wrong. Davey, look who it is!'

My son is startled. 'Oh, it *was* you – earlier,' he says, addressing Joe. 'We thought we saw you in the church car park . . . eh, we weren't sure it was you . . . as we heard you weren't coming.'

'Well, here I am – large as life,' Joe said with a grin.

'That priest made a good fist of the ceremony, did you not think so?' says Davey, obviously trying to make conversation.

'Did he? I wasn't actually *in* the church.'

'Well, he was certainly very warm, anyways,' I say. 'Karen, would you pass me up the water jug like a good girl?'

'I trained him well. He used to be my curate in Ennis. Don't you remember him?'

Slowly, the memory of a previously bearded and shaggy-haired young priest who had helped out at Vanessa's funeral comes back to me. Could this be the slightly older, more serious man who had married Rob and Tammie today?

'He's changed a lot – the hair, no beard,' I say. 'In fact – it's been a day for changes. I wouldn't have recognised Rob if I'd bumped into him on the street. Very thin, very trendy –'

'Very gay.'

I nearly choked on a stringy bit of Italian ham. 'What did you just say?'

'Ah, Johnny, cut the pretence. I said Rob looks very gay.'

It all made perfect sense. I was done with my starter. I was never a big fan – slimy indigestible meat – but after this, it would really have choked me.

I lower my voice and glare at Joe. 'So you *did* know when I asked you – when I had a *go* at you outside St James's after the wedding rehearsal?'

'Always suspected it.'

'And *you* let my Nessa go ahead and *marry* him, knowing what you knew!'

'I knew nothing definite. It didn't seem to fit in with his job or his lifestyle, so I thought, yeah, maybe he's genuinely committed to the strict doctrine of his faith – the "no sex before marriage thing" – and it's *us* – even someone senior like me *within* the Church – who are out of step, because we've all turned our backs on what the rule-book stipulates.'

Before I can respond, the wine-waitress offers a choice to my dinner companion and he selects the white.

I put my hand firmly over my glass.

'Not drinking, Johnny?'

'You know why not. I want to keep a clear head. And, listen, *Bishop* –'

Davey speaks up on my left. 'Ah, Dad, one glass won't do any harm. Help you relax.' He tries to offer me a glass of red – the waitress has left the bottles on the table.

'No!' I growl.

'So, how you've been keeping, Bishop Joe?' Davey leans forward to ask.

'You mean after my breakdown and all the subsequent problems I've had since we last met?' Joe takes a sip from his wine.

Davey has the good grace to look embarrassed and focusses instead on my plate. 'Are you not eating your starter, Dad? That's good Parma ham. You shouldn't let it go to waste.'

'Take it, so.'

He has his fork on the meat before I finish speaking.

'Only Rob —' Davey continues, chewing the Parma — 'mentioned that you were going to be out of the country for today. That's all. We weren't expecting to see you.'

'Well, plans change.' Then as the serving trolley with the fish course begins to rumble around the table, he concentrates on Davey, leaning forward to continue his inquisition. 'So, you and Rob are still in contact – despite what happened to Vanessa?'

'I don't arrange to see him by *appointment*, if that's what you mean. Maybe after the friendly matches, if he stays on, well yes, we'd certainly say hello. But he was probably training hard to make the overseas tour for the last while – I haven't seen him for months – apart from when I ran into him briefly at our local club in Dublin – he was giving a masterclass or something to the kids' summer camp.'

'And was that the last time you saw him before today?'

'Yes.'

'Does Tamsin go to all the matches like Vanessa used to do?'

'Bishop, if you don't mind me saying, you're in the wrong job! You should have been a police interrogator. What's with all the questions?'

'Idle curiosity, that's all. But does she?'

'What – oh, Tamsin? I hear she's not sporty. No interest in rugby apart from maybe photographing the corporate side the odd time.'

'That must suit Rob – to have free rein to relax a bit after his matches.'

'And do *you* go – eh, *Bishop* – to Rob's matches?' I ask.

'Occasionally. He invited his father and me to one of the Munster matches at the Aviva. V.I.P. treatment – best seats – food after and everything.'

Karen interrupts. 'Excuse me, Joe, Johnny. The waitress is checking if you opted for the lamb or salmon?'

'The lamb, of course,' I reply.

'And you, Joe?'

'Wicklow lamb, just like the bride!'

The waitress smiles, makes a note and departs.

Karen turns to Joe. 'Lamb in August?' She laughs. 'That's one hairy old lamb! Eh, no reflection on the bride, of course.'

421

In the lull after the main course, people began moving around for a bathroom break, and I notice a bit of movement at the principal table: Frank and one of the little twins are clearly saying goodbye to everybody. I wonder why they're leaving before the speeches.

I stand up and give Joe a nod to follow me outside – we need to discuss our respective plans.

For my part, I had only agreed to come to this wedding with the intention of standing up and making a speech of my own – at the right time, of course – so all the guests would know just how Rob had failed his first wife. I have the notes in my jacket pocket.

But since I belatedly realised that Tamsin Roche was not some faceless Greystones rugger-hugger but in fact little Tammie – my resolve has begun to weaken. Throughout the day, as I have enjoyed Mrs Roche's hospitality and observed the evident rapport Tammie has with her new twin sisters – and the mother-in-law – the *mothers*-in-law, I conceded that humiliating the girl by publicly attacking Rob, was not the way to go. God knows, the poor girl is probably going to be humiliated enough in the future.

Joe's plan – as far as I can grasp – aims to focus on the 'soundness' of the marriage: whether Rob was *really* free to enter into a commitment with Tammie.

As we make our way back to the table, I am just about to plead with him to consider the young bride, when Rob, completing his walkabout through his various guests, notices his uncle resuming his seat beside me.

'Uncle Joe. Not in Rome, after all. Able to dine, if not to officiate. My mother thought she spotted you in the church car park, but I put it down to all those G & Ts at brunch in Blackrock.'

'Well, I hear you had the pleasure of Tom instead.'

'As celebrant?'

'What else?'

'Yes, he was most obliging on all matters in the run-up to the Big Day. And – why are *you* sitting with the Walshes and not with your own family?'

'Johnny invited me as his guest.'

I could have kicked him – bishop or no bishop! I saw immediately the altered expression on Karen and Davey's faces. I had wanted to keep this to myself: now I just looked sneaky – all along plotting behind their backs.

At the top table, the best man is banging a microphone.

Rob excuses himself. 'I'm up in a minute.'

'Your favourite bit, Johnny!' Karen laughs as she tries to pour me a glass of wine.

I reach instead for my suit jacket on the back of the chair. 'No thanks, pet. I'm going to make a break for it – the bathroom – outside for an imaginary cigarette – anywhere but here! See if I can cut it down to only one or two boring speeches!'

423

'Dad! That's rude, sit down.'

Davey looks cross, but I still escape, just as Finnuala Roche is about to begin.

———

Outside on the timber decking, looking at the gardens lit below by occasional spotlights scattered throughout the vegetation, I think about Tammie. It's her I'm concerned for. Suppose Rob begins to unleash that short temper of his? Or withdraws affection – or more – just like he had with Nessa? Of course it all makes perfect sense now – after what Bishop Joe said – but why the heck is Rob marrying *women*?

Maybe he's changed. Maybe Tammie and he will have a rake of kids and they'll do a family portrait, the babbies propped up on a velvet sofa for one of those old celebrity magazines that Vanessa was always buying. That would quash the rumours once and for all that he's not really a ladies' man.

When I see those golden highlights, I am inclined to doubt it.

———

By the time I'm back in the Sugar Loaf suite, Rob is on his feet.

'*When I first came across Tamsin, I couldn't believe my luck. She*

424

was the most warm, funny woman I had ever met. She was everything I longed for in a partner: caring, considerate, calm. I need calm. Spending your working life with your head wedged between two 110-kilo men, you need your personal life to be calm!'

Laughter from the guests.

Karen and Davey, now sitting on the same side of the table, are getting a bit giddy. 'Dad!' Davey whispers. 'Doesn't this all sound very familiar?'

'She and I have a similar family background. We are both only children who, along the way lost a parent – through one means or another. I am happy to say that I got my father, Frank, back with the added bonus of my lovely half-sisters, Molly and Milly. Tamsin wasn't so lucky. But she could have had no better woman to take over the role of solo-parenting than her mother Finnuala here. They formed a little team and supported each other with strength and fortitude after the premature passing of Greg.'

There's a warm round of applause for Mrs Roche, who nods her head in appreciation. Rob rattles his page and resumes.

'As an accomplished and talented photographer, my teammates who are here today have met Tamsin at many charity fund-raising events. What many of you will not know is that she offers her services voluntarily when we are promoting the Children's Hospital charities and many others – too numerous to list. This generosity imbues every aspect of her character and it is one of the traits that makes me love and appreciate her greatly.'

Davey, slurping his wine, mutters, 'I'm all into recycling, but I've definitely heard bits of this speech before!'

'Ladies and Gentlemen, please charge your glasses! I stand before you all today, family and friends of many years, on this my wedding day, and I am delighted to present Mrs Tamsin Cunningham. My beautiful, understanding, generous wife. My love, my life, and without doubt, my best friend. A toast: Tamsin Cunningham!'

'Tamsin!'

'Tamsin Cunningham!'

The sheep, I think. The Wicklow sheep.

I'm wondering if, after all, I *should* make my move – water down the comments a bit, yes, but still mark his card – for Tammie's sake. I'm feeling responsible for her now, knowing what I do. After all, she has no father to mind her.

But the priest – Father Tom – beats me to it and is on his feet. He begins:

'It was a *great* pleasure for me to officiate —'

'Sit down, Tom,' says Joe.

One of the waitresses – trying to be helpful – runs over to him with a roaming mike.

Joe walks out into a space between the tables. He smiles, first at the groom, then at the bride.

'Excuse me?' Terry grabs his own mike, not recognising the rather under-dressed man in the middle of the room.

'And you too,' Terry. I have the floor.'

'Now, hold on a second—'

If the younger guests in the room had been bored up to now by the speechifying, well, suddenly they're all agog. A hushing, murmuring Mexican-wave rumbles around the room and all the whispered conversations cease.

426

Bishop Joe, carrying his portable microphone, moves nearer the top table and addresses the guests in the round.

'Some of the older folk and family members present might recognise me as Bishop Joseph of Waterford and Lismore, but I am also the groom's uncle. And it is in this private capacity that I have come here today.'

'*Johnny!*' Karen is trying to whisper to me but, in view of all the wine she's sculled, it's quite loud and other people at our table turn and look at us both. 'What's he up to? Is he drunk? *Do something!* After all, he's your Plus One!'

And she's right. If I had doubts before, one look at Tammie's worried little face and the comforting arm her mother extends to pat her on the shoulder, is enough to propel me into action. I follow Joe onto the floor and extend my hand for the mike. He thinks *I* want to go first and launch into my roasting of Rob – so he hands it over.

But I've changed my mind and want him to do the same. I blow into the microphone – and hope I can remember the words. 'Eh, what Bishop Joe wanted to say to you all – was – we've had a wonderful meal here today – and no doubt we're all grateful to the staff – the chef – and Mrs Roche, of course. But there's somebody else we should be grateful to – who didn't get a mention. You might like to join us in saying the "Grace After Meals". *We give Thee thanks, Almighty God—*'

The older folk – thankfully – parrot the words. I can here 'pings' as phones nearby are switched on to check messages, the younger generation once again bored, having thought they were in for something exciting.

When the short prayer is over, I fumble for the Off switch, because Joe has his hand on the mike again.

'What did you do that for?' He tightens his grip on the shaft. 'Give it to me!'

'No. This isn't the time or the place.'

'*What?* Have you lost your bottle?'

There are murmurs of disquiet and shushing from the nearby tables – the mike is clearly still on.

'That's *enough*,' Rob is coming towards us. Clearly angry, he says into his own mike: '*Security?*'

A burly uniformed fella with a walkie-talkie ploughs up through the tables, followed by the tall debonair hotel manager we met when the wedding party arrived this afternoon. They swoop in and demand their equipment.

'That's it, gents,' says the security-man. 'Time to go. Give it here.'

Then I hear an appeal from the top table. 'No, gentlemen, give it *here.*' It's Finnuala, Tamsin's mother, who has her hand outstretched for the roaming mike. The manager takes it from me and walks towards the top table, while the bouncer lets go of Joe's arm and we both slink back to our table.

All around us, guests are becoming subdued, putting down or even turning off their phones as the slim woman in the lavender dress begins to speak.

'Evening, everybody,' she opens, 'and I'm sorry that I'm back tormenting you again so soon. Firstly, let me *thank*

Rob's uncle, Bishop Joe – *and* Mr Walshe – for spotting my oversight in proceedings and not acknowledging our celestial Boss! Nicely done. Now, while we give the much-thanked staff an opportunity to clear and reset the room for some dancing, can I ask you all to join me in the atrium where Rob and Tamsin will cut the cake – and where, I believe, there is some Prosecco on ice to wash it down.'

There is a short, polite ripple of applause as the guests begin to scatter.

———

In the atrium, guests mill around as Rob and Tammie pose for the traditional cake-cutting ceremony. The cake isn't a big elaborate thing with loads of layers – like last time – it's just a big square, with lemon icing and pictures of a camera and a rugby ball made out of coloured marzipan on the top. Neither are there any little 'Mr and Mrs' people waltzing on top of it. They have the cake propped up at an angle, so the photographer can capture the sugar decoration. I accept a glass of Prosecco from a little lassie wandering through the guests with a tray. I don't know where the other pair have got to, but I'm not alone for long.

Bishop Joe sidles up, looking narked.

'I'm sorry, Joe, about – earlier.'

He sips his drink. 'You let me down, that's all. I thought you were still mad at Rob.'

'Oh, I am, don't be under any illusion.'

'And you need to make people aware – of what you think you saw – you know, in Sicily – in case Rob isn't always this calm and complaisant with Tamsin.'

'I'm sorry I ever told you now – about my part in the fall. But the guilt – was eating away at me.'

Joe raised his eyebrows in disbelief and shook his head.

I said nothing, just drained the remainder of my fizz. I was eager to try and get the conversation back onto an even keel. 'Are you – still whizzing around on that bike of yours – frightening the life out of the poor Waterford cows in your gaudy strip?'

'I get out fairly regularly – not as much as in County Clare. I tend to head out to—'

'Gentlemen, if I might have a word?'

It's our hostess.

'Mrs Roche,' says Joe.

'Finnuala, please. Mrs Roche is my thankfully long-deceased mother-in-law. I just wanted – to thank you – not for saying "grace" earlier but for having the grace not to say what you probably had intended to.'

I'm not good with riddles, but Joe has the benefit of a Jesuit education, so he's all over it.

'What did you expect us to say?'

'Well, in your case – *given your day job* – something about the suitability of the marriage to your nephew. And in Mr Walshe's case – maybe some words of dissatisfaction about the groom. Would I be correct?'

I look at this pretty, beautifully presented woman who

must be of an age with myself – and I'm dumbfounded. She *knows*! There was nothing that either Joe or I could have shared that she didn't already know.

'I like to think that I have reared a modern daughter – a 21st century daughter – who is pragmatic and understands the nature of compromise and of sharing. From what I know of Rob's own family circumstances, that was a prevalent concept in his household too.'

'But – Mrs Roche – Finnuala, do you not aspire to *more* for Tamsin?' Joe seems genuinely upset.

'Tamsin will have a good life with Rob, and if that means sharing him occasionally, she is perfectly capable of coping with that. Married men have affairs all the time – and women cope.' She sips from her glass of fizz. 'Anyone enlightened these days knows that one's sexuality is no longer binary – it's often on a spectrum.'

This is all double-Dutch to me. Joe rubs his chin and I think he looks sceptical.

Finnuala waves to the lassie with the tray and swaps out her glass for a full one.

'Gentlemen?' she asks.

We decline.

'Johnny, today must have been particularly hard for you – memories of Vanessa and all that. But you *had* a daughter. *You* understand the lengths that a parent will go to, to secure a child's future. You, above anyone, should understand me.'

'Maybe I do, but I'm sure that if I had the knowledge at

the outset that *you* did I would have handled it differently.'

'Well, that's immaterial now.' She took a mouthful of her drink. 'We'll iron out some of Rob's problems over time. We've already come a long way in the couple of years they've been together. As Tamsin would say, "This is her day, her time". We need to leave the past in the past.'

Back in the Sugar Loaf room, Davey is waving at me.

'*Dad!* Come back to us. Here. Sit down. Are you OK?' He puts an arm around me.

'I'm fine, fine. No need to fuss.'

The staff have moved everything around in preparation for the dancing. Our table has been shoved God knows where.

I can't find my original chair and immediately start fretting about my jacket. 'My keys are in the pocket. Can you see it anywhere?'

Karen is going along the row of unoccupied chairs, trying to find one with a jacket on it. 'Did you and Bishop Joe have words? He seemed a bit – cross, after you said that prayer.'

'No, nothing like that. I suppose – he thought I was stealing his job!'

'*Ah ha!* Here we are. This is yours, isn't it?' She seizes a chair and lifts it out from against the wall. 'Do you want to check the pockets?'

'I'll do it in a minute.' I'm not being difficult with the lass, but suddenly I feel drained – weary – as if the emotional tension of the whole day has finally caught up with me.

Karen calls Davey over to our new seats and, as if she recognises the exhaustion in my face, says: 'Will you get us a couple of drinks, Dave? Johnny, would you take something stronger than water now?'

I turn her down. 'I was thinking I might drive you lot home.'

'But we've booked to stay in the hotel tonight!' Karen does that fake 'ticking-off' thing she often employs when 'reprimanding' my son. '*Davey*, did you not even tell your dad there's a room for him here?'

'Ah, I'm not in the mood for a posh hotel like this,' I say, and I most certainly wasn't. 'I'll probably just head back out to yours, if that's OK. I can get a taxi.'

'Well, whatever you want, Dad.' Davey looks at me with a worried expression on his face.

But that *was* what I wanted. It wasn't the length of the day that had exhausted me, it was the *strain* of keeping myself in check. It was the discomfort at watching that poor girleen walk up the aisle to God knows what. It was my spinelessness at not confronting Rob, for fear of what he might unexpectedly throw back at me.

I was willing to sacrifice someone else's daughter to preserve the memory of my own, to salvage *our* innocent, affectionate relationship – hers and mine — unblemished, regardless of what was the right thing to do, and of that I was not proud.

'You're still here.' Joe pulls up a chair.

'Yes. *That* was unexpected.'

'What was? Finnuala?'

'I can't understand how she'd turn a blind eye – *willingly*.'

'I'd say not so much willingly – as pragmatically.'

The waitress drops over a tall clear drink to the bishop. He pulls a note out of his trouser pocket but she refuses it, reminding him it is still a free bar.

He continues. 'Finnuala strikes me as a woman who believes that men are base material that can be *moulded* into whatever is required.'

'That Tammie will turn him?'

'It doesn't work like that, Johnny. Your sexual orientation is what it is – instinctive and embedded. I think the best Finnuala can hope for is that he'll identify as bi-sexual. As long as he plays fair by Tamsin and gives her what she wants, he can be discreet about the rest.'

'Fat chance of that if you'd opened your big gob – sorry, Joe – to all and sundry like you were intending to do.'

'Yeah, I suppose I should thank you for shutting me down. I don't want to lose my new job already.'

'Rob would have been livid. Can you imagine?'

'Oh, he'd probably just have wriggled out of it. Sometimes there are advantages in your uncle having been incarcerated in a mental hospital as a result of a breakdown. He'd have said I was having a relapse – thence not being up to performing the ceremony, arriving dishevelled and not dressed smartly enough to pass as a guest. That I only crashed the meal to cause trouble — deliberately.'

'And what about me? What would he have said if I'd blabbed?'

'That we're both off our rockers – you consumed with grief from your sad loss, and me having the official record of being of "unsound mind". But Johnny, remember: he's employing a media adviser these days. Be *careful* where Rob is concerned. Don't push him too far.'

I appreciated what he was trying to say, but it didn't make me feel any better about myself.

'Thanks.'

'I'm heading off now.' The bishop drains his water, puts his arm into the sleeve of his trench coat. 'If you're ever in Waterford, call in. Mind how you go, Johnny. Look after yourself.'

When he had left, I watched Karen and Davey out in the centre of the dance floor, jiving, and felt relieved that at least *one* of my children had been lucky in love. I thought it was probably wise to follow the bishop's lead and take my leave. I beckoned to them to come over to me.

They panted back to the chairs, looking for a drink.

'I'll take the key of the house off one of you, if that's OK. I'm going to head.'

Karen hugged me. 'Take it easy, Johnny. And we'll be back in time tomorrow to take you out for a bit of lunch before you head for home.'

'Will I come up to Reception with you to organise a taxi,

Dad?' Davey looked like a teenager instead of a nearly-forty-year-old man, with the shirt open down to his navel from his exertions on the dance floor.

'No, son, I'll be fine. I'll just wait up there in the foyer until the driver comes. You two enjoy the rest of your night.'

'Bye, Johnny. Safe home.'

I give my daughter-in-law a kiss on the cheek.

'See you tomorrow, Dad.'

'You will.'

Chapter 35

Johnny sits in a foyer armchair, waiting for the taxi to pull up at the set-down. A large brandy is on the marble table in front of him; he has finally succumbed to a real drink. The night porter, dressed in casual clothes, comes in the revolving door. He is carrying a bundle of newspapers which he lobs on top of the polished cherrywood reception desk. 'Oh, great!' the head receptionist says. 'A selection of the Sundays from Dublin!'

'You're welcome.'

'I'll pay you later. But go and get something to eat before you change into your uniform.'

The porter leaves and the receptionist cuts the binder of the bundle. She lifts the top copy – it's an edition of the most popular Sunday on sale. She glances at it quickly.

'*Oh look!*' she calls out. 'That's our wedding in the Sugar Loaf suite!' She holds it up for her colleague. The caption reads: '**Robbie Hooks Up Again!**'

With precision timing, the groom comes out of the bar and she calls him over.

'Look, sir! You've made the front page. Would you like this copy?'

Rob smiles and glances at the newspaper. He tucks it under his arm and then somebody catches his eye. He walks deliberately in the direction of the armchairs.

'Great things, newspapers – how fast they can turn things around. As for social media—' He extends his arm in an all-encompassing arc. Then, he bends down, leaning in towards the marble table and lifts Johnny's brandy glass. He swirls its contents around and around in his hand.

'Did you have a good day today? I hope so. *Remember*, Johnny. A promise is a promise.'

The Missing Hour

Sicily

July 2019

Hotel Giorgio, Castelmola, Taormina
July 13th 2019
12.55pm

'*Daddy? – I need you – Can you come down to the Villa? Quickly. 'It's Rob . . . I'm afraid—*'

He listens to his daughter's sobbing for the umpteenth time. This is the last recording he has of her, her final plea for help, and he hadn't got there in time. He presses the voicemail number again.

'*Daddy? – I need you – Can you come down to the Villa? Quickly. It's Rob . . . I'm afraid—*'

He would have to tell the police everything later. How Rob

was strangling the life out of her, how she had sounded afraid of something when she left the message. That stuff about him vanishing off on his own! The 'no sex' business – no sex with *her* anyways. No great evidence of them enjoying themselves even on their honeymoon.

That bastard Rob is down at Reception now, checking if there is a room he can book here, because he wants out of the Villa. Press crawling all over it, he says. He thinks he'd be better off somewhere quiet, *to 'grieve in peace'*. To grieve, my arse, when it's him that's led to this in the first place. When he volunteered earlier to come back in the taxi – (*'I'll keep you company, Johnny'*) – he had his own agenda. Always has, that Rob. It's not *only* about getting a room – he certainly won't be welcome up here to haunt me, a constant reminder of her death – but more likely he's here to agree *what* we'll say in our statement to the Carabini or whatever they're called, later this afternoon.

He knows how I feel about him. He'll say it was all in my head – that I imagined what I saw. That he wasn't fuckin' *'strangling'* her, but engaging in some kind of bondage yoke, before *actually* fucking her. Chance would be a fine thing, with that fella. He'll do the distraught widower act and complain that I had a habit of turning up uninvited *'ruining their intimacy.'* Interfering. *'Didn't he even crash our honeymoon – how usual is that?'*

But there is this: Johnny presses 'Voicemail' again.

'Daddy? – I need you – Can you come down to the Villa? Quickly. It's Rob . . . I'm afraid—'

440

It's time to talk to the shyster now. The plan is to travel back together in a taxi and present a united front in case there's media waiting. He's even writing the headline for them: **'Father and Husband Devastated by Their Tragic Loss.'** *Bollox!*

He's back from Reception, sitting in the shade at the little table for two. With a baseball cap *and* sunglasses, the fool! As if the staff in this hotel don't know exactly who he is and what has happened. Sicilians are like the Irish, love the bit of gossip. And, in fairness, it's more than that, they have been genuinely concerned and upset at the accident, probably in no small part worried what it'll do to their tourist trade, with the journalists asking so many questions. He waves across at me, as if greeting an old friend. Does he *really* think he's 'incognito'?

The 'chat' begins. What exactly is to be said to the police? Where were we when she fell? Where was Vanessa immediately *before?* Will we say she fell off the fence? Or climbed over it – to fetch something – something she had dropped? And slipped? (*Slipping summarily dismissed – too dry.*) Lost her balance then? What could she have dropped?

The locket. The locket she was wearing that's now missing. Yes, that makes sense.

Better not make too much of the punches thrown after she fell. Just our frustration at not being able to do anything while we waited for the emergency services. No malice in it at all. (*That's where he's wrong; I wanted to punch his fuckin' lights out.*)

Then there's a lull, and he wonders about the surveyor chap turning up. Where *exactly* were we, when they came into the garden? He remembers, the manager was there too. He's not pleased about that.

He's trying his best to make it all fit logically, time-wise. He gets a bit anxious when I don't seem to be chipping in with suggestions. He obviously hasn't considered that I might intend to tell the truth.

You're very quiet, Johnny. Anything on your mind?

Not a thing, only my dead daughter! Egotistical wanker.

Time to be frank. (*Not actual Frank cos we know what he thinks of him.*) Just the truth.

That the new husband was trying to strangle his wife. That the father interrupted the scene. That in the kerfuffle, the poor unfortunate daughter ended up flipping over the dilapidated fence and fell down the cliff. God knows what their row was over, but he was a controlling and jealous bastard and I have my suspicions.

Listen to the message. Listen to her fear.

I play it again.

'*Daddy? – I need you – Can you come down to the Villa? Quickly. It's Rob . . . I'm afraid—*'

He's not too bothered by the voicemail. He sips his sparkling water and takes off his baseball cap. And then he grins.

'*It's nice to have it,*' he says, '*that last sound of her voice.*'

He says it would be a shame to lose it, or erase it – even

accidentally. A daddy needs his girl and a girl needs her daddy, even when her daddy makes a mistake. Even when a daddy gets it wrong and makes a bad judgement call. Even when a daddy *imagines* that her sexy attractive husband is — what, trying to *strangle* her? And what's all this nonsense about her new, fit husband not desiring her! What a bizarre notion for a daddy to have, when the police inventory of the objects taken from the honeymoon suite will show a bumper pack of condoms – *and* a packet of oral contraceptives.

He laughs. *'How potent did she think I was?'*

He goes on.

How sad it would be if everyone were to learn how *obsessed* her daddy was with her. How he couldn't bear to see her happy, couldn't stomach seeing another man hold her and touch her! How his jealousy made him make that fatal mistake, made him lose that famous temper, made him tear her out of the arms of her lover, made her lose her balance, made her fall over that fence and fall, fall, fall to her death! *All* because he loved her.

'You killed her, Johnny. Is that what I tell the police?'

Hotel Giorgio, Castelmola, Taormina
July 13th 2019
13.55pm.

'Signor Walshe? Your taxi is here.'

THE END

Printed in Great Britain
by Amazon

17739886R00261